# ODD BIRD

# ODD BIRD

Lee Farnsworth

This edition published in 2020 by Farrago,
an imprint of Duckworth Books Ltd
1 Golden Court, Richmond,
TW9 1EU, United Kingdom

www.farragobooks.com

ISBN: 9781788423113

For Mum. Thanks for the chromosomes,
tuna fish flan and everything, basically.

# Chapter 1

'Claire and I dissolved our pair-bond,' I said.

I was surprised to hear myself say that. Not because Claire and I were still together. Not because I was in denial. No, I was just surprised because I had promised myself I wouldn't tell Phil yet. After all, it had only been five months since the dissolution.

The pint glass, which had been ascending towards Phil's mouth, stalled in mid-flight; I saw it stall. He knew I saw it stall. It began to ascend again.

'Was it because she had a face like a cracked plate, Bird?' he asked, across the rim of his glass.

'I'm not with you,' I said.

'Because she looked like a clock stopped at twenty past eight?'

'Phil, are you trying to infer that Claire is po-faced?'

'Only on a good day.'

'Claire isn't po-faced,' I said.

'Shame nobody told her face.'

I should have stopped there. I could already hear the kind of mood he was in. I could see it in the way he was leaning back, one arm draped along the chair back. Plus there was that look. I definitely should have stopped there.

'Would you accept that I have seen a lot more of Claire's face, po or otherwise, than you have?' I said.

Phil shrugged. A nod, you see, would have been a concession.

'Well,' I said, 'take my word for it: she isn't. You probably think I'm not objective when it comes to Claire, but nobody else has ever suggested that she was po-faced. "Lovely" – yes. "Po-faced" – no. You might suggest this is because those more sensitive to my feelings have shielded me from the truth. It's possible. However, I have an alternative hypothesis. You see, I only ever saw Claire looking po-faced in *your* presence, Phil. I am, therefore, forced to conclude that Claire was prone to episodic, stimulus-specific po-facedness. Basically, she didn't like you.'

Unperturbed, Phil downed the final swallow from his glass. 'Did she decapitate the bluebird of happiness, or was it you?' he said, wiping his mouth along the length of his index finger.

'It wasn't like that,' I said. 'We wanted different things. She went to Cardiff.'

'She wanted to be Welsh?'

'She got a lectureship, of course. I'm pleased for her; it's what she's always strived for. I thought that we would carry on seeing each other at weekends, holidays, etcetera, but she wanted to discuss the future.'

'Lucky escape,' said Phil. 'Pint?' With one hand pressed down on the small, wobbly wooden table, he pushed himself up and out of the spindle-backed chair.

I looked up into his mallet-shaped face. 'Do you really think so?'

'It's a tried and tested cure for sombre reflection and I'm definitely having one.' Phil tried to extract a few more drops from his empty glass.

'I meant about Claire.'

'Definitely. Anyway, let's talk about birds instead, Bird.'

'Phil, we both know that you know nothing, *absolutely nothing*, about ornithology.'

'True, but I am not expecting to be appointed Dean of Contemporary Relationship Studies any time soon either,' he said, reaching over the table to take my glass. I curled my fingers around it in a tiny act of defiance, but he quickly twisted it from my grasp and stood back, triumphantly, a brace of glasses in his hands.

Surprising myself again, this time with the speed and spontaneity of my reaction, I slapped my hand down hard on the surface of the table.

As I fought to ignore the stinging sensation radiating through my hand I became aware of the voice of James Blunt wafting from the small speaker mounted on the wall above our heads.

Sensing the stares of the couple on the next table I turned to them. Their cutlery was frozen in mid-air. Apologising, I explained that it had not been my intention to elicit a startle response. The male nodded and the female started to chew again, slowly. I turned back to face Phil.

'I will take my Swan Song now, please,' I said.

'Bollocks,' he said, closing his eyes. His head lolled back. Expelling a long, deep sigh he said, 'There's no way I'm doing that without beer.' He headed over to the corner of the wooden bar as if towards a gallows, leaving me alone at the table to consider my impulsivity.

I picked up the empty brown glass ashtray from the table and began to turn it over in my hands, exploring its lines and angling it against the light coming from the bare bulb overhead. What was I going to say? I looked across to Phil, leaning against the bar, provoking the new barmaid.

For months I had been agonising about Claire. I had hoped the ache would ease with time but it continued to find new ways to branch, and fork and twist. I hoped that dedicating myself to the identification of a new mate would help to ease it, but I didn't know how to initiate the process and the need to talk to someone had become more insistent, *but Phil?* There were at least seven billion *Homo sapiens* who were better listeners than Phil.

Returning, Phil slid my pint across the table and sat cupping his own in his lap. 'Fix You' by Coldplay was playing and Phil looked up at the speaker and said, 'Ready when you are, Bird.'

'I am entitled to a complete song, as you know,' I said.

'Hmm… it better not be "Bohemian Rhapsody",' he said. 'Thinking about it, perhaps I should get another couple of pints. And some crisps. And a cyanide capsule.'

I told him that crisps weren't permitted.

'That's not in the rules,' he frowned. 'We never said anything about crisps.'

'The rules, as they were explained to me, *by you*, stated that under no circumstances should the Swan Song be interrupted. Crisps are simply a savoury interruption.'

'When I devised the rules of Swan Song, I didn't know that they were going to be turned against me,' he sulked.

'When I *consented* to the first Swan Song, I didn't know that you were going to try to convince me that your girlfriend's dependency on moisturiser was evidence of human evolution via an aquatic intermediate.'

Phil grinned, baring small, closely packed teeth. 'Good times. Arctic Monkeys I believe.' Stroking his pint he continued, 'I've got a new theory, by the way. It's about the beauty enhancing properties of car windscreens. Have you ever noticed that when you drive—'

Wise to his distraction tactics, I told him that I wasn't listening and picked up the brown ashtray again and tried to compose my thoughts.

As Coldplay faded I looked at Phil and then at the speaker, and hoped to avoid a ballad. But from the very first 'Oooooh' I recognised the voice of Mariah Carey. Phil grinned; I rolled my eyes. I can identify the vast majority of birds of the British Isles by their song or calls alone, but by the mid-nineties I had entirely lost the ability to differentiate the songs of Mariah.

Unfortunately, the rules of Swan Song were explicit and so I had no choice. 'The topic of my Swan Song this evening is Claire and my pair-bond quandary,' I said. Phil closed his eyes for a second time and pulled his stubby-fingered hand down his broad face and stubbly throat.

Feeling no sympathy for him, I continued: 'When the Cardiff opportunity arose, Claire said she wanted to talk about our pair-bond and the future and, well, given contemporary life-expectancies, the future is a very long time. I wasn't expecting to have that discussion and it's fair to say I was *very* ill-prepared for it. And I don't just mean that I hadn't made notes.'

I paused. Phil was peering at me through splayed fingers. How could I make him – the most lay of laymen – understand? We sighed simultaneously.

'You see, Phil, I'm not good at making those kinds of choices,' I continued. 'And you aren't either. *We* aren't. We aren't even supposed to make them. In the natural world it is the female who makes such choices.'

Phil's fingers closed like blinds. While I had been unprepared for the 'talk' with Claire, I was very prepared for such signs of dismissiveness from him and I took no heed.

'Well, the preliminary discussion didn't go well, it's fair to say. I learned that though the female is the ultimate decision maker there are some, Claire included, who don't appreciate being reminded of this. She got quite upset and left abruptly, informing me that I had a week to tell her what I wanted.

'And I did give it a lot of thought, but the days continued to pass and I still didn't know what to do. As you know I lost male guidance and support at a crucial stage of my development and I can't draw on those formative experiences… and so I decided to go back over the scientific literature about mate selection strategy.'

Phil rubbed the left side of his face with his hand and looked up to the ceiling, thus making his laryngeal prominence more, well, prominent.

'There are a number of observational studies in individual bird species but there are no systematic reviews. However, I came across some interesting theoretical modelling work out of Berkeley.'

Phil was now shaking his head. This struck me as odd because he works in 'talent acquisition' and so it was highly unlikely he would be familiar with the Berkeley work, much less have an informed opinion about it.

Fighting my curiosity, I pressed on. 'The Berkley Group postulate that a "pooled comparison" strategy is probably optimal, though the "threshold" strategy is also effective under certain conditions. Essentially, the pooled comparison strategy involves the screening of a sample of a number "n" of potential mates, followed by the selection of the best of that sample. The optimal n is apparently *five*. I appreciate, of course, that there are limitations concerning the application of a theoretical model to a real-life human courtship situation, but given that such skills are not innate to our gender, I thought this was instructive.' Phil was still shaking his head and I was beginning to think that he had trapped a nerve.

'The problem is, my personal n is one, as you know,' I said. 'Claire is my entire n. I could have included Katie Thomson but I didn't because we were both only nine at the time, and it only lasted for the duration of a bus trip to Alton Towers. And so, you see, it's little wonder I was feeling so uncertain.'

Phil expelled a short blast of air through his lips. While not technically an infringement of Swan Song, this was a deliberate provocation. I could have castigated him, but I knew that the most effective way to punish him was to continue unabated.

'With just two days left until her deadline, I decided to tell Claire that I wanted to make it work. But I just couldn't quite bring myself to do it and I started thinking about the nature and function of love.'

At this point Phil raised his glass to his mouth and took long, deep gulps, half-emptying it.

'As far as we can tell man is the only creature that feels love with such intensity. Approximately ninety per cent of mammals, including the other apes, don't form pair-bonds, but we do. These bonds often last for a lifetime. We believe that love is an almost uniquely human phenomenon and we think we know why. Love almost certainly developed as a consequence of the transition to bi-pedal motion. Upright walking led to a narrowing of the birth canal which in turn meant that human infants had to be born small, pathetic, helpless, and incredibly demanding. Couples who worked together stood a much better chance of successfully rearing those infants. Love evolved as a *powerful* reward system, promoting formation and maintenance of strong pair-bonds. The key word here is *POWERFUL*.'

Phil covered his face with his hands again but given that his ears were still unconcealed there were no legitimate grounds for objection.

'I thought about my feelings for Claire,' I continued. 'I've always admired her intellect and enjoyed her company and I do care about her, but it wasn't a *POWERFUL* feeling, not even in the beginning. There have been glimpses of something deeper I think. I felt very close to her when she came birding with me on our Papua New Guinea trip. And when her sister became ill my desire to comfort and protect her *was* definitely powerful, but isn't that just empathy?'

Phil's hands parted and then his lips parted too, but I wagged a finger and his mouth closed again, grumpily.

'I used to tell myself that this was what love was, for me anyway. But if I'm not capable of feeling love that intensely, if I have a dysfunctional love reflex, why do I long for something more? Why do I sense that there is more? Why have I always felt like something is missing? Might it simply be because my n is underpowered?'

I stopped speaking for a femto-second to check in on Mariah and discovered that she was now sounding highly distressed. Realising I had little time left, I began to speak again, now more hurriedly.

'As the critical meeting with Claire drew nearer I became increasingly anxious. What would I say? We met at Tacos and I was feeling more settled after the initial exchanges, but as I was assembling my first fajita she just came right out with it. "Do you want me stay, Simon?" she said.

'Well, of course I said it wasn't just about what I wanted, etcetera, and she said that she knew that, but she wanted to know what I wanted anyway.' I pressed my lips together and gave a long double-nostril sigh. 'Well, I got into a terrible flap and… and I told her about the pooled comparison strategy… She didn't even let me finish. She said that she had decided to go to Cardiff because at least *they* were unambiguous about her.

'I don't think she was particularly disappointed. She said that she felt that our relationship had "run its course" and then she calmly finished her burrito and left. Perhaps she was slightly relieved. I don't feel relieved though. I miss her.'

Phil finished his pint and rested the rim of his glass against his forehead.

'What have I done, Phil? I'm thirty-four. It took me thirty-two years to meet Claire and now she's gone and I am unpaired once again. Even if I do meet a female who elicits a more profound and sustained love response, she might not feel that way about me. After all, they don't make a sexy behavioural ecologist calendar, do they? Society has decided, for whatever reason, that footballers and firemen are more attractive.'

Mariah emitted a final, exhausted vowel string.

'Thank you for listening Phil,' I said, sitting upright in my chair. 'I would be very happy to take questions now.'

Phil raised his eyebrow. 'I do have one question,' he said.

'Really?' I said, hopefully. 'What is it?'

'Are you glad you won't be bringing po-faced children into the world?'

# Chapter 2

*March. Empirical University, London*

The breeding dynamics within guillemot (*Uria aalge*) colonies – or 'loomeries' – are fascinating. The manuscript I was reviewing had so thoroughly transported me to an Orkney Island cliff top that I completely failed to notice the opening of my office door.

'There you are, gorgeous man, hiding away as usual.' This shrill interjection slid away into an avalanche of giggles. Jolted back first to England then London, South Kensington, Empirical and finally my desk, I looked up to see Pippa striding towards me.

*Yes*, said the voice, which had become gradually more insistent as the months post Claire's departure rolled past.

'Oh, hello, Pippa. How are you?' I said, hurriedly scribbling a note in the margin of the manuscript. What did she want? And 'gorgeous'? I wished she would stop calling me that. And how could sitting at my own desk in my own office be considered 'hiding away'?

'Sooo?' said Pippa.

'Hmm. Overall, I think it's a nice piece of work. Auks are notoriously difficult to study but the research has been conducted with real rigour. There are novel insights and I think it certainly merits publication. Some of the conclusions seem a little speculative though.'

'What?' Pippa frowned for a brief glorious moment and then giggled again, more violently this time. 'No, silly. Saturday. *Supper.*' She stepped, uninvited, behind my chair. Instinctively, I tried to swivel it, though it lacked swivel functionality, but it was too late – she was already behind me.

As Pippa began to massage my shoulders she said, 'It's going to be so much lovely fun and I so want you to meet my gorgeous friends.' Pippa's fingers were surprisingly strong and the sensation was not unpleasant, but I wished that she would stop. *Why was she massaging me? Did I look tense? I didn't feel tense, did I?* I began to feel tense.

'Ah yes, sorry. Saturday. Look, Pippa, I just don't think I would be very good company. I—'

'Silly old Dr Doldrums,' said Pippa, giggling and further ratcheting her finger force. 'I'm not taking no for an answer this time.' Another flurry of giggles.

Pippa's giggles were a departmental phenomenon. Always enthusiastically delivered, they lacked selectivity, proportionality and social coherence. Basically, Pippa giggled loudly, all the time, at everything and often alone (see Figure 1b). For this reason, many in the department felt uncomfortable and even claustrophobic in her presence, and some perceived her to be a pest.

Pippa made me feel uncomfortable too, but then almost everybody did. I didn't want to go to her party and frankly I didn't want to go to anybody's party. My state of mind was such that I would have probably tried to wriggle out of a quick pint with Darwin, Maynard Smith, Lorenz and Lack.

Pippa abruptly stopped massaging and moved to sit on the corner of my desk. She was a tall, robustly constructed female, and she wore her hair cropped short which made her head seem relatively small. On this particular occasion she was wearing a grey crew-necked sweater which only acted to accentuate, in my eyes at least, a certain pigeon-like quality to her appearance.

'Anytime from seven pm,' she said.

Pippa's insistence was entirely understandable. On three previous occasions I had cited imaginary commitments to escape the pull of her social vortex.

'It's nice of you, it really is Pippa,' I said. 'I promise I will come next time. But I just don't feel ready for the social scene yet.'

'That's why my supper is exactly what you need. You have to start having some fun again, Simon.' She reached out towards me, clasping my hands in hers. 'You need to get yourself a new puppy.'

If I did have a need at that moment it was to get my hands back.

'Why on earth would I want a puppy?' I asked. I cast my eyes over towards the door, hoping that nobody would be looking in through the window.

'You know,' she giggled. 'When a beloved dog dies they say that you should get a new puppy straight away. And it's been, it's been a while since you know, Claire…'

'Ah, I see.' I glanced at the door again. 'I'm not altogether sure that Claire would welcome the canine analogy.'

Pippa giggled for a long time about that. Just when I thought that my forced smile would surely falter, she said, 'It's just a few friends, some drinks, supper. It will be fun. And my puppies are all house-trained,' she erupted.

I waited for her to subside. 'Can I think about it?'

'That's your trouble; you think too much, Captain Clever Clogs.' Pippa inched across the desk towards me, escalating my discomfort. 'Sooo?'

'OK… OK. I will come to your party, Pippa. Thank you.'

'Great! Great! *Great!*' said Pippa, leaping up and clapping her hands like a birthday princess. I smiled and drew my hands slowly back into the safety of my lap. 'I can't wait. It's going to be *so-much-fun!*' she said, rubbing my hair gleefully. Then, finally, she left.

My office seemed cavernous following Pippa's departure and my guilt grew loud. The truth was that my mind was still far from made up about Pippa's party. I had accepted simply to buy myself time, freedom and a swifter return to the Orkney Islands.

Figure 1a. Normal giggle response

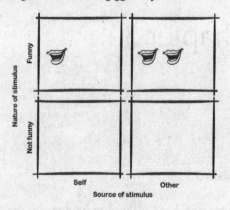

Figure 1b. Pippa giggle response

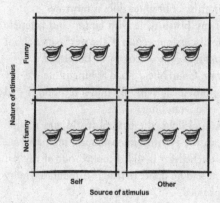

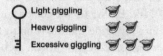
Light giggling
Heavy giggling
Excessive giggling

# Chapter 3

The morning was striped with rain. I had planned to head out to the Chilterns to take in the soothing soaring of the red kites (*Milvus milvus*), but decided to wait for the promise of brighter skies tomorrow.

Instead, I settled down at my bistro table with laptop and cafetière and got started on writing the discussion section of the next paper about our captive zebra finch (*Taeniopygia guttata*) colony at Empirical.

A trip down to the bakery on Churchfield Road at lunchtime was my only brief escape from self-imposed captivity. By mid-afternoon, I had descended into a grade three (moderate) fug.

I had been deprived of natural light, the natural world and natural pursuits for too long. Back on the Pleistocene savannah, man evolved to run and my inner ancestor ached for it still. I looked out of my flat window. The contemporary me had no desire to trudge through the rainy streets, but *he* would not be pacified.

I cut across Acton Park – noting the irate calls of the ring-necked parakeets (*Psittacula krameri*) – and then made my way through the quiet back streets towards Gunnersbury Park. By the time I got on to Bollo Lane I was finally beginning to get into my stride and was running through the shallow brown puddles rather than side-stepping them. As I approached a commercial building on the right-hand side of the road, I became aware of a huge flock of pigeons (*Columba livia*) packed together into a grubby avian blanket that draped over the left-hand side of the corrugated roof. I stopped briefly to estimate the size of the population, concluding that there were at least fifteen hundred individuals.

The birds, taking comfort in their mass and presumably from the warmth of the surface they were gathered on, were largely unaware of and undisturbed by my presence. In fact, only a single bird appeared to respond. It flew from the ridge of the roof, its wings making the sound of a toy sword frantically slicing the air. As I watched its panicked flight over Gunnersbury Works and under a swirling papier mâché sky, I remembered.

*Genitals*, I thought. *Pippa's party*.

Mumbling, I started to run again, constructing excuses by the stride.

***

I completed two loops of Gunnersbury Park and then headed back to the flat the most direct way. I arrived muddy and panting like a Labrador (*Canis lupus familiaris*). As I slipped off my running shoes and socks before entering the building, I could tell that the ancestor was satisfied.

In the shower, I stepped away from the jets to soap myself. I bent to rub away the thickest of the mud from the insides of my shins and then stood so that the jets of almost-too-hot water drilled into the backs of my shoulders. It was then that I felt the first waves of love for the shower well up within me.

*Hello endorphins*, I thought, *I've been expecting you*.

My love began to spread, like a puddle. Soon, I was loving the minty-cucumberiness of the shower gel. The love puddle deepened and I wanted to swim in my love for the shower. I wanted to stand on the top of a hill, spread my arms above me, arch my head back and sing of my love for showers and for cleanliness of all varieties. This love was not in any way diminished by the paucity of songs about personal hygiene, or the lack of nearby hills.

'I'm gonna wash that man right out of my hair,' I sang. I sang it over and over, getting louder and more confident with each recitation. Knowing only the chorus, however, and despite my love, I eventually tired of the repetition.

The desire to sing of other things, things like cafetières, zebra finches, cucumbers and Gunnersbury Park came upon me. I knew of no such songs of course, but I didn't blame the songwriters for that. In fact, my love for songwriters had never been greater because, at that moment, I loved *everyone*.

And everyone included Pippa. I loved Pippa for inviting me to 'supper', especially because I had turned her down consistently before. *Supper could be fun*, I thought, as I lathered my buttocks. *I should go*, I thought.

*I will go*, I thought.

# Chapter 4

Baseline neurochemistry and doubts were restored by the time the cab pulled on to the Victorian terraced street. As I opened my wallet to pay the driver, I almost asked him to take me straight back to Acton.

Elsewhere, curtains were drawn and blinds were lowered, but light poured from the bay window of number 21, clearing a low brick wall and illuminating the pavement.

As I approached the green front door I detected the muffled sound of the Gypsy Kings coming from within. I paused at the threshold, deliberating between doorbell and silver-horse-shoe knocker, but the door flew open before I could choose.

'Simon! Gorgeous man! There you are,' said Pippa. 'I was beginning to think you'd changed your mind.' I just had time to observe that she was wearing a vivid pink blouse and matching lipstick before she engulfed me.

I felt the warmth and force of Pippa's giggle-breath in my left ear. The bottle of red wine (*Cabernet Sauvignon*) I was holding would have prevented me from matching Pippa's enthusiasm, even if I had felt it. With a final happy trill, she released me, taking the wine from my hand.

Turning into the pale yellow hallway, she lifted her voice above the Gypsy Kings to yell, 'Simon's here.'

Closing the door she took my hand and pulled me down the narrow hallway. I immediately detected a delicious piquant meaty aroma that awakened me to a gnawing, post-run hunger. The aroma grew stronger as we made our way along the hallway, passing a neat row of framed rosettes. Alerted by the tapping of our footsteps on the wooden floor, a female wearing a red polka dot apron over a black dress stepped into the empty doorway at the top of the hall. Watching us approach, she sipped from a fluted glass.

'Ah, new blood,' she said.

'Judy, you are just *terrible*,' said Pippa, slapping her playfully on the bare elbow as she stepped, giggling, past her into the kitchen. Confused by this exchange, and also unsure if Pippa intended me to follow, I remained in the hallway in a state of mild bewilderment, awaiting further instruction. From the kitchen I heard the sound of cupboard doors opening and then Pippa's voice: 'Don't take any notice of Judy, Simon. She's gorgeous and *wonderful* but she's also very, very cheeky, I'm afraid.'

As Judy eyed Pippa across the kitchen I took in her profile and I heard the familiar, cynical voice stir.

*No*, it said. *Cheeky she might be but gorgeous she isn't.*

*Please don't,* I pleaded. *Not tonight. Please.*

\*\*\*

About *that* voice: it had always been there I suppose, but I didn't recognise it for what it was until one morning shortly after returning to Empirical from my Miami postdoc. I was sitting in the Life Sciences library with a large pile of bound journals on the desk before me. Though working conscientiously, I became aware of an attractive bespectacled female seated just a couple of rows away from me. Once, I looked up to see her paused in reflection, her eyes towards the low ceiling, her pen gripped in her teeth. At that moment, a female librarian of late middle age was pushing a trolley up the aisle towards us. As I watched, the attractive female stopped the librarian to make a brief whispered enquiry.

There was something about the brief interaction between those two females – one significantly more attractive than the other to my eyes – that made me consider my perception of attractiveness more deeply than I ever had before. How was it that one face could awaken desire in me and another, still a female face after all, well, didn't? How was it that I was able to make such rapid, instantaneous assessments of attractiveness?

As the librarian trundled past my desk, I took another fleeting look at the attractive female, now writing again, and then lifted myself from my seat and headed into the tall rows of shelves to see what science could tell us about this phenomenon.

In those rows I discovered that these flash judgements of beauty originate in a brain region known as the paracingulate cortex. I haven't smiled too often in the Life Sciences library over the years, but I grinned when I saw that cognitive neuroscientists often abbreviate the name of this brain region to 'PC'.

\*\*\*

Back on the perimeter of Pippa's kitchen, I told my PC, as I had so many times before, that I didn't want or need his opinion and that I wasn't the slightest bit interested in how 'gorgeous' he thought Pippa's guests were. I told him that all I wanted from the evening was to spend time with friendly people who preferably weren't quite so giggly or tactile as Pippa.

*Why don't you take the night off?* I suggested.

*I have to remain vigilant at all times,* he said. *You know that.*

Pippa reappeared, framed by the doorway. Placing two glasses down on the central island, she beckoned me towards her. Puzzled but obedient, I mumbled an apology to Judy and stepped past her towards the centre of the kitchen. There, Pippa hooked her hand into my arm and turned me around.

'Simon, meet my dear friend, Kim,' she said.

The female henceforth known as Kim was standing over a dark grey worktop with her back towards us; she had long, straight chestnut coloured hair that draped down the back of a billowing white blouse. She turned to face us.

'Kim,' said, Pippa, 'This is Simon.'

The Kim female smiled at me. I may have smiled back, I really can't be sure.

*Code Alpha,* said the PC. *I repeat, Code Alpha.*

I felt a combination of elation (dopamine) and terror (adrenaline) seize me. I tried to speak only to discover that I had lost the capability to vocalise.

*What are you doing?* I asked.

*It's for your own good,* said the PC. *It's to stop you saying something ridiculous.*

*But all I can hear is the sound of blood rushing through my ears. How is that supposed to help?*

Though thoroughly discombobulated, I could at least see that the lips belonging to the Kim female were now moving and I noticed that they were in fact moving in synchrony. I thought that they were very clever lips for doing that. They were very red lips too. I liked red. Kim had very clever, very red lips, I decided, and I liked them. But realising that the clever red lips must be moving for a reason, I became disconcerted.

*Oh my god. She's talking.*

Worse still, given that the lips and face were oriented towards me, I came to the conclusion that Kim was talking to *me*. By force of will, I fought to wrench back control from the PC. I just managed to hear her say 'carrots' before her clever red lips came to a halt.

Carrots? I was deeply confused by 'carrots'. Nevertheless, I deduced that I was now expected to respond. I did the best I could.

'Erm, hello,' I said.

Then to avoid sustained eye contact I glanced down and observed that Kim was holding a kitchen knife in her pretty right hand. The tip of the blade was pointing towards my abdomen. First an association and then a tentative understanding began to coalesce. *Carrots? Knife?*

'Sharp,' I said. 'Slicing.'

'What?' said Kim.

I looked down towards the blade again. This time she looked down towards the blade too.

'Oh shit! I'm so sorry!' She laughed and turned back to the counter, placed the knife down and quickly wiped her pretty pink hands on a white checked tea towel. Turning back to me, she took my right hand in hers. Her skin felt cool, soft and slightly damp.

'Don't worry. You are quite safe,' she said. 'Pippa won't let me hurt you. Will you Pippa?' Releasing my hand she glanced, still smiling, over my shoulder towards our host.

I did not take *my* eyes from *her* though. Her hair was long and lustrous, indicating that not only was she currently in good health, but also that she had been in good health for several years. Her skin was pale and her features small, suggesting that a high concentration of oestrogen and just the tiniest trace of testosterone were circulating in her immaculate bloodstream. Brown irises floated in still seas of unblemished white sclera. Best of all, she was highly symmetrical; I reminded myself that I had always wanted to form a pair-bond with a highly symmetrical female.

Next I noticed a tiny black full stop of a mole just above her left eye. I marvelled at the way her slender eyebrow guided my eye towards it, as if by design. *Even her imperfections are perfect*, I thought.

'Absolutely not,' said Pippa, taking me by the hand. 'Let me give the poor thing some lovely bubbles to soothe his nerves.' Somehow a glass of champagne found its way into my hand and Pippa took my arm once more. 'OK ladies,' she announced, 'I'm taking Simon through to meet everyone else.'

'We'll be through with the dips and bits in a minute,' said Judy.

'Help? Can't I help?' I said, desperate to stay in the kitchen beside Kim. Having met her I had no desire to meet anyone else, ever again.

But Pippa tugged me along. 'Come on you,' she said, giggling.

# Chapter 5

The PC and his cognitive co-conspirators might have allowed me to speak again, but they had disabled my short-term memory. I immediately forget the names, relationships and occupations of everybody Pippa subsequently introduced me to. The PC only wanted me to remember Kim.

When Pippa announced that dinner was served she immediately took me by the elbow. 'Come with me,' she said. We were the first to enter the dining room. Pippa took the seat at the apex of the black glass table and patted the seat to her left to indicate that I should sit beside her.

'Now, where's Janet?' she said.

'Which one's Janet?' I said.

When a curly-haired female in a red dress appeared, Pippa waved at her frantically, saying, 'Janet, Janet – over here.'

'Oooh, isn't Janet glamorous, Simon?' said Pippa as Janet obediently placed herself in the seat to my left. Kim had just stepped through the double doors but I managed a muttered affirmation. 'Janet works at Empirical too,' said Pippa.

'Ah, yes, I thought…' I said. I did not say, 'You look very different without safety goggles,' though the thought did offer itself.

As I watched Kim slip into a seat at the other end of the table, Pippa said, 'Janet studies zebra fish don't you, Janet? That's a big coincidence don't you think, Simon?'

'Remarkable,' I said.

'Zebra fish. Zebra finch,' Pippa giggled.

Remembering my manners I smiled.

Kim must have sensed that I was observing her because as she opened her napkin she flashed me a brief friendly smile. I smiled back, shyly, and then feigned a sudden deep interest in the bread basket. When I turned back to her, a male whose name I could not recall had inserted himself between us, blocking my view of her almost entirely.

As I took a first soothing sip from the red wine Pippa had poured for me, I felt utterly devastated and yet at the same time mightily relieved that I wasn't the one sitting beside Kim.

\*\*\*

Of that dinner, I remember a rich beef and black olive casserole. I remember Pippa insisting that I had to feel Janet's 'sexy' arms, honed by hours in the stable yard. I remember Pippa and Janet talking about horses and horses and more horses. I remember nodding. Most of all I remember discovering that I had already become sensitised to Kim's voice and especially to her laughter.

\*\*\*

After dinner Judy's boyfriend Aman proposed a trip into Ealing for a late drink, winning Pippa to his cause with a slew of flattery and an exhibition of advanced hugging techniques. As Aman pulled open the pub door, the turbines of Saturday night revelry droned out on to the quiet street.

We followed Aman along the transitory channel he created through the tightly packed crowd. I apologised to a half-dozen or more strangers before emerging into a clearing at the far end of the bar.

We barked drinks orders at each other and then at a gaunt barman in a black T-shirt who served us with all the enthusiasm of an inmate. Then we settled into yelled and fragmented conversations supplemented by lip-reading and hopeful nods.

Kim slipped off to the rear of the pub with Aman and Judy. The rest of us formed a huddle around the back of a large burnished red leather Gladstone sofa. I ached for Kim to join us, though I had no idea what I would say to her if she did. On the brighter side, Daniel – the male who had been seated beside Kim at dinner – stayed with us and I became more confident that he and Kim were not paired.

The Eileen and Paul pairing went home after the first drink (in addition to companionship, caring and copulation, pairs also have better excuses).

The crowd had thinned a little by then and Pippa and I were able to conduct a conversation without first having to place mouths directly beside ear canals. I was considering how best to ask her for more information about Kim, when she glanced over at Janet and Daniel who were chatting together and said, 'Simon, aren't you going to do something?'

'Possibly,' I said. 'About what?'

Pippa giggled, of course, though as was often the case I wasn't sure why. 'I think someone must have put kryptonite in my wine,' she said, cryptically. 'My superpower has *totally* deserted me this evening.' When I asked her what she meant Pippa explained that she had a reputation as a matchmaker. 'Judy and Aman. Paul and Eileen. All my handiwork,' she said proudly.

In light of this additional information I looked over at Janet and Daniel anew. Daniel was leaning in towards Janet, talking. He broke off briefly in order to hitch up his glasses (I had noticed that he habitually did this with his knuckle) and then he began to speak again.

'And you suspect that she does not wish to pair with him?' I said.

'I do,' she smirked. 'Look at how she's backing away. *Poor* Janet.' Pippa winced theatrically and then began to giggle and so I laughed too.

Pippa was still laughing about Janet and Daniel when Judy and Aman came to say their goodbyes. 'Where's Kim?' asked Pippa.

'In the bathroom,' said Judy. 'Hiding from…' she grimaced and behind a raised palm Judy jabbed a finger towards Daniel.

After Judy and Aman departed I became fascinated by the ladies bathroom. I was looking over there for signs of Kim's emergence when I heard a shriek. Spinning around I discovered that an inebriated female in a toy-green beret had slopped beer down the front of Janet's red dress as she returned to her social group. She offered a series of imperfectly pronounced and highly repetitive apologies, but Janet didn't look upset, though she did announce that she was going to leave.

Daniel promptly announced that he also intended to leave and volunteered to accompany Janet while she waited for a cab.

'You'll be OK on your own for a minute won't you, Simon?' said Pippa, giggling. She explained that she thought she ought to protect Janet from Daniel's advances.

\*\*\*

It had been an evening of unusually intense socialisation and so I enjoyed a moment of replenishing solitude. I leaned against the Gladstone, metabolising and observing the dynamics of the transient ecosystem before me.

All along the length of the wall opposite, drinkers sat around small square drinking tables. They were packed so closely that leaving for the bar or bathroom could only be achieved with difficulty. Amused, I watched a bearded male of perhaps twenty-eight years of age lift a booted foot over the horizontal thigh of a friend as he attempted his exit.

Feeling a sharp prod in my ribs, I turned. It was Kim. How long had she been there?

*It's her,* said the PC. *The beautiful one.*

*I know,* I said. *I'm not completely hopeless.*

*You are beyond hopeless,* he said.

'I said, "What's funny?"' said Kim. She took a sip of white wine, eyeing me.

'Oh, hi Kim,' I said. 'Sorry, I was miles away. Was… was I smiling?'

'Borderline purring,' she said. 'What were you looking at?'

'Nothing,' I said. She cocked her head and took another sip. 'I was just thinking. I was thinking a silly thought.'

'I like silly. Tell me about silly.'

'It's not the sharing kind of silly, unfortunately. It was more of a highly personal, idiosyncratic kind of silly.' I was beginning to appreciate why the PC had silenced me earlier.

'Simon, I'm tired and you don't know me very well, but basically I'm impatient by nature. If you don't tell me what you were thinking right now, more innocent root vegetables *will* suffer.'

I laughed because I thought her comment was amusing, but also because I needed time to think. It seemed to me that I had to quickly choose one of two possible strategies: a) tell her the truth and destroy my credibility, or b) make something up. I much preferred b), but b) took imagination. Which left a).

'I was just thinking,' I said… 'I was just thinking that there are lots of pairs packed in here and yet most are not actively interacting with neighbouring pairs. They are oblivious to those sitting on the next table. And so they look, well… like a colony of gulls. A bit… Some of them… A bit… How long have you known Pippa?'

Kim looked at me and sipped in silence.

'I told you it was silly,' I said. Embarrassed, I looked back over at the drinkers.

'Actually, it's more weird than silly,' said Kim.

'I hope not,' I said. 'I wouldn't like to think that I was the kind of person who would stand in the middle of a busy pub smiling weirdly.'

'Well, it's not disturbing at least. Frankly though, I was hoping for something more obviously silly with less of an undertone of weird.'

'Could we say it was unorthodox?'

'Definitely.'

'I'm sorry,' I said. And I was. I knew that it was highly, highly, profoundly unlikely that Kim would ever consider pairing with me. However, I wanted very much for her to at least like me.

'Don't be,' she said, cheerfully. She touched my arm. Surprised, I micro-flinched. *Had she detected it?* 'It's not your fault,' she said. 'You were just standing in the middle of a pub, on your own, surrounded by late-night drinkers, grinning like a simpleton. How were you to know that anyone was watching?'

'Thank you,' I said. 'I feel better now.'

'I remember,' she said, pointing her glass at me accusingly. 'Pippa told me: you're the Birdman of Acton. How did you become a birdwatcher?' she asked.

I checked her face. She seemed genuinely interested, in a beautiful kind of way. Genuine interest in my work is about as common as a Siberian rubythroat (*Luscinia calliope*) and so I checked her expression again, just to be sure.

'Actually, I'm not a birdwatcher,' I said. I had said that a lot over the years, though it rarely seemed to help. For reasons I never really understood, denying that I was a birdwatcher only seemed to cement the misperception.

'I see,' she said. 'Birdman is a strange nickname, for somebody who isn't a birdwatcher. Is it possible to appeal against nicknames?'

'I'm a behavioural ecologist. I study the behaviour of birds. Specifically I study their mating behaviour.'

'So you are more of a bird-voyeur? Is that better?' Her eyebrows certainly didn't appear to think so.

'I don't actually watch them copulating. There isn't much to see, frankly; the whole thing is usually over very quickly. The point is, what

I do is very different to what is commonly known as birdwatching or birding. Birdwatchers are usually focussed on trying to spot as many different species as they can. It's a wonderful hobby, but I'm an academic. I study one species at a time, intensively.'

'Ah. Now I get it. You're a bird-stalker.'

I smiled again. I had been teased about my vocation many times, but this was easily the most enjoyable. And I suddenly realised that I was actually feeling relaxed and at ease in the company of a beautiful woman, for the very first time.

'Flamingos,' she said.

'I beg your pardon?'

'Flamingos are the third kind of bird I know,' she said. 'You've got me thinking about the birds I know. I remembered sparrows and swans earlier, and now I just remembered flamingos. I know swans because they are graceful and they pair for life. I know flamingos because they are pink and beautiful. And as far as I am concerned a sparrow is basically any bird that isn't a swan or a flamingo. What do you know about flamingos, Simon? Do they pair for life, like swans?'

'No, they form strong monogamous pair-bonds, but usually only for a single breeding season. Occasionally they do pair for more than one year. Actually, almost ninety per cent of bird species are monogamous. That's part of the reason that we find them so interesting to study.'

'Why does that make them so interesting?'

'Well, because the mating strategies of many birds resemble our own. Most birds are socially monogamous. *Homo sapiens* are also socially monogamous, which means that we are very unusual mammals.'

'But…'

'Yes?'

'But, if you are only interested in understanding people why don't you just study people?'

I smiled. 'Scientists have learned from long and bitter experience that people don't like it if you camouflage yourself and stare at them for long periods through binoculars.'

Kim laughed. I enjoyed the ensuing sensation and only wished that I knew how to make her do it again. 'I study birds first and foremost because I like to study birds. But what we learn also contributes to the wider understanding of the rules that govern all nature, including *Homo sapiens*.'

'I'll take your word for it. Tell me something fascinating that I don't know about flamingos.'

'Did you know that they dance?'

'Actually, I did know that, I saw it on TV. Are you impressed?'

*You have no idea*, said the PC.

'Very,' I said. 'Did you know that flamingos apply "make-up" in breeding season?'

'You are kidding. Really?'

'Really. They secrete carotenoid pigments from their preen glands and they spend hours applying them to their feathers with their beaks. It makes them look pinker, thus healthier, thus more attractive.'

'That's great! I love flamingos.' She leaned in towards me. 'Do you think they might eventually evolve handbags?'

'It's just a matter of time,' I said.

Above the crowd I spotted a pale pink hand and a vivid pink sleeve and Pippa's head bobbing in and out of view. I quickly tried to conjure up a final flamingo related factoid before Pippa arrived, but then a large male carrying two empty glasses half-stumbled clumsily into Kim. Frowning she turned upon her assailant.

'Sorry love,' he said.

Kim took a half step back away from the male and examined his face. Her frown softened then evaporated. 'Michael?'

The male's expression melted too. 'Kim? It's Kim, right? The Dorchester? The Comms Awards?'

'Right,' she said, nodding, remembering, smiling. The smile was very unlike any she had shared with me and there was something I really didn't like about it. Pippa stepped beside me and I shared an anxious questioning glance with her.

'I, I lost your number. I looked everywhere for it,' said the male.

'Sure you did,' said Kim. The lupine smile had suddenly, happily cooled.

'I did. I really did,' Michael insisted.

Kim didn't seem to have heard him. She introduced Michael to Pippa and then to me. His hand was large and his grip unnecessarily firm. As he shook my hand his pale grey eyes met with mine for just a moment and then I was released and forgotten and Kim was the focus of his attention once again. The PC is not able to accurately evaluate male-attractiveness, but as I watched him watch Kim I quickly developed a very bad feeling about this Michael.

'Look, Kim,' he said, 'at least let me buy you a drink by way of an apology.'

'No, thank you, Michael,' she said. 'There's really nothing to make up for. Actually, Simon hasn't quite finished telling me about the behavioural ecology of flamingos…'

I flinched for the second time when I heard the words behavioural, ecology and flamingos spill so thrillingly and unexpectedly from her clever red lips.

'When Michael left, I said, 'If you think flamingos are interesting, Kim, wait until I tell you about bowerbirds.'

But Kim was watching him retreat to the bar with his two empty glasses and I realised she hadn't heard me.

'Kim?' I said.

# Chapter 6

I spent most of that spring in Kent studying marsh harriers (*Circus aeruginosus*), but I was usually able to meet Pippa for coffee or lunch at least once a week. Initially we met on campus, either in the coffee room on the third floor or in the Life Sciences refectory. The only trouble was that Pippa laughed too loudly and too frequently and I became aware of the glares of other diners.

We started to meet at a busy café I found on Cromwell Road. It had low ceilings and wooden floors and one of those coffee machines that required frequent noisy violence to dislodge the grounds. Outside the open windows, buses passed every few seconds. Even Pippa didn't seem loud in there.

Away from the prying eyes and ears of Empirical, our friendship strengthened. Over those lunches I heard a lot about Duke, her eight-year-old, sixteen-hand American Saddlebred stallion.

One time she pulled out an old-style flip-over photo album. At a suitably restrained pace I flicked through pictures of Duke inhaling, exhaling and ingesting, hoping that the small plank conveying my sandwich would arrive soon.

'He's a bay, but you can see that, and he has adorable little hooked ears,' she said. 'He's totally gorgeous, very cheeky and a shameless flirt.' I looked up from the album; while my expertise in mating behaviour does not extend to equines I was fairly confident that horses progressed rapidly from grazing to penetration. Flipping over another page I let the thought pass unspoken.

'Who was the girl I sat next to at your supper?' I asked. 'Did you meet her through horses?'

'Janet?' said Pippa. 'Do you like her?'

'No… I mean, she seems very nice, but no. I was just wondering if you met a lot of your friends that way. Like Judy? Or any of the others?'

Somehow, I couldn't bring myself to reference Kim directly. For one thing, I didn't want Pippa to conclude that I was spending time with her in order to find out more about Kim. More significantly though, I was too shy to admit or even to hint about my feelings.

I didn't anticipate that this approach would be problematic. Pippa would be sure, I thought, to speak about Kim from time to time and I would eventually gain confidence.

Pippa and I talked about a lot of people, of course, over the weeks and months after her supper. We talked about mutual acquaintances from the department. We talked about our families, friends and notable equestrians. We laughed about Daniel's continued pursuit of Janet and I heard the backstories of other supper guests. But Pippa never spoke about Kim, not even once.

This seemed strange to me because Pippa and Kim had seemed close and because I was almost certain that females do not typically invite random strangers into their kitchens to slice their vegetables.

*\*\**

Then, a few weeks later, Pippa invited me to an exhibition of equine art and photography in Surrey.

'It will be such fun. Lots of people will be there. Aman apparently knows a lovely place for dinner afterwards. You just have to come, Simon.'

Hoping that 'lots of people' might encompass Kim, I eagerly accepted the invitation. I even bought a new shirt.

Aman drove us down to Surrey in his grey BMW. Judy sat in the passenger seat but spent most of the journey facing Pippa and I in the back. When we hit the M25, Aman slid a Van Morrison CD into the player, but I was listening, without success, for mention of Kim.

I got to know Judy and Aman better that evening. I stood before countless paintings of galloping horses with flying manes. Pippa enthusiastically introduced me to two of her 'delicious' single friends from the stables. But they weren't Kim, and Kim wasn't there.

# Chapter 7

I was back at the same old table, sipping the same old beverage alongside the same old male conspecific. The song coming from the speaker was different but Leo Sayer hardly felt like progress.

Phil leaned back to undo the top button of his jeans – a sure sign that he had achieved an advanced state of relaxation. 'How's it all going, Bird?' he asked.

'Define "all",' I said.

'You know – the whole heterosexual hurly-burly; dating and humping and shagging and that.'

Scowling, I shushed him. 'It isn't. It isn't *going*.'

'You always have to have a succession plan, Bird. You should have developed a succession plan long before whatsherface got the hump.'

'Claire. Her name was Claire.'

'You broke up with Claire without a succession plan, didn't you?'

'I can confirm that I did not have a "succession plan", whatever that is, at the time that Claire and I severed our pair-bond.'

'Bird, Bird, Bird.' Phil shook his head.

'Have *you* got one?'

'Of course. Cammie would never leave me, but if she dies I will probably seek solace from Ruby or Kate from the office, after an appropriate period of mourning of course. I might also consider her sister – if she lightens up a bit.'

In order to end the great succession plan debate, I opened the menu binder and peeled apart its plastic pages, though I knew it, including the spelling mistakes, from memory.

Phil was not to be silenced. 'I've been thinking: you should have your landing gear—'

'Something tells me that you are referring to my genitals,' I said, as I tried to decide between vegetable chilli or hunter's chicken.

'Bingo. You should have your "genitals" cryogenically frozen.'

'Now, I know I should be able to figure out why I should have my genitals frozen, but for the sake of time, could you...'

'Sure. So, you know there are these people who have had their heads cryogenically frozen? Well, I was thinking, they are going to need a decent set of "genitals" if they ever come back – and yours have got low mileage.'

'Vegetable chilli,' I said, closing the menu and placing it by my glass.

'Alternatively, if you aren't quite ready to kiss your balls goodbye, you could compensate for your lack of succession plan with some internet action.'

'I'm not doing that. I can't,' I said.

'Why not?'

'Well for a start it's a very unnatural way to screen potential mates and it places too much emphasis on physical attributes. And besides, I don't want my picture all over the internet.'

'It's hardly a taboo, Bird. Everybody does it.'

'I don't want to walk into the department at Empirical wondering if people have been looking at my profile. I'd be wondering if they were gossiping about me. I bet the students google the lecturers.' I slid the menu across the table towards him. 'Pick something.'

'You should try it.'

'I wouldn't feel comfortable. I don't want people I know, or strangers – and basically that's everyone – to be able to read a lot of personal stuff about me.'

'You don't have to say anything original. Most people just say that they "love to laugh". They say "My friends tell me that I'm sexy and funny and loyal". They say "Carpe diem" or some Kahlil Gibran bollocks. That's what the women do anyway. I haven't looked at the men yet.'

'Are *you* registered on a dating website?'

'No. I browse from time to time, that's all.' Phil didn't seem embarrassed, but then Phil never did. Nor did he feel moved to offer an explanation. '"Love to laugh", what kind of shite is that anyway? I know, Bird, why don't you say "I dislike pain and avoid it wherever possible". No, hang on a minute, that might seem a bit sinister. How about, "I like to consume food when I am hungry"? Don't mention the birdwatching though, whatever you do.' Phil opened the menu and peered down at it. 'Maybe speed-dating would be better for you,' he said, nodding in agreement with himself. He looked up from the menu. 'That way, only twenty or so strangers will see your face. You get to talk to each of the girls for three or four minutes. That's usually more than enough, trust me.'

'I don't think so. I get very uncomfortable when I meet attractive women, though I suppose the courtship interactions are very short under those circumstances. But, no, I don't think I would be very good at it.'

'You would be fine if you had your trusty wingman by your side,' he said, grinning malevolently. 'I'll show you the ropes.'

'You can't do that. What would Cammie say?'

'*She* wouldn't mind.' He sounded confident, as always.

'Of course she would.'

'She wouldn't.'

'Doesn't that bother you?'

'No.'

'It would bother me.' Recognising my error immediately, I braced myself for a reiteration of the merits of the 'succession plan', but instead Phil appeared to become engaged in a primitive form of reflection.

Breaking his silence he said, 'Look, I know for sure she won't mind because… well, we've done it ourselves a couple of times.'

'Done what?'

'*Speed-dating*.' Phil said this as though I was the stupid one.

'Together?'

'Yes.'

'Why?'

'Just for fun… And to see who won…'

'What?'

'I told Cammie that I would get more call-backs than her and she disagreed and so we put it to the test.' He took a sheepish sip. 'Four times,' he said, wiping his mouth.

'Well, you two are quite something, aren't you? You are probably the only established pair in all of human history who compete at speed-dating.'

'We can't be held responsible for the death of the contemporary imagination,' he said.

I shook my head in wonder. 'Cammie won, didn't she?'

'I had a cold last time.'

'What's that got to do with it? I might be a novice when it comes to human courtship rituals but I'm pretty sure there is no actual athleticism required in speed-dating.'

'I wasn't at my best.'

'You lost.'

'It was close.'

'Cammie won all four times, didn't she?'

Phil sort of nodded. I enjoyed it. Then I realised why Phil had initiated a conversation which would inevitably end this way.

'You think you can beat me, don't you?'

He nodded. 'I'm taking multi-vitamins.'

\*\*\*

I was at Hazeley Heath when Phil called me the following Saturday morning. He sounded excited. He had found a speed-dating 'match' for twenty-five- to thirty-eight-year-olds in Soho the following Friday.

'We will probably be the youngest blokes there,' he said.

'Surely not.'

'Everybody lies about their age. Don't be surprised if you bump into your uncle.'

'Don't they check?'

'Oh absolutely, Bird. All speed-dating in the capital is overseen by a guy who used to be in charge of security at the Pentagon. The doors to the speed dating "*facility*" only open if they recognise your irises.'

Before agreeing to participate I insisted on speaking to Cammie first to be sure that she was fully aware of what we were planning to do.

'Why would I worry?' she said, in her liquefying French accent. 'But, Simon, you must beat him – for both of our sakes.'

\*\*\*

The speed-dating 'facility' was a narrow, sett-like basement in a bar called *Destiny*. The walls and central brick pillars were painted matt black. Red leather booths ran along one side of the basement. A black mirror-backed bar ran along the other flank. We were greeted by a male leaning against a black pillar, clutching a clipboard. 'Marc' was scrawled on a badge clipped to a red lanyard that hung around his thin neck. He highlighted our names on his list and passed us our very own badges and lanyards. I was number five for the evening.

When Marc issued Phil with number six I asked him if he had seeded us.

'No, mate. No,' he said. 'They're just numbers. Make sure you both get your free drink at the bar.'

In fact, as we walked over to the bar I noted that Phil seemed very pleased to have been allocated number six. Behind the bar, a dark-haired girl in a black vest was enthusiastically hugging a short blonde girl in a white vest. They broke and chatted animatedly in what sounded like a Slavic language. They looked happy to see each other and I felt cheered by their display of intra-gender affection. While waiting for the girls to return to their duties, we introduced ourselves to males two and three. They both seemed much more relaxed than me.

When the blonde girl disappeared through a matt black door, the dark girl turned her attention to us. All traces of warmth immediately left her face. She looked down at my badge and up at my face.

'Sex on the Beach, yes?'

'I beg your pardon?' I said.

'Free drink is *Sex on the Beach*.'

'Of course,' I said, looking at Phil, eyebrows raised. 'Of course it is. Could we have two beers instead and we will pay the difference.'

'Beer is full price until happy hour.'

'When is happy hour?'

'Seven.'

'It's six fifty-three…'

Phil must have believed that his negotiation skills were superior to mine because at this point he jumped in. 'If we promise not to buy any discounted drinks after seven fifty-three could we get the happy hour price early?'

'Happy hour end seven thirty.'

I touched Phil on his arm to alert him that I was resuming control. 'Thank you. We will have two of your finest *Sex on the Beach* please.'

We witnessed the full sexual act. The dark-haired girl placed several cubes of ice in brightly coloured plastic beakers, thus immediately creating the illusion of volume. She then poured a carefully measured shot of peach schnapps into each beaker. Bypassing the time-consuming carton-shaking step she opened the cartons of first orange and then cranberry juice with blunt scissors and poured the juices into the two cups. I noted that she had allocated the juices in markedly different proportions in our respective cups, perhaps reflecting an instinctive understanding of our individual fruit preferences.

'Do you have a website where I can download the recipe?' asked Phil. I wonder if she would have stirred them if he hadn't said that. She nudged the two beakers across the bar towards us and nodded. With this final highly efficient gesture the drinks became ours. Thanking her, for some reason, we reached for them and stepped away from the bar.

As we headed for the sanctuary of a pillar I told Phil that I preferred the colour of his drink. 'Cheers,' I said. 'And thanks, Phil.'

'No problem. Why?'

'Well, I'm very impressed with what I've seen so far. It's *so* much better than I expected. I've got a really *great* feeling about tonight.'

'You won't win.'

'No, I mean she's going to be here. I just know she is. I think I've always known that my female – the one that I have waited all these years to find – would be lured by a complimentary cocktail with an erotic name.'

'When did *you* get so cynical?' he said. He took a sip of his cocktail, shuddered and looked at his watch. 'Six fifty-eight,' he said.

Glancing over at the bar I said, 'Let's wait until five past – just to be sure.'

\*\*\*

Over the next fifteen minutes the anxious-looking, lanyard-wearing congregated. Conversation, such as it was, was dominated by personal speed-dating history. Then Marc appeared amongst us blowing on the referee's whistle which was also attached to his Swiss Army lanyard.

I did not need to draw upon my knowledge of game theory to comprehend the rules of speed-dating. Marc's whistle was to be the signal that heralded the start and end of our four-minute 'dates'. At the end of each 'date' the males were to move, clockwise, to the next table. Marc urged us to believe that the most important thing was to have fun.

I leaned over and whispered to Phil that there were certain similarities between what we were about to do and the courtship of many species of birds, except of course that in those cases it was the female who moved from territory to territory in her quest to choose the best mate.

'You should ask if they can change it,' said Phil.

I frowned. 'Don't be ridiculous. I just thought you might be interested.'

'And *I'm* just saying,' Phil's voice grew stern and louder, 'that if it's important to you, you should speak up.'

'Everything OK, guys?' said Marc.

'Fine,' I said.

'Sorry, Marc,' said Phil. 'Number five was just explaining that he's a birdwatcher. Don't know if any of you ladies go for that kind of thing. Can't imagine why you would.' All eyes fell upon Phil, and then on me.

'Actually I'm an avian behavioural ecologist,' I said.

'Right...' said Marc. 'That's cool. I don't think we have ever had a birdwatcher here before actually... Well, if there aren't any questions, I'm going to give you five more minutes to fill your glasses and then we will begin. Have fun guys.'

'I reckon I'm ahead already,' said Phil.

\*\*\*

Barbara, my first date, was a pleasant primary school teacher from Wandsworth. Almost immediately, she told me that she had recently experienced the termination of a long-term pair-bond. Her wound gaped before me. She spent almost the whole four minutes describing the termination and apologising for describing the termination. Just before Marc blew his whistle at the end of the round she asked me what my favourite bird was.

I said goodbye to Barbara and moved on to table number six to sit in the seat just vacated by Phil. From table seven he flashed me a demonic grin.

Fiona, a pleasant-looking female with a round attractive face, beautiful braided hair and an orange blouse was waiting for me. I smiled and introduced myself, but she glowered.

'Is it true that you thought it would be more *natural* for the women to move around?' she said, her voice strident. 'What's more natural about it?'

I spent the next four minutes failing to make Fiona understand. I didn't find out anything about Fiona at all, apart from the fact that she sometimes clung stubbornly to initial perceptions.

The next five dates plotted much the same course. If I didn't get challenged directly about my views, I encountered restrictive body language.

According to the PC the female at table number four, my final 'date' of the evening was the most attractive of the females. As I approached the table I decided that the best strategy was to tackle the female circulation issue head on.

I cleared my throat. 'Hi Charity. I'm Simon, and I never intended to suggest that the females should be the ones to move around the tables. All I was saying was—'

'What are you talking about?' she scowled.

*Very clever, Phil,* I thought. *Very clever.*

# Chapter 8

*July*

With summer came another invitation from Pippa, this time to a ball in aid of the cancer charity that patiently provided the funding for her never-ending PhD. The thought of spending a whole evening making innovative excuses to avoid the dance floor chilled me, but I clearly heard Pippa say, 'Everyone will be there.'

At last – everyone.

I hired a tux and had my black shoes re-heeled. I developed a number of ways to greet Kim and a series of discussion topics. I went to the Life Sciences library to garner new flamingo facts.

These mental preparations spawned a large clutch of imagined scenarios. In one such flight of fancy, I was standing at the bar of a generic country house hotel in my tux when I saw Kim. She was standing, alone, beside a huge, gilded framed portrait. Though this Kim was merely an embellished memory, I felt the PC stir. She wore a long diaphanous, low-cut, pale pink dress. Looking over at me, her gaze was undeviating. Her hair was swirled around her head, but in a good way, and she clutched a small pink strapless purse in her pretty pink hands. Her smile, ethereal at first, solidified. She began to sail across the room towards me. I felt a pang of imaginary guilt when I caught myself assessing her imaginary breasts.

'Lovely to see you again, Dr Selwood,' she said. I felt her fingers rest lightly on my forearm as we air kissed. 'Do I remind you of any South American wading bird in particular?'

\*\*\*

But Kim did not attend the charity ball.

I sat between Pippa and her friend Margot, a recently divorced equine vet, and 'Dukie's aunty'. If I had been a collector of gruesome foaling anecdotes it would have been one of the best nights of my life.

\*\*\*

By the following Friday I had largely regained my appetite for both food and life. I spent the latter part of the morning in the Life Sciences library. Heading back to my office at lunchtime, I opened the door at the top of the stairs. The stairwell was of the concrete variety found frequently in multi-storey car parks, but minus the urine. As I stepped out on to the landing, I heard the reverberation of two female voices from below. I recognised instantly that the dominant voice was Pippa's.

Before the ball I might have leaned out over the stairwell to announce myself, but I was still feeling a little distant.

Pippa giggled – the stairwell echoes made her sound demonic, in a head-girl kind of way. I heard her say, 'You remember Paul, don't you? Well it's his idea. Judy is coming, and Aman if he gets back in time. Kim will be there too.' I inhaled, long and deep. Kim! 'It's in Walpole Park. The weather is supposed to be gorgeous tomorrow and I'm going to be making a *lovely* picnic. Are you sure you won't come?'

The second female voice was gentler and less distinct – Janet I suspect – and it was difficult to hear precisely what was said.

'Boo you. It's such a *great-big-shame*,' said Pippa.

When the two females parted, I waited until I heard a door close and for the sound of heels clopping down the staircase before I began my own descent.

At last, I thought. At last I was going to see Kim again. And tomorrow!

I bounded down the stairs and returned to my office in elevated spirits, fully expecting to find some kind of note on my desk. But there was no message.

I checked the white board.

I checked my phone.

I checked my email.

Oh well, I thought, I'm sure Pippa will be back later.

\*\*\*

Towards the end of the long afternoon, and now feeling somewhat miffed – did Pippa just expect me to be free at short notice? – I headed down to the second floor. I eventually found Pippa in the tissue culture suite. Had she been too busy to pass by my office?

I pulled up a stool alongside Pippa's laminar flow hood while she pulled off her gloves.

'Hi,' I said, expecting that would be all it would take to set off a communication chain reaction that would result in me being invited to Pippa's picnic.

'Hi, Simon,' she said.

'Cell lines flourishing?' I said, nodding at the stack of flasks in the hood.

'Not especially,' she said.

'Oh dear,' I said, recalling Pippa's reputation as the 'Stalin of the cell line'. 'Are you still OK for lunch next Monday?'

'Would I ever cancel a lunch date with the gorgeous Dr S?' she said. 'Of course I'm fine for Monday. Silly Simon.'

'Great,' I said, and waited.

Staccato banter and erratic giggling followed, but still Pippa did not invite me to her picnic. By this point I was feeling frustrated and even a little hurt, but it was almost time for Prof's examination meeting and I had to go.

In desperation I said, 'Anything fun planned this weekend?' as I returned the stool to its original position.

'No, not really,' she reached for a new bottle of culture medium, red as cough syrup, from a box on a trolley by the side of the hood. 'Just hanging out with a handsome Duke.'

As I strode, glowering, towards Prof's office, I realised that Pippa hadn't giggled about her handsome Duke remark. Not so much as a titter.

***

Why hadn't Pippa invited me to Walpole Park? I returned to my office after the exam meeting, perplexed and frankly sulky. Back behind my desk, I immediately searched Walpole Park and discovered that The Ealing Blues Festival was taking place over the weekend.

The blues: I owned a copy of BB King's Greatest Hits (a random gift) and a two disc 'Blues Legends' compilation, though disc one had been missing for years. Over the years I had tried and repeatedly failed to like the blues. To my ear it was dull and monotonous and all of the songs sounded so similar. However, Kim was attending a blues festival and so, therefore, was I – invitation or not.

Should I go on my own? Having considered this for a few minutes I reasoned that if I was to go anywhere on my lonesome, a blues festival must be just about the best place. Might Kim think it was a little odd though? Worse still, might she consider this an indication of low rank?

I considered my other options (i.e. Phil) and quickly concluded that it would definitely be best if I went on my own.

Still concerned about the rank implications, I immediately began to research the history of the blues in order to impress Kim with my knowledge of the genre. It was nearly seven pm when I slung my backpack over my shoulder.

I got as far as the door, and even laid a hand on the handle, but then returned to my desk and picked up the phone. I hesitated anew, and then dialled.

Phil answered almost immediately. I felt pleasure and disappointment jostle with each other.

'Hi Phil. Would you care for a spontaneous beer?'

***

I waited until I had dispatched approximately fifty per cent of my second beer before I mentioned the blues festival.

'Apparently, there's a blues festival in Ealing tomorrow.'

'I've never been to a blues festival,' said Phil. 'How does it work? Do the organisers pick one song and then all the bands agree to play it over and over for two days?'

'Don't be ridiculous,' I said. 'The blues is a vast, diverse and infinitely flexible musical form. Texas, Chicago and Memphis have all spawned distinct sounds.' I took a sip from my beer and cautiously eyed Phil. 'I'm thinking of going.'

'You don't like the blues.'

'That's not true.'

Phil shook his dice-like head. 'Yet more hidden depths to the one they call Bird. What are your favourites?'

'Erm… "Hummingbird" by BB King. Love that.'

'I can already see just how wrong I was. Any other recommendations?'

'Erm… "Little Red Rooster" by Howlin' Wolf.' My desk research was paying off sooner than I had imagined.

'Of course. Anything else?'

'That one by Muddy Waters.'

'If you are thinking of "The Ugly Duckling", I'm pretty sure that was "Dirty" Danny Kaye.'

Soon, the concept of a rapid-fire 'Birdie Song contest' was firmly lodged in Phil's mind. Escape was impossible.

Phil clapped his hands. 'Right. Sudden death. Me first, OK?' He took a fistful of peanuts and tossed his head back, because you can get more peanuts in that way.

He shifted the bolus of peanuts to the side of his mouth and said, 'Ready? "Swansong for a Raven" – Cradle of Filth,' he said. Reading my face, Phil chomped the rhythm of his pleasure. 'That counts as two goes. Right?'

'It does not. Who are Cradle of Filth?'

'They're an extreme metal band.'

'They might be, or you might have made them up.'

'I could have, but I didn't need to. Can't you go?'

'"Pretty Flamingo" – Manfred Mann,' I said, imagining Kim exactly as she had looked in the pub after Pippa's supper.

'"When Doves Cry" – Prince.' Phil picked up the tumbler of peanuts and poured another batch into his curled mitt.

'"Stool Pigeon" – Kid Creole and the Coconuts.'

'"Albatross" – Fleetwood Mac.'

Damn him – I'd been saving that one. '"Blackbird" – The Beatles.'

'"Blue Jay Way" – The Beatles,' said Phil with borrowed nonchalance. Fear flickered in me. I could see how badly he wanted to win and I also knew, from bitter speed-dating experience, just how loudly and how long he could crow over a victory.

'"Ain't Nobody Here but Us Chickens" – Louis Jordan.'

'"A Chicken Ain't Nothin' but a Bird" – Louis Jordan. That dude really loved chicken,' said Phil.

I was searching. There had to be a song about the robin (*Erithacus rubecula*).

'I'm afraid I must press you,' said Phil.

I grinned when it came. Of course: '"Rockin' Robin" – The Jackson 5.'

'"When the Red Red Robin Comes Bob, Bob Bobbin' Along" – Bing Crosby.' Phil pointed his hands to the wood-chipped ceiling. 'Thank you Gran,' he said; then planting his elbows on the edge of the table, he leaned forward, chin on knuckles.

What about the raptors, I thought. Yes. '"Fly Like an Eagle" – Seal.' Would Phil realise that eagle was not a species? Observing him, I prepared my defence, but it wasn't defiance that I saw in his eyes.

'Anything by the Eagles, he said.'

'Song plus band, Phil. Song plus band.'

'"Kookaburra Sits in the Old Gum Tree" – by… by Nick Cave,' he said.

'Not a chance.'

'"Fools Thrush In" – Elvis.'

'Nope.'

'"Pheasant Valley Sunday" – The Monkees.'

'Ingenious, but still no.'

'"I Wanna Owl Your Hand" – The Beatles.'

'*Pathetic.*'

\*\*\*

The victory pint is the sweetest, but I curbed my gloat, mindful of my wider objective. I waited until a little of the chuckle and spar were back in him to make my play.

'I think it should be good, tomorrow. The festival,' I said.

Nothing.

'There is something primal, earthy and raw about the blues. I don't think any other music is so evocative of its roots. Do you know what I mean?'

Nothing.

'Did you know that Ealing was where British blues was born? The Stones played some of their early gigs at the Ealing Club.'

Phil looked around the bar, absently.

'Plus, I think it's good to support local community events and the musicians who are still trying to perform authentic music… I'm definitely going.'

'Do you want me to come with you, Bird? Is that it?' Phil cleaned a molar with a hooked finger.

'No, that's *not* it… I mean, of course, it would be great to have you along, but I assumed you would be busy,' I said, though in reality I considered it highly unlikely that Phil would be busy.

'What time does it start?'

'I was going to go along at about three-ish?'

'Pheasant Valley Sunday?' He inspected his nail.

'Sorry Phil. It's not me, it's the rules. You know I would give it to you if I could.'

Phil said he would let me know if he changed his mind about the festival.

# Chapter 9

*Saturday*

Phil called at lunchtime to say he would be with me sometime between three pm and four pm, 'If you still need me that is.'

'Only come if you want to,' I said.

'I'm sure you would make the same sacrifice for me.'

And so on.

At four forty-five pm I was still sitting on my battered cream sofa, listening, for the third time that afternoon, to the surviving CD of my 'Blues Legends' compilation and gleaning what I could from the sleeve notes. There wasn't a molecule of fraternal gratitude left in me when the buzzer interrupted Little Walter.

\*\*\*

I tried to hurry Phil towards Walpole Park without revealing my anxiety. He stopped on Ealing High Street first for a pasty and then, just a few yards later, for a coffee. I waited outside on the pavement, my thigh jiggling.

It was almost five thirty pm by the time we first laid eyes on the festival entrance, but the sky was a clean midday blue and the air was thick and warm with no hint of evening. We were just twenty-five metres from the entrance when Phil cut across the park to dispose of the scrunched wrapper and cup. I waited by the entrance for him, trying to absorb the optimistic boogie-woogie piano emanating from within the festival enclosure.

'Sounds really good, doesn't it,' I said, when he returned.

'Have you got a tissue?' he asked, holding up his hands.

*\*\*\**

The enclosure was littered with clusters of pink-armed drinkers. They sprawled on picnic blankets, picking chips from polystyrene cartons. They sat folded like living paperclips in camping chairs. They stood in groups holding yellow pints out before them like liquid handshakes. Few seemed to be taking much notice of the music.

I let Phil stride ahead so I could discreetly search for Kim, or even Pippa. I stopped when two young boys ran out in front of me; the largest boy tripped, then got to his feet and punched the smaller boy on the chest and ran off. Ahead of them, a shirtless man in white calf-length trousers wavered and smoked.

I had met Kim only once but the festival enclosure did not seem at all like her natural habitat. *I bet she's gone*, I thought.

From the large blue and red marquee on the right-hand side of the enclosure I heard applause for the end of a tenor sax solo. I stopped to applaud too, and looked to Phil, hoping for some sign of enthusiasm or appreciation, but he had veered towards the beer tent.

*\*\*\**

Plastic glasses in hand, we wandered around the festival enclosure. I looked for Kim amongst the passers-by, amongst the stall browsers and amongst the faces of the condemned as they queued for the chemical toilets.

At a second smaller stage at the rear of the enclosure, a band led by a young adult male with long red hair and purple flared cords was playing rocky guitar blues. It took me a few minutes to realise that he reminded me of Janis Joplin. With a voice stretched taut, he sang the world-weary songs of older men. We stayed for the end of the set, but I wasn't listening. I was scanning the audience, alert as a bodyguard at a political rally.

*\*\*\**

We looped back to the main marquee. Phil went back to the bar and I stepped inside to lean back against one of the outer posts, silently cursing him for our late arrival. On the stage, a male in a black cap adjusted the height of a central microphone.

'One, two. One, two.'

Were there, I wondered, other numbers, thus far overlooked, which could provide greater acoustic insight?

'Simon?' said a familiar voice. I turned. Pippa stepped in front of me. For a fraction of a second I got to see Pippa as experienced by door-to-door salesmen. Then a squeal heralded the return of the old Pippa. She flung herself upon me, pressing me back against the post.

'What a gorgeous surprise!' she said.

'Hi Pippa,' I said, with the breath available to me. Over her shoulder, I saw Kim, in a pair of green shorts and a loose-fitting black and white striped T-shirt.

The PC wakened with a start. *Yes! It's her. At last. And this time she has pins.*

I didn't respond to him, but I hadn't failed to note that her legs were long, slender, smooth and flawless, like a manikin's.

Kim smiled and waved a forelimb, which was also very pleasant. I flapped mine as best as I could – like a penguin attempting to turn underwater. Releasing me, Pippa said, 'You are a very naughty boy, you know. You didn't tell me you were coming.'

'You didn't tell me *you* were coming,' I said, only partially suppressing my censure.

'Oh, it was a last-minute thing... You remember Kim...'

*Frequently,* said the PC.

'Yes, of course. Hi Kim.'

'And Kim, you remember Simon...?' said Pippa.

'Yes, absolutely. Didn't Pippa buy a saddle from you?'

'I...I...' I stammered, and looked to Pippa for help, but she looked as stricken as I felt.

'No, no. Kim,' she said, 'you... you, met Simon at my...'

'I know, P,' she said, reaching out for her hand. 'I'm joking. Simon taught me almost everything I know about flamingos.' She looked at me. 'Simon knew I was joking, didn't you, Simon?' I nodded and attempted to recover.

It seemed like the kind of moment when two people who previously met at a dinner party might kiss. I always felt like I had received insufficient training about how such decisions were made and so I defaulted to female choice. Unfortunately, Kim didn't move towards me.

'What are you doing here anyway, Simon?' said Pippa. 'I didn't know that you liked the blues.'

I had prepared an answer for that question during the long sofa hours of the afternoon, but was unable to recall it in my moment of need.

'Don't I?' I said. 'I mean, didn't you?' Convinced that I was about to be exposed as some kind of predatory heterosexual, I panicked. 'I'm here with my friend. He's a *huge* blues fan. He's at the bar.'

'No he isn't.' Phil stepped alongside me holding two beers and grinning ominously. I was at his mercy and he knew it. 'Sorry I took so long. They usually have twelve bars at blues festivals, and I should know. How many blues festivals would you say I've been to over the years, Bird?'

'Lots and lots,' I said.

'Well, lots, anyway,' he said.

'Yes, lots.'

'Really?' said Pippa. 'Why do you like the blues so much?'

'It's in my blood, ma'am, I guess,' he said. He looked over at the stage, his eyes misted. 'Back on the Harrogate delta, the blues coursed through our veins like watermelon juice. After supper, Pappy would play his beat-up ol' guitar, for me and little Sissy.' His voice had slowed and deepened. I hated him.

'How lovely,' said Pippa. 'Did he teach you to play?'

Phil swallowed. 'No M'. When Sissy left…' he closed his eyes. 'When Sissy left, Pappy smashed up that ol' guitar and he never did play it again. I wasn't even allowed to hum 'til I was fully growed.'

'Oh my god,' said Pippa, her hand clamped over her mouth.

Kim was not so taken in. 'I'm curious, Phil. What's your favourite kind of blues?' she asked.

'I love 'em all,' said Phil, unperturbed. 'The thought of choosin' just one kind of blues makes me sad, so sad, but I do 'specially love the harmonica. Folks roun' here calls me "Phil Harmonica".'

'I just bet they do,' said Kim.

My anxiety was mounting. If Phil continued in this vein I feared that Kim's assessment of me as a potential mate would suffer by association.

Desperate, I called upon my emergency platonic safe word. 'Philip…' I said, pausing to let it permeate, 'Philip, why don't you tell Pippa and Kim, who aren't yet familiar with your sense of humour, what you really think about the blues?' Phil glared, but I sensed a begrudging acknowledgement.

'Of course, Simon,' he said – and Phil called me Simon as rarely as I called him Philip. 'I love the primal, earthy, rawness of the blues,' he said, 'I don't think any other music is so evocative of its roots. And of course Ealing was where British blues was born, and so I wanted to come and Simon was kind enough to accompany me.'

Phil(ip) was beautifully behaved, if a little sullen, for the next few minutes. Kim and Pippa pointed over to their encampment beneath a drooping willow and beside railings.

'Come on,' said Kim, linking arms with Pippa. 'Michael will be wondering where I am.'

'Michael'. I had definitely heard Kim say 'Michael'. The implication was obvious, even to me, and devastating. So Kim had paired with Michael. I tightened my grip on the marquee post and cursed myself: this wouldn't have happened if I had known more about flamingos when we first met. I felt my heart pound powerfully within my chest and I ached to sprint out of the marquee and out of the festival exit. Somehow I felt sure that this act would be more therapeutic if I also bellowed.

I didn't run though, or bellow, I just swallowed, hard. A moment later the desire for physical escape had been replaced by a sudden crushing weariness. I discovered that the obliteration of hopes, no matter how slender was exhausting. Suddenly I wanted Kim to go away so that I could lie down on the grass and start to sleep away all thoughts of her.

'Do come over and join us,' said Pippa.

'That would be lovely. Thank you,' Phil said.

This was now the last thing I wanted. 'Philip, I thought you were really keen to see the next band.'

'Oh yes, I am. Thank you for reminding me, Simon,' he said, compliantly. 'I hear they have a mean harp man.'

As Kim tugged her away, Pippa told us that we were welcome to join them whenever we wanted.

\*\*\*

The singer had long kinked hair, a green waistcoat and a disappointing north-west accent. At the end of the first song – which didn't feature a harmonica incidentally – we were informed that we had been listening to a Booker T and the MGs original.

Phil leaned in to say something at the start of the next song, but I couldn't hear him. He redoubled his efforts: 'I said, "You really like that *hoochie-coochie* mama, don't you?"' I felt the fine spray of his spittle in my ear.

I shrugged my shoulders and watched the singer – his face contorted like a constipated infant – while digging in my shorts pocket for a napkin. This was not a topic that I wished to pursue and so I said: 'Was this Al Green?'

In the applause that followed the song the singer asked the sparse crowd if we wanted to hear something from their new album. I tendered a tepid, courteous affirmation, but Phil cupped his hands around his mouth and yelled, 'Frankly, I'm ambivalent.'

The singer looked out across the crowd. He looked directly at me. I wanted to tell him that I wasn't the one that yelled. The bass player was looking at me too. A juvenile male holding his father's hand just in front of us also turned to look. Finally, the two men on the stage looked at each other, shrugged, and began to play again.

'Come on, Bird,' said Phil, 'Phil Harmonica needs to find him some chitlins.'

\*\*\*

We ate sitting cross-legged on the grass outside the marquee.

'I bet Pippa and Kippa have a blanket,' said Phil, chewing. 'Can *we* have a blanket next year, Bird?' He waved three limp chips in the air. 'I can see why you like her,' he said.

I pretended to concentrate on my falafel wrap. Phil picked up the burger again, dipped it in ketchup in the white polystyrene tray and then pointed it at me while attempting, python-like, to swallow the previous mouthful. It looked painful. His own plastic glass was drained and so without asking he took a sip from mine. 'But I have to say she is pretty stupid,' he said. 'She completely bought that whole delta-papa thing. I mean—'

'Not that one, you dodo,' I snapped.

'Gotcha,' he grinned. 'So you prefer the other one?'

'Yes,' I mumbled. 'I think she is the most attractive female I've ever met.'

'Sure, she's attractive,' he said, 'if you are into that whole natural, timeless, classic, flawless thing. But, that's your problem right there, Bird. A woman like that is always going to be difficult. She'll be difficult to get and difficult to keep. You know that don't you?'

'Oh, I don't expect her to select me as her mate. I just – I just like the way she makes me feel. I met her at a party and once I became accustomed to her beauty, I found that I was actually able to converse with her. I wanted to see her again, that's all.'

'Hey, I didn't say you shouldn't try, Bird.'

'Well it's too late in any case. She has clearly formed a pair-bond with this Michael since I last saw her. I'm clearly not her phenotype.' I managed to deliver the sentence cleanly, giving Phil no indication of just how difficult I had found it to say.

'Hmm,' he said. He chewed his burger for a while, silent but for the hum of mastication. Still chewing, he clambered to his feet and placed the burger container in a nearby bin. He sat back down in front of me, leaning back on his arms with his legs splayed before him. A splat of ketchup was webbed in the hairs beneath his knee cap. I tried not to look.

'Tell me about him?'

'Who? Why?'

'Just curious. I mean to know what kind of bloke a girl like that would go for.'

I told Phil what little I had been able to observe about Michael. Phil seemed curious. He even asked questions.

He looked over his shoulder towards the willow (*Salix babylonica*). 'We should probably go over there in a minute.'

'Why? So I can be confronted with concrete evidence of their pair-bond?'

'Don't worry, Bird, chances are they won't actually be fucking,' he said. When I protested he apologised with hands held high. 'I know – I know – I know. I'm just saying we don't want to look rude.'

This was highly suspicious. 'When did *you* become concerned about etiquette?' I asked.

'Point taken. But *you* don't want to look rude, do you?'

'I suppose not...' I said, annoyed with myself for privileging courteousness over self-preservation. 'But can I trust you?'

'What do you mean?' I saw him take pleasure from my question and then attempt to conceal that pleasure. He wiped the ketchup from his knee with a finger and licked it.

'I mean I am not going over there unless you promise that you won't try to make a fool of me,' I said.

'OK,' he shrugged.

'OK, what?'

'OK. You – can – trust – me – Bird. You know, you really remind me of Pappy when you get all arsey.'

# Chapter 10

Pippa's social group was gathered on two adjoining picnic blankets, one tartan, one robin-egg blue. Pippa was kneeling beside a hamper, pouring wine into the gaping mouths of the plastic glasses stretched towards her. I recognised Paul and Elaine from the party. At the back of the furthermost blanket, I recognised Michael. Most of all I recognised Kim's head resting on his shoulder. I groaned.

'Jesus. I hope they aren't the kind of couple who feed each other finger foods,' whispered Phil as we stepped around the deckchairs of a neighbouring group.

'Agreed,' I said from the corner of my mouth. 'From there it's just a short step to mutual regurgitation.'

'And is that a rabbit reversing out of his shirt?'

'Philip,' I cautioned.

'I know.'

The faces began to turn towards us. Pippa saw us last, but was first to her feet, snapping a breadstick in her haste.

'Simon! Great! Now we are going to have even more lovely fun. Look everyone, Simon! And his friend.' The group rose. I shook hands with Michael last. I noticed fading, crescent-shaped bruises below his eyes. And his nose seemed a little larger than I remembered, or was I just standing closer?

Kim introduced Phil to Michael: 'Mike, this is Simon's friend Philip. He's an authority on the blues. Aren't we lucky?'

'Is that right?' said Michael, oblivious to her sarcasm. 'I don't get it at all, I'm afraid.'

'What happened to your face?' said Phil. 'Looks like you've got the black and blues.'

Michael laughed, fortunately, and reached up to touch his face. 'It's no big deal,' he said. 'Judo. Landed flat on my face.' He wiggled his nose to prove it wasn't broken.

Kim tucked herself back underneath his arm. He was a full head taller than her. They looked like a campaign poster extolling the merits of sexual dimorphism.

'Boys,' she said, but I thought I detected suppressed pride.

Pippa handed plastic glasses to Phil and myself. We sat cross-legged on the blue blanket beside Kim and Michael, who had descended to the blanket as one.

'In judo, aren't you supposed to use the skill and strength of your opponent against him?' said Phil.

'Well, yes – sort of,' said Michael.

'Then, why practise?' said Phil. 'Aren't you setting yourself up for a fall, so to speak?' Michael smiled and Phil charged on: 'I mean, I hate to think how strong and skilful you must be to get hurt like that,' he said, pointing to Michael's face and grimacing.

Michael laughed good-humouredly and patted Phil roughly on his chubby arm. 'How do you keep in such great shape, buddy?'

'Actually, I was really into chess-boxing for a while,' Phil said, 'but I got banned for poking an opponent in the eye with a bishop.'

Kim turned to me. 'Does your friend ever take a break?'

Michael placed his hand on her beautiful knee cap and said, 'Believe it or not, honey, chess-boxing is a real sport. It's this weird-freaky hybrid thing. They alternate games of chess with rounds of boxing.'

'I'm into bare-knuckle bingo now,' said Phil. 'It's not for the faint-hearted – apart from the bingo.'

Michael was much amused by this and he dipped his head as a little red wine escaped from his lips. Kim tutted and reached over to wipe his chin with a napkin and I tried to control my breathing.

'No seriously though...' said Phil, tugging at a paw-full of flesh through his T-shirt, 'I need to get myself fit. Can you teach me judo?'

'I could introduce you to some people,' said Michael, reaching past Kim to take some vegetable crisps. 'But I don't coach, myself.'

'You could teach me the basics though.'

'You need to join a club.'

'I will,' said Phil. 'But why don't you show me some simple stuff now; just a couple of simple throws. I promise I won't hurt you.'

'Here?' said Michael, laughing and patting the blanket. Phil nodded.

It was clear that Michael had no intention of doing this, but Phil kept trying, cajoling and entreating until I almost felt moved to call upon the safe word again, but he and Michael seemed to be getting on surprisingly well. After a while I was beginning to feel excluded and so I turned to listen to Paul and Elaine's conversation.

A few minutes later, I felt a tap on my shoulder. 'How's it going, Bird?' said Phil. He was standing above me, with the sun behind him. I squinted.

'Bird!' said Michael, smirking. He was standing to Phil's side with his thumbs hooked in his shorts.

'Mike and I are going for beers.' So now it was Mike, was it? 'Want one?'

Small flies were floating in the remnants of my wine, but instinct told me to decline. I watched the two men head off like Tarzan and Cheetah. When they reached the end of the row of stalls, Phil looked up at Michael and patted him on the back as they turned towards the beer tent.

*\*\**

Here was my opportunity to speak with Kim and yet, adjusting, as I still was, to the painful news of her pairing, I couldn't bring myself to initiate a conversation. When Paul and Elaine invited me to join them as they left to explore the festival I gratefully accepted.

After circling for a while, we returned to the improvised settlement. Pippa was distributing quiche and Kim was passing around salad. Phil, with his legs stretched out in front of him, was taking up too much space. I decided I would quietly speak to him about it.

When Phil saw me approaching he flung out a string-puppet arm in my direction. 'The Birdman comes home to roooost,' he said, now clearly intoxicated. This was unusual – I had rarely seen Phil drunk since our university days – but more than that, it was worrying. Phil had few social inhibitions at the best of times – what might he say when compromised?

'Ha… Birdman,' said Michael, tapping Kim on the arm. He was clearly also worse for wear.

A burst of whooping and applause reached us from the main stage.

'I think I will go and see what's going on over there,' I said.

\*\*\*

I returned to my old perch inside the perimeter of the marquee.

'You can go to The Swan on your own from now on, you disloyal hominid, bastard,' I muttered.

An elderly black American bluesman was on stage. His skin was dark and leathery. Wiry grey hair sprung out from beneath a straw trilby. He sat perched on a low stool, playing earthy, old-style tunes on a golden-yellow electric guitar while stamping a shiny black shoe on the stage. Between songs he told colourful stories from his times on the road with some of the names from the sleeve notes of my blues compilation.

I imagined myself on a creaky old tour bus in a world far from London; a world of dust, sweat, whiskey and tobacco. I found a little solace in these thoughts, though I don't like dust, sweat, whiskey, tobacco or bus journeys.

As another song began, my eye was drawn to the left-hand side of the stage. There, a mother and child were swaying gently to the music. The girl – in a purple princess dress and a plastic tiara – was clinging to her mother's hip. She looked tired but totally at peace. I may have expelled a little sentimental sound.

I felt a finger poke me in my ribs.

'This is getting to be a habit,' said Kim, leaning in to make herself heard above the music.

*Yes*, said the PC. *Yes, yes, yes!* It's fair to say that he does not recognise the sanctity of the pair-bond.

'Oh. Hi, Kim,' I said. 'What's getting to be a habit?'

'You were smiling… *again*,' she said. 'Did you even know?'

'Was I?'

She nodded. 'What kind of bird are we this time?'

'Just plain old *Homo sapiens*.' I pointed over to the princess.

'She is adorable,' she said, 'but I didn't think you were interested in *Homo sapiens*.'

*You'd be surprised*, said the PC.

'Easily my favourite mammal,' I said.

'And your pal? What species would you say he was?'

'Awaiting verification on that,' I said. 'I've only managed to narrow it down to the genus.'

'Whatever he is, I need to keep him away from Mike; they egg each other on.'

I glanced away from the stage to catch her expression: if she was disgruntled I was unable to detect it beneath all that beauty. Looking back to the old bluesman, I apologised anyway.

'Stop it,' she said gently bumping the top of my thigh with her hip. 'He's not so bad. Mike's pretty drunk too.'

'You know, it's funny. I haven't seen Phil drunk for years, literally. Mind you, I've never seen him rapidly form a social bond either.'

'He's drunk all right. They are over there playing some stupid game.'

'Oh yes, he's hyper-competitive with other males.'

'No kidding. They started trying to spin paper plates, like Frisbees, into the hamper.'

'And then Phil devised a scoring system?'

She laughed. 'Yes he did. It got pretty complex. They've started to attract spectators. I decided to leave them to it.'

'Totally juvenile,' I said, though it actually sounded like good fun.

'They were having a blast,' she said. 'So much so that Phil seems to have completely lost interest in the blues, which is kind of surprising, don't you think?'

Alert to the danger, I kept my gaze on the stage. 'It's a shame. This guy's really good.'

We stood, side by side, listening to an acoustic rendition of 'Rollin' Stone'. The bluesman stared down at the stage, shaking his head slowly from side to side as if entranced by the rhythm.

'Yeah, that was cool,' she said at the end.

I nodded. 'I like its simplicity. There's something very ancestral about it. I can still hear Africa in it and echoes of *the* original music, the music that gave birth to pretty much all the music that we hear today. I like the way that we can trace the way music evolves too.' Hearing my enthusiasm begin to spill over, I checked myself and said, 'Sorry.'

'What is it with you and the apologies?' she said, smiling.

'Sorry.'

'Of course you are.'

I smiled. 'Have you enjoyed yourself this evening, Kim?' I asked in order to change the subject, but also because at that moment nothing in the world, not even marsh harrier or zebra finch courtship, was so fascinating to me.

'Yes, it's been nice,' she said. 'I'm not mad about the music, but it's always good to see Pippa. I wish Mike hadn't got so drunk, but I'm not going to say any more about that because you would only feel the need to apologise again.'

The next song opened with a harmonica wail and Kim laughed and said, 'Phil would love this.'

'I expect so,' I grinned.

We listened on, applauding the solo and eventually the song. I enjoyed being alone with Kim and yet the sadness of the melody had amplified my loneliness. The bluesman leaned towards the microphone, holding it in one hand and announcing a break. Barely lifting his feet, he shuffled off to further applause.

Kim looked back beyond the food stalls in the direction of Pippa's settlement. I was surprised to see that darkness had enveloped the park.

'I'd better go back,' she said. 'I should get Mike home. Are you coming?'

I said I would stay to see the rest of the act. The truth was I wanted to avoid witnessing the inevitable reunification rituals practised by human pairs. That and I didn't want to see Phil.

I watched Kim leave. When she got to the burger stand at the corner, she stopped and turned back towards me. She smiled. I gulped.

I said 'Sorry' quietly to myself as she set off again.

***

I was trying to decipher the residual emotions I was feeling when I saw Phil round the corner by the burger stand.

He smiled when he saw me. He actually smiled. I turned away from him.

'Ho Bird. Kippa said you would be here. Can we go now?'

'You can go if you want to,' I said, my eyes still fixed on the stage. Then the anger welled up in me and I blurted, 'And stop calling me Bird.'

'What's wrong with you now, Bird? I've just spent a whole evening with that hairy arse – *for you*. I think I might actually be getting a fur ball.'

'Don't even try it,' I said and this time *my* spittle lashed *his* face. 'I didn't expect you to be charming. I just asked you to not make a fool of me. But you couldn't, could you? Not even once. What was that "Birdman comes home to rooooost" thing?'

'Ah, yes,' he said, mildly, 'sorry about that – necessary evil. The creation of a temporary rift between us was essential to my strategy. Don't worry – I still like you, Bird.'

'"Strategy"? Do you really expect me to believe that you had a "strategy"? Do you think I'm totally stupid?'

'No, I don't think you are stupid… but there are multiple forms of intelligence, Bird, and you have a low FQ, we both know that… That's why I decided to help.'

'What's an FQ?' I snapped. 'No, actually, don't bother.' I turned back to the stage.

'IQ, EQ, FQ. It's basically the kind of intelligence associated with getting laid. Yours is stunted. Which is why you need a wingman… a wingman who knows what is best for his Birdman buddy.' He patted himself on the chest. I stared at him. I expect my mouth was hanging open. 'Look,' he said. 'You like Kim. Kim likes Mike. Bummer. I can't make her like you more – even my capabilities have limits – but I figured I could make her like him a bit less. From what you said, during the briefing—'

'"Briefing!" There was no "briefing". I just said "don't make a fool of me".'

'Whatever. We both know what you meant.' I objected – vociferously. Phil quietly waited for me to finish. 'From what you said, I suspected that Michael was the alpha male type and thus highly competitive,' he said. 'You also suggested that he liked a drink and so I thought I would hang out with him, get him a little bit shitfaced and then progressively make him look like an idiot. I thought the judo might—'

'*You* were the one that was drunk, Phil. *You* made *yourself* look like an idiot. *And* you dragged *me* down with you.'

'I wasn't *drunk*. I was just pretending.' He actually looked offended, which I didn't know was possible. 'Watch,' he said. He shrugged his shoulders a couple of times, cleared his throat and then threw out the string-puppet arm. 'The Birdman comes home to roooost.'

I was speechless.

'And as for making myself look like an idiot – that was a sacrifice I was happy to make… You are probably feeling like you should buy me a beer.'

'I am not,' I said, 'I'm going home.' I started walking dejectedly towards the festival exit.

'Cool. You can buy me a ruby on the way,' he said.

# Chapter 11

*December*

After the blues festival Pippa and I reverted to weekly lunches and pretending Kim didn't exist.

I was in an unusually good mood for our first week of December lunch. Mats Carlsson, my Swedish collaborator, had called me that morning to notify me that we had been awarded funding for our study of pied flycatcher (*Ficedula hypoleuca*) courtship and mating.

'I mean, a whole summer of studying polyterritorial polygyny, Pippa,' I said. 'It doesn't get any better than that, does it?'

'Sounds positively painful,' she said. When she eventually regained her composure, Pippa invited me to her 'fabbie Christmas lunch'.

'Are you cooking a turkey?' I asked.

'Yes. Yes, I've ordered a huge bird. Twenty pounds!' Pippa's face lit up like a festive decoration.

'I'm sorry, Pippa. In that case, I'm afraid I won't be able to come. The females are artificially inseminated you see and I just don't think it's ethical.'

Pippa's hand shot up over her mouth. 'Oh, I see… I'm sorry. Simon… I didn't know that you—'

'Relax Pippa, I'm being humorous,' I said. 'Must be the funding news.' Pippa giggled, but I knew not to read anything into that. Thanking her for the kind offer, I explained that unfortunately I was already committed to Christmas with Mum and her mate.

\*\*\*

We returned to the cacophonous café for lunch at the beginning of the first week of January. Pippa told me all about Christmas, and especially about her festive gathering, freely dispensing great abdomens of laughter. But when her salad arrived she became suddenly quite serious and I thought she might be experiencing quinoa remorse.

'Pippa? Are you OK?'

'Yes, yes, I'm fine. I've got a huge favour to ask you though… What are you doing on March 9? It's a Friday.'

'Hmm. Let me see. I'm busy on March 9 next year and the year after, but I do believe I'm free this year.'

Pippa laughed, briefly. 'Great. I wondered if you would be my plus one.' She was now looking more sheepish than pigeonish and I prayed to Darwin that I hadn't just agreed to participate in mixed-doubles dressage or something of that ilk.

'Great! Great! Great! It's going to be so much lovely fun. You remember Kim and Mike, don't you?'

I remembered Kim very vividly indeed. I began to remember her bumping her green shorts against my thigh at the blues festival.

'Simon?'

'Sorry, yes of course I do, yes. Lovely. Couple.'

'They are a *wonderful* couple. And now they are a wonderful *engaged* couple,' said Pippa, her eyes ablaze. 'They announced it at *my* Christmas lunch.'

I began to imagine the scene in Pippa's dining room: I saw Kim and Michael grinning, kissing and clinging. I saw Aman and Judy, Elaine and Paul and, for some reason, David and Victoria Beckham all rushing around the table to congratulate the happy pair. I saw Pippa laughing then crying then laughing again.

I'm afraid I wasn't feeling as thrilled and delighted for them as a decent *Homo sapiens* should have been. I was only glad that I had declined Pippa's Christmas lunch invitation, thus sparing myself the requirement to conjure up joy in real time.

Becoming aware of an enquiring look from Pippa, I said, 'Fantastic.'

Pippa pursed her lips. 'Look, Simon, I know you probably had a teensy little crush on Kim. Everybody does. She wouldn't have been right for you though.'

'I, I didn't… I never… I don't think…'

'Look, Kim has always been…' Pippa glanced up for a few moments, calculating. 'You're too nice for her, Simon. No that sounds wrong.' She looked up at the ceiling again. 'Put it like this: I love Kim, but she's… complex. She enjoys the power she has over men a little too much, in my opinion.' Pippa put down her fork and reached for my hand. 'You are a nice guy, Simon – a lovely guy but lovely has never floated Kim's boat, and it doesn't bring out the best in her either. She would break your gorgeous heart.'

'Well, umm… it's…'

Pippa squeezed my hand. I had never seen/heard her go this long without giggling. 'Kim needs to be with someone like Mikey. They are made from the same stuff.'

'Hmm.'

'I will find you a lovely girl, Simon, just give me time.' She patted my hand again. Brightening again she said, 'I could see exactly what was going to happen from the first time we saw Kim and Michael together. I can *always* tell.'

I prickled; Pippa was demonstrating classic hindsight bias, which is annoying at the best of times but especially so when expressed by someone with scientific training. I was on the very verge of telling her that she shouldn't claim predictive powers until these had been validated with a statistically robust sample of randomly selected couples observed under standardised conditions, but then I reminded myself that it wasn't Pippa's fault that Kim had chosen Michael.

'It's a contemporary fairy tale,' I muttered.

Pippa cocked her head. 'They are having a little engagement party for their London friends, and *we* are invited.'

'Actually, they invited you plus one, P.'

'Well, yes, I suppose.' Pippa picked a chick pea from the top of her salad with finger and thumb. 'But I know Kim will be so excited if you can come. And she has *lots* of gorgeous friends…'

'Hmm.'

# Chapter 12

My plan for the engagement party was simple: arrive late; smile where possible; leave early. By the time we did arrive, poor Pippa, the engagement party had already been underway for almost an hour.

She frowned when we reached the outside door, gave the knot of my tie a twist and smoothed the front of my jacket with her palm. It was my yellow tie; my favourite. I hoped that people would like my tie so much that they wouldn't notice how 'practical' my shoes were.

'There,' she said. 'Gorgeous again.'

'Thank you, Pippa. You look lovely too.'

She beamed, leaned over to kiss me on the cheek and slipped her hand inside my arm. I knew that she had been excited about her new dress – a midnight blue cocktail thing – for weeks and hoped that she would be happy enough for both of us.

We walked down a narrow corridor and stopped at the top of steps looking down and out over the long, narrow gallery below. The walls were smooth, white and bare, except for a huge black and white photographic image of Kim and Michael projected across the back wall.

*For the love of Darwin*, I thought.

The gallery floor below us was full of guests sipping champagne. Nobody noticed us. To our right, a jazz quartet was playing, but nobody noticed them either. From our elevated vantage point we were unable to locate Kim and Michael in the crowd. I spotted a waitress and led Pippa down the steps towards her. The waitress didn't know where the 'happy couple' were.

We now had champagne, but we had lost elevation. We stood in the centre of the floor, rotating like twin periscopes.

I'm afraid the PC was opportunistically gorging on the female guests. I was more concerned about a trend I had observed amongst the male guests: most of them were not wearing ties. Those ties in evidence were thin and usually black. Tie or not, shirt collars were universally unbuttoned. Suits were slim-fitting with slim lapels. Shoes were pointed, like the beaks of gannets and lacked practicality. Ironically, given the sensibleness of my footwear, I was the one who started to feel uncomfortable. My suit felt underpopulated. I didn't even like my tie anymore.

Pippa shot out a hand and let out a squeal like a hungry guinea pig (*Cavia porcellus*) when she spotted Aman and Judy. My confidence dipped again because Aman was looking sharp in an electric blue suit and brilliant white shirt.

Pippa asked them if they had seen Kim and Michael.

'They were over there when we last saw them,' said Judy, pointing towards the back wall and the picture. We made our way over towards the projected image only to discover that Kim and Michael had flown.

'What a wonderful picture,' said Pippa, slipping her arm inside mine again.

I grunted an acknowledgement and stared at it. Why didn't I like it? Black and white Michael was standing behind black and white Kim. He was wearing a white T-shirt and his arms were thick and hairy with prominent veins. He was pulling Kim back against his chest. His left arm was pressed – a little too forcefully for my taste – across her breasts; his right arm was across her abdomen. He was staring, almost defiantly, into the camera. Kim's arms were raised above her head and looped back around his neck. She was looking lovingly up towards him but, given the limitations of human spinal flexibility and field of view, I doubted that she was actually able to see him from that angle.

Despite the distress it caused me I was unable to take my eyes from the picture until the moment when the jazz quartet stopped playing. The saxophonist tapped the microphone and, more than generously, thanked everyone for their attention and announced that 'his old friend' Mikey was going to say a few words.

We watched Michael and Kim, their faces set in wide grins, step out of the crowd to flocked applause. Behind me a guy whistled, loudly. Kim and Michael turned to face their guests with their linked hands raised like victorious gladiators. When the applause subsided they dropped their hands, but their grins were indelible.

They looked spectacular. Michael wore a dark grey suit and moved across the floor with the easy physical grace of a predator. I, of course, was much more interested in Kim. I hadn't seen her in almost seven months but she was still, unfortunately, the most beautiful creature, winged or otherwise, that I had ever seen. She wore a strapless pink chiffon cocktail dress with a flowing calf-length train that made me gulp. *Pretty flamingo*, I thought.

Standing there before their applauding friends with cameras flashing, they looked like the kind of couple that you might see in a fragrance ad; I have always had deep reservations about fragrance ads – why do modern *Homo sapiens* entrust their eyes to make decisions on behalf of their olfactory system? – and yet I knew that I would feel compelled to purchase whatever Kim was promoting.

Michael looked into Kim's eyes then lifted her hand to kiss it. She looked back at him adoringly, which, while not enjoyable to witness, seemed entirely reasonable under the circumstances. He moved over to the microphone. I wanted him to look nervous; he looked anything but. He beckoned Kim to come to stand closer to him.

Michael started to speak but the PC and I were looking at Kim and the dress. She filled me up and hollowed me out. I was so engrossed in her that I only realised that Michael had said something worthy of applause when I noticed Pippa's frantic motions to my left. She smiled at me, and I smiled back as fully as I could.

I don't remember much of what Michael said, only that some dodo called Russ kept making 'witty' interruptions.

I paid more attention when Kim took the microphone to speak of her great love for Michael. It was a particularly challenging part of a particularly challenging evening and so I stopped listening again and gave the PC free rein to drink her in in all of her flightless glory.

I forgot about Pippa until I heard her applauding again at the end of the speeches. When I turned to her she smiled and with this she finally lost control of her lachrymal glands and a tear made a dash for her chin.

She dabbed it away with a tissue and I gave her shoulder a friendly one-handed rub.

***

Aman went to the bar after the speeches and Pippa, Judy and I made our way through the guests towards the gaggle of well-wishers surrounding Michael and Kim. I mentally rehearsed my congratulations and my smile but I could feel my trousers flapping, which didn't help me to feel at ease. Kim spotted us and the kissing, hugging, squealing and handshaking commenced. I hope I gave a convincing display of mock elation.

The jazz band began to play some old Chet Baker thing. Pippa was talking to Kim and Judy and another female and I found myself standing with Michael and two males. Keo was a slight Japanese male with very long, straight black hair. Umberto was a quietly spoken, brown-shoed Italian and a handsome one, I suspected. Both were old advertising colleagues of Michael's.

'Simon's into birds,' said Michael.

'Right,' said Keo. 'Cool.'

'I'm a behavioural ecologist,' I said.

'Of birds though, right?' said Michael.

'Yes, that's my core specialism,' I said. To avoid more tortuous explanations and self-justification, I congratulated Michael on his speech, though I couldn't recall a word.

'Yeh, definitely…' said Keo. 'She got you, man. I had you pegged as a life-long player, Mikey. You were my idol, man.' He turned to me, 'Mikey was like the Assassin of Ass. I used to say that if I ever get, you know, reincarnated, then I wanted to come back as Mike's dick.'

Michael laughed, evidently enjoying the recognition. 'What can I say? I met my match.'

'No shame in it,' twinkled Umberto. 'You had a good run, for an English guy.'

Michael laughed again, louder this time. Holding Umberto's face and gently patting him on the cheek, he said, 'No you don't, polpetto; I won't let you wind me up. I'm happy, that's all there is to it. We're both happy and we're tired of the game.'

My estimate of Michael's cumulative pair-bond count (or 'n') grew steadily as I listened. It was clearly considerably in excess of five. *No wonder he always looks so confident*, I thought.

Behind me a female squeezed past on her way to congratulate Kim. Michael's eyes darted to her and he leaned forward conspiratorially. 'Hypothetically though…' he whispered.

Keo and Umberto laughed boisterously and Keo and Michael clapped raised palms. Embarrassed, I turned to see just what kind of female could have inspired a polygynous quip at such an inappropriate moment. Kim was hugging the female and grinned at me over the girl's shoulder. I waved and tried, despite everything, to feel happy for her.

# Chapter 13

I spent the rest of the evening in a social grouping with Pippa, Judy and Aman. I removed my tie and, after burning through all of my excuses, I danced dutifully and drank therapeutically. Consequently, as the evening progressed I began to dance more experimentally.

At one point I danced straight into Kim and Michael.

'Why, Dr Selwood, I do believe you are doing the flamingo,' said Kim.

\*\*\*

As midnight approached, Pippa, now bare-footed, and Judy were still dancing. Despite the versatility of my shoes, my feet ached. Pippa pleaded for another half an hour and so I headed to the bar for a last/final round of drinks. I arrived in the queue just shortly before Michael's loud friend Russ. He stood beside me checking his phone. I felt myself tense when an advantageous space at the bar opened up directly in front of him.

However, before this scenario could play out, I heard a female voice call my name. I turned, expecting to find Pippa, but it was Kim. Her cheeks were pinker now. Her hair was down. Her beauty was undiminished.

'Hi Dr Selwood,' she said. 'Having fun? I worry when you aren't grinning for no reason.'

'I'm great, thanks, Kim. I was just trying to establish an imposing bar presence.'

'Ah I see. Well, I will let you get back to that in a second, but can I have a quick word with you first?'

'You've got a nerve. Anyone would think this was your big night,' I said. I was beginning to realise that I really didn't need another drink.

Kim stepped away from the queue, moving over to the long gallery wall on our left. I followed, obediently. Her strapless dress afforded me a first glorious opportunity to observe the top of her back and her shoulders. She had the loveliest shoulders I had ever seen. Previously, as far as I was concerned, female shoulders – millions of years of evolution notwithstanding – were merely the twin anatomical structures connecting the female neck and female arms, but Kim's shoulders really helped me to appreciate them in their own right. I suspected that Kim's gall bladder and pancreas were probably very beguiling too.

Upon reaching the wall she turned and her beautiful red lips took centre stage: 'I just wanted to say I'm, well, I'm really happy for you and Pippa. You look great together.'

'No! *No!* It's not like that,' I said. Alcohol *may* have made me a little more emphatic than I needed to be.

'Oh, I see,' said Kim. 'Fuck buddies.'

I gasped. 'Well, I know that bonobos use sex to ease tension and maintain social cohesion, but I hardly think... well, what I mean is Pippa and I aren't paired, not even transiently. Truthfully, we have no courtship or mating aspirations.'

'Oh,' said Kim, 'I just thought... it doesn't matter, I was obviously wrong, but I do think it's a shame. Maybe the two of you should give it a try...'

'No!' I said, and again I may have been a little too emphatic.

'OK... OK... but I still think it's a shame. Pippa's lovely and well, you're... interesting, intelligent. And cute.' She smiled. 'If I hadn't met Mike... well, who knows?'

The emotions that I was feeling in that moment were, it is fair to say, mixed. 'Thank you,' I said.

'You are welcome,' said Kim. She glanced behind me and instinctively I turned to see what she was looking at. It was Michael of course. He was standing a few feet away on the edge of the dance floor, beckoning. 'I have to go, Simon,' she said.

I wanted her to stay. I wanted her to stay so that I could enjoy her face, neck and shoulders but also because alcohol had made me uncharacteristically competitive. I was aware that this might be the only chance I would ever have to frustrate, just a smidge, the 'Assassin of Ass'.

'What made you think Pippa and I had paired?' I asked. It did the trick.

'I just know that you've been spending a lot of time together. And you came together this evening. And you are single, aren't you?'

'I remain as yet unpaired, yes.'

Kim looked as if she was about to leave again, but then hesitated. 'What kind of girls *are* you interested in? You never know, I might know someone.'

*Ask her if she has a clone*, said the PC.

'I really have no idea what I'm looking for,' I lied.

'Simon… do you like… *girls?*' Kim spoke slowly, as if formulating a hypothesis.

This question did not please me. There I was, self-medicating with German bottled beer because Kim had formalised her pair-bond with the 'hitman of humping' and now she was, questioning my sexuality. How could she suspect that I was homosexual? Hadn't she seen my shoes?

'Yes, Kim. I do like girls!'

'I thought you did,' she said, both palms up in a gesture of contrition. 'How come you don't know what kind of girls you like then?'

'It's, well it's just not that easy to describe. The concept of "type" is much too… well, simplistic.'

'Oh really? Enlighten me professor.' She was clearly amused, but I didn't care. We were still talking and Michael was still waiting.

'It's about value.' I shuddered inwardly at my own words; face to face with by far the most attractive female I had ever known I was commoditising human romance, and at her engagement party.

'Value?'

I nodded. 'Each of us has an innate sense of our value in the mating "market place". Each of us is "programmed" to behave in the way that helps us to achieve the best possible legacy for our genes. We all try to get as much as we possibly can from what we have to "trade". We subconsciously adjust our mate selection to reflect that value.'

I was interrupted by Michael's friend Russ who stepped past us, clutching three beers and saying 'Kimono!' loudly. I gave him a disdainful glance as he walked over towards the seating area.

'That's the crux of it,' I said. 'Oh, apart from the fact that throughout the animal kingdom, humans notwithstanding, the female is more discerning, because mating is potentially a bigger investment for them, and so, usually they are the ones who make the mate-choice decisions. The whole theory is pretty well established. I could email you a couple of the key articles if…'

Kim smiled. 'That sounds great, Simon, but I should probably get the wedding plans pinned down before I hit the books.'

'Right. Yes. Good point.' I was aware that my explanation had become too academic, as usual, and yet there she still was, shoulders and all.

'And what's your "value", Simon? Have you got any articles about that?' she said, playing with me again.

'It's not like that. All I know is whether I am attracted to someone or not.'

'Come on, Dr Selwood…'

'No really. It doesn't work that way. It's fairly binary. Either I am attracted to a female or I'm not.' I was so drunk that for a second I even considered telling her about the PC and then I came to my senses.

Kim looked around towards the makeshift dance floor again. Was she hoping to be rescued? An Asian girl in a layered red dress and high-heeled shoes was heading, like a novice ice skater, in our direction.

*That's a yes on the binary front*, said the PC.

'Hi Manjit,' said Kim brightly. She waited for the girl to pass and then she whispered, 'Yes or no?'

'That's not fair. I can't decide just like that.'

*Liar*, said the PC.

'Liar,' said Kim.

'Look, I'm not prepared to stand here and evaluate every female guest like, like… livestock.'

*You don't need to*, said the PC. *That's why you've got me*.

'I think Manjit's cute,' said Kim, turning to the bar where the girl was now standing. 'Russ says she's naughty too.'

The fact that Russ had, presumably, copulated with the female Manjit did not increase my desire to pair with her.

I said, 'Sometimes I do worry that *my* programme might be malfunctioning. Do you think that's possible?' Kim's brow of finest porcelain wrinkled momentarily. 'I mean, *should* I be attracted to Pippa? *Should* I be attracted to Manjit? Are my mate expectations unrealistic? The problem is, despite my *profound and irrefutable* heterosexuality, I just don't seem to be attracted to very many females. I sometimes worry that my own programme is erroneously eliminating value-matched females, thus skewing my mating matrix. Do you think that's possible?'

'I'm not sure I understand, Simon,' she said. She reached out to give my hand a gentle, encouraging squeeze.

'Oh.'

Kim let go of my hand but I could still feel where her fingers had touched mine.

'But...' she sighed. 'But for some weird reason, I am curious. For some reason I do want to know what a "mating matrix" is. Why is that?'

I had no idea. Nobody had ever wanted to hear about it before. I decided to explain without delay in case Kim changed her mind. 'Every individual has his or her own mating matrix you see. It assesses the correlation between those whom they find attractive and those who find them attractive in return. It's a simple hypothetical concept, a model, a framework, but it's useful. It works like this: let's assume that I am attempting to complete my personal mating matrix. For the sake of argument, let's say that I simultaneously evaluate every age-appropriate single female in London.'

'That sounds a bit greedy, Simon.'

'No. It's *hypothetical*, thus eliminating any actual greed.'

'It's hypothetically greedy. How many women *do* you want?'

'No. That's not what I'm saying at all. I'm naturally monogamous. I just need to find a female to monogamise.'

'That's cute,' she said, squeezing my hand again. 'Life would be a lot easier if we all lived that way.'

'And it's the truth, honestly it is. But what if I am making it difficult for myself to find a stable pair-bond by eliminating all but the most highly valued females? What if the upper left-hand box of my mating matrix is destined to remain vacant?'

Kim said that she still didn't follow and so I tried to explain the mating-matrix concept again. Twice more I failed.

Eventually Kim laughed. 'Sorry Simon, I'm still not getting it.'

'It's not your fault. I'm just not explaining it coherently.' I patted down my pockets but they were empty except for a few jangling coins. 'Wait there for a second, Kim. Please.'

The girl behind the bar loaned me a biro and a pink receipt slip. I leaned on the bar and quickly scribbled the mating matrix (Figure 2) on its reverse. I felt confident that Kim would now understand, but when I looked over to where she had been standing, she was gone and my heart, which had rallied for the duration of our conversation, sank again.

Figure 2. The Selwood Mating Matrix

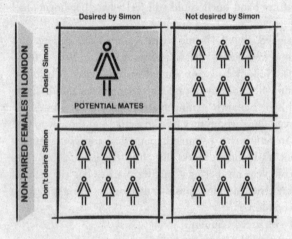

# Chapter 14

*April. South Kensington*

On my final day before heading off to Sweden to participate in the long-awaited pied flycatcher (*Ficedula hypoleuca*) study I was excited, impatient and ridiculously busy. In addition to briefing Gustavo, my PhD student, and preparing for the trip, I had a couple of undergrad teaching commitments. Last but not least I had promised my mum that I would get a haircut.

***

The pre-lunch tutorial overran by ten precious minutes. It was my own fault. I couldn't bring myself to stop the passionate debate amongst the four second-year students about the ethics of cutting ocelli (eyespots) from the trains of adult male Indian peafowl (*Pavo cristatus*) in order to evaluate the impact on female choice.

Placing the board eraser down, I sighed. The extended discussion had left me, yet again, without enough time for that haircut. Oh well, was my hair really so out of control? I looked over to the window to assess my reflection. The shadowy outline of my head resembled a common puffball fungus (*Lycoperdon perlatum*). Yes, it was overgrown, but surely there would be a barber in Uppsala who would relish the opportunity to try his/her hand with brown hair. I left my office and set off down the stairs towards the refectory for a sandwich.

Then I remembered how my mother had implored me to get a haircut and I also recalled my first meeting with Mats Carlsson at the Madrid congress. My clothes always look crumpled from the moment, or even shortly before, I put them on, but Mats's looked straight-from-the-store crisp and his bronze hair also looked immaculate. Might Mats interpret my lack of preening as a lack of respect?

I looked at my watch. I had forty-five minutes until my final lecture of the academic year. When I reached the bottom of the stairs I started to jog down the corridor.

When I got out of the building, I started to run more energetically, thus awakening the ancestor. I was still running when I arrived at Joe's on Cromwell Road. Through the shopfront, I could see Joe cutting the back of a head of gull-white hair. Fortunately, there was nobody waiting in the row of red chairs that lined the wall of the shop, and so I stepped inside.

Regrettably, Joe's client had a lot of hair for a male of advanced years. He also had a lot of strongly held views. Joe and his customer shared a collective disdain for just about everything and everyone. Joe kept refraining from clipping to vent his views. I eyed my watch anxiously. I couldn't be late for the lecture. Should I leave?

When I eventually got into Joe's chair, I thought about telling him that I was in a rush, but meeting his steely-blue eyes in the mirror I decided against it.

It has always seemed to me that the final five minutes of any haircut makes no discernible difference to the final outcome. I longed to tell Joe that I was satisfied, but daren't because Joe hadn't yet completed berating Blair. It was only as he dusted my neck with a long-haired brush – with a ferocity presumably intended for the former Prime Minister – that I found the courage to tell him that I had to go.

I shoved a ten pound note in Joe's hand and ran to the barbershop door. Fifty metres down the road I remembered I had left my lecture notes on the shelf beneath the mirror and so I ran back.

When I finally got back to Exhibition Road I thought I heard a female voice yell my name. Curiosity, courtesy and perhaps some embryonic courtship instinct brought me to a halt. Where was she? Who was she? Was she calling me or another Simon, the kind of Simon that gets hailed by females?

I was about to set off once again, when I spotted a beautiful female in a pale grey trouser suit, waving, at me. She looked a bit like Kim. No, she was Kim.

*I know*, I said, pre-empting the PC. *It's her.*

'Hi Kim! What… what are you doing here?'

'Hi Simon.' We kissed. I smiled. 'I just needed to get out of the office today,' she said. 'I needed more light, more oxygen and fewer people. I mean… fewer colleagues. It's nice to see you though.'

Kim seemed different. What was it?

'I didn't know your office was close by,' I said.

'Didn't you? It's a twenty-minute walk, that's all. I only live about ten minutes away,' she said pointing back across Cromwell Road. 'I sometimes meet Pippa for lunch.' Why had Pippa never told me that?

'Well, it's nice to see you. How are *you*? Oh, and also Michael?'

'I'm fine,' she said. She looked sombre for a moment and then the smile was back but even then she didn't seem quite her carefree self. Was this what a morning spent working in public relations could do to people?

'Listen,' she said, enthusiastic now. 'I don't have to be back at work until two pm. Do you have time for lunch?'

I looked down at the treacherous face of my watch; it was 12:58 pm. I cursed the entire first-year Zoology intake, even the intelligent ones.

'I would *love* to Kim. Really I would but I'm already late. I'm giving a lecture in less than two minutes.'

'I'm sure a clever man like you can think of an excuse,' she said. 'Unless… unless you don't want…'

'I do want. I just can't,' I said. 'I have to go right now or I am going to find myself endangered. *Sorry*.' I turned to face the university, poising myself to run more quickly and yet also more elegantly than ever before.

'Wait,' she said, clutching my forearm.

'I can't Kim. Sorry.'

'You can't give a lecture looking like that either,' she said. Instinctively, I looked down at my crotch. 'You've just had a haircut, haven't you?'

'Yes. How did you know?'

She smiled. 'You've got little bits of hair stuck all over your face.' I laughed and thanked her and began to swipe at my face with my palms. 'That won't work,' she scoffed. 'Let me.' She put her handbag down on the pavement and then leaned in towards me, her eyes locking into mine as she approached. When her lips were within just a few short centimetres of my own she began to gently blow on my face. I felt her warm breath gently massage my lip and then my left cheek. I closed my eyes so that I could experience the moment more deeply. In one long, continuous breath she covered my entire face, finishing with a final breath-blast on the end of my nose.

I opened my eyes and was surprised to discover that it was still daylight. A lady pushing a stroller, talking on a mobile phone, hurried by, oblivious.

'There. That's better,' said Kim, picking up her handbag. 'Bye, Simon.' She began to walk down Cromwell Road towards the pedestrian crossing. I stood there, paralysed. My eyes were still able to move within their orbits and they followed her down the street, greedily. When she reached the pedestrian crossing, she stopped and turned back. Seeing me standing there frozen in time and space she smiled and then winked, and then the traffic stopped for her and she crossed the road.

\*\*\*

I arrived at the lecture theatre acceptably late but unacceptably breathless. As I fought to regain homeostasis, I apologised to the class, blaming a fictional crisis in our zebra finch colony. I felt a pang of professional guilt and resolved to be the consummate educator for the remainder of the lecture. However, it wasn't so easy to stay focussed. The problem was that while it was the fourth time that I had given the same 'Introduction to Ethology' lecture it was the first time that a stunningly beautiful female had ever blown on my face. I found I could expound on Tinbergen's four principles very effectively while simultaneously trying to make sense of what had just happened.

Face-blowing seemed like an unusual thing for a paired female to do – even a thoughtful and friendly one. It seemed a bit… well, intimate, wasn't it? And if this was a typical response to a little facial hair, did it explain why so many members of the Life Sciences faculty wore beards?

# Chapter 15

I was slightly late and so I couldn't understand why our usual territory was unoccupied with not so much as a wet beer ring on the table. Had he forgotten? I frowned and scanned the pub and observed Phil waving from the far side of the lounge. Odd. Then I noticed that Cammie was with him. I went over, hugged her, and apologised to them both for my tardiness.

It was good to see Cammie and it was even better to hear her. I was touched when she said that she had wanted to see me before I went away. When I returned to the table a few minutes later with drinks I was in good spirits.

'So, how are things in the world of finch fucking?' said Phil.

'Don't feel the need to answer that, Simon,' said Cammie with a tired roll of her eyes. Cammie rolled her eyes at Phil almost as often as she rolled her Rs. As I observed their playful bickering, I wondered if different types of disapproval prompted different kinds of eye-roll.

\*\*\*

Later, when Cammie went to the bar, Phil leaned in to interrogate me.

'How's your pipeline coming along, Bird? And, more to the point, has your pipe been smoked since I last saw you?'

'Do you know, I think I would actually be prepared to spend a full day working in "executive talent acquisition" if you would agree to never ask me about my pipe or pipeline again,' I said.

'I see. Nothing… still. Absolutely nothing.' He pushed a fistful of crisps into his mouth and began to grind his disappointment into them.

'Precious little, yes.'

'You wouldn't survive a day in ETA, Bird,' he said, allowing me to glimpse just how thoroughly the crisps had been masticated. 'There's a lot of crossover, you see, between the core competencies required for talent acquisition and booty acquisition. You would only embarrass us both.'

So I told Phil about the Kimcident. I could claim that I did this in response to his provocation but I think I probably wanted a second opinion, even from him. Though not a formal Swan Song, Phil listened without interruption. In fact, he was so quiet that I thought he might be choking, but his eyes weren't bulging more than usual. I stopped when I got to the winking part.

'And then what happened?' he asked, nodding.

'The lecture,' I said, slightly taken aback.

'You didn't go after her?'

'No! I told you. I was late. Besides, what would I say? "Excuse me, Kim, I think you may have missed a stray follicle on my mandible"?'

'You could have asked her if she fancied a go at blowing your pubes off too.'

I objected to that, of course, but Phil spoke over the top of me, saying, 'Bird... Bird... I'm joking. Mostly. But you should have arranged to see her after the lecture, or this evening.'

'I was busy getting ready for Sweden *and* I had already arranged to meet you *and*, and this one's a significant impediment, she's paired, Phil. Had you forgotten that?'

'Firstly, even I don't think I'm that good company. Secondly, screw Sweden, and finally, I think she's the one that's forgotten she's "paired".'

'I went to her engagement party. Doesn't that count for anything in your seedy little world?'

'All's fair in love and executive placement my timorous friend.'

Phil was still shaking his head when Cammie arrived carrying three pints on a silver tray.

'Ah, bless her,' said Phil, leaning over to kiss her with deliberate sloppiness on the hand, then on the elbow and finally on the back of the neck as she sat on the bench beside him. He turned to me, 'She has tiny little hands, poorly evolved for the task of carrying pints, but see how she adapts?' Cammie rolled her eyes. 'OK, Cammie,' he said. 'We need a feminine perspective. Bird, tell her exactly what you just told me.'

I told the story again. I was quicker and more efficient this time, but Phil kept butting in anyway to explain what really happened – apparently unperturbed by the fact that he hadn't been there to witness it. He even mimicked the blowing action used by Kim, and with surprising and unsettling accuracy.

Cammie listened silently until I finished and even then she hesitated. 'Is that it? Is that the end?' she said.

'Yes… Oh, no, I did make it back for the lecture,' I said. 'Luckily.'

'You didn't arrange to meet up with her?' she said. Phil gave a large that's-what-I-said shrug.

'No I didn't,' I said.

Phil, adopting a thin mocking voice, said, 'Come now, Cammie. Kim is engaged and surely Bird should be applauded for the level of maturity and respect that he has shown.'

'But Phil, this girl – Kim is it? – she is fleerting with Simon. And it is not that subtle fleerting; this is an invitation.' Phil super-shrugged once again. 'You do know that she was fleerting with you, Simon? Don't you?' she implored.

I felt shame and excitement well within me. The bad news was that I had failed to recognise an apparently blatant display of feminine proceptivity, but, on the more positive side, there had apparently been a blatant display of feminine proceptivity. And from Kim. Directed at me. This was good, wasn't it?

'Simon?' said Cammie.

'Well I did think it was an unusually friendly thing to do,' I said. 'But I wasn't one hundred per cent sure that she was signalling her receptivity.'

'So, George Clooney, how sure were you – roughly?' asked Phil.

'Twenty per cent, maybe?' I said. Phil and Cammie groaned. 'Anyway, what makes the two of you so sure?'

'Trust us,' they said, in unison.

'Simon, I don't understand how you could fail to see this,' said Cammie.

'Well to be fair,' said Phil, 'she was only blowing on his face, winking and fluttering her eyelashes.'

'Fluttery will get you nowhere with me,' I said, ruefully.

'Simon, take it from us, she was definitively fleerting with you. What are you going to do about this?' said Cammie.

I didn't have a clue.

# Chapter 16

*Heathrow Airport*

My eyes opened in response to the gentle motion of the plane pushing back from the terminal building then closed again. I was shattered. Thoughts of Kim had kept me awake in Acton. Over and again I had asked myself: *why did she blow on my face?*

As we waited for our slot, I squeezed my eyelids together more tightly as if this could keep the insistent Kim thoughts at bay.

They remained closed during take-off. Only when I heard the electronic chime inform us that we were at cruising altitude did I accept that sleep's sweet escape was beyond me. I unclipped my seat belt and got up to retrieve a manila folder from the overhead locker.

The gentleman seated to my left nodded politely as I dropped back into my seat. I nodded back, but I was in no mood for conversation. I pulled out the grey tray table and began to spread my collection of pied flycatcher papers across it, confident this display of academic ornithology would nullify his desire for interaction.

In addition to preparing me for the work ahead, I hoped that the articles might release me from memories of Kim's pursed lips and sweet breath.

Leaning forward, I began to read Skoglund's 1998 paper. On reaching the end of the one page introduction I realised that I couldn't remember a thing. I got out of my chair again to retrieve a determination-enhancing highlighter pen from my backpack and started over.

Shortly afterwards the intro page was thoroughly striped, but I had still absorbed nothing. The same questions persisted: *why did Kim blow on my face? Had she tired of blowing on Michael's face already?*

Sitting upright with my back pressed against the seat, I pleaded with myself to focus. For five long months I had waited impatiently for this study to begin. At times I had felt like a child before the world's most tedious advent calendar and now I was finally on my way to Sweden and I wished I wasn't going.

I told myself that I was being ridiculous. After all, we were to be the very first group to fully characterise the role of polyterritorial polygyny in a native pied flycatcher population. And yet, though such opportunities present themselves rarely, it wasn't thoughts of polygynous passerines that tantalised me that morning. I tried again to convince myself to feel excited about the fieldwork ahead. It didn't work.

I gave in, silently apologised to Skoglund and slid him back into the folder.

I turned to my neighbour, thinking that a conversation might actually prove to be pleasantly distracting, but he was now sleeping with his head cocked back, his mouth horribly open.

Next I tried capitulation. I permitted myself to think about Kim for the duration of the flight, on the understanding that I would focus exclusively on the pied flycatcher from the moment we landed in Sweden.

I began to consider the events of the previous day. Could it be that Phil and Cammie's interpretation was correct? Had Phil's judgement ever been right before? Over the next few minutes I came to a number of firm yet mutually incompatible conclusions about the implications of the Kimcident. I dismissed all of the pleasing conclusions immediately, dwelled on the pessimistic ones and then started again.

What was the status of the Kim–Michael pair-bond? Had she deliberately evaded my question about Michael or had she just not heard it? Was I right to sense that she seemed heavy-spirited? Was this heaviness related to her avoidance of the Michael question? Round and round I went.

Somewhere high above the North Sea I convinced myself that Kim and Michael's pair-bond had ended. This gave me a few moments of joy and then, almost immediately, I began to worry that it hadn't. I rounded on myself for my mean-spiritedness, and then began to worry that they had parted but would get back together. Then, that she would meet someone else by the time I landed in Sweden. I worried that she would be attracted to my handsome colleague Barry, if they ever met. Or Umberto. Or even Russ.

Deciding that I felt better when I was working, I reached for the manila folder again and pulled out a paper about the migratory habits of the pied flycatchers of Spain. As I attempted to read it, an irony began to coalesce in my mind: the pied flycatchers had spent the last month or so making the four thousand mile trip from West Africa to Sweden. Now I was flying to Sweden too. But the pied flycatchers were flying there to breed whereas I was flying *away* from the one female with whom I wished to pair. It seemed to me that while they were obeying ancient instincts, I was totally disregarding mine.

My sleeping neighbour coughed, shifted and placed his hand on mine, lying on the arm rest. I carefully removed my hand, laying it across my lap and started to consider the biological significance of the feelings that coursed within me.

From an evolutionary psychology perspective, I was impressed. These intense new feelings were clearly nature's way of making sure that I didn't let Kim get away, now that she had demonstrated some interest in me. In this context, obsession and anxiety weren't flaws – they were powerful tools. I saw with greater clarity than ever before, why our species had become so numerous.

Impressive or not, I knew that I mustn't yield to the feelings. I *was* going to Sweden and I had important work to do. But *how* to overcome them? First, I told myself that Kim was out of my league and so it hardly mattered that I was out of her country. Next, I told myself that if she was interested in me in any meaningful way then surely she would endure a brief absence. Finally, I even tried to convince myself that my trip would be a valuable test of her desire.

A few rows back, a baby – a very small one by the sound of it – began to cry with immediate intensity. This crying woke my neighbour with a start. His eyes brimmed with alarm and confusion as they met mine. They relaxed again, when he realised that I was not his wife, presumably.

The baby fell silent and I returned, like an addict, to my obsession. It was as if my mind had been hacked. I chided myself again for failing to gain control of my emotions. It wasn't as if I could return home. I needed this study and, besides, there was my professional reputation, the reputation of Empirical and the department. *And* it was just a few weeks.

And yet going to Sweden still felt very, very wrong.

In search of distraction, I leaned over to the right, resting my right arm on the arm rest and looked down the aisle. Across from me, and in the row in front, a lady was reading a tabloid article about the state of the nation's sex life. A couple of rows down from her, a pair of feet wearing Nike running shoes the same vivid green colour as my highlighter pen bobbed in the aisle. Just beyond them, the breakfast trolley was making its way back towards us, row by row. My eyes came to rest on the back of the cabin attendant's navy blue, pin-striped skirt. And then the realisation came to me – complete, whole and irrefutable.

'You want to mate-guard her,' I heard myself say, aloud, my voice tinged with self-mockery. That was it: the reason I didn't want to go to Sweden anymore was to prevent other males from engaging Kim in courtship.

'I beg your pardon,' said a voice.

Horrified, I looked directly across the aisle towards its source. A gaunt middle-aged female with unconvincing black hair stared back at me. Prominent angry ridges had fixed her brow. What could I say to her? I decided to say nothing.

She repeated the question. 'What did you say?' She spoke calmly but assertively, in precise, unbroken English with a northern European accent, perhaps German.

I apologised for disturbing her, but the gaunt female was not satisfied. She remained assertive but became less and less calm over the ensuing exchanges.

In my peripheral vision, a juvenile male, seated in the chair immediately in front of my own, kneeled up on his seat. I briefly turned towards him. He rested his chin on the back of his seat and stared at my face with a neutral, unblinking expression. He held a damp-looking biscuit in a damp-looking hand. I had, it appeared, become in-flight entertainment.

A second female voice, his mother I assume, rapped out a command to the boy in Swedish. He didn't move. She repeated the command, this time as a slow, gentle growl and he slid, reluctantly, out of view.

Then the cabin attendant arrived with the trolley. She turned to me, dispensing her efficient auto-smile for the umpteenth time that morning.

'Would you like some breakfast today, sir?' she said. She was young and her dark hair was drawn up in a bun-net thing. Her make-up was thick and orange and she looked as though she had been fired, like a pot.

I shook my head. I wasn't hungry. I only wanted her to move on without incident. But the stern lady interrupted, saying, 'I insist that you must apologise to this young lady.'

The attendant turned towards the stern lady, saying, 'One moment, madam, I will be with you very shortly.' She returned her gaze towards me and I was awarded a second brief smile for my patience.

'No,' said the stern lady. 'That is not it. That is not it at all. I wish for this gentleman to apologise to you for what he said.'

The attendant frowned and looked at me. Then she turned to face the stern lady more fully. 'I beg your pardon, madam?'

'This man made lewd commentaries about you a few moments ago.'

The attendant span back to me; abhorrence quickly appeared and then equally quickly vanished; I imagine she was recalling techniques learned in some kind of 'Difficult Passenger' workshop.

'Excuse me, sir,' she said, with forced composure. 'Please tell me what you said,' I sighed and braced myself for turbulence.

'He said that he wanted to *mate* with you,' said the stern lady. The attendant pretended to ignore her and repeated the question.

And so I told them everything, I had to. I undid my seat belt and shifted to the edge of my chair so as to be able to keep my voice lowered. I spoke in a hurried shorthand whisper. I told them about Kim, the haircut, about my eight weeks in Sweden and even about the basic principles of mate-guarding. When I finished, the boy was kneeling up on his chair again, looking at me. To my left my neighbour was pretending to blow his nose to mask his amusement.

When I finished speaking, I covered my face – my warm, warm face – with my hand.

The attendant turned to the stern lady and then back at me. She said, 'OK sir, I understand. Now… would you like to have some breakfast today?'

\*\*\*

A little later the first officer announced that we would be landing in Stockholm on time, which meant that I still had eighty-five long minutes to endure in seat 23C.

Now all I wanted to do was read. While the other passengers chewed on chilled, compressed croissants, I retrieved the Skoglund paper and opened out the tray table again. I tried to ignore the feeling that the stern female was watching me but finally I could stand it no more and turned to face her.

She smiled. 'I hope you understand why I was concerned,' she said.

'Yes, I do.' I said.

I started to read again. A little later she tapped me on the elbow with a long bony finger. I looked into her grey eyes. 'You should call this Kim,' she said.

I smiled meekly and turned back to the sanctuary of Skoglund.

# Chapter 17

From the train to Uppsala I looked out over the open and gently rising farmland, taking in the scattered red barns. Almost immediately I broke my Swedish promise and thought of Kim; I just couldn't keep thoughts of her at bay. And yet, I observed, my thoughts weren't overtly sexual in nature. Why was that? Was it normal? Did my genes lack ambition? Or were they trying to tell me something?

***

The three buildings of the Evolutionary Biology Centre (EBC) were arranged in a C-shape around a neat rectangular lawn. Mats's cramped office was on the ground floor of the long three-storey brick building that formed the spine. He made us coffee dark as liquorice and then strode over to the wall to point out the study locations on the map pinned to it. From my chair I nodded and watched his finger zig-zag back and forth over the map but my mind was elsewhere.

I was with Kim in a red barn. She was wearing a red checked shirt knotted at the waist to reveal her magnificent imaginary abdomen. We were lying on a great pile of straw and she was leaning over to blow a stray strand from my face. The fantastical scenario escalated and I regained confidence in my genes.

Mats coughed. 'I was just saying,' he said, 'that you will meet the other members of the team tomorrow. Each will lead on one of the potential female choice criteria. Wolfie, who recently joined us from Munich, will lead on the role of male plumage characteristics. Charlotta will be responsible for studying the impact of song and she has agreed to pick you up in the morning.'

As Mats sidled back to his chair I was inwardly vowing to contact Kim.

\*\*\*

After a short tour of the well-equipped EBC labs, Mats showed me to a small vacant office with blank white walls and empty grey bookshelves. When he left, promising to return at the end of the afternoon, I shut the office door, leaned heavily back against it and closed my eyes. Fatigue and the effort of suppressing my Kimpulses for the last hour had left me feeling spent.

At the desk, I struck another deal with myself: I was allowed twenty minutes of Kimvestigation before tackling my outstanding Empirical work.

\*\*\*

The apartment Mats had found for me was pristine, angular and basic but comfortable. I felt anything but comfortable though.

The elation that had accompanied the discovery of Kim's number on the Cucumber Communications website was short-lived. What should I say to her?

Since an actual conversation was out of the question because a) I was terrified and b) I didn't think Kim would be won over by a series of short stuttered sentences, I spent the evening composing a text message. After typing and deleting, typing and deleting I opted for paper and pencil. By the time darkness finally fell, the apartment floor resembled a small indoor driving range covered in small white balls.

Exhausted, frustrated, discombobulated, I slipped into bed with Skoglund.

# Chapter 18

As I lay in my narrow bed that night, the PC and his cognitive collaborators bombarded my Kimagination.

I was awake at three thirty am as the first edge of dawn arrived. I was still awake at four thirty am and also at five thirty am. It wasn't until six thirty am, when the chirpy alarm tone jolted me from a dream in which Kim was blowing downy feathers from my face, that longing had finally given way to fatigue.

I showered, dressed and mulled. I mulled my way around the local convenience store. I mulled over breakfast and while scrabbling together a packed lunch. I mulled while sorting out my field kit in my backpack.

Finally the time to depart approached and I knew that the time for mulling must end. I picked up my phone and began typing without even referring to my notes, impressing myself with my pluckiness.

>Hej Kim. Sorry I couldn't
>stop the other day. My treat
>when I get back from the
>land of meatballs? S

I liked it: 'Hej' demonstrated informality, wit and rapid cultural assimilation; 'My treat' hinted at courtship intent and assertiveness, while '?' softened both; 'land of meatballs' was a little irreverent and I recalled Phil telling me that females were attracted to displays of humour; 'S' was informal and just a little bit intimate. Yes, it was very good.

There was just one thing that I still needed to decide before heading down to the courtyard: should I sign off with a kiss? After debating this briefly I told myself I would live courageously or die trying. I typed xx into the phone. Then I read the message one last time and deleted the second x – this was no time to lose my head.

I sent the message.

It went.

I stared down at the phone for a few moments, as if expecting a receipt to spool from it, and then stuffed it in the thigh pocket of my combat trousers, picked up my backpack and headed out. The phone thudded heavily against my thigh as I trotted down the wooden stairs to the courtyard.

\*\*\*

It was ten past the hour when an old white minibus bearing the university logo pulled into the courtyard. The window lowered as it pulled up to the pavement. A female with white-blonde hair obscured by an orange baseball cap beamed at me.

*No* said the PC, sulkily.

'Sorry. It wouldn't begin,' said the blonde female.

'What wouldn't?'

'The minibus.'

The passenger door gave a warning croak as I opened it. Behind my seat, the minibus was piled high with oak-plank nest boxes. On closing the door my nostrils filled with a wonderful citrusy sawmill aroma which briefly took me back to childhood journeys in Dad's van. I felt that old loss try to pull me down but as the minibus tyres crunched over the stone chippings, Charlotta turned up the radio and its grip loosened again.

Later, raising my voice to penetrate the loud pop music, I asked Charlotta about her experience with pied flycatchers.

'I have never studied them in the field,' she said, 'but the literature suggests that song complexity varies significantly between age-matched individuals. Perhaps the females evaluate male song to identify high-quality males, but nobody has proved this definitively. I am very excitable to learn more.' When we stopped at a junction she turned to me, her pale eyes dancing.

I warmed to her enthusiasm as we made our way out of the city and towards the study site at Fiby. Instinct told me I would enjoy working

97

with Charlotta and I began to hope we would form a social allegiance too. Might she, in time, be able to offer a new perspective on the Kimcident?

Some twenty minutes later I smiled again as we entered the woods because she reached over to turn the radio off. Was this reverence?

The bright morning light threw spinning shadows across the dusty grey dashboard and I stared out of the passenger window into the hardiest oaks in Europe. We were just a few miles south of the Limes Norrlandicus, a boundary formed by nature rather than by the random designations of *Homo sapiens*. North of this line Sweden became less hospitable, the lowland surrendered to the hills and the oak surrendered dominion to the conifer.

Soon we pulled off the road on to a gravelly single track, following it into a secluded car park. Mats and a male were already unpacking the 4x4 outside a single-storey, redwood cabin with a white door and frames.

Charlotta snatched up the handbrake and it protested like a disturbed jay (*Garrulus glandarius*).

Wolfie was a tall and over-nourished male. Shaking his hand I noted his thick, dark, bushy hair. Had it really only been twenty-four hours since my fateful visit to Joe's?

I told Wolfie that I was looking forward to working with him.

'Absolutely,' he replied with a sharp nod. 'I with you also.'

*\*\*\**

In the cabin, the four of us sat around a chipped wooden table and Mats outlined the plan for the day. We had calculated that we needed to erect three hundred and fifty nest boxes to get sufficient data for the study. We agreed to divide the reserve in half and Charlotta suggested that she and I should work together, since we would be travelling back to Uppsala in the minibus at the end of the day.

'Oh. What about height?' said Mats, at the closing of the meeting.

'Don't worry about that, Mats,' I joked, 'you have other qualities.'

'I meant the nest boxes,' said Mats.

Recalling my reading, I suggested two metres. Mats and Charlotta nodded and Charlotta began to return her packet of biscuits to her backpack, but Wolfie said that studies had shown that pied flycatchers preferred higher nest boxes.

'You are right, Wolfie,' I said. 'But if we go higher than two metres we will have to lug long roofing ladders around the reserve for the next couple of months. I just don't think that's practical. Skoglund showed that pied flycatchers prefer nest boxes to naturally occurring holes as long as they are at least one and a half metres above the ground. Two metres is a good compromise.'

Mats and Charlotta nodded once more and Wolfie offered no further objection.

\*\*\*

Charlotta and I pencilled out a route on a photocopied map of the nature reserve. Next we loaded a green tarpaulin mini-skip with a dozen nest boxes from the minibus, grabbed a tool belt and finally a short aluminium ladder from behind the cabin. Swinging the loaded mini-skip between us like a very large and unresponsive toddler, we headed across the car park towards the footpath.

'Hang on a second please, Charlotta,' I said, as we approached the gate into the reserve. Resting the nest box mini-skip on the ground I pulled my phone from my thigh pocket. It was now eight thirty am in the UK and I thought perhaps Kim might be up by now, even at a weekend.

'Ah. There is no signal here I'm afraid,' said Charlotta.

Groaning, I checked the phone anyway. Charlotta was right and as the phone sank back into the depths of my pocket, I told myself that this was for the best because now nothing could distract me from the work.

\*\*\*

I felt Kim's presence throughout the day. As we erected nest box after nest box, it was as if warming thoughts of her were delivered to me on the brittle, angled sunbeams breaking through the canopy.

\*\*\*

One hundred nest boxes, nine hours, two packed lunches and zero pied flycatcher sightings later, Charlotta and I were back in the minibus, though now it was empty and echoey. My back ached and I removed my hiking boots and socks to rub my feet.

Charlotta turned the radio on again as we left the woods. She also invited me to join her and friends for pizza that evening.

We were just outside the city when I heard the sound of an incoming message from my backpack on the backseat.

'Now you have signal,' said Charlotta cheerily.

Though I was desperate to read the message, I decided to wait for the privacy of the apartment.

\*\*\*

I felt calm enough to make a coffee before checking my messages and judged that I was already developing effective coping strategies against love's ravaging power.

Mug in hand, I examined the phone. My optimism ramped when I saw there were not one but two messages. But the first message was from Phil and the other was from my service provider. At that moment I hated my service provider and I didn't feel very fond of Phil either.

I threw myself back on to the bed, all coping strategies and optimism dissipated. Perhaps Kim hasn't checked her phone, I thought. But an immediate retaliatory thought said that *everybody,* and especially PR people, regularly check their phone. Personal experience told me that there was an inverse correlation between perceived message importance and response time. Desolate, I concluded that I was not important to Kim. She had prioritised other texts, other communications, other people.

I felt a brief flare of irrational anger which quickly gave way to a deeper dejection which no amount of running would alleviate.

\*\*\*

While I was in no mood for company, I was in even less of a mood to be alone.

Charlotta introduced me to her mate, Kevin. Though she made his name sound hyphenated, Kev-in still struck me as a very disappointing name for a Swede. She also introduced me to her friends, Bertil and Nelly. Nelly had big eyes, a torrent of curly black hair and lovely skin the colour of fallen sycamore leaves. The PC, who never dwells on romantic disappointment, was delighted to meet her.

Our table was at the back of the patio beside steel railings. Beyond the railings the green Fyris rushed. I sat at the end of the table, with the females to my left and right and the river before me. Charlotta and Nelly made every effort to make me welcome, but my mind wouldn't still. As they spoke my eye was repeatedly drawn back to a lone black-headed gull (*Chroicocephalus ridibundus*) bobbing on the Fyris; he fought against its urgings and aggressively pruned his neck, as if punishing himself.

***

Despite my great fatigue, I slept for only a short while that night and then lay on my back in the darkness, staring up at the black sky of the ceiling, thinking sorrowful Kim thoughts. It was dark and so I knew it was between midnight and two am, but reached for my phone for a more precise assessment.

To my surprise, there was a message and this time it was from Kim. Had the incoming message woken me? Excited, I pulled myself up in bed and fumbled frantically for the switch on the reading light.

>*Hi S, hope you are enjoying the*
>*pine flysnatchers. Lunch would*
>*be nice. Let me know when you*
>*get back Kx*

The message seemed unambiguous. Kim had belatedly tossed a few crumbs of friendship my way. There seemed to be nothing left to mull. I sighed, put the phone back down on the bedside table, turned off the light and began to mull anyway.

***

Next morning, though I already knew the seventeen words by rote, I read Kim's text again while slowly chewing toast. In order to prevent myself from spending the day considering my response, I responded.

>*Hi K. Will do. See you soon x*

And then I tossed my phone in my backpack and my backpack over my shoulder and pledged myself to the pied flycatcher.

# Chapter 19

By lunchtime we had finished erecting all the nest boxes and we divided up to scour for males. We didn't see or hear any pied flycatcher males though and wandering, alone, from nest box to vacant nest box turned out to be the perfect conditions for brooding.

\*\*\*

Despite Charlotta's cheeriness on the drive back to Uppsala, I was still feeling grumpy and so I decided to call Phil when I got in.

'You were wrong,' I said, immediately swooping in for the kill.

'OMG! You mean Elton John has *not* been abducted and replaced by a hoarse Borough Market trader,' said Phil.

'You were wrong about Kim.'

'It seems to me you live your life like a mango on the wind,' he sang, mournfully.

My pique was already peaking and I strained to maintain my composure. I told Phil about the exchange of texts with Kim. 'So clearly she was *not* signalling her receptivity, Phil, was she? Admit it, you were wrong.'

'Hang on a second, Bird,' he said. I thrummed my finger tips on the apartment window sill and waited. 'That's better,' he said. 'Now, what are you telling me?' Hearing a noise in the background I asked him what he was doing. 'Nothing,' he said, 'carry on.'

'I'm saying that perhaps you are the one with the low FQ, Phil. I'm saying *you* misinterpreted her signals, not me.'

There was a new, louder noise in the background. This time the rushing sound was unmistakeable.

'Did you just go to the toilet while I was talking to you?' I asked, now openly belligerent.

'I was still listening,' he said.

'You're disgusting.'

'What's disgusting about it? Are you telling me that in all the years we've known each other we've never talked at a urinal?'

'It's acceptable when we are urinating simultaneously, as long as we stare at the wall; you know that as well as I do.'

'Think yourself lucky I didn't need a dump.'

Knowing that nothing I could say would make Phil feel regret, I decided to abandon the subject. 'Admit it, you were wrong about Kim.'

'What makes you say that?'

'She rejected my approach. You made me make a fool of myself.'

'She didn't reject it. She just didn't embrace it. It doesn't change anything. She was coming on to you, no doubt. Probably the sight of you in your moss-coloured corduroys...'

'I don't wear those anymore.'

'Well there you are then, that explains everything. Maybe she just couldn't resist you. And maybe she felt bad about it afterwards. I don't know. But she definitely came on to you, Bird.'

'Kim is not the kind of girl to "come on" to people in the streets, Phil. She just happened to bump into me, a friend with hair clinging to his face and, knowing that I had a pressing professional engagement, she responded as any good friend would.'

'I've known you a lot longer than her, Bird, and that's not how I would respond.'

'No, *you'd* probably urinate.'

'Well that would probably get most of it off,' he cackled.

I shuddered. 'She just formalised her pair-bond, for Darwin's sake. I'm sure she and Michael are happily wandering from one intimate photoshoot to another. We have no evidence to the contrary.'

'Ah, gotcha,' said Phil.

'Got what?'

'I understand.'

'What do you understand?'

'Don't worry, I understand. *Fully.*'

Phil continued to claim that he understood, while refusing to specify exactly what it was that he understood. When the call ended I felt even worse. Berating Phil had not proved to be the salve I had hoped it might be.

# Chapter 20

After four long days Mats spotted and captured the first male. We all went back to that first nest box with him.

'Dr Selwood, would you please do us the honour of welcoming our first guest,' he said.

Mats insisted and so I took the ladder from him and placed it against the gnarly trunk of the oak and made the few short steps up to the box.

Holding my ear to the box, I could hear the scratching of tiny feet on the planking.

I paused to take my fleece off. As I pulled it over my head, I pulled up my T-shirt too, exposing my stomach.

'Will you be keeping your trousers on, Dr Selwood?' asked Mats.

Charlotta laughed, saying, 'This study may be even more fun than I thought.'

Tucking my T-shirt back into my cargo trousers, I began to wrap the fleece around the box, forming a makeshift net as I sometimes do when I am feeling a little rusty.

*Don't worry*, I told myself, *it's a male. It's females that evade you.*

I slid my hand beneath the fleece, lifted the lid of the nest box a little, slipped my hand into the box and fanned my fingers. I felt wing tips beating lightly against my palm. As I lowered my hand slowly towards him he pecked me once and then I felt him move back into the rear corner of the nest box. Following him, I curled my fingers gently around him and lifted.

Letting my fleece drop to the ground, I stepped carefully down the ladder. At the bottom, I passed the bird gently from hand to hand, examining him – my first pied flycatcher. He opened his mouth once in a silent protest then rested passively in my grip.

He was beautiful. An imaginary line extended back from the hinge of his tiny black beak along his length to the tip of his protruding tail feathers. Beneath this line, his plumage was pure white. Above it, he was liquorice brown-black. He might have slipped into a long dark cape. Between his black bead eyes there was a small white patch, shaped like a pair of binoculars.

Before travelling to Sweden I had educated myself about scoring of male pied flycatcher plumage, which varies from brown to black during breeding season. However, Wolfie insisted on explaining the scoring scheme to me.

'I would say this bird's head and back feathers are at least ninety per cent black,' said Wolfie. 'Would you agree?' I nodded. 'Good,' he said. 'This makes him a six according to our scale. We may not see a darker bird all summer.'

As Mats noted the measurement in the PDA, the bird silently protested again, revealing a grey mouth.

'The scoring takes a little practice,' said Wolfie.

'Dr Selwood will pick it up very quickly, I am sure,' said Mats.

Next we aged the bird, weighed him and measured the length of his tarsus (shin).

'This is a big, strong boy,' said Mats entering the last of the data.

'And very handsome,' said Charlotta.

I quietly apologised to the bird as I took a single drop of blood from a wing vein, depositing this in a plastic capillary tube. 'It's actually a very good deal you're getting,' I told him. 'We get lots of data, but you get a complimentary nest box with a lovely narrow entrance hole. The females will love it.'

Finally, I shifted him in my hand for ringing with Mats, Wolfie and Charlotta still watching on. I closed the numbered aluminium ring on his right leg and then placed two coloured rings on each of his legs according to the pre-planned scheme.

Getting up on to my feet I raised him up in my closed hands. 'Best of luck, young man,' I said, then I opened my hands and he was gone.

Wolfie led the way back to the cabin with Mats and Charlotta following closely on behind. I hurried along at the tail with the ladder.

'Dr Anderson, I think Dr Selwood shows promise, but let's not take any chances,' joked Mats.

'Don't worry, Dr Carlsson,' said Charlotta, turning back to grin at me, 'I will monitor him very closely.'

# Chapter 21

The number of new male arrivals increased daily. Charlotta needed to capture their lusty early morning song and so she arrived outside my apartment at three thirty am every morning, smiling.

We saw Mats and Wolfie at the dawn briefing meetings and occasionally at lunch, but Charlotta was my main human contact.

I learned that she had grown up in Göteborg (You're-the-boy) with a mother who was the neighbourhood wildlife rescuer. For young Charlotta sharing a home with a tame hooded crow (*Corvus cornix*) and a magpie (*Pica pica*) that greeted visitors with a sharp 'Halla' didn't seem strange. Nor was it odd that their garden pond was home to a disabled mallard (*Anas platyrhynchos*) that had hatched in the family airing cupboard.

Charlotta and I didn't only speak about birds – she told me about meeting Nelly at university, about her PhD and her love of music – but mostly we spoke about birds.

One particularly lovely, clear morning just before we entered the woods, a magnificent male Ural owl (*Strix uralensis*) flew across the road in front of the minibus. Charlotta and I spent the last minutes of that journey happily trading owlnecdotes.

\*\*\*

When the female pied flycatchers started to arrive the study transitioned into Phase 2 (Pairing) and then in to Phase 3 (Nesting).

My workload increased steadily with every phase and I was getting back to the cabin later and later in the day. Mats and Wolfie had usually departed already by the time I returned, but Charlotta always waited for me patiently. Usually she was in the cabin but sometimes if she was in a hurry she would already be seated in the minibus. I felt guilty for delaying her, but somehow I always got distracted by a pairing attempt or some other fascinating piece of pied flycatcher behaviour. It didn't seem to matter how late I was though, Charlotta always greeted me with a wide grin.

\*\*\*

The evening drives back to Uppsala developed a routine of their own.

As we left the trees behind Charlotta would turn on the radio and as soon as the right song arrived, she would begin to sing. She had clearly learned all of her lyrics by ear, and after hearing her rendition of 'Champagne Supernova' which included the lyric 'walking fastly from the cannibal' I learned to listen out for such gems. I nearly managed to convince her that Adele was chasing penguins (*Sphenisciformes*).

Snow Patrol was her big steering-wheel-beating favourite of the season though. Whenever it came on she would sing and then as the first chorus neared she would urge me to sing with sharp jabs of her elbow, but I refused to yield.

\*\*\*

One morning, when Charlotta was recording nearby, I waited for her as she tried to get a clean recording of a vocal unpaired male. Unusually, the male was on a low branch, only a few metres above the nest box, rather than way up in the upper branches. Under these circumstances she should have been able to get a perfect recording, but a nearby great tit (*Parus major*) was competing for top billing.

'Mammaknullare!' said Charlotta, removing her headphones in frustration.

'What?' I said.

'Sorry, I mean motherfornicator,' she said. She laughed, apologised again, then folded up her tripod and picked up her large parabolic microphone which, with its furry black cover, reminded me of Julie Christie in *Dr Zhivago*. 'I give up. I will come back later, with a rifle, perhaps,' she said, walking westward on the path towards the next nest box. I picked up my ladder and followed her like an apprentice window cleaner.

We spoiled ourselves that lunchtime, pausing to sit on one of the few benches within the reserve. A shaft of sunlight warmed our backs. Charlotta even took off her baseball cap before unfolding her sandwiches on the bench; made with dark rye bread and neatly wrapped in greaseproof paper, they made my own sandwich look thick and irregular by comparison.

Charlotta sighed contentedly. 'Tonight, I will drink beer and I will listen to pre-recorded human song,' she said.

'Yes, I can see how that might be appealing,' I said, my reply distorted by bread and cheese.

'We are going to William's English Pub. Will you join us?'

I didn't reply at first. I was tired, but that wasn't all. By then I had spent several evenings with Charlotta and friends and I didn't want to overstay my welcome. I got along well with lovely Nelly and lucky Bertil, but Kev-in and I had clashed about hunting.

'It's Saturday, Simon,' said Charlotta.

'Perhaps, but since the concept of weekend is yet to evolve in the avian consciousness, tomorrow is just yet another extremely long day.'

'Simon, it's *Saturday*.'

'OK, OK, I'll come. For a while.'

'Yay,' she said, refolding the greaseproof paper around the remains of her sandwich.

# Chapter 22

By the time the study entered Phase 4 (Laying) I was head over heels in love.

I loved their plumage and their melodious warble. I loved their nests, woven with such care and precision that the central depression looked as if it had been removed with an ice-cream scoop. I loved the stoic way they tolerated me lifting them from the nest boxes when I counted their beautiful pale green eggs.

With more to observe all the time, the days grew ever longer. On Day 20, after several glorious days, there was drizzle (or 'dugga') and so I returned to the cabin for lunch. Turning on the kettle, I told Charlotta and Wolfie about the highlights of my morning. Charlotta expressed interest, but Wolfie just seemed hungry. I made a pre-emptive apology to Charlotta, explaining that I didn't think I would be back until at least seven pm.

'I'm finished recording for the day and so I can help you this afternoon… if you would like,' she offered pushing back the peak of her cap.

Wolfie opened a can of coke with a loud chuck-fizz and took a direct slurp from it. 'Actually, I think I need your help, Charlotta,' he said. 'I just saw a new male. He was singing more loud than I ever heard. I think you should record him.'

'Thanks, Wolfie,' she said. 'I will get him tomorrow morning, when he is in full voice. Which nest box is it?'

'He was singing very loudly when I came here.'

'Perhaps you *should* go and check him out now, Charlotta,' I said. 'He might be paired by tomorrow.'

'Absolutely,' said Wolfie, looking even more serious than usual. 'This is possible.'

Charlotta eventually agreed to go with Wolfie, but when I left the cabin for the afternoon she was still sitting at the table and her parabolic microphone was still stowed in the back of the minibus and her characteristic enthusiasm seemed to have deserted her. Perhaps the early mornings are finally catching up with her, I thought.

\*\*\*

The dugga cleared after lunch and so I expected Charlotta to be sitting in the sunshine when I returned, but she wasn't on the bench and she wasn't in the minibus either and so I went to check inside the cabin.

Charlotta and Wolfie's faces were illuminated by Charlotta's laptop screen. She waved at me when I entered and then looked back at the screen, pointing to it as she spoke. 'So you see there is at least a ten-fold difference in song repertoire across the males.'

'Fascinating. Absolutely fascinating,' said Wolfie, which seemed odd because he was looking at the side of Charlotta's face, which was devoid of sonographic data.

Charlotta smiled proudly down at the laptop.

'Do we know yet if the best singers gain advantage?' I said, stepping around behind them to look at the screen.

'Not yet, but very soon,' said Charlotta.

'I look forward,' said Wolfie.

'Where's Mats?' I asked.

'Oh, he's gone already,' said Charlotta, standing and folding her laptop. 'Wolfie wanted to see my data so we're going to drop him off on the way.'

\*\*\*

When I offered to sit in the back of the minibus I hadn't expected Wolfie to accept so readily. Charlotta turned the radio up so that I could hear, but the back of the minibus was warm and I quickly dropped into a head-lolling doze.

I woke with a start to the sound of Wolfie chanting 'Monster' by The Automatic. His voice was deep and light on intonation, like Kraftwerk at reduced speed.

Charlotta caught my eye in the rear view mirror. 'Do you like this one, Simon?' she asked.

'Absolutely,' I replied.

# Chapter 23

I arrived back at the apartment to find two missed calls from Phil. I was hungry and tired and not at my most Philanthropic. Telling myself I would call him later, or tomorrow, or eventually, I started to prepare pasta.

It was draining and the tomato sauce was beginning to bubble when he called again.

I looked down at the phone vibrating in my hand and then at the rinsed prawns and the chopped parsley. '*It's not rude*,' I told myself. '*It's Phil.*' Then with a gasp of self-directed exasperation, I answered.

'Hi Phil, I'm about to sit down to eat.'

'No worries,' he said. 'You'll mostly be listening anyway. First thing to say is it wasn't easy. You really didn't give me much to go on, Bird. I'm not moaning, I'm just saying. I got there in the end though, as I always do.'

Stirring the tomato sauce, I said, 'What are you talking about?'

'Don't interrupt, you'll get indigestion. You didn't tell me Kim's surname—'

'What?' I turned off the gas ring, moved the saucepan to the back of the hob and simmered. 'What have you done?'

'You didn't tell me Kim's surname and so I decided to target Mike instead. A less astute friend might have monitored Mike's movements over a few days, but that would be really time-consuming. I mean, I love you, Bird, and I want you to have a life, but basically I've already got one. So, anyway, I decided to infiltrate his judo club.'

The words 'target' and 'infiltrate' were already haunting me. 'You infiltrated?' I said.

'It took a while. Have you any idea how many judo clubs there are in West London? Oh, and you owe me a hundred and fifty quid. I had to sign up for a ten-week programme. No rush though, you can pay me when you get back.' Phil's tone was bright, light and proud, like an infant, proudly showing off a new finger painting. 'You're lucky I didn't have to buy any gear,' he said.

'What have you done?'

'Slow down, Bird, all in good time. The first two classes were pretty boring – just learning how to fall. I mean, I could teach *them* that. I did find out about club night though. And so I went along and that's when I saw Mike. He was pretty surprised to see me.'

'He remembered you?'

Phil snorted. 'Of course he did. Couldn't remember you though, even after I showed him a picture.'

'You spoke to him, about me?' I could feel my blood start to denature.

'Nah. We talked for a bit about judo and shit. I tried to get him to come for a beer, but he said he had to go. I was ready for that. "Say hi to that lovely girlfriend of yours for me," I said. "What was her name?" He said "Kim" but it didn't sound right. He hesitated or something. So I said, "How is she doing anyway?" And he hesitated again, definitely. I could see he didn't know what to say, so I asked him another question before he could make something up. I said, "I bet she smokes a mean love pipe, doesn't she?"'

I closed my eyes. I knew that Phil had not said that, but I also knew that he had been tempted to say it. The possibility made me shiver. 'What *did* you actually say?'

'I said, "Will we be seeing the two of you at the blues festival again this year?" Clever, no?'

'What did he say?'

'He said – his exact words: "Very unlikely, I'd say." Then he opened up and said they had broken up. He looked a bit choked actually. I offered to smoke his love pipe to cheer him up but he said he wasn't "in the right place". I said that was bullshit because Kensington was probably the best place for cocksuckers.'

'Is this true?' I said.

'Yes. Except the cocksucker bit. You have to give it to me though, don't you, Bird? I come through for you time after time.'

Often with Phil thank you is the hardest word. I told him that I appreciated his efforts and then made him promise to stay away from Michael and Kim.

After the call I reheated the pasta and the sauce and I stewed. I tossed the pasta and sauce together but I had lost my appetite and so I put a lid on the pan. I went to sit at the small table by the window. I looked out across the courtyard.

What did it mean?

# Chapter 24

While I meditated on the Kimplications, the study was progressing into its most crucial and fascinating phase (5); the female birds were dutifully incubating their clutches and their mates were attempting to entice secondary females and this was the activity we were most keen to characterise.

Consequently, I stalked my sector with heightened vigilance and I was duly rewarded. When I arrived at the cabin briefing on Day 28 I was eager to share my news. Before the meeting began I made myself a strong, sweet coffee, bumping into Charlotta as I turned away from the aluminium sink. Chuckling we shuffled out of each other's way.

'Wolfie, I think our colleagues are very tired this morning,' said Mats, eyeing us from his seat at the chipped table.

'There was karaoke at William's pub last night,' said Charlotta.

'Dr Anderson refused to leave at a reasonable hour,' I said.

'Because *Dr Selwood* refused to sing.'

Mats shook his head tolerantly. Wolfie slowly chewed a heavily speckled banana.

\*\*\*

Though I was highly sleep deprived, when Mats called for someone to open the review of the previous day's observations, I immediately volunteered.

'OK, first,' I said, 'I observed three males who have established secondary pairings. One of these was over half a kilometre from his primary nest box.' When I had provided a full account of these observations, Mats thanked me and asked Charlotta if she would like to go next.

'Actually, I haven't quite finished, Mats,' I said. The previous afternoon I had been fortunate enough to witness a paired female copulate with a male other than her mate. Technically we describe such events as extra-pair copulations or EPCs. Up to this point, we hadn't observed an EPC in our study population and so, naturally, I was excited as I shared my news with the team.

'You observed an EPC?' said Wolfie.

'Yes,' I said.

Three pairs of eyes were fixed on Wolfie. 'Does anybody else think that it is odd that Simon is making so many observations? He has observed five polygynous pairings. I have only witnessed one so far and, Mats, I don't think you have seen any. And now he has also observed the first EPC,' he said, his arms spread wide. There was silence in the cabin. Wolfie appeared to have finished but then picked up again. 'Charlotta, you have spent a lot of time with Simon recently, I think. Did you see these pairings, or this copulation?'

Charlotta glanced at me quickly. 'I wasn't with Simon until late yesterday afternoon.'

'Let's move on, shall we?' said Mats authoritatively. Wolfie tossed his banana skin towards the waste basket by the cabin door where it hung limply over the rim.

***

The awkward tension endured and I was glad when the meeting concluded. As Mats rinsed his mug and I retied my bootlaces, Charlotta came over to say goodbye.

'I will come and find you after lunch,' she said.

Wolfie, who had been thrusting sandwiches into his backpack, coughed. At first I thought this was just a case of common frog (*Rana temporaria*) in the throat; however, he was actually preparing himself to say something significant.

'I am sorry to return to this,' he said, clearing his throat again, 'but I think we should independently validate all of the secondary pairings. That way we can be—'

Mats marched over to Wolfie from the sink. Bending over the table to face him, his hands clasping the table edges, he said, 'No, Wolfie. That *won't* be necessary.'

Wolfie, his face vermillion, got to his feet. Watching him walk across the cabin, I resisted the urge to clear *my* throat. I resisted the urge to say that the reason I was always the last to return to the cabin was because I was careful, precise and thorough in my observations. I resisted the urge to say that after dedicating fifteen years to the observation of courtship and mating behaviour I knew it when I saw it. In deference to Mats, I said nothing. I just tied a double bow in my laces and tried to figure out what on earth I had done to upset Wolfie.

# Chapter 25

On Day 38 a female flew past my hand, her wing brushing it. This was not so unusual; however, the newly hatched pulli (nestlings) squirming in the nest box she vacated were the first I had seen. The five naked lives writhed up towards me like the fingers of a strange, mutant hand. Their bright yellow mouths instinctively gaped for food.

I was still feeling buoyed by the transition into Phase 6 (Feeding) when Charlotta joined me to help me complete my nest-box round. She was uncharacteristically quiet though. As the path narrowed to single file she dropped in behind me.

'Everything OK, Charlotta?' I asked, turning to face her and walking backwards along the path (not easy when carrying a ladder).

'The song is over,' she said, her eyes looking down towards the path, her voice edged with sadness. 'I have now recorded all of the unpaired males.'

'Did you get all the data you needed?'

'Yes,' she said, though strangely she seemed to take no pleasure from this.

'Congratulations,' I said. 'It's a huge piece of work.'

We arrived at nest box 319, an awkward one. It stood at the edge of a small bank which rose steeply from the footpath. Charlotta stepped heavily on to the bottom step of the ladder to make sure it was pressed firmly into the hard earth. She climbed and lifted the nest-box lid. Standing on the path below, I opened up the PDA. Hearing Charlotta yelp, I looked up in time to see her jump back off the ladder. She landed solidly on her right leg but her left foot slipped down the bank towards the path and so she finished in an unnatural half-standing, half-kneeling posture. The ladder fell back towards her and I yelled a warning, but she caught it, straight-armed, above her head. Her orange cap lay in the grass by her side.

'Jesus,' she said, placing the ladder on the ground and twisting around to face me.

'Are you OK?' I asked, still holding the PDA, like an indecisive traffic warden.

Charlotta shook her head, then slid down the bank on her buttocks and ran to me. She threw her arms around my neck and began to lacrimate like a neonate. I put my arms around her and self-consciously patted her shoulder with my free hand. She felt lighter and more fragile than I expected – like a bird. Her hair smelt like the woods.

'Charlotta, are you OK?' I asked, again.

She pushed herself away, apologising and rubbing her eyes with the heels of her dirty hands. 'I'm sorry,' she said, brushing herself down. 'Shitting vessla made me jump.'

She explained that a weasel (*Mustela nivalis*) was sitting in the nest box, eating the eggs. To avoid the possibility of a nasty bite – weasels do not easily let go – she chose to leap.

'You look like a grief-stricken racoon,' I said. Charlotta punched me on the shoulder, and it hurt. 'I just meant your eyes are dirty, that's all,' I protested.

She sniffed, gave me a sad–angry look and punched me on the other shoulder. I was about to remonstrate with her but then I noticed that her hands were shaking.

\*\*\*

I drove the minibus back to Uppsala for the first time that evening *and* we didn't even listen to the radio. Charlotta sat quietly staring out of the window. As we turned into Luthagsesplanaden, she said, 'I need a drink.'

\*\*\*

I had never been in William's when it was so quiet. I glanced around, taking in the chimeric surroundings while Charlotta was at the bar. The walls were Irish green. The bar, also green, was trimmed with Union Jack bunting. The carpet was bullfinch (*Pyrrhula pyrrhula*) red and branded with black heraldic Ws. The sixties-inspired chairs were turquoise and chrome legged. The aroma was medieval.

Charlotta bought two pints of Guinness. We sat at a small table by the window at the rear of the pub, looking down over the cathedral.

'I've never seen you drink Guinness before,' I said.

'I just felt like it,' she shrugged. She took a small sip and licked away the small foam moustache from the tip of her lip.

'Guinness: the pied pint,' I said taking a sip of my own. Charlotta smiled for a moment and then began to stroke wavy lines through the condensation on her glass with the tip of her finger. 'That vessla really shook you up, didn't it?' I said.

'No,' she said, her voice deepening as it sometimes did, when I said something stupid. 'I don't mind the vessla.'

'OK. Good... It's just we've never stopped for a drink on the way home before...'

'Perhaps I wanted to make the most of the time with you before you leave,' she said, her eyes still fixed on her glass.

I hadn't thought about leaving. There was still so much to do and it was difficult to imagine being back in London. I knew every path, every tree, nest box, sound and aroma of the nature reserve. But Charlotta was right. In a few weeks I would be back in London, dreaming again of escape.

Charlotta took another sip. 'Did you know that things were not so good between me and Kev-in?'

'No, I didn't,' I said, which was true. 'I'm sorry to hear that,' I said, which wasn't. I had grown fonder of Charlotta, Nelly and Bertil over the summer, but I had never warmed to Kev-in and his tiresome hunting tales, his powdered tobacco and his surliness. She deserved better.

'Didn't you?' she said, looking enquiringly into my eyes.

'No, I didn't,' I said. Sensing she was not satisfied by my brief answer, I continued. 'Well, it did occur to me that the Nelly–Bertil pair-bond was more evident than the Charlotta–Kev-in pair-bond, but I just assumed you didn't go in for public displays of affection.'

'Or private displays of affection, actually. Though, I am a very touching person.'

'Oh. I see.'

122

'I would have ended it a long time ago, if Kev-in didn't try so hard.'

'*Really*?' I couldn't imagine Kev-in trying hard at anything other than recreational slaughter or perhaps skinning.

'Yes, Simon, *really*! Is it so hard to believe that he would fight for me?'

'No. No. *No*. I didn't mean that. It's just that Kev-in doesn't seem like, you know, the loving kind.'

'Well, he is.' Her voice had softened again. 'I wish he wasn't.'

Relieved to have narrowly avoided offending her, I said, 'If you ever need to talk about it with someone who lacks experience or competence… just say the word.'

Her eyes pooled again. She reached her hand across the table to rest it on my own. 'Thank you, Simon. That's very sweet… I wish you didn't have to go so soon.'

Sometimes I wonder how people lacking a rudimentary understanding of evolutionary psychology are able to navigate their way through the twisted branches of life's canopy.

Fortunately, I knew exactly what Charlotta was doing. In chimpanzee troops, bonds are forged by touch. All members of the troop groom others, but the subordinates groom most. Charlotta's hand on mine was, I was sure, an ancient echo of this instinct. By listening and empathising with her intimate concerns I had earned Charlotta's gratitude. I feared that she was now feeling upset *and* subordinate, which I didn't want.

I took action. To restore relationship parity I told Charlotta an intimate secret of my own.

I told her about Kim.

I told her everything. I told her about our meetings and about how the Kimcident had haunted my summer.

My strategy worked beautifully. As she listened, Charlotta gradually withdrew her hand. She started sipping her drink again. In fact, for someone unaccustomed to stout, she drank it surprisingly quickly. When she declined a second drink I took this as a sign that she was already feeling better.

I was only glad that I had been able to help.

# Chapter 26

We held an extended dawn cabin briefing on Day 50 to finalise our plans for Phase 7 (Fledging). Before the nestlings fledged, we needed to measure, ring and blood each and every one.

'We should divide into two teams,' I said. 'It's the only way.' I paused for reaction, but there was no debate. 'Charlotta, if you agree, it makes sense for us to pair, given that we travel together.'

'I absolutely don't think so,' said Wolfie. 'We should randomise.'

'Randomise?' I said, scornfully. I glanced at Mats, concerned that I had overstepped my authority, then I promptly overstepped it again. 'How on earth do you suppose that Charlotta and I will be able to skew weight, tarsus length and, and... and genetics, Wolfie?' I stammered.

'Individual assessments of tarsus length have been shown to vary by as much as ten per cent,' said Wolfie calmly.

'Which is,' I said, less calmly, 'precisely why we went through standardisation training seven weeks ago.'

Wolfie looked unhappy, but Mats intervened, saying that he also thought it made sense for me to pair with Charlotta and he mounted no further resistance.

\*\*\*

After the meeting, Mats and I carried our ladders together across the crunchy gravel of the car park in the day's early warmth.

'I don't know which has been the most interesting to observe this summer,' he said, after a few silent yards, 'the birds or the humans.'

I laughed – it seemed like the right thing to do. Mats eyed me expectantly, and so I spoke, because there was nothing else to laugh about. 'Both are fascinating, that's for sure,' I said.

Mats stopped to remove his backpack, retrieving his binoculars and hanging them over his neck. 'My wife is quite hooked,' he said. 'I have to update her every evening before she will feed me. She says it is like *Big Sibling*.'

We walked on to the gate of the reserve, silent again but for our footfall and the gentle shifting of our backpacks. I held the gate open so that he could pass through. Ladders and gates make for a tricky combination.

When we were both safely through I asked, 'What fascinates her the most?' My question was cleverly designed to deduce what Mats was talking about without revealing that I had no idea what he was talking about.

'Oh, women love all of this. You know that.'

'Yes. They do, don't they,' I smirked, none the wiser. 'Does she think it's funny?'

'Oh, yes, she certainly does.'

My questions weren't getting me very far, but I persisted. 'What makes her laugh the most?'

This must have been a good question because it stopped Mats in his tracks. 'Hmm. Perhaps when Wolfie learned to whistle like a flycatcher and then asked Charlotta to record it.'

'Yes, he does seem quite interested in all of that. Does he plan to study song more seriously?'

Mats frowned and searched my eyes. 'Simon, Wolfie is *much* more interested in our sonographer than he is in sonography. You do know that, don't you?'

The idea had never once occurred to me, but I said, 'I had my suspicions of course. Does Charlotta know?'

'Not at first, I think, but she isn't totally deaf.' We started walking again, heading slowly towards the fork.

I smiled. 'What does she think?'

'I think she is a little embarrassed. But she is too distracted to take much notice.'

Ah, so Mats knew about Charlotta's troubles with Kev-in. 'Yes,' I sighed. 'It can't be easy for her.'

Mats lowered his brow. 'Have you spoken with her, Simon? Be honest please.'

'Only once and that was a couple of weeks ago,' I said. 'She hasn't mentioned it since, but she seems to be almost back to her old self over the last few days.'

'Good. It's best that you have spoken, I think.' Mats looked into the bank of oaks ahead of us. 'Thank you, Simon. I appreciate your professionalism.'

After we parted, I couldn't shake the nagging feeling that I still hadn't fully grasped what Mats was talking about. Professionalism?

\*\*\*

Charlotta drove quickly that evening, given the limits of the minibus, and, for the first time in a few days she sang too. It was good to witness the return of her old energy. It wasn't difficult to see what Wolfie liked about her when she was in that kind of form.

For only the second time since the vessla incident, Charlotta pleaded with me to join her and her friends for drinks.

'Just for a couple of hours,' I said. 'You and I have got a big day tomorrow, you know.'

I expected her to chide me, but she just grinned and said, 'Yes we do, don't we.'

# Chapter 27

*Next day*

Placing the nestlings in a net sack, I carried them down to Charlotta at the small fold-out camping table. She weighed and ringed the first and passed it across to me.

The young bird looked fluffy, foolish and feckless, as young birds do. It had the typical brown plumage pattern of the female, with some additional pale speckling on the mantle and crown. I fanned out a wing to investigate the development of the flight feathers.

Charlotta gave a small double cough. I had learned only a few Swedish words but I understood that the double cough vocalisation meant 'hurry up, slack-arse'. I apologised, she smiled and I thanked Darwin that I had not been randomised with Wolfie.

\*\*\*

That evening I treated the ancestor to a refreshing loop around the campus. After my shower, I sat naked at the table by the open window with a glass of orange juice, awaiting the expiration of perspiration. Realising that I hadn't checked my phone all day, I peeled my backside from the plastic chair – like an RSPB windscreen sticker – and went to find it.

There were two messages. I ignored the one from Phil but quickly opened the second and dropped to the bed, still dripping but now also exhilarated.

>Hi S. I'm famished! Where
>are you? K xx

I read it again. Then I paced back and forth around the bed, reading it, over and over. Ostensibly, it was a request, from Kim, for information about my location, possibly motivated by a desire to see me. But what did it really mean?

Kim's message provoked the ancestor to renewed restlessness, and so I continued pacing, thinking, pacing. Two kisses! What did that mean? Try as I might, the combination of message and residual endorphins made it impossible to quell the rising euphoria.

I checked the message again and saw that Kim had sent it a full eight and a half hours earlier. This began to concern me, because something always does. Would Kim believe that I was deliberately withholding my reply to maximise my desirability? This concern refused to budge, possibly because that is probably what I would have done if I had received her message eight and a half hours earlier. As it was, I found myself in the unfortunate position of being pressurised into replying immediately so that Kim wouldn't think that I was deliberately delaying my reply. It was frustrating, but what choice did I have? I certainly couldn't tell her that I had just received the message because then she would know that I had replied immediately, which I had.

I replied.

>Hi K. Great to hear from you!
>Still in Sweden. Back soon.
>How are you? S xx

The waiting began. Within minutes, I was wishing I hadn't replied so quickly. I suspected that Kim would probably delay her reply – which would be deeply unfair.

Unable to bear sitting in the apartment alone with a pregnant mobile phone, I headed out.

\*\*\*

I sat at the bar in Buddy's, trying to make conversation with the barman and a local drinker sporting a neo-Viking mullet/pointy-goatee combo. Neither of my companions had any idea that, at two million breeding pairs per annum, the pied flycatcher was one of the most abundant birds of Sweden. I was telling them about their miraculous annual migrations and idiosyncratic mating strategies, but the Viking somehow managed to steer the conversation towards death metal, of all things. I'm sure that it never crossed his mind that the barman and I weren't the slightest bit interested in his obsessions.

He was still reeling off the names of obscure American bands that had been influenced by the Swedish sound, when the text landed.

'Shit man. That's loud,' he said.

I checked to see who it was from and then excused myself and stepped outside on to the street so that I could read it in an environment conducive to pacing and reflection.

>Hi S, how long can it take 2
>watch a few birds? ;) When
>u back? K Xx

As I read and reread the message I was feeling woefully maladapted. Over the last two million years, few, if any, of my male ancestors had ever found themselves twelve hundred miles away from the female they desired. Why me? Call this progress?

I paced several agitated laps around two concrete waste bins, telling myself not to reply immediately this time. Then I sat down on a concrete bench and replied.

>Hi K. I'll be back in a few
>weeks to honour my promise.
>How's life? S xx

***

When the minibus pulled up some six hours and fifteen minutes later, I had still received no reply from Kim.

Fortunately, I was with Charlotta all day and her mood, which never waned even as afternoon sloped into evening, buoyed me. Every time I looked her way she was smiling. I had never met anyone who enjoyed ringing quite as much as her. And despite my anxieties about Kim, I couldn't help smiling back. As I returned the final clutch of the day to its nest box she started to fold away the table and I heard her begin to hum the Snow Patrol song.

'I consider myself a very lucky behavioural ecologist you know,' I said, lifting the nest box lid.

'Why?' said Charlotta, pausing as she leaned over her backpack.

'Well, I can't imagine a more wonderful colleague,' I said. 'I'm not sure I could've made it through the summer without you, Dr Anderson, to be frank.'

'Thank you, Dr Selwood,' she beamed.

\*\*\*

I ran up the stairs and rushed into the apartment, leaving the door open behind me in my haste. There was a message from Kim, thank Darwin.

>Hi S, this cute guy I know is
birdwatching. Should I sprinkle
myself with sunflower seeds?
Pls advise. K Xx

I stood by the window in beautiful agony. I was now almost certain that Kim was possibly signalling her availability, maybe.

I sent a carefully considered reply which was encouraging and yet slightly ambiguous – frankly, I had absolutely no idea what I was doing – and then headed out for a hard, purging run, with the phone clutched tightly in my hand.

Kim's reply came in as I was running over a small bridge across the Fyris. I stopped and read it while leaning on the metal bridge railing, the river breeze cool on my shins. This time I was approximately quite certain that the content of Kim's message was not inconsistent with courtship. I set off on my run again, driving the ancestor harder still.

For the next three miles, I mentally composed a reply. I finally sent it from the top of the stairs outside the apartment, before retrieving the apartment key from my shorts.

After that, messages pinged between us all evening at a frequency of nine per hour (median). I fell into bed shattered yet quasi-elated.

# Chapter 28

Day 53 was Bertil's birthday. When I arrived at the restaurant that evening, I was worried and agitated because I hadn't heard from Kim all day.

Bertil's friends and family were gathered near a long table covered in a pale blue checked cotton tablecloth, over by the side of the rear patio. I didn't recognise Charlotta at first because she was wearing a new pink and white 'Happy Birthday' baseball cap. She came over towards me and proudly handed me a cap of the same design, but in blue and white. I dutifully slipped it on and went to greet the birthday male.

I was hugging Nelly when I heard Charlotta say, 'See'. I turned. She was talking to Kev-in as he buttered a crispbread. '*Simon* doesn't mind wearing the cap,' she said.

Things, I deduced, were not greatly improved between them.

I was browsing the menu when the call came in. 'Kim' said the screen display.

Kim was calling.

Kim was calling my phone.

Kim was calling me from her phone.

My pulse quickening, I excused myself and went to stand beside the whitewashed restaurant wall.

'Hi Kim,' my voice sounded surprised and happy, even to me. But did it also creak, just a little?

'Hi, Simon. I thought we might try an *actual* conversation. What do you think?'

'I think it's… a great idea…' I looked over to the table. Charlotta was looking over at me and I waved. 'I can't talk for long. Birthday party.'

'Oh. I'm sorry. I can call back tomorrow…'

'No. I mean yes, but we can talk for a few minutes now… It's good to hear you.'

Kim bombarded me with questions about my trip and about Uppsala. I didn't really get much chance to ask her anything. I certainly didn't get a chance to ask about Michael. I kept glancing at the table. Everybody was seated now and Charlotta was waving a menu at me.

'Sorry, Kim, need to go,' I said.

'Oh, OK. I could do some online dating instead, I suppose.'

Even as a joke I hated that. 'Don't,' I said.

'Why ever not, Simon?'

I swallowed. 'I've heard… I've heard that a flamingo dies every time somebody logs on to an online-dating site.'

'Hmm, that does seems like a high price to pay just to trade messages with men who aren't as intelligent, funny, tall or as single as they pretend to be.'

'Exactly,' I said.

'So what do you suggest, Dr Selwood?'

When a female pied flycatcher approaches to evaluate a male he makes a characteristic high-pitched plea, often from within his nest box. I suspected that Kim was now waiting for me to make my plea to her.

'Wait for me… Please. Kim,' I said.

After what seemed like an eternity, I heard Kim say, 'OK.' I will never be able to adequately explain just how good I felt, just for that moment. 'I will wait for you, Simon, until August 1.'

I began to edge towards the table, mouthing a silent apology to Bertil across the patio and calculating. How many days was that? Eight? Ten? It was going to be tight. I saw Charlotta point me out to a waiter. He began to walk over to me with his pad and pencil.

'Thank you,' I said.

And then Kim told me to enjoy the party and she was gone.

I gave the waiter my order quickly, unthinkingly and tottered over to sit beside Charlotta.

'Is everything OK?' she asked. 'You look worried.'

'Oh, yes, I'm fine,' I said, adjusting my visor. 'In fact, I'm good. And thank you for my lovely cap.' I briefly grasped Charlotta's hand, having observed that females often did this to convey gratitude and/or affection.

Kev-in glowered. Rather than indulge him I turned to raise a glass to Bertil; after all, if Kev-in wanted the cap so much, why hadn't he taken it when Charlotta first offered it to him?

# Chapter 29

I made my play on Day 60, aka July 26. I suggested that given that we were now at the tail end of Phase 7, I might be more productively employed by making a start on the paternity analysis in London.

To my great relief the vote was carried by three to one. Only Charlotta voted against it.

As I loaded my backpack I kept glancing across the cabin to watch her scrubbing her mug. Mats was watching her too and I caught his eye. We could both see just how much she was going to miss the study and our woods.

\*\*\*

To cheer Charlotta up, I suggested that we should do something to celebrate the end of the study. She nodded, but at first my suggestion didn't have the desired impact. It wasn't until late morning – after I had just returned a brood of eight nestlings back to nest box 67 – that she began to speak about it with enthusiasm.

'Just the four of us?' she said.

'Five, surely,' I said, frowning.

'No, there are only four unless you count my parabolic reflector.'

'What about Nelly and Bertil? And Kev-in?'

'I think we should do something as a team,' she said, her blues eyes fizzing, 'I want to say goodbye to you properly... We want to.'

\*\*\*

That evening I booked a Friday lunchtime flight and immediately called Kim. She didn't answer, but called me back a little later.

'Sorry. I was in the shower,' she said. I felt the PC stir.

'No problem,' I said, chirpily. 'I've got great news.'

'Have you?'

'Yes, I'm flying home on Friday July 29.' I said, though it still felt more natural to think of it as Day 63. 'And that is just three days away,' I trilled. 'What are you doing on Saturday?' There was a long pause on the other end of the line. 'Kim? Are you there?'

'Sorry, Simon, my towel slipped. What did you say?'

'I said, "What are you doing on Saturday?"'

'This Saturday?'

'Yes.'

'Simon, I'm sorry. I didn't know... I have to go away for a few days... Actually, it could be longer...'

I felt the talons of a yellow-eyed devil pierce my flesh. Where there had been excitement and anticipation now there was only fear, struggle and chaos. Away? Away where? Why? With whom?

'Simon?'

'Yes,' I said.

'I'm joking.'

'That's good,' I said, though I still felt confused. Joking?

'Simon, I'm sorry. I thought you would think it was funny. Besides, you deserve it. You've been gone for *seven* weeks.'

'Nine. On Friday,' I said, still trying to compose myself.

'Really? Well, whatever, it's very rude to go away for so long. Are you finally going to take me out for lunch?'

'Yes,' I said.

# Chapter 30

Mats, Wolfie and I sat hunched around a Thai restaurant table, sipping beer in a partition fashioned from lashed bamboo poles.

Bamboo blinds blocked out all natural light and the walls and ceilings were black. Illumination was provided by fluorescent rope lights coiled like tropical snakes around the bamboo enclosures. However, despite the curious décor, it was the large white-framed glasses Wolfie was wearing – the kind favoured by keyboard players in the 1980s – that fascinated me most.

To distract myself, I glanced down at my watch again. 'Where is she? She hasn't been late since the first morning,' I said. Moments later a waiter approached the table. Stepping aside he revealed a female. The female was not wearing a cap. She wasn't wearing a fleece, cargo pants or walking boots. She was wearing a pretty knee-length navy dress, spattered with tiny red flowers. But she was Charlotta all the same. Charlotta had come as a female – a *beautiful* female.

Shyly she stepped into the bamboo enclosure to join us.

*Yes*, said the PC, meekly.

*I'm sorry? I'm not sure I caught that,* I replied.

*I said yes.*

*Yes? After sixty-two days?*

*I think I probably owe you an apology,* he said.

Charlotta and her surprise legs slid into the vacant end seat, facing Mats, with myself and Wolfie at either side. As she bent to place a small handbag by the side of her chair, I looked across the table at Wolfie; his moist, bulging eyes swam behind the thick lenses.

Charlotta sat upright again and looked at the three of us. 'What?' she said.

'Charlotta, you look wonderful,' said Mats. 'You have taken our words.'

'Thank you, Mats,' she said, smiling self-consciously.

'Absolutely,' said Wolfie. 'Absolutely!'

'Thank you, Wolfie. A double absolutely – that's very sweet.'

It was my turn. 'Charlotta, you look… well you look… I mean, I agree.'

'Thank you, Simon.' By now she was beaming, and a little flushed. 'It's just a dress. Have you guys never seen a dress before? Shall we look at the menu?'

I glanced at the menu, then at Charlotta, then at the menu and so on. She really did look amazing. Was it the fluorescent lighting? I looked across the table at Wolfie's big pink face. If the light *was* responsible for enhancing Charlotta's attractiveness, it was clearly a gender-specific wavelength.

I shook my head and turned the menu over. Why had Charlotta changed her appearance so dramatically? Had Wolfie's courtship efforts finally won her approval?

'I'm feeling adventuring,' said Charlotta, 'I'm going to try something new.'

I raised my glass high, 'Lady and gentlemen, esteemed collaborators, a toast: to female choice…'

\*\*\*

Silence hung heavily in the moments after the toast.

Mats broke it: 'I'm intrigued to hear your thoughts, Simon,' he said. 'What criteria do you think the female pied flycatchers are using to select males?'

Charlotta protested, 'Hey, no shopping talk.'

'Don't worry, Charlotta, I don't have much to say,' I said, 'I honestly don't know.' Mats raised a single caterpillar-like eyebrow. 'I can see you think I am being cautious for the sake of it, Mats, but I really don't know. We know the males vary considerably with respect to plumage, size and song complexity, etc., but I don't think we can make firm conclusions about which combinations of factors are most attractive. We have a lot more work to do.'

'And will you come back next summer to help us?' he asked.

'I would love to.'

'Yay,' said Charlotta, clapping her hands. 'I can't wait.' She squeezed my shoulder.

Wolfie was holding a prawn cracker bearing an impression of his incisors. 'I must say, I think this is a very surprising discussion,' he said. 'How can you say we can't make conclusions about female choice?'

'At this stage I just have hypotheses,' I said, finishing my beer.

'This is ridiculous,' said Wolfie, sitting back and placing the prawn cracker on his plate beside a scrunched black napkin.

'Wolfie!' said Mats. The sudden conviction of both men made me laugh and I began to choke. Charlotta passed me a glass of water, but when I tried to speak again I sounded like an old accordion.

Wolfie leaned on the table. 'The conclusions are very clear. I will make my proposal to Simon right now.'

Clearing my throat I said, 'Wolfie, that's very nice of you but it's going to be hard enough to say goodbye as it is.' I was awarded with a rare grin from Mats.

'The females prefer dark males,' said Wolfie. 'They prefer males with complex song. This is all irrefutable.'

I looked across the table at Wolfie and then at Mats. Mats gave an almost imperceptible nod.

'Wolfie, you may be right. The problem is that we can't prove it. Not yet.'

'Absolutely irrefutable,' he said.

I refuted it. He re-refuted me. Charlotta tried, without success, to restrain us. Finally I said, 'In conclusion, we can't be certain that the females are choosing males at all. It's entirely possible that they are selecting the territories with the best resources rather than the males who are occupying them.'

'Yes, it is possible,' said Mats.

'This is unprovable,' said Wolfie, but the force of his initial indignation and insistence was greatly diminished.

'Would anybody like another drink?' said Charlotta.

'Perhaps,' I said, 'perhaps the finer details of female choice must remain forever beyond our grasp... But I think there might be a way...'

I pushed a paper place mat into the centre of the table and began to draw.

'Thank you, Simon,' said Mats, 'but I think perhaps Charlotta is right. We have had enough scientific debate for one evening.'

\*\*\*

After the darkness of the restaurant the brilliant evening light was quite an adjustment. On the pavement, I said my farewells to everyone.

Mats asked Charlotta if she would like a lift. Wolfie awaited her reply, his eyes fixed on her like a dog on a ball.

'Thank you,' said Charlotta. 'But I think I will walk.'

Mats crossed the street to his car, with Wolfie trailing behind.

'Which way are you going, Charlotta?' I asked.

'I will walk with you for a while,' she said.

'Isn't it out of your way?'

'Not so much.'

We started to walk down the slope towards the university building. Mats honked the horn of the 4x4 as it pulled alongside us, startling us both. Wolfie's expressionless face stared at us through the passenger window.

'Poor Wolfie,' I said, 'his eyes were melting like polar ice-caps when you arrived this evening.'

'Really?' she said. 'I hadn't noticed.'

'Come on Charlotta – really?'

She smiled. 'I may have noticed a little… But I am not attracted to Wolfie.'

We stepped out into the road to let a couple pass on the pavement. I wondered if this was a good time to ask her about Kev-in.

As we stepped back on to the path Charlotta bumped into me. 'Sorry,' she said, 'I think I may have had a little too much Thai beer.' She slipped her fingers inside my arm. I pretended not to notice, but in truth I was aware of little beyond the coolness of her finger tips against the soft skin of my wrist.

'Better safe than sorry, no?' she said.

'It's nice to walk without a ladder isn't it,' I said.

'I want to know your reaction, not Wolfie's.'

'Mine?'

'Yours.'

'Why?'

Charlotta laughed. 'Apparently, we are both not so good at noticing.'

As she spoke, I began to feel the effects of the old neurochemical cocktail taking hold of me and I cursed the PC.

We reached a junction and paused to let a car crawl past. Charlotta's fingers curled around my wrist a little more. 'What did *you* think when you saw me this evening, Simon?'

'I thought...' I swallowed, 'I thought you looked beautiful,' I said as we stepped back into the road.

Charlotta stopped walking. Tightening her grip on my wrist, she said, 'And now? Do I still look beautiful?' Her eyes docked with mine.

I nodded.

'Good,' she said, brightly. Her grip softened again and we began to walk past the university main building because that is what Charlotta had decided.

'Now, I will come back to your apartment for coffee,' she said.

'No coffee,' I said, panicking. 'Didn't replenish. Hate waste.'

Charlotta stopped us again. 'Simon.'

'Yes.'

'I have no intention to drink coffee.'

'But–'

'Tonight, Simon, I think we should make love, not coffee.'

'I've got tea b—'

'We don't need tea. Or coffee. Or a kettle. Or even a kitchen. A bed would be nice, but even this is not essential.'

'Kev-in?' I pleaded.

'I told you about Kev-in before. Remember? The last time I tried to seduce you?'

'Oh...' I was now even more confused. When had Charlotta tried to seduce me? 'Have you... severed your pair-bond?' I spluttered.

'Not yet. Not quite. But that doesn't matter. This is our last chance, Simon. It is a most beautiful way to say goodbye. No?'

'But Kev-in?'

'Simon, it is not only birds that engage in extra-pair copulations. Did you know that?'

Three men talking loudly in Swedish passed on the opposite side of the street. As I listened to their voices trail away up the hill, I realised that I very much wanted to copulate with Charlotta. I wanted to run up the steps to my apartment with her. I wanted to fumble in my pockets for my door key, feeling her arms around my waist, her face pressed into my back. I wanted to hear her whisper 'Hurry up, Simon'. I wanted to press her back against the wall of my kitchen, feeling her body against mine and my mouth against hers. I wanted to slowly, slowly lift the hem of her dress up over her hips, her stomach, her breasts, her slender upstretched arms.

'Simon?'

'No,' I said.

'Why?'

'Kim.' The street suddenly seemed very quiet.

'Has... has she been in touch?'

'Yes.'

'Does she want you?'

'I don't know.'

Charlotta looked down at her feet and sighed. She released my hand and walked ahead. She felt too far away. I followed her.

'Charlotta.'

'Yes.'

'Sorry.'

She shrugged.

'Hold my hand, Charlotta.'

'Sure.'

We walked on in silence until we reached Johannesgatan.

'This is where I will say goodbye,' said Charlotta.

I didn't want Charlotta to go. It was much too soon. Coffee was impossible and copulation out of the question, but I was pretty sure I had some milk and I wanted to make Charlotta tea and then I wanted to sit and sip it with her on the balcony until it got dark and then light again.

But I just said, 'Goodbye, Charlotta.'

She reached up, squeezing my face between her hands, forcing me to look into her eyes. 'I will miss you very much, Simon.'

'Charlotta, I...'

Charlotta kissed me, admonishingly. Then she released my face and started to back away.

*Stop her, you idiot*, said the PC.

But Charlotta was already running down the hill towards the city.

# Chapter 31

Only when we were airborne did I finally believe that my homeward migration was actually going to happen.

Primarily I felt excited and Kimpatient, but I also felt relieved. I had been tempted by Charlotta, the PC would not allow me to deny that, but I had not succumbed. Should Kim ask, I would be able to assure her that no female had blown on my face for the whole n = sixty-three days.

I turned my attention to developing a protocol for the courtship encounter to come. Kim had already agreed to join me for a woodland walk. It was likely that by the time we returned to the car that female choice would have already occurred. I intended to do everything humanly possible to influence that choice and there were still important decisions to be made about clothing, kit and supplies, logistics, emergency conversation topics and, perhaps most crucially of all, music for the journey.

Knowing that females were more attracted to musicians than behavioural ecologists, I reasoned that my music choices might help Kim to see what kind of musician I could have been, if only I had been blessed with rhythm, coordination, charisma and access to an instrument at an early stage of my development.

I spent the return flight huddled over a piece of paper, agonising over my shortlist.

***

Next morning I awoke at pied flycatcher o'clock. There were still five hours and fifty-three minutes until I was scheduled to arrive at Kim's.

Unable to sleep, I drank coffee, rehearsed conversation starter topics, revised my music choices and jittered.

*** 

I arrived much too early because I had allowed for the declaration of a national state of emergency with multiple checkpoints between Acton and South Kensington. To prevent Kim from detecting me, I parked down the road and waited there, drumming my fingers on the dashboard.

*** 

There was no answer from Kim's flat. I checked the intercom. It was definitely the right button. A flock of dark possibilities circled me. I pressed the button harder.

The intercom crackled with the most ecstatic static of all time and then I heard her. 'Hello? Simon?' I closed my eyes in thanks. 'Sorry, I'm running a bit late,' she said. 'Come up.' The intercom fell silent, the outer door buzzed and I pushed against it and then I heard her say 'I'm on the first floor'.

I bounded up the stairs two at a time. Clearly Kim hadn't woken at three am, she wasn't adhering to a meticulously planned protocol and she almost certainly hadn't laid her clothing out the night before, but at least she was in.

*** 

Standing in the centre of her lounge on a white rug, I completed a slow, rotisserie-like scan of the room. I took in a shocking-pink sofa, vivid against the white wall, a yellow armchair and white shelving laden with books, but I detected no evidence of male territoriality.

At the far end of the lounge there was a large framed print in a modern black wooden frame. It was Collier's *Lady Godiva*, though I didn't know that at the time. Drawn, I went over to examine it more closely. I was examining it when Kim entered. She was bare-footed and wore faded, ripped-knee jeans and a pale blue T-shirt. At the sight of her my heart strained against its tethering, like that goat (*Capra aegagrus hircus*) in *Jurassic Park*.

'Beautiful, isn't she,' she said, stepping lightly towards me.

*Magnificent*, said the PC.

I had already decided that if Kim blew on my face I would keep my eyes open this time, but she simply kissed me on the cheek and squeezed my arm.

'You look well,' she said.

'Thank you.'

'Must be all of that time spent outdoors. It suits you.'

'Nature reserve,' I said, picking two prominent words from the sentence I had composed but was unable to utter. She seemed to know what I meant.

'The picture doesn't really work in this room,' she said, looking over at the Collier. 'It's too traditional, but I just love it. I've got another pre-Raphaelite print in the bedroom.'

I was about to select two words from red, power, innocence, hair and horse, but Kim disappeared back into the hallway. She returned holding a pair of newish running shoes.

'Will these be OK?' she asked.

'Suitable footwear.'

'Good. I've got a hoodie. Do I need anything else? A machete?'

\*\*\*

Kim was in my car.

At the Brompton Road junction, I remembered to initiate the Jeff Buckley CD I had selected. The Buckley moans built as I waited for a gap in the traffic.

'Simon…' said Kim, meekly, 'Simon, there's something you need to know before we go any further.'

I was sure it was going to be about a male. We hadn't even made it as far as the A4, and the acetone of reality was already about to wipe clean my whiteboard of hope. My entire 'date' with Kim was going to consist of a U-turn.

I applied the handbrake. 'OK,' I said, stoically.

'Music makes me travel sick. Sorry.'

\*\*\*

145

It took forty minutes to get to Quarry Wood. Fortunately, I had resumed full sentence mode well before we entered Berkshire and my topics worked well. After we finally pulled off the dual carriageway Kim turned to look out of the window at the passing fields and hedgerows. Glancing across at the hand resting on her knee, I was delighted to observe that she was not ringed.

\*\*\*

We stepped between the posts marking the wood's perimeter and stopped to read a poster about a missing dog. Ahead of us, beyond the initial clearing, was the familiar stand of tall beeches and the heavily trodden footpaths which divided like the branches of an evolutionary tree. High above us was the strident repeated phrasing of a mistle thrush (*Turdus viscivorus*), one of the summer's last singers.

'What's that one, Simon?' asked Kim, generously. I explained, without elaboration, suppressing the instinct to tell her how easy it was, with a little practice, to tell the difference between his song and that of the common thrush (*Turdus philomelos*) or the blackbird (*Turdus merula*).

It was a beautiful, warm summer's morning, but the cornflower sky was barely visible through the leafy lattice-work high above us, and the air in the woods was pleasantly cool. The path forked again and again as we made our way around the western perimeter of the woodland plateau.

We fell into single file as the path narrowed and snaked through a patch of blackthorn and fern in a clearing. She waited for me to fall in step as the path widened again.

'So, why did you bring me here, Simon?' she said.

Quarry Wood had always been a special place to me, but as I stood there, contemplating it through the eyes of Kim of Kensington, I wished I had suggested a gallery or an exhibition.

I tried to explain. 'I came here first with my Dad when I was eleven. I was in the school performance of *Wind in the Willows* and he said that these woods inspired Kenneth Grahame. He was in a particularly good mood. It was autumn and the leaves were deep and they smelled fantastic. We kicked them up into the air. We had a balancing contest along the length of a great felled beech and we ran. It was a perfect childhood afternoon. This is where I fell in love with nature.'

'Were you hoping its magic might work on me?'

'Everybody falls in love with nature if they give it chance,' I said. I was one hundred per cent serious, but Kim laughed. 'It's true,' I said, perhaps a little indignantly.

'Thank you, Simon.'

'What for?'

'For bringing me here.'

'It's just a shame it isn't autumn. It's really stunning in autumn.'

'It's perfect.'

***

Our footpath merged with the bridleway that ran down to the bottom of the old quarry.

'This is my favourite part,' I said, explaining that Dad and I called it 'the bobsleigh run' because of its curved banks. 'We used to race down to the bottom. He fell over once. It was hilarious.'

'Want to do it with me?'

'Sure. Do you want to race?' I said.

'No. I just want to run… Did you ever hold your dad's hand?'

'No! I was eleven.'

'Yes, but you were reading a book about talking animals.' She held out her beautiful ring-less hand. I took it eagerly, wanting to believe more than ever in the theory that hand-holding evolved as a way of demonstrating pairing.

'I feel ready now, don't you?' she said.

We ran, tentatively at first but picked up speed and laughter. Kim whooped twice. Halfway down, her hair came out and we halted by a fallen trunk which lay across the path; she quickly pushed it back into a hair band and tugged me down the slope once again.

'That was fun,' she said at the bottom. 'Let's do it again.'

'Now?'

'Yes now… But hey, if you can't make it back to the top, you could always wait for me here.'

147

'I think I will be fine…' I said, 'but it's probably best if you hold my hand.'

***

Back at the top Kim announced that she wanted to race. I was just ahead on the approach to the fallen trunk but I overshot the bend. Kim cleared the trunk and laughed as she overtook me on the inside. She shouted a challenge to me and pushed on, intent on victory.

At the bottom, we were both breathing heavily. 'Fun,' she said, between gasps.

By then the ancestor had fallen in love with her too.

***

We picked a central path to the top and began the slow walk back. Kim reached for my hand again.

'Safety first,' she said. Guiltily, I dismissed thoughts of Charlotta.

A greying, lightly bearded male and a chocolate lab with an oversized branch clamped in its jaw passed us on their way down. It pleased me to think that the male would assume that Kim and I were paired.

'You are very lucky you know,' she said.

'Yes, I've got slightly longer legs and I was more familiar with the course.'

She jabbed my ribs. 'I meant about your dad. You're lucky to have that kind of relationship.'

'Hmm,' I said. Lucky was definitely not the way I felt about Dad, but I didn't want to say anything that could blemish our date or adversely influence female choice.

'My dad's a shit,' she said. 'I haven't seen him in years.'

'Hmm,' I said.

'Your dad must be very proud of you.'

A grey squirrel (Sciurus carolinensis) skittered across the path just ahead of us and ran up the trunk of a young beech and as it disappeared from sight I tried to find the best way to address Kim's question without further recourse to hmm.

'Simon?'

'He died,' I blurted. 'He died not long after my thirteenth birthday.'

'Oh, Simon.' We stopped walking. Kim placed an arm around my waist and stroked the back of my head. It had been a long time since I had told anyone about Dad and I felt a genuine resurgence of grief, but I also found pleasure in Kim's gentle caress and guilt about that pleasure and fear in case the PC, misinterpreting that pleasure, should send inappropriate guidance to my genitals.

I was quite relieved when we started to walk again.

'It changed me,' I said.

'What happened?' she said. 'If you are OK to talk about it.'

'I'm fine,' I said. 'It was a very long time ago. A freak accident at work.'

'And how did it change you?'

'It's a long story.'

'And we are on a long walk.'

'OK,' I sighed. 'Dad got it into his head to create an aviary at home. "Something we can do together" he said.'

'And of course you loved it.'

'I loved building the aviary with him, and choosing the birds together, and when the birds first arrived, but I quickly got bored.'

'Bored? How could anyone get bored of birds?' Kim smiled gently.

I smiled back. 'Put it down to immaturity. I liked riding my bike, making dens; juvenile male stuff. Dad wasn't bored though; he kept adding new species and extending the aviary. Mum said the birds scared her. "All that flapping". And she was annoyed about all the time Dad was spending out there. She wanted him to do stuff to the house. "What's the point of marrying a carpenter otherwise?" she said. But Dad was always too busy with his birds. Then one evening when I got back from school Dad was taking a load more wood and mesh out of his van to build a second aviary and Mum locked him out; she told him to sleep in his "blessed" aviary. He slept in his van instead. Soon after that she asked him for a divorce.'

'I'm sorry, Simon, that must have been tough.'

'It was. I was angry with both of them and scared. I stayed awake at night willing them back together. It was so strange going to visit Dad in a rented cottage. It smelt like gravy and boiled cabbage and the walls were covered in brown floral wallpaper. Dad didn't seem to mind. The second time I went to visit him he'd run out of bread and squash, but he was very proud of the progress he had made with the second aviary. He asked if I wanted to help build it and I shook my head. I thought Mum might take him back if he would only give up his birds. He asked me if I would rather help him clean out the first aviary instead. I burst into tears, told him he was an idiot and asked him to take me home.

'And that was the last time I saw him. He fell on a construction site. He died still believing I thought he was an idiot.'

'I'm *sure* your dad knew you loved him,' said Kim.

'I hope so,' I said. 'But to prove it to everybody else I dedicated my adolescence to his birds. If I wasn't at school I was attending to them. My uncle moved the aviary back to Mum's for me. I don't suppose she was very happy about that, but she didn't try to stop it. She even let me finish constructing the second aviary. I sold my bike to buy food and nesting materials. And so while all my classmates were discovering females, I was busy breeding.'

'I see,' she said.

We continued on up the hill in silence. Eventually that silence became oppressive. Knowing that we would soon be back at the car I started to scroll through my remaining conversation topics. I wanted to recreate the kind of mood we were in after the run and before it was too late. One question kept pushing itself to the fore, but I kept rejecting it. And then, as the slope began to level off, I asked it anyway.

'What happened with Michael, Kim?'

Kim looked at her feet. 'I don't want to talk about Michael,' she said.

I nodded and grunted and we continued for a few more yards. 'It's over though?' I said.

Kim sighed heavily and stopped walking. She looked away from me towards the mesh fencing that ran along the southern edge of the woods and then faced me again. 'Michael and I promised that we would forsake all others and, well, it turned out that wasn't quite as easy as Michael expected. And so, no, I'm not with him anymore. There – that's it.'

'I'm sorry, Kim,' I said, now feeling very selfish for pressing her. 'I'm not like Michael. I can see why you might find it difficult to trust males right now, but I'm not.'

'No, you aren't, are you?' she said, eyeing me thoughtfully. 'Let's not talk about the past anymore though, Simon, OK?'

'Yes. I'm sorry I shouldn't have—'

Kim leaned forward and pressed her clever red lips against mine, stopping them in their tracks. Down the hill by the old quarry, a green woodpecker (*Picus viridis*) laughed.

'There,' she said, 'I think we both probably feel better now.'

# Chapter 32

I was hooked on a new cocktail. It didn't come with a slither of lemon peel or a floating fruit segment. There was no straw or brightly coloured plastic stirrer. It didn't even come with a glass.

The recipe? Large measures of dopamine and phenylethylamine, a splash of serotonin and just a squeeze of oxytocin. That was how the PC rewarded me for finally forming a bona-fide pair-bond.

Love's cocktail suffused even routine experiences with a delicious novelty. I got huge pleasure from the first time Kim asked me to pick up something on the way over to her flat (olives, as it happens), from our first trip to the cinema (*Bourne Ultimatum*, as it happens) and from the first time we met up with a group of her friends (narcissists, as it happens).

And the pleasure I got from accompanying her to Tate Britain to see her beloved Waterhouses and Rossettis was, frankly, ridiculous. I learned that there are few joys in life comparable to gazing at a painting of a beautiful female with a beautiful female.

Love, was, as I had suspected, POWERFUL.

\*\*\*

I still found ways to worry, of course. I worried about the bird-like brevity of our initial copulations. When this issue resolved I started to worry about Michael again. In the beginning I was glad that Kim didn't ever mention him, but as time went on I couldn't quite banish the feeling that he was out there somewhere, like a sparrowhawk (*Accipiter nisus*).

I suppose I worried because I sensed that Kim was not quite as intoxicated as me. My suspicions were heightened on our four-week anniversary. She was asleep, but I was awake, despite a post-copulatory surge in prolactin. I was enjoying lying there beside her too much. Her bedroom door swung silently open and a wedge of angled grey light poured up over the bed, gently illuminating her face. I decided to observe her for a while before going to turn the light off.

She moved slightly and the white sheet slipped, exposing the superior margin of her breast. As familiar with Kim's breasts as I was by then, this was enough to trigger a resurgence of desire. I smiled. She shifted again, ascending closer towards consciousness. I felt my smile broaden. Her eyes briefly flickered.

'You OK, honey?' she whispered, her voice laden with sleep.

'I'm thriving.'

She smiled again as her eyes closed.

Powerful, uncontainable emotions swirled up within me and, selfishly wishing to keep her awake a little longer, I said, 'I believe I am in love with you, Kim, though this is yet to be validated by functional MRI analysis, you understand.'

'Thank you,' she said.

I lay there evaluating her response for a long time. I tried to convince myself that gratitude and/or courtesy was almost the same as reciprocity but I failed. I told myself she was tired. I told myself not to worry. I told myself to be patient. I told myself to sleep, but I didn't, not for ages.

\*\*\*

There were professional benefits of the neurochemical cocktail. I harnessed the energy it yielded to analyse the pied flycatcher bloods swiftly.

Over the phone, Mats and I discussed which journal we should target. He had his heart set on JAB or *The Auk*, the top ornithological journals. I had a feeling that we could do even better.

'I think we should submit a letter to *Nature*,' I said, pausing to let Mats absorb my suggestion. 'Because of its impact factor of course, but also because it could be in print in a couple of months and then we would definitely beat the Finns.'

'Yes, but do you really think we have something worthy of *Nature*, Simon?'

'Absolutely. I mean yes… I do.' I began to doodle on a pad with a pencil.

'What is it?'

'I don't know, quite… yet.'

Mats, still unconvinced, changed the subject: 'How much longer do you think you need to complete the analysis of the blood samples?'

'Oh don't worry about that. I will finish the last repeats tomorrow,' I said, doodling on. 'I can start to do the paternity analysis on Wednesday.'

'How did you complete this so quickly?' It felt good to hear the surprise lift Mats's tone.

'Well, we have a high-throughput system at Empirical, and, on top of that, I'm using performance enhancing substances… but don't worry, Mats, they are all endogenous.'

*\*\*\**

Dinner at Papa's was one of the first of our pair-bond routines. That evening, as she reached for a second piece of bruschetta, Kim said, 'Are you OK, honey? You seem preoccupied?'

I apologised, and explained. 'I'm trying to think of a way to get our paper into *Nature*.'

Kim took one of her tiny bites and with a hand arched over her mouth to conceal the dark mysteries of mastication she said, '*Vogue* knocked you back then?' She chewed a little more. 'And why is *Nature* a problem?'

'It's *the* elite science journal. They only accept eight per cent of the papers submitted. They reject everything which isn't brilliant, novel *and* brimming with wider implications. And we haven't nailed our novel, wide-reaching brilliance yet.'

'I know you will think of something,' she said. 'You're my absolute favourite behavioural ecologist.'

'Hmmm.'

'And I've decided that spiced flysnatchers—'

'Kim, it's catchers. *Pied. Flycatchers.* How many—'

'I know,' she said. 'I just like to see you getting arsey. Anyway, I've decided that they are my second favourite bird. They would be number one, but the boys are a bit too sneaky for my liking.' She reached out to lift a tiny fragment of chopped tomato I had dropped on the white tablecloth and placed it on the rim of her plate.

*Sneaky?* I thought. *Sneaky?*

Salvatore, the jovial pot-bellied owner of the restaurant and an unabashed admirer of Kim, arrived to personally take away our plates. Kim stood to hug him and I waited to shake his hand. Lost in thought, I stared at the rolling grey hairs protruding from his open-necked shirt.

'Simon,' said Kim, touching me on the arm, 'Salvatore was speaking to you.'

'Oh, I'm sorry. Sorry, Salvatore,' I said. 'I was twelve hundred miles away.'

\*\*\*

By the following Monday I had cross-matched a sizeable sample of the DNA fingerprints of the nestlings and parents. I called Mats.

'Mats, what would be your guess regarding the levels of extra-pair paternity in our pied flycatcher population?'

'Ahh. I don't know, Simon. I am not one for guesses.'

'Come on, Mats. I'm interested to know your hunch.' Mats wouldn't be drawn until I snared him with my version of 'Play Your Birds Right': 'OK, Mats, the average level of EPP in socially monogamous birds is eleven per cent. Do you think that the incidence with pied flycatchers is higher or lower than that?'

'I don't know.'

'Mats!'

'OK, OK. Let me think. The males are very vigilant during the fertile phase. They are rarely more than ten metres from the female. So I would say lower.'

'How much lower?'

'Simon, please…'

'OK. They are… *higher*.'

'Really? This is interesting,' said Mats, flatly.

'It looks almost twice as high so far.'

'Well, well.'

155

'Mats, I think we have our answer. We should write our *Nature* paper about deception. The males behave as if they are unpaired to lure a second female. The females are closely guarded but still manage to copulate with neighbouring males. Gram for gram, the pied flycatcher is clearly a very sneaky passerine.'

\*\*\*

I called Kim straight afterwards.

'Higher,' she said. 'It's obvious. That's how the girls get their own back.'

'Honey, it doesn't work *quite* that way…'

'Trust me.'

'Anyway, we are going to write our *Nature* letter about deception, but I can tell you all about it tomorrow evening. I'm really looking forward—'

'Ahh…'

That sounded ominous. 'What?'

'I've got to go to Paris now. EPCON pulled the meeting forward. Sorry, honey.'

'That's OK,' I said. Then I tried harder to sound jollier: 'We aren't joined at the pelvic girdle. I will get to work on the deception paper so that I can dedicate myself to you at the weekend.'

'I could… see you on Thursday…' she said, 'but no… Phil wouldn't like that.'

I told her that Thursday would be great and that Phil wouldn't mind, though I knew that he would accuse me of being henpecked, again. But I could tolerate a torrent of abuse from Phil in order to get my next dose of neurochemicals.

# Chapter 33

Mats and I wrote the deception paper over an intensive five-day period and submitted it to *Nature* on September 4. And then we waited.

\*\*\*

Every week for the last fifteen years, 'Post Room Mary' had slid copies of *Nature* into Empirical campus pigeonholes. On October 18, she placed a copy into my hand. Nothing special about that, except this time I wasn't merely a subscriber – I was also a contributing author.

'Congratulations, Simon, love. Your parents must be very proud,' she said in her soft north-eastern accent.

'Thank you, Mary. Yes, Mum is and I think Dad would have been.'

'Well, I'm proud of you too, if that doesn't sound daft.'

'Thank you, Mary. It doesn't. Do I get a hug?'

\*\*\*

Back at my desk, I stared at the beautiful magnified image of an enucleated oocyte on the cover of *Nature* and wondered if life would ever get better than this. Suddenly I had love *and* success.

Ripping the plastic wrapper off, I opened the journal and ran my finger hurriedly down the contents listing and then thumbed through the pages to check that the deception paper was actually there, in full, in print.

Later, unable to settle at my desk, I went through to the molecular biology suite to speak to Gustavo.

Marek, a bearded research associate from the group in the top bay looked up as I entered. He got up off his stool and nudged the girl in safety glasses sitting next to him. Marek began to clap, though he was still wearing his lab gloves. As I walked down towards the end bay, smiling, applauding lab-coats gathered in each of the bays. Gustavo stepped out to shake my hand. Touched, I managed to say a few clumsy, bashful words of thanks.

\*\*\*

All afternoon emails poured in from collaborators, mentors, associates. I set about replying to them but handshakes and good wishes kept bursting through the door. Prof was especially delighted and made me promise to update my entry on the departmental website.

I bumped into Pippa in the corridor mid-afternoon. When I told her about our *Nature* success, she insisted on stopping passers-by to inform them how 'clever *and* gorgeous' I was.

\*\*\*

By October I was seeing Kim and Phil on alternate Thursdays. Fortunately the publication of the deception paper happened to fall on a Kim Thursday.

When I arrived, she was seated by the window and there were two flutes and a bottle on the tall pedestal table.

'Pippa called you, then?' I said.

She nodded. 'Apparently, everybody is predicting very big things for you, Professor Selwood. You aren't really just a common or garden birdwatcher at all, are you?'

'I'm sorry if you feel that I have deceived you,' I said. 'If you want to end it, I wouldn't blame you.'

She toasted my success then leaned over to kiss me on the neck, sending a delicious shudder through me.

I reached into my backpack to pull out my copy of *Nature*. When she had finished skimming over it, she closed the journal and kissed me again. Then she tapped the image of the oocyte with an immaculate nail.

'Next time,' she said, 'we need to get *you* on the cover.'

# Chapter 34

And just when I began to worry that my current level of optimism and wellbeing couldn't possibly be sustained, things got even better.

Roger Turnbull, Chair of the Ornithological Trust, Fellow of the Royal Society and living god called to ask me to contribute a chapter to a volume he was editing. Suspecting a prank, I almost told him to 'shove his chapter up his tight, little multi-purpose cloaca'. Fortunately caution prevailed.

I began to write when and where I could. Early one Saturday morning, I had settled myself on Kim's pink sofa and had just fired up the laptop when she stepped into the doorway, wearing only one of my old conference T-shirts.

*Yes*, said the PC. After four months, he still greeted her as if unaware of our pair-bond.

'Oh, no you don't,' said Kim, striding across the lounge towards me, her eyes hawkish on the raised lid of the laptop.

'Kim, you know I have to work on this.'

'I *know* it's Saturday. I *know* that you are going to take me back to bed until I remember how you convinced me I needed a head-to-toe Gortex outfit. I *know* we are then going to go out walking in our Gortex outfits. That's what I know.'

'Kim… I can't.'

She closed my laptop, lifted it from my lap and turned towards the door. I watched her buttocks rise and fall beneath the hem of my T-shirt in a gentle, alternating rhythm – like two halves of a peach attempting to reunite.

\*\*\*

We ate thick-cut cheese sandwiches at the top of Leith Hill. A cool wind snapped angrily at our jackets. With our hands wrapped around polystyrene cups full of soup purchased from the tower café, we looked over to the distant South Downs, mauve in the blanched winter light. We sat huddled together on our bench, watching two bickering blond children attempt to outclamber each other on an amputated oak skeleton.

The temperature dropped further after lunch and the wind shepherded us back to the car. The village was lit up like a model in the valley below.

The breeze through the village brought the smell of chimney smoke to us. A white pub stood prominent amongst the stone houses and as we passed it a warm yellow light washed across our legs.

'That looks cosy, doesn't it?' said Kim.

*A warm welcome to walkers and their furry friends*, said a sign by the door.

In the corner of the lounge, an old gent with a nose like a burl sat at a table alone with a glass and a newspaper spread out before him. He slowly turned a page when we entered, but not his head. Otherwise, the bar was empty. No staff appeared to welcome us or to stroke us. I went to the bar while Kim set up camp at a small redwood table by the door.

'Hello?' I said. Nobody came.

Over at the table, Kim was shifting beer mats from our table to the next one. She pulled a tissue from a 'handy' pack. Frowning she started to wipe circles across the table top. 'Ask them for a damp cloth please, Simon.'

'I can't do that,' I whispered. I looked over anxiously to gauge the old man's reaction, but he was still reading.

I heard footsteps behind the bar. A stout, bustling woman with tightly curled grey hair and a navy blue apron had arrived. She tipped like a teapot, with one arm in the small of her back, to take a bottle from a refrigerator cabinet and then disappeared again.

*Surely she saw me*, I said to myself. I turned to shrug at Kim but she was checking her phone.

'Hel-lo,' I yodelled. 'Hel-lo?'

A man with wild, bristly dandelion-grey hair and fierce black eyebrows appeared. He leaned on the bar before me with hairy-knuckled hands. His abdomen beached itself on the bar.

'Ah, hello,' I said.

'Hello,' he said curtly, as if he suspected I was a fundamentalist aerobics instructor. Unable to detect desire for companionship in his demeanour, I ordered drinks. I know that he heard my order because he reached for two glasses – a windowed half pint tankard hanging from a hook on the bar and a wine glass. As he pulled my beer, his eyes flicked towards Kim.

'Is that your lady friend?'

'It is,' I said proudly. 'We are just down here for the afternoon.'

'We don't have any Pinot Grigio open. Chardonnay will be OK, won't it?' he asked, though he was already pouring it. 'I'll make it a large one,' he said.

'Actually, I think a small one will be fine… Thanks.'

'Right you are,' he said. He looked over at Kim again. 'I wouldn't go letting her sober up though, if I were you.'

'I beg your pardon,' I said, though I had heard him clearly. Is that what everybody thought when they saw me with Kim?

'Oh, don't mind me,' he said as he went back to pouring the wine into the measure. 'I've got a dry sense of humour. That's why I sell drinks, or so Glynys says.' He placed Kim's glass of wine down by my beer. 'Ten pounds sixty-three please.' His mood suddenly seemed greatly improved. Lacking the courage or the wit required to verbally slay him, I asked him what kind of crisps they had.

'Let me see. We've got plain, cheese and onion, salt and vinegar, and sour cream and chive.' The last of these flavours was delivered with a condescending warble. 'Oh, yes,' he said, 'and organic otter and watercress.'

'Otter and watercress?'

'That's right, young man. Very tasty – so I'm told.'

'In that case,' I said, 'I will have one pack of salt and vinegar… and one pack of otter and watercress.' I felt pleased with that. At least I wasn't going to let his unsavoury attitude go entirely unchallenged.

'Excellent choice, sir,' he said. He groaned and gasped his way down to the stack of boxes and emerged, red-faced, holding up two packs of salt and vinegar crisps between the finger and thumb of his left hand. 'Unfortunately,' he said, 'we appear to have had a bit of a run on otter and watercress. We had a darts match yesterday, you see. We'll be getting another delivery on Tuesday; perhaps you could pop in then.'

\*\*\*

161

'What's wrong?' said Kim, as I returned to the table with the glasses in my hands and the crisp packets dangling from my mouth, like nesting material.

'Nothing.'

'Why did you get two packets of salt and vinegar?'

'Don't ask.'

Kim took one of the packs from me. 'Did you enjoy your afternoon, Dr Selwood?'

'I did.'

'And are you glad I made you come?'

'Definitely.' I became fascinated by the precise way that Kim was splitting open her crisp packet. It was the first time I had ever seen her open a packet of crisps. 'I *have* to work on the chapter tomorrow though.'

'A couple of hours is fine.' Kim lifted a single crisp from the little foil platter she had created.

'I've only got three weeks left,' I said, picking up three large crisps.

'What is it again?' said Kim.

I sighed. I loved everything about Kim, except perhaps her inability to remember anything about my vocation. 'I have been asked to write a chapter for the forthcoming *Oxford Handbook of Avian Behavioural Ecology*.'

'This is another one of those important things that doesn't sound important, isn't it? Is it more or less important than *Nature*?'

The sound of slow strokes, like sandpaper, on the floorboards behind me, made me turn. The old man was making his way to the bar, glass in hand.

'It's *important*. Roger Turnbull is an ornithological deity and it's a tremendous honour.' My words had not affected Kim's expression. 'It's like… It's like being selected to play for my country.'

'At *birdwatching*.'

'Kim,'

'I know. I know. I just love to see your face when I use the b-word.' She snipped off approximately one-sixth of a crisp with her perfect teeth.

'Do I undermine your work?' I asked. I tried to take a small bite from my own crisp, but it split.

'Yes, you do. Does "PR is just systematic gossip" sound familiar?'

'Hmm.'

162

'I just don't understand why you are writing a chapter in some dusty old academic's book? You should be writing your own book.'

'My own book?' I stopped chewing.

'Why not?' she said. 'Who's going to read this birdwatching manual anyway?'

'It's a *handbook*.'

Unimpressed, Kim took a final crisp and slid the rest of the packet over towards me.

'Do you think they sell little bowls of olives here?' she asked.

'I very much doubt that, honey.'

'I'm just saying that if you insist on wasting our precious weekends, you should be writing a book of your own.'

'What would *I* write about?' I asked. 'Lorenz studied greylag geese for fifty years before he wrote a book about his insights, and *he* was a Nobel Laureate.'

'I'm not saying that you should write a book for scientists. I think you should try to reach the public. I love all the little facts you've told me about birds.'

'Little facts? Are you sure they aren't actually little-wittle facts?'

'You know what I mean. Look, people love birds don't they? When I go to the garden centre with Mum we can't move for great sacks of peanuts. And people are fascinated about sex too.'

'Ah, so *that's* why they also sell lots of fat balls in garden centres.'

Kim laughed. I still liked that. 'I'm serious,' she said. She lifted her glass, took a sip of her wine and shivered.

'Oh yes, sorry. They didn't have PG. It's Chardonnay.'

'It doesn't taste like Chardonnay either. It's… tinny.' She slid the glass towards me, but I declined. 'I think you could write a book about how similar birds and people are when it comes to sex.'

'Whoa, Kim. That's way too anthropomorphic.'

'You could call it *The Feathered Ape*, or something.'

I shook my head. 'Catchy. Do you think that if I wrote it well enough people would overlook the fact that humans don't actually have feathers?'

'Think about it. Birdwatchers would want to read it. Birdwatchers' girlfriends might even want to read it—'

'There are female birdwatchers, you know.'

I think it might even appeal to quite a few relatively normal people...
Can I try some of that?' Kim reached for my beer, lifted it to her mouth,
took a sip, tilted her head to one side to consider the taste and then
shivered again – seismically this time. Pulling a new tissue from the pack
lying on the table, she started to dab her tongue.

'Would you like me to get you something else?' I said.

'Yes please. I think sparkling water would be safest.' I found my wallet
and summoned the courage to face the barman again.

'Oh and, honey, ask if they have olives, please,' she said.

# Chapter 35

Christmas: another first.

I was excited about spending time with Kim and apprehensive about staying with her sister Sara and brother-in-law Tony at their 'little hideaway' in Dorset. I wasn't ungrateful, but a week being treated as the subordinate male is a long time, even for a behavioural ecologist.

\*\*\*

Kim began to supplement my wardrobe in November. 'Early Christmas presents,' she called them. At first it was just a black V-neck jumper. Then another jumper (blue, chunky) appeared and a pair of distressed jeans which distressed me whenever I wore them because they always slipped down to expose my lower back and the upper reaches of my rump.

Finally, on the evening before we were due to leave, she gave me a pair of black leather boots that made me look like a member of a poorly provisioned paramilitary organisation. Then, fittingly, she marched me through to the bedroom where she oversaw the packing of my case.

'How many times do you think Tony will call me "Mike"?' I asked.

'He called you it once,' she said, lifting my great horned owl T-shirt from the case like a beautiful forensic scientist at a horrific crime scene.

'It's for running purposes only,' I said. 'And I only met him once.'

\*\*\*

We drove down on Christmas Eve, stopping off en route to exchange Christmas gifts with Mum and my stepfather.

It was early evening when we turned off the road on to the grey stone drive. I got out of the car to open the wrought iron gates. It was a still moonless evening, but at the top of the rise beyond the gates I saw the upper storey of a grey stone house. Lights were blazing from every visible window.

As we drove on to the parking area at the front of the house a set of external floodlights was triggered.

Sara showed us up to our room. Tony and Kim's mother, Marjorie, stayed in the kitchen, but three small, excited pyjama-clad juveniles trailed behind us, chittering.

'I'm afraid the little parasites are wondering if you have Christmas gifts for them in those bags,' explained Sara, as she lifted the black iron latch of the bedroom door.

Sara told us that the main window had originally served as the opening to the hay loft and informed us that it would give us a magnificent view of the estuary the next morning. Standing beside it, I gazed out into the vast darkness beyond the parking area, while taking in a lungful of the marvellous new-carpet aroma. Hearing another latch opening behind me, I turned and followed Sara and Kim into the adjoining brown-tiled wet room. While Kim paid close attention to the shower briefing, I stood beneath the gleaming square shower head letting the possibilities wash over me.

Leaving the children bouncing energetically on our bed, Sara took us for a tour of the rest of the first floor.

\*\*\*

Tony and Marjorie were still seated at the black, granite-topped island when we returned to them.

'Simon, I forget: are you red or white?' asked Tony, getting to his feet.

'Red, I think,' I said, glancing at Kim who had pulled out a wooden bar stool. 'Shall we quickly freshen up first though, honey?'

'Don't worry, Simon, there will be plenty of opportunity to get Kim into the wet room,' said Sara, passing a bottle and the corkscrew to Tony. Everybody, with the exception of me and possibly also Marjorie, seemed to think this was a very funny thing to say.

'No, I just meant…' I stammered as the children bounded into the kitchen. They began to plead with their mother for chocolate decorations from the Christmas tree.

I asked Tony how they found the house, because that's what people do.

Apparently oblivious to the tantrum mounting on the other side of the granite surface, he sat on the vacant stool beside me and explained that they had fallen in love with the area when they came down, free of progeny, for a spring bank holiday break. 'We decided we wanted a space where we could connect with the landscape,' he said. 'This will be our haven from the craziness. There are fabulous walks and we want to start sailing again, don't we, Sare?'

'Sare' was unable to respond promptly. By now, she was gripping the wrists of her eldest, Matthew (Spiderman pyjamas), trying to make him understand that he shouldn't slap Mummy – even if it was only on the knee – when he didn't get what he wanted.

'Sare,' said Tony.

'Just one second, darling,' she said.

After receiving a firm final warning and no chocolate, the pouting children, led by Matthew, heaved themselves back up the stairs and Tony and Sara dedicated themselves fully to the tale of their acquisition.

'Tell Simon about the deal you negotiated, Tony,' said Sara. Marjorie timid by nature and predominantly interested in her grand-progeny, had said little since I arrived, but something about the way that she lifted her glass told me that she had heard the story before.

As it was, Tony was unable to complete his tale of merciless guile, before the children thudded back down the stairs and into the kitchen with little Tabitha (Sponge Bob pyjamas) at their head.

'Mummy?' she said.

'Daddy's talking, Tooshi,' said Sara.

'But, Mummy…' said the child, bringing her hand out from behind her back and holding it out like a branch, 'are these sweeties?' The roll of pink foil-wrapped condoms unfurled from her hand, dropping to the floor. I shot a look at Kim across the island. Her eyes were closed.

'No they aren't,' said Sara, calmly taking the condoms from the child's hand. 'And…' looking at me and then back at Tabitha, 'what have I told you about going through other people's things?'

'But what are they, Mummy?' asked Tabitha.

Sara paused to think, but Tony knew just what to say. 'They are Simon's special shower caps, Tooshi,' he said.

\*\*\*

After supper, the children's gift-anticipation hysteria intensified. At nine pm they were circling us like an unimpressive war party. I tried to concentrate on Tony's impromptu Christmas Lecture (Working Title: The Mind-set of the Serial Entrepreneur), but the juveniles were noisy and, frankly, more interesting.

When Tabitha finally fell to the floor and began to wail, Sara scooped her up and barked bedtime commands at the exhausted girl's siblings.

Marjorie went to bed not long after the children and I hoped that the end of my evening might be in sight, but Kim and Sara disappeared into the lounge to look at photos. Tony brought out a smoky single malt of impeccable, unquestionable, reputation-enhancing reputation, and mentored me on the importance of resilience and self-belief.

\*\*\*

My spirits rallied when Kim closed the bedroom door behind us, but hers did not.

'I'm tired,' she said, unbuttoning her blouse, her back towards me.

'And you're grumpy,' I said, flopping back fully clothed on the bed. 'It's not my fault the children went through my bag.'

'I don't mind that.' She slipped out of her jeans and disappeared into the bathroom with her toiletries, shutting the door behind her.

A few minutes later she startled me awake with a shake of my thigh, and ordered me to clean my teeth. When I returned, she was in bed and the bedside lamp was extinguished, but light was creeping in beneath the uneven bottom of the bedroom door. I slid in beside her. She was facing away from me towards the freestanding wooden wardrobe and her respiratory rhythm suggested she was still awake. A few moments later, the light on the landing was extinguished and we lay there in total darkness.

'Are you going to tell me why you are grumpy?' I asked.

'I'm not grumpy… I'm just tired,' she said, grumpily.

Perhaps she is, I thought. After all, I was tired. 'Happy Christmas, honey,' I whispered, kissing the back of her neck.

'Happy Christmas, Dr S,' she replied, reaching for my hand beneath the duvet.

I may have been asleep already when she turned on the lamp and faced me, her eyes electric. 'They didn't take any interest in what you do,' she said. 'Not even about your *Nature* paper thing. They hardly acknowledged it.'

'I think they let their *Nature* subscription lapse,' I said, shielding my eyes from the lamp's glare.

'I *must* have mentioned it three times.'

'At *least* three. Sara did kind of ask me about it.'

'Barely.'

'She was slicing cheesecake.' Touched by Kim's concern, I fought to keep my eyes open and reached for her hand again. 'Don't take this the wrong way, Kim, but I don't mind. We don't become behavioural ecologists for the adoration.'

Kim sighed, rolled over and turned out the lamp again. I let my eyes close and then rolled on to my back so that she could rest her head on my chest.

When I woke the next morning I couldn't tell whether I had heard Kim say 'I mind' or if I had just dreamt it.

***

It rained for the whole week, and Tony and Sara's desire to 'connect with the landscape' did not extend to getting a damp face.

Despite the balm of Kim's constant presence, the ancestor quickly became restless. Junior Monopoly, I discovered, does not generate a lot of endorphins. I took him out running along the estuary cycle path every morning and I went down to the Bowling Green Marsh RSPB reserve. I saw great flocks of avocets (*Recurvirostra avosetta*) and black-tailed godwits (*Limosa limosa*) descend beyond the high water point only to lift again when a passing peregrine (*Falco peregrinus*) spooked them. They filled my field of vision with a magnificent living tessellation of black and white. I returned to the grey house uplifted, and better able to face the rigors of the Pictionary contest awaiting me.

***

We left after breakfast on New Year's Day. It was a bright morning and, underestimating the temperature and the wind chill factor, the whole family came out to the front of the house to see us off, setting off the floodlights. As Sara and I stepped out of a brief self-conscious embrace she shivered and I quietly urged Kim, now holding her mother, to hurry so that everyone could get back inside.

Kim was still tearful on the short walk to the car. I was about to reach out to her, but little Tooshi unexpectedly wrapped herself around my right leg, like ivy (Hedera helix). Instinctively I reached my hands into the air and looked down at the little pink face shining up at me.

'Don't go yet, Dr Birdman,' she grinned. 'Please... Please...'

Kim laughed away her tears. 'I think I have a competitor, Dr S,' she said. With her help, I prised Tabitha from my leg and carried her back to her mother.

'What are you smiling about?' asked Kim as I started the car.

'Oh nothing; just that it's nice that the two lowest-ranked members of the group were able to form an allegiance,' I said. 'That's all.'

# Chapter 36

*January*

We spent a Saturday evening with two of Kim's colleagues and their respective silverbacks. I wore the new blue print shirt Kim bought me for the occasion. Neil the Cardiologist got us a table at the 'best oyster bar in the city'. Afterwards, Damien the Solicitor dragged us through the chill night air to the 'best little cocktail bar in the city'. There, cut off from the females by a mysterious invisible sheepdog-like force, I consoled myself with several of the best little mojitos available.

\*\*\*

Unusually, we stayed at my place that evening.

I woke first, and slipped into the lounge with the laptop. However, the mojitos had turned against me like irate Cuban gangsters and I did little more than preen the Turnbull text.

\*\*\*

Our overly ambitious plans for that day had included shopping and – a gesture to the natural world – a walk around Kew Gardens. Neither happened.

After brunch in Richmond, we returned to the flat and sat side by side on my battered cream sofa, steeping in aftermath. Two coffee mugs bearing the logos of lab equipment manufacturers, sat tantalisingly on the glass-topped coffee table. I lacked even the energy required to reach for mine. I could feel the boundaries between myself and the sofa blurring.

'Did Neil say anything about Bel last night?' she asked.

'Let me think. Hmmm. No, I'm pretty sure Neil spoke exclusively about himself.'

Kim shook her head. 'You shouldn't let them dominate you.'

'They don't dominate me. They are too busy trying to dominate each other. They don't even notice me.'

'It looks like domination.' Kim reached for her mug.

I didn't have enough energy to protest *and* watch her sip and so I just watched her sip. Impressed by her resilience I felt a timid flicker of desire. *Perhaps the worst of the hangover is behind me*, I thought. Digging deep I reached for my own mug and nestled it in my lap. I hoped that my thighs could convert the heat into the energy required to lift it to my mouth.

By chance, I discovered that if I closed my right eye I could almost superimpose the top right-hand corner of the copy of *Nature* on the table top with the corner of my tatty cream rug. For a few moments, the perfecting of this alignment seemed to me to be a singularly worthwhile pursuit. I slid into a deeper slump, tilted my head and squinted. On achieving my dubious objective, I gave a small subconscious grunt of satisfaction.

Kim reached again, this time to rest her hand on my leg. The slumping-squinting spell was lifted. Taking extra care with my mug, I leaned over to press my lips to her temple. Her hair smelled good – like hairy apricots. I felt desire flicker again, but the desire for sleep still seemed greater.

'When we've finished this,' I nodded down at my mug, 'shall we slip under the duvet for a bit?'

'Hmm. Is little Dr Selwood up to making house calls?' she said.

I smiled. Of course he was. Kim and I would make slow, lazy, languorous love. Afterwards we would sleep deeply and contentedly. All was well with the world.

It was with the simple chambers of my simple heart filled with this simple happiness that I replied, saying, 'Yes, I think he might prescribe a course of copulation.'

Kim's reaction was instant and ancient: she withdrew her hand from my lap and twisted her face into a snarl, a vestige of a more violent and precarious way of life.

'*Copulation*. You would like to *copulate* with me would you?'

Suddenly, I was very awake. 'I'm sorry, Kim. It was a bad word to choose. I'm tired and I don't select words well when I'm tired.'

'But the rest of the words were just fine, Simon. How do you explain that? And *technically,* "copulation" is spot on, isn't it? That is what we were, note, *were*, about to do. It's not like you said you wanted to *marinade* me or to… I don't know…' she looked around and then slapped her hand flat on the table, leaving an imprint which immediately began to evaporate, 'to *coffee table* me, is it?'

'I think I might have lost the thread of your argument,' I said, more out of hope than anything else.

'The point I am making, Simon, is that I am not buying the bullshit about fatigue and vocabulary. The reason I am upset – and yes, Simon, I am very upset – is that the word you chose was an entirely appropriate way to describe the sexual act, when conducted by pied flycatchers or baboons or some other ape.'

'Actually baboons aren't apes. They are new world monkeys.'

'Simon,' she snapped, 'don't you *dare* try to lecture your way out of this…'

'I'm sorry, Kim. I've admitted it was the wrong word to use. In my defence…' I put my mug of coffee down on the shabby carpet and held up my hands in submission, 'it's a term that I use so often professionally that it just sort of slipped out.' I stopped speaking to assess the situation. Sensing that Kim was still some considerable distance from pacified I decided more talking was my best option. 'Obviously I don't actually think of our love-making that way; it's barely even analogous to the copulation of baboons.' Kim's eyebrows were still bunched. More talking was required. 'Primates have a pretty uninspiring sex life. Most only mate when the female is in oestrus and their sexual repertoire is usually limited to dorso-ventral copulation.' Kim's eyes flashed. 'Oh yes, sorry, I should explain: that's when intromission takes place with Mr Monkey positioned posterior to Mrs Monkey. It's less intimate than human love-making – which is predominantly ventro-ventral – because it precludes communication of emotional status via eye contact.' Realising as the words gushed out that such talk might inadvertently reduce the likelihood of future dorso-ventral excursions of my own, I backtracked. 'Which isn't to say that there isn't a place for dorso-ventral love-making – in the context of committed, loving relationships.'

'Simon, please stop,' said Kim, her mug now on the coffee table and her hand over her eyes.

'I was just explaining how different we are from primates.'

'Thank you, I think, but learning all of this scientific terminology for monkey sex, does nothing for me.'

'Ah, I see… Yes… Well there are lots of sexual positions that we *don't* have scientific names for. For example…'

'Simon, *don't*.'

'Let me just explain this, I really do think it might help. There isn't a technical term for "the wheelbarrow" for example. If you pushed me – and that wasn't supposed to be funny – I would say it was really just an inclined variant of dorso-ventral copulation, but – and this is the point I really wanted to make – I don't think that it has ever been observed taking place in nature.'

'Simon, for fuck's sake, STOP… TALKING!'

I stopped talking. I cradled my mug between my palms. It was barely warm now. Kim began to laugh.

'Am I allowed to speak if I only ask what's funny?' I said.

'You are funny, Simon.'

'Am I?'

'You don't have the first clue about women, do you?'

'No, I don't. I never have.' More silence. 'I'm sorry.'

Kim expelled a long lung-squeezing sigh.

'Maybe it's a good thing,' I said. 'I mean, I imagine a lot of females would feel reassured knowing that their mate lacked polygynous tendencies.'

Kim said nothing but eventually she did place her hand back on my thigh. Was our first argument over? And since I hadn't actually disagreed with her, did it even count as an argument? Whatever had or hadn't happened, I was glad that the snarling had passed, but I still wanted to do something to reinforce our pair-bond.

'I've been thinking about that book idea of yours,' I said.

'Have you?'

'Yes, I have.' I hadn't. 'I am going to do it.'

'That's great, Simon. I'm really pleased.' She scootched her beautiful bottom across the battered cream sofa towards me.

'I love you, Kim.'

'I love you too – "Mr Monkey".'

I smiled, relieved. All the same I decided this would not be a good moment to solicit a copulation.

# Chapter 37

*February*

With the morning's writing goals accomplished, I sneaked back into Kim's darkened bedroom. Though I hadn't detected it when I woke, a delicious eau de Kim was unmistakeable now. Kneeling at the bottom of the bed, I carefully lifted the rolled kingfisher-green throw off the bottom of the bed, and placed it on the floor. Next, I lifted the end of the quilt over my head. Kim stirred, and I froze. Above me, her left foot shifted out a little and then she stilled once more. Like a fossorial rodent, I began to make my way up the bed until my nose touched against the inside of the ankle. I sniffed it and then pressed my nose and lips gently to her wonderful, soft skin. I had no problem accepting that the outer layers of my own epidermis were dead, but Kim's?

I edged a little further north and then paused again to enjoy the ridiculous rigidity of shin beneath skin. High above me, Kim moaned. Duvet and sleep distorted her words, but I could still make out my name and the muffled syllables of protest. Her left leg moved again, bumping against my arm and I heard her fingers forage along the bedside table in search of her phone. I pressed my lips to her shin.

'It's *really* early,' she moaned. 'Come here, you silly boy.'

Transitioning to a reptilian form, I crawled up the bed towards her. Though I tried to keep low, I lifted the quilt. She pulled her legs up reflexively and moaned again. 'Si-mon… Quickly… I'm cold.'

Emerging from beneath the duvet, I lay on my back, and with Kim's head nuzzling into my neck I drifted into a thin asleep. When I woke, I eased myself out from beneath her and crept out to the kitchen to make coffee. She was awake when I returned carrying the tray.

'Hmm, that smells good,' she said.

'Oh that… It's just male *Homo sapiens*,' I said.

'Hmm. Are you Colombian?' she said, propping herself up on her elbow to take the mug from me. I put my own mug down and slid back under the duvet beside her.

'Now, in a second I'm going to ask you a very important question, but before I do, please note that I am holding a mug of coffee over your duvet,' I said.

'What is it?'

'Would you like to copu-now or would you prefer to copu-later?'

'Very funny… the word doesn't bother me anymore. I'm still trying to get over doing it with a *birdwatcher* though.'

'Doing what?' I smirked.

'Copulate. *Copulate*. I *copulate* with a birdwatcher…' Then pressing her hands together and looking upward she said. 'Forgive me, father.'

'Bless you my child, but tell me this: how will you copu-manage when your birdwatcher goes birdwatching this summer?'

'This again?' Kim sat up, planting the pillows against the headboard for support.

'Come and visit me at the weekends, Kim.'

'Honey, didn't you tell me that you don't get weekends off when you are part of an elite birdwatching SWAT team? What would I do while you and your binoculars are off from dawn until dusk?'

'It's a very historic and cultural city. There's a cathedral, a castle, the Linnaeus Museum and a botanical gardens.'

'Oh. I didn't realise…' She adjusted the pillows again. 'If only they had a museum of evolution as well.'

'Actually, they—' Kim's impish grin pulled me up short. Sulkily, I reached for my mug and considered another approach. 'You could bring Pippa…'

'That's a great idea. She could catch up on her botany while we copulate… I still don't understand why you need to go anyway.'

'There's still a lot of work to do. We still know very little about female choice. We don't know if they are choosing male attributes or territories—'

177

'And it would also be "fascinating" to see if they are using different "criteria" to choose their main male and the males they shag opportunistically,' she said, stroking my arm. 'I know, honey. You told me before.'

\*\*\*

Two weeks later we were out for breakfast in South Kensington. Kim tore a tiny piece from her croissant and said, 'Oh, I almost forgot, Neil and Belinda have invited us to join them for a week at their place in Montenegro in the summer.' I imagined Neil telling me that Montenegro was the best little country in south-east Europe. 'It looks amazing,' she said.

'Just one problem...' I said, though for me this was actually a miraculous solution.

'You shouldn't let Neil intimidate you, honey. This holiday would be a great chance to get to know him better.'

'I'm not *intimidated* by him,' I said. I did not say that I would jump at the chance of knowing Neil *less* well. 'I will be in Sweden for most of the summer, remember?'

At which point Kim really let fly.

1. Hadn't I been the one who designed the studies? Why did I have to do the grunt work too?
2. What about *The Feathered Ape*? How was I supposed to get that finished?
3. Was she supposed to go without a holiday every summer?

I countered each of these points.

1. It wasn't grunt work it was fieldwork. It required considerable skill and I loved it.
2. *The Feathered Ape* was a side project, albeit an important one.
3. This year I would be finished in Sweden by mid-July and so there would still be plenty of time for a holiday.

Kim did not give up: 'Can't you at least ask Mats if he could find someone else?'

'No, Kim, I can't. We do the work as a team. We analyse the data as a team. We write the papers as a team. I don't want to let Mats down… And I don't want to let Charlotta down either.'

'And *who* is this Charlotta?'

\*\*\*

Mats was very good about it.

I told him that Gustavo's zebra finch studies were at a very sensitive stage, which was true. I didn't tell him that Gustavo was perfectly capable of managing the colony single-handed.

Mats said that he had been thinking that it probably didn't need four of us for the new studies. He might even have meant it.

\*\*\*

Phil was not so good about it.

I called him on Wednesday to ask if he would mind meeting somewhere between Acton and South Ken, rather than at The Swan, because I was going back to Kim's afterwards.

'Sure,' he said. 'Where were you thinking? East Acton? Turnham Green?'

'Very funny. I'll think of somewhere and text you tomorrow.'

'No, I'll choose it,' he said. 'You'll only choose some poxy place that's full of chrome. I think I'm allergic to chrome.'

Phil found a pub devoid of chrome and lustrous surfaces of all kinds. I didn't complain because I knew he would be ready, and I wasn't. Instead I tried to impress him by telling him about Kim's desire to protect our pair-bond.

'You told her about Charlotta?' he said, jaw hanging even more loosely than usual. 'Why would you do that?'

'I'm always rigorously honest and transparent with Kim,' I said.

'Oh, highly, highly commendable,' he said. 'Shrewd? Not so much.' He turned to the back of the pub. 'Fancy a game of pool, Bird?'

\*\*\*

The pool table was old. A large brown stain across the baize might have been the residue of a recently spilt pint or it could have been from a homicide.

Phil and I were both unaccomplished and infrequent pool players and, though we hadn't recorded results systematically, it seemed to me that victories had been shared evenly over the years. However, Phil insisted that he was the least unaccomplished player.

He broke and we both played a couple of fruitless strokes before I was left with a straight yellow into the middle pocket. As I bent over the table to take the shot, cringing again at the stickiness of the cue shaft against my thumb, he came to stand right beside me. An old tactic.

'You won't put me off,' I said, still in position, my eyes fixed on the yellow.

'I don't need to.' I pulled the cue back ready to strike. 'You've got to hand it to Cruella,' he said. 'She really clipped your wings this time.'

Forgoing the shot, I stood. 'Referencing Disney movies makes you sound very childish you know,' I said.

'Jesus, you even sound like her.' He came in closer and whispered, 'I get it: she's listening isn't she, Bird? Is there somewhere we can go where it's safe to talk?'

I bent to take the shot again. 'Why can't you two get along?'

'I've been wondering about that too,' said Phil, strumming his fingers against his chin. 'Could it be that *I know* she's evil and *she knows* I know?'

The yellow ball visibly arced right on the uneven table and touched the right-hand side of the pocket, coming to rest on the lip.

Phil crouched, eager to sink the pot. To unsettle him I moved to stand over the pocket and adopted a puzzled frown. 'You are just mad that I'm not able to get out as often as I used to,' I said.

Phil did not rise from the table. 'They call it house arrest, don't they?' He struck and the yellow dropped and a second yellow was nudged into open play. Phil moved around the table for his next shot. 'Honestly though,' he said, looking around again for the blue chalk which we had tried and failed to locate for the last ten minutes, 'I didn't think even she could come between you and your nerdy-birdy science. Has she put your sexy camouflage gear on eBay yet?'

I didn't admit, even to myself, that Phil had unsettled me, but he was definitely the least unaccomplished pool player that evening.

# Chapter 38

*March*

Kim informed me that I needed media and presentation skills training for when the book was finished. I reminded her that I had only written three chapters and that I hadn't even approached any publishers.

'We need to start creating an audience for your book now,' she said.

I reminded her that I had already done quite a lot of teaching, and speaking at scientific meetings.

'That's OK,' she said, 'most of that can be corrected.'

\*\*\*

She got clearance to use a meeting room in the Cucumber Communications office.

As we waited at the pedestrian crossing, I looked up at the grey building looming in front of us; languid sunlight reflected off the glass.

'You are going to love Maddie,' Kim said. 'She's great.'

We crossed the street and climbed the concrete steps towards the building. Stopping at the top, Kim grabbed my coat lapel and pulled my face down. She flicked the tip of her tongue against my top lip, before releasing me. 'There. You can get some more sugar this evening, *if* Maddie says you've earned it,' she said, heading for the doors.

'Hey, that's not fair.'

Kim looked back over her shoulder. 'Perhaps not, but I bet it will do wonders for your attentiveness.'

\*\*\*

The Cucumber Communications office was vast and open-plan. A pale green carpet gave it a savannah-like feel. Desks were gathered in vast herds on either side of a wide walkway. Nobody looked up as Kim and I walked through.

'What do all these people do?' I whispered.

'Mostly, they monitor each other's productivity,' she said.

She led me to a glass meeting room in the corner of the floor. In the centre of the room, four tables had been pushed together like an attempt to represent the Selwood Mating Matrix via the medium of modular office furniture.

'Maddie should be here soon,' she said, looking at her watch. 'Why don't you go through your slides one more time and I'll go and get you a coffee.'

Maddie – escorted by an office assistant – arrived almost as soon as Kim left. She was pencil thin with fashionably chaotic blonde hair and wore a sleeveless black dress, shiny black high-heeled shoes with a golden toe-tip and black glasses with stern, rectangular frames. Everything about her looked expensive.

'*No, I don't think so,*' said the PC. '*But then again…*'

'Maddie Millard,' she said, extending a long, bony hand, as if it was covered in a long black silk glove. 'You must be the talent.'

I was about to bumble something self-deprecating, but Kim returned and I was forgotten as Kim and Maddie gave little screams of pleasure and went into an elaborate, highly choreographed display of mutual embracing and exclaiming. I stood watching them while the PC struggled with Maddie.

As the intensity of their display began to taper, Maddie, still holding Kim's arms, turned to me, saying, 'Isn't he the handsome one? How long did you say I get him for?'

'Yes, we're quite pleased with him,' said Kim. 'He's yours for as long as you need him. How's Charles?'

'Insatiable,' said Maddie, placing the back of her hand against her forehead with exaggerated theatricality. 'One does weary a little of the same old willy – no offence Simon – I'm thinking of going at it with face-paints.'

Kim laughed. 'And Teddy and Millie?'

'Inconsolable,' said Maddie. 'And they already have face paints…'

'Didn't I tell you she was fantastic, Simon?' said Kim, taking hold of Maddie's hands 'Strip the Willow' style.

'I can't believe I was worried,' I said, now terrified.

'Oh you! What could *you* possibly have to worry about?' said Maddie. 'I can handle handsome or brilliant, but I'm powerless against the combo.' Turning to Kim again she said, 'I don't know if I can do it, I really don't.'

'Have you read what he's written so far?'

'Yes. Loved it. Absolutely L-O-V-E-D it. Just couldn't put it down… Charles was furious.'

Shortly after that and following a slightly less elaborate display, Kim pulled the glass door closed behind her and left me alone with Maddie.

\*\*\*

The change in Maddie was immediate. She marched across to the flip chart, tossing the cover sheet over the back, as if offended that nobody had done this already. She began to write an agenda for the day in exuberant red marker pen. As she walked me down the list, she pointed at each of the items with the pen, and placed an emphatic tick alongside each.

'Is there anything else that you wanted to cover, Simon?'

'No,' I said, 'that looks pretty comprehensive.'

'Good. OK, let's get started. Let's get into your presentation now so that I can identify your areas for development… oh, and any strengths. And I want you to imagine that I am a journalist.'

Fiddling with the remote control, I turned on the projector. While the projector warmed up, I slid a stapled printout of the presentation across the table to Maddie.

'I thought you could use this to make notes,' I said. Maddie began to leaf through the pages, expressionlessly. On the screen the first slide flickered into view, disappeared and then reappeared.

'OK, I think I'm ready,' I said.

'Great,' said Maddie, without conviction. 'Although, I've seen it now, haven't I?' She held up the printout, pursed her lips and placed it down on the table. 'Don't ever give out handouts, Simon.'

'I wouldn't do normally,' I said, 'but I thought that it might be—'

'Please start when you are ready. I have to go to meet Michael Palin in a few minutes.'

'But I thought—'

'No Simon,' she rolled her eyes, 'I'm not meeting Michael Palin. But if I was a *journalist*, I might be, and I definitely wouldn't have all day…'.

'OK, I see… Right… The central idea I explore in *The Feathered Ape* is—'

Maddie held up her hand. 'Sorry, Simon. There is one question I wanted to ask you before you get going: how did you come to develop such a chilling view of the world?'

'I'm sorry, Maddie, did you say chilling?'

'Yes, Simon, I did say "chilling". From what I can tell,' she waved my book in the air, 'to you, relationships are little more than "strategies" and you have no more affection for people than you do for sparrows. Why is that?'

'No. No. That's not it,' I spluttered. 'I didn't say—'

'But what are you saying, Simon? I would really like to know, not least because it's my parents' golden wedding anniversary this weekend, and I am hoping that if I understand you better I might not feel so devastated by your assertion that their unshakeable, post-reproductive love for each other serves no useful biological purpose.' The words left her mouth like blowdarts.

'I—'

The door swung open and Kim stepped back in.

'Sorry,' she said, 'I just remembered, Maddie, I totally forgot to ask if you wanted a drink.' Maddie twisted to face Kim in the doorway. 'How are you both getting on?' Kim asked.

I could no longer see Maddie's face, but I heard the sweet cheeriness return to her voice. 'We are doing just fine,' she said. 'We are nearly done with lesson number one.'

'Ah yes. You must never, ever, ever, trust a journalist, Simon,' said Kim.

'He's a very quick learner,' said Maddie. 'A cappuccino would be lovely.'

\*\*\*

At lunchtime, the three of us sat around a low table at the back of the ground floor café. A doleful wind pleaded against the window. I watched Maddie, moving chunks of feta around a box with a plastic fork.

'His presentation skills aren't bad.' Turning to me, she said, 'Except…?'

'Except that if I ever use that many bullets again, it should be to shoot myself.'

'That's right. But you get your message across well enough.' I hadn't been given permission to speak but I thanked her anyway. 'The only problem is that it's the wrong message.'

'Is it?' I was dumbfounded.

'Your audience isn't preparing for an exam, Simon. Think of your presentation as a *trailer*, rather than a lecture. Nobody *has* to read your book. If you want them to read it, you are going to have to win them over.'

I shifted in my seat.

Kim leaned forward, wobbling a white spoon at me, 'She's right honey. You have to grab them.'

Maddie pushed her plastic salad container to the centre of the table. 'Everything is a drama, Simon. I'll give you an example: what's that thing Attenborough did?'

'*Planet Earth*,' I said.

'Right, *Planet Earth*. *Planet Earth* is a drama. The trailer features lots of chases, teeth, claws and death and very little grooming.' She paused to sip her juice through a lipstick-preserving straw. Kim was nodding. 'I need you to send me a revised presentation by the weekend. And I warn you,' she began to tap the table with a highly lacquered fingernail, 'I don't want to see a single mention of monogamy.'

'But that's the point,' I said, looking to Kim for support. 'That's why birds are a useful model to help us to understand human reproductive strategy. I can't ignore that.'

Maddie stirred the last of the ice in the plastic glass. 'If they buy the book, Simon, they will find that out. But if you tell them about it now, they won't bother buying it, that's the reality. Look, sex sells, if it's dirty and disreputable. Monogamy just isn't commercially viable. It's ruined my life, and it will ruin every chance your book has – if you let it.'

'So you want me to just turn the science on its head?'

'Look, Simon. It's just a matter of emphasis. Selfishness and infidelity is an important part of the story too, right? And they are much more profitable.'

'I'm not writing the book to make a profit.'

'Maybe not, but you must want people to read it. Otherwise, why are any of us bothering, right, Kim?'

I turned to Kim, hoping that she would rescue me from this madwoman.

'Maddie's right, honey,' she said. 'People are going to love your book, but we need them to pick it up first. Like Maddie said, it's just a matter of emphasis.'

'I need to think about this,' I said.

'Couldn't you just eat him?' said Maddie.

# Chapter 39

*May*

I opened the door of Kim's apartment. Hearing the TV burbling in the lounge, I smiled because it meant she was already home.

Kim was sitting on the pink sofa with her feet curled up beneath her; her laptop was open but discarded on the seat beside her. She gave me a happy wave, moved the laptop to the floor and hurriedly beckoned me over.

'This is nice. I thought I would be back before you,' I said as I leaned over to kiss her.

'Shhh. Let me just watch this for one second, honey,' she said.

It was not unusual for Kim to be intent on the news. On several previous occasions we had waited anxiously to see how the media would cover stories concerning her clients. But I wasn't aware of any imminent mergers, launches or other such milestones.

I turned to the screen where they were showing images of Facundo Zalde. I knew only that he was a tennis player and probably a very good one, since prominence and excellence are closely correlated in competitive sports. What had he done now? Had he won a tournament or acquired a new hairband?

The footage showed him sitting in a courtside chair with a black eye and a strapped elbow. Kim was still intent on the screen, but I was not aware that Facundo Zalde or any manufacturers of elasticated support-wear were clients.

'Remind me exactly how we are trying to manipulate the attitudes of the populace today,' I said.

She whacked me on the thigh with a folded copy of the *Evening Standard*. 'Shush!' She pointed at the screen with two hands, like the loveliest parking marshal ever.

'Which account is it?' I whispered.

'What? Oh, it isn't. Listen…'

'You don't even like tennis… Do you?'

'No, not really… It's Facundo. Apparently his wife caught him in flagrante with two fans.'

'Oops. Double fault.'

'She went berserk – she hit him with one of his own racquets, which is kind of beautiful when you think about it.'

I looked over at the screen again. The camera zoomed in on a vacant seat in the players' box. Then, switching to archive footage they showed Facundo Zalde in a white tuxedo posing for photographs with a stunning blonde woman in a black dress with slender shoulder straps.

*Yes*, said the PC.

I turned to the un-pixelated beauty by my side. 'Kim, it's just tittle-tattle.'

'Don't be so dismissive,' she said, this time jabbing me with the newspaper. 'Don't you see? This could be the opportunity you've been waiting for?'

'Don't be silly,' I said. 'I've never even met Mrs Zalde. And besides, I love you.'

Kim smiled. 'I mean infidelity is back in the news, you fool. This could be the opportunity we've been waiting for.'

I stared at Kim. Had we been waiting?

On screen a journalist was holding a microphone outside the Houses of Parliament. Kim muted the TV. 'The media is going to start asking questions about why men stray again, Simon. It's going to be a big story because Facundo is a big story. He already has what most men want, but it wasn't enough. The media will be looking for an angle. You *have* an angle.'

'But I'm not a vulture, Kim. I am not about to start passing judgement on couples in a crisis. Don't you think they deserve to be left alone?'

'Simon…' she paused, perhaps seeking patience. 'Simon, they are not going to be left alone. There is just no way that's going to happen. They are going to be torn to pieces. And I'm not asking you to tell the world what you think about them. I'm asking you to tell the UK what you know about polygyny. You never know, you might be able to help to take the emotion out of the situation. You could actually help…'

I laughed and got up. 'Do you expect me to believe that? I'm making a coffee, do you want one?'

'No,' she said, reaching out to stop me. 'No, I don't expect you to believe that. I don't even believe it myself. But I want you to do it anyway. I want you to post something about polygyny and extra-pair copulations on your blog.'

I looked down at her hand holding mine. 'OK. I will get to it in the morning. Coffee?'

'No thanks,' she said, 'I had too much at the office today. And, tomorrow will be too late; we aren't operating on an evolutionary timescale here.' She picked up her computer and placed it on her lap and looked down at the screen. 'I'm going to reach out to some people. Oh, and post something on Twitter too.'

'Really?' I stopped in the doorway. 'Do you think that's going to catch on?'

'Definitely, you'll see. You need to start tweeting like a pied flycatcher.'

'Pied flycatchers *don't* tweet,' I said.

'Well, they should,' she said.

# Chapter 40

*May*

When Kim and I first paired Pippa seemed a little distant. I assumed this was because *Homo sapiens*, regardless of gender, don't like being proved wrong.

When she told me that she had paired with a male called Sebastian (the Equestrian) I realised there were probably multiple factors contributing to her recent atypical behaviour.

When I suggested that we would love to meet Sebastian, Pippa said that he was away a lot.

'No rush. We can validate your mate choice whenever it's convenient,' I joked, but Pippa said he really was away an awful lot. 'Why don't I make a lovely supper for the two of you instead?'

\*\*\*

Pippa furnished us with Italian white wine and then briefly left us in the lounge with the Buena Vista Social Club. It wasn't long before we heard a loud shriek in the kitchen. A giggling Pippa briefly reappeared, to announce that, 'owing to unforeseen circumstances', there would be no guacamole with the nibbles.

We were alone again when Kim's phone rang in her handbag. Releasing my hand, she retrieved it. 'I'll turn it off,' she said, apologetically. But, with her finger still poised above it, her expression hardened.

She stood, said 'Hello' into the phone, and then signalled at the stereo with three sharp jabs of her finger. I padded over to silence it and she walked over to the bay window. She stood there with the phone to her ear and her back towards me.

'That looks important,' whispered Pippa when she returned with the nibbles tray. I nodded. We tried to listen, but Kim said little more than 'yes', 'sure' and 'uh-huh'.

Kim was still looking out of Pippa's bay window on to the street, when Pippa went through to finalise supper and so I went to help.

I was consoling Pippa who had discovered a large pile of grated cheese she had forgotten to incorporate into the lasagne when Kim walked in, waving her phone in the air.

'That was the BBC,' she said.

'Great,' I said because she seemed happy.

'Great!' said Pippa.

'Yes, it is great! I've got you an interview with Radio 4 in the morning, Simon.'

'How exciting!' said Pippa, clapping like a member of the sea lion family (the Otariidae).

I was not excited. I did not clap. 'I have a meeting with Gustavo in the morning. Can we do it another time? What's it about? I don't even know what it's about?'

Kim spoke calmly, at first. 'It's about infidelity and it's going out live, so there is no other time to do it. And I worked my tits off to get you this. It's an amazing opportunity and you are lucky that they had a last-minute cancellation. They usually get around *three million* listeners.' I felt three million muscle fibres contract in unison. 'Imagine if just *one per cent* of them go on to pre-order your book, Simon.'

'It's just *so* exciting,' said Pippa. 'What programme is it?'

'It's… It's *Woman's Hour*,' said Kim, throwing Pippa a look laced with something other than gratitude.

'*Woman's Hour*! When do you think we should come clean about the fact that I am not actually a female?' I asked.

'Don't worry, I broke it to them, gently,' she said – gently. 'They need someone who can talk about what science tells us about infidelity and they don't care about your gender. They want your perspective, not your allegiance.' The kitchen fell silent except for the whirr of Pippa's oven. Kim stepped towards me, wrapping her arms around the back of my waist. 'I know it seems a bit scary right now, honey, but you will be great.'

Still holding me, she turned to Pippa, 'I'm really, really sorry, P, but we have to go. We have got *lots* to do this evening.'

\*\*\*

At 9.55 am the next morning I was sitting in Kim's office wearing a large black pair of headphones, staring at a grey microphone mounted on what looked like a steel imitation limb. I badly wanted to be sitting with Gustavo in the lab talking zebra finch. Kim was sitting beside me. 'You are going to be great,' she said. I nodded.

I felt wired and tired. When we got back to Kim's flat the previous evening I spoke to Maddie on the phone. 'Remember to smile when you are speaking, they will hear it,' she'd said.

Then I'd rehearsed with Kim until two am, at which point I could no longer think. I fell asleep before Kim had even made it into bed, but I woke an hour later and stayed awake.

'Just remember what we practised and what Maddie taught you,' said Kim, calmly. 'You will be fine.'

I nodded. '*Get through this,*' I said to myself. '*And then never do anything like it ever again.*'

'Hello. Dr Selwood, can you hear me?' An assured young female voice came through the headphones. I looked at Kim who put on her own headphones.

'Hello, yes, this is Simon Selwood. Yes, yes, I can hear you.'

'Great. We are about to begin. When we do, you will hear Terri introduce the segment. Shortly after that she will address questions to yourself and Mrs Meyer. OK?'

'That's fine,' I said. But it wasn't fine. The situation was totally unnatural. My ancestors might have spoken to two or three hundred people in their whole lifetime and I was about to address millions. I wasn't adapted for this.

'Good luck,' said the voice.

I took a sip of water and sat waiting, swallowing and thinking up questions I didn't know the answers to. Kim reached out for my hand. I smiled, best as I could.

'Let's turn now to the topic of infidelity,' said a new voice, warm and soupy. 'It's a topic as old as relationships, but we have recently been reminded of its impact by the emergence of allegations about Facundo Zalde. I have been joined on the line by two experts…' – *I am not an expert. I never said I was an expert* – 'with different perspectives on infidelity. Cathy Meyer is a counsellor who works to help couples to protect their relationships from temptation, and Dr Simon Selwood is a biologist from Empirical University who has just finished writing a book' – I turned sharply to Kim, but she was looking away – 'about what we can learn about our own instincts by studying the sex lives of other creatures. Cathy, Simon, good morning to you both.'

'Good morning,' I said. My voice, muffled by the headphones, sounded thick and alien. I could hear Cathy Meyer's voice more clearly. She sounded older than me. I have never accurately guessed a physical appearance from a voice, but that didn't stop me imagining a small wiry female with curly greying hair.

'Let me turn to you first, Cathy.' I felt myself relax just a little and glanced at Kim again. 'We've been reminded once again of all the pain and anguish that infidelity causes. Why does it still happen? What can we do?'

Cathy Meyer began to speak. She sounded confident. Would I sound confident? 'Well, Terri, in today's society, couples have less support and are exposed to more temptation than ever before. The sheer numbers of people we meet and the time we spend away from our loved ones have both multiplied manyfold over the last century. It's perhaps inevitable that these things happen. However, I believe that fidelity is a *skill* which can be learned. In my work I help couples who are committed to each other to learn and, and this is crucial, to *practise*, those skills.'

Cathy Meyer stopped speaking. I swallowed. I was sure I was about to be asked for my opinion. What was my opinion?

'And what does that actually involve, Cathy?' said the Terri voice; a reprieve. I looked at Kim again. She was miming deep, exaggerated breaths. Apparently I was in labour.

'The crucial first step is to help the couple to develop a shared definition of fidelity,' said Cathy. 'My experience is that every couple has a different definition. It is so important to make sure that both parties share and *own* that definition. Then we work on practising the behaviours that reinforce their choices and learning to recognise and avoid the behaviours which undermine them. Finally, we establish a framework for regular review.'

I listened carefully. The longer Cathy Meyer spoke the more I prayed that I wouldn't be asked for my opinion about what she'd said. My opinion had formed by then and it wasn't positive. I didn't disapprove exactly; after all, what harm could it do? But I doubted that the effectiveness of Cathy Meyer's approach had been validated with a large sample of randomly selected couples and matched controls.

'Dr Selwood, over to you now,' said the Terri voice. 'Do you think that the biological forces which compel people to stray are just too strong to fight? Are we hard-wired to be unfaithful?'

I played back the question in my head. Biological forces? Compelled? Stray? Somehow, before I was even aware that I had formulated a response words began to rush from my mouth. I heard myself say, 'I'm not familiar with Cathy's approach, but I am sure that there are things which couples can do to protect the sanctity of their relationship.' I liked 'sanctity'. To avoid Kim's eyes I stared intently at the grey cage-like mesh that formed the head of the microphone as I went on. 'Actually, human beings are among the most monogamous of mammalian species. I don't think we would get so outraged when we hear about infidelity if polygamy was the norm. That said, polygamy does have a small but important part to play in human mating strategy.' That sounded OK. I felt OK. I looked at Kim and she nodded eagerly.

Terri was speaking again. Why so soon? 'In the high-profile case which we have all heard about it is the male who is the transgressor. Clearly we can't judge on the basis of one couple but, Dr Selwood, in your opinion are there significant differences between the genders when it comes to infidelity?'

I was speaking again: 'Well the first thing to say is that polygamy has probably been an adaptive trait for both sexes throughout the history of our species. There are more similarities than differences between the sexes in this respect, but polygamy has probably served different purposes for the two sexes. It is almost certainly true that, as a consequence of asymmetries of parental investment…' – I silently cursed myself for using technical language, Maddie would hate that – 'it is likely that in early societies men were less discerning about some aspects of mate choice, because there were fewer implications for them.'

Kim was still nodding.

'Cathy,' said Terri, 'do you see these differences when you work with couples? Realistically, do you think those different biological roles can ever be reconciled?'

As I waited to hear Cathy Meyer's answer, I glanced over at the small digital timer on the table in front of me. Two minutes and forty seconds had elapsed. There were less than five minutes to go.

'Overwhelmingly, the couples I meet want the same thing,' said Cathy. Did she sound a bit irritated? 'If I can just say, I think all of this evolutionary psychology nonsense does nothing but harm.' Yes, she was definitely irritated. 'We are asked to accept that men have a deep primal need for sexual variety. We are supposed to believe that to limit that is somehow to deny the poor things their birth right.' I frowned and looked over at Kim. She frowned back and began to scribble a note on a piece of paper. I watched the letters appear while Cathy Meyer was still talking. 'It is nothing but self-interest dressed up in a load of pseudo-scientific rubbish. It's not what I see and I really wish people would stop saying it.'

Where did that come from? I looked back at the microphone and tried to recall what Maddie had said about dealing with aggressive journalists. Would those techniques work here? And what was the technique anyway? I remembered Maddie before me, stirring her latte and saying, 'Address the question, Simon – not the emotion.'

And so I tried, I really did. I calmly explained that male and female *Homo sapiens* were very similar in their attitude and behaviours within sexual relationships, and that in fact both genders are occasionally motivated to pursue infidelity.

I heard Kim push the piece of paper towards me across the desk, but I didn't have time to look at it because Cathy Meyer was already hissing her reply. I had to trust myself.

Again I replied calmly. From the corner of my eye I could see Kim holding up a piece of paper with *The Feathered Ape* written on it and I managed to squeeze in a plug while maintaining a conciliatory tone. I was rewarded with a thumbs up from Kim.

Cathy Meyer was not impressed though. 'I meet couples every day who want to work at their relationships and I think they would have a better chance if people like Dr Selwood would stop talking all of this pessimistic, deterministic nonsense.'

I looked at Kim and shook my head. Cathy Meyer hadn't listened to a word that I had said.

'Simon, a final word from you,' said Terri. 'Monogamy is under fire and the scientific community is partly responsible. Do you accept that?'

'I don't accept that at all,' I said. 'Science doesn't have a vested interest in perpetuating views about the pros and cons of monogamy. Science seeks to shine a torch...' – I winced because that cliché would earn me another of Maddie's black marks – 'on the truth, whatever that—'

'It's male-dominated science,' said Cathy.

It was the second time that Cathy Meyer had interrupted me and this time I felt myself flare. 'Do you seriously believe that male scientists are secretly clubbing together to do research which will help to justify polygyny?' I asked.

'Don't be ridiculous.' The voice of Cathy Meyer rasped. 'I'm simply saying that you – don't – have – any – evidence. It's – all – supposition,' she emphasised every word, speaking slowly, patronisingly. Afterwards Kim told me Terri tried to step in. I honestly didn't hear her.

'And where is *your* data, Cathy, huh?' I said, 'I mean, at least evolutionary psychologists aren't charging couples by the hour to test *their* speculative hypotheses.'

Silence in the headphones. Had I been cut off?

'I'm afraid we will have to end it there,' said the Terri voice. 'My thanks to Cathy Meyer, Director of *Love for Life* in London, and to Dr Simon Selwood from Empirical University.'

I swung my chair around to face Kim. Her beautiful mouth was open. I looked down at the note, lying by my right hand. *Stay calm and SMILE!* it said in big green letters.

# Chapter 41

*June*

My *Woman's Hour* interview did not go viral. Three million predominantly female listeners just got on with their lives. Maddie was nearly complimentary but the person who was most impressed was not drawn from the *Woman's Hour* core demographic.

'You totally gave her the bird, Bird,' said Phil, his arm around my shoulder.

***

Then, two weeks later, I received a call in my office.

I had been expecting to catch up with Mats about PF2, but instead a pleasantly round and almost viscous female voice said, 'Am I speaking to Dr Selwood?'

I imagined that the speaker was tall and athletic with pale skin, long red hair and freckles. The PC gave his provisional approval.

'Speaking,' I said.

'Fantastic,' said the viscous female, who introduced herself as Dr Nat Foserby.

Believing Dr Foserby might be a prospective collaborator I listened and stared out of the window at the collared dove (*Streptopelia decaocto*) grey sky. When Dr Foserby explained she was calling from a television production company I immediately leaned forward, elbows on my desk, alert to the presence of a predator.

Flustered, I regurgitated my *Woman's Hour* experience. 'Which is why I don't do media work,' I said. 'Well, that and not being approached.'

'I don't want to film you,' she said. 'I just want to kick some ideas around.'

'What kind of ideas?'

'The kind of ideas I heard you talking about. And the ones in your blog.'

'You've read my blog?'

Now, bear in mind that at this point I had never met anyone – other than Kim – who had read my blog. This was a moment to treasure, like my sighting of a myrtle warbler (*Dendroica coronata coronata*).

'And you don't want to interview me?'

'No, I just want thirty minutes of your time.'

'Hmmm.'

It did seem like a great opportunity to show Kim that I was trying to generate publicity without any risk of actually generating publicity and so I consented.

***

Phenotypically, Dr Foserby was not the female I had imagined; she was short, blonde, full-faced and freckle-free.

And our telephone conversation had also given me no clues about the breadth of her gesture vocabulary; these gestures weren't simply expressive – they were positively narrative.

She bought me a coffee and we sat at an empty table in the Life Sciences refectory. To kick us off I asked her what kind of ideas she wanted to 'kick around'.

'OK,' she said, 'I was really intrigued about what you wrote in your blog about the way that computer models have been used to simulate the outcomes in small, early human groups. I want to know more about that. I want you to tell me *everything* you know about early human groups.'

I hesitated. 'You do know that I am an *avian* biologist, don't you?'

'You mean birds, right? Yes, I knew that. I enjoyed what you wrote about birds' – she joined her hands at the thumbs to simulate flight – 'I even bought a feeder for my garden after reading it – but I am most interested in what you can tell me about humans.'

'You've read most of what I know already. I'm a bit sketchy on humans I'm afraid. If you don't believe me, you should ask Kim, the female I'm paired with.'

Nat was not deterred and so I reiterated what she had read already. She opened out a large pink moleskin notebook and started to take notes. Several times she looked me in the eye and repeated a word such as 'Africa', 'Clan', or 'Hunter', nodding sagely.

'Thank you so much,' she said when our time together was at an end. 'It's been very interesting and very valuable.'

'Has it?'

'Yes, it really has. You've helped me a lot. You see, Dr Selwood, we want to find a way to simulate life in an early human group, but not in a computer model – I want to do it with real people, as a kind of experiment.'

'But there are still a few societies who live traditional hunter gatherer lives. Why don't you show people what life is like in those groups, rather than attempting to simulate it?'

'We would watch that,' she said, 'you and I. We already think the human journey is fascinating.' I watched her walk two fingers slowly up the slope of her arm on the long trek towards her shoulder, 'but we want to reach a wider audience. We want to engage everyone in the original battle for survival.' She fell silent, looking across the desk at me. 'We would love you to help us, Simon.'

'Oh sweet Darwin. You are making a reality TV show, aren't you?' I said, leaning across my desk towards her, my torso suddenly heavy with the weight of disillusion.

'No,' she said. 'This is more… simulation TV, I think.'

I expelled incredulous, syllable-free air and breathlessly explained that I couldn't be involved any further and that I really, really needed to get back to my zebra finches.

To plug the awkward silence as we walked back to the refectory entrance I asked Dr Foserby about her PhD. It was in ceramics, apparently.

***

As my birthday approached Kim had pressed me for gift ideas though I told her that since pairing with her I felt entirely satisfied. That said

I was just a little bit delighted with the nicely preserved first edition of David Lack's *Ecological Adaptations for Breeding in Birds* that Charlotta sent me. It was a truly lovely gift, but owing to the double kiss inscription I decided to keep it at the office.

\*\*\*

Kim took me gift foraging to the Westfield retail metropolis. In our second department store of the morning, I watched her run a finger along the shoulders of a row of grey and navy jackets that hung from the kind of long chrome rail that could cause Phil to develop a rash.

'Do I want a jacket?' I asked.

'Probably not… We are looking for something with stopping power,' she said, now appraising a pile of neatly folded black shirts. 'We'll know it when we see it.' A moment later she was gone, stepping between the shelves and a couple of low tables piled with lightweight jumpers and polos. She headed towards the middle of the floor, coming to a halt by a display of bags and began to explore the compartments of a light tan leather satchel-style bag which hung down from an angled chrome peg by a woven shoulder strap.

'This is a lot nicer than that old backpack that you hump around with you, don't you think?' she said, as I arrived at her side.

It was five years since I had acquired my backpack. I purchased it only because the zip of my previous long-serving backpack was irreparably damaged and still thought of it as my 'new' backpack. The external webbing was perhaps a little frayed but I didn't use that and its core 'carrying' functionality was undiminished.

'Hmmmm,' she said, offering the leather bag up to my face as if I were a dray horse. 'Smells good, huh?'

'It does,' I said. 'I can never understand why leather should smell more delicious than food. It makes no—'

'Do you like it?'

'It's nice.'

'It's beautifully made,' she said. I nodded. 'It would keep your papers much flatter.' I nodded again, though I couldn't recall a journey during which the condition of my papers had deteriorated markedly.

'Try it on.'

I was under the impression that bags, like ties, were all the same size, but Kim had already moved towards me. With a beautiful upward sweep of her head she signalled that I should lift my arm and then she slipped the bag over my shoulder, like a harness, and directed my attention to a long mirror mounted on a white square pillar just across the floor. I stepped over towards it, aware of the gentle slapping of the empty bag against my hip.

Standing before the mirror I had to admit that the bag looked good. I jiggled it a little – the jiggle is to the man bag what the air tunnel is to the motor vehicle – and it still looked good. What would Phil say though? Should I keep the backpack for The Swan? But then what would Kim say about that?

Kim's smiling face appeared in the mirror over my left shoulder. She stepped to the side to make a bag-related adjustment and then looked towards the mirror again. It amused me that she believed the mirror bestowed some additional power of discernment versus the naked eye. She smiled back and then she began to shorten the strap.

'Oh, yes,' she said. 'How did it go with the lady from the TV production company?' I started to play with one of the zips.

'Simon?' With my hand I assessed the capacity of the inside pocket.

'*Simon?*' Kim grabbed the hand.

'It was a stupid waste of time. They are making a reality TV programme about early human evolution.'

'What was stupid about it?'

'The reality TV part.'

'What did she want you to do?'

'I'm… I'm not sure.'

A young adult male with long sapling-like limbs and sprouty dark hair approached the mirror and asked Kim if we needed help.

'No, thank you,' said Kim, passing the bag to him. 'We were just looking.'

'Didn't you like it?' I asked as I watched the assistant return it to the display.

'It wasn't you.' She moved right across the aisle and lifted a rich red, zip-front cardigan. 'Hmm. Really soft,' she said, feeling the knit with her fingers.

'You're disappointed, about the TV thing, aren't you?'

201

Kim put the jumper down and I saw her tongue press gently into the side of her cheek, an expression sometimes associated with deliberation.

'Actually, I think I am more perplexed.'

'Why?'

Kim picked up another cardigan of the same design, but this time in woodpecker green. 'Well, it's just that I've heard you say you wish more people took an interest in science. You say you don't understand why people aren't more interested in evolution or human origins and then an opportunity arises, maybe, to get people interested and *you* dismiss it.'

'Kim, they aren't making an educational programme.'

'Why did they contact you then? Have you thought about that?' When my answer didn't come Kim dropped the cardigan back on to the display. 'Let's come back later, OK? I need a coffee.'

\*\*\*

That weekend I considered the relationship between disappointed and perplexed. Eventually I concluded that though perplexed was probably better, it wasn't totally unrelated to disappointment. Given this emotional phylogeny, I decided that perplexed was not something I wanted Kim to feel. On Monday morning I stared at my phone for quite a while before I finally called Dr Nat Foserby.

# Chapter 42

*June*

Phil finished his Swan Burger (quarter pound burger plus two spicy boneless wings) and pushed his plate to one side. He did not undo his jeans button. He did not lean back. Instinctively, I pulled my own plate closer.

Sure enough, he reached out for one of my chips. I pushed his hand away.

'No, Phil.'

'You are never going to eat all of that.'

'Maybe not.'

'Well why can't I have a chip then?'

'You didn't ask.'

I watched Phil calculate. 'Can I have a chip, please?'

'No.'

'Why not?'

'I don't know.'

He sat forward. 'You know what I was thinking?'

'"How many Swan Burgers could I eat in one sitting?"' Reluctantly I pushed the last of my fish and chips across the table to him and dabbed my mouth with a red napkin.

'No. I was thinking that the London Wetland Centre is less than ten miles away and I've never been.'

I retracted my plate. 'One more sarcastic comment from you and I will personally scrape this little lot into the bin.'

'Honestly.' Skilfully snaking his hand past the open sauce bottle Phil picked up the two longest remaining chips. 'It's a shame, when it's so nearby, and when my bessie mate could explain what's going on.' He snipped the exposed chips, leaving potato stubs between his stubby fingers. 'And it must be especially interesting at this time of year.'

'How's that?'

'Don't play dumb, Bird. There must be a lot of eggs and that going on. Sperm competitions, maybe?'

I laughed. 'That's a good one.' I watched his face but detected no scorn. 'You really don't know do you?' He shook his head, though this may, in part, have been to facilitate a swallow. 'Many wetland birds winter in the UK, but they breed in the far north. You might see some young lapwing, gadwall or ringed plover, but if you're hoping for an orni-orgy you are going to be sadly disappointed.'

'There will be birds though, won't there?'

'For sure. Oh, and the sand martins won't have fledged yet.'

'That's good then. What about Saturday?'

'You really want to go?'

'Defo.'

I hesitated. 'If you don't show, Phil…'

'I'll be there.'

'Actually, why have I never thought of taking Kim there – isn't that crazy?'

'Take her another time,' said Phil, tearing a strip of batter from my fish.

***

Cammie dropped Phil off at the car park at nine thirty am as agreed. He was wearing an orange American college sports T-shirt. We began to walk to the entrance and I said, 'Well I'm not sure what you are going to see today but I feel confident that all the birds will see you.'

'Sorry, Bird,' he looked me up and down, 'didn't know I had to come as a shrub.'

***

I was braced for a difficult morning, but Phil was like a highly curious nephew, albeit one unable to form new memories.

We stopped in at the Dulverton hide first. I passed him a pair of bins from my backpack.

'Thanks, Bird.' He pressed them to his eyes and looked out over the window to the main lake. Then he flipped the bins into the magnifying orientation.

'What's that, Bird?' he pointed to a bird bobbing on the water beside the nearest scrape.

'It's a male northern pintail.'

He pointed again. 'What's that, Bird?'

'It's a female northern pintail.'

'Ah.' And again he pointed. 'What's that, Bird?'

'It's that male northern pintail you asked me about before, only now he's dabbling.'

'Really? He looks pretty committed to me. Will she do that too?'

We spent a good twenty minutes in Dulverton and Phil didn't even ask for a snack. And then we headed up the path towards the next hide for another round of 'What's that, Bird?'

\*\*\*

When we left the WWF hide, heading right, for the sand martin (*Riparia riparia*) nest bank, he said, 'I can see how you could get into this.'

'A lot of people get an awful lot of innocent pleasure from it.'

'Yes, they must.' Holding my spare bins in front of him, he scuffed the bottom of his trainer against the path. 'Bird…?'

I readied myself for another tufted duck (*Aythya fuligula*) question.

'I want to tell you something and I don't want you to be mad with me.'

'Do you need the toilet?'

We reached a narrow planked footbridge. Phil stepped on to it, grabbed a handrail and looked out towards the white bat house across the lagoon, squinting against the reflected light. 'It's… It's about Mike,' he said.

I inhaled deeply. 'What about Michael?'

Phil sucked his lips and briefly trained the bins on the bat house and then let them hang freely around his neck. 'Michael didn't cheat on Kim. Kim cheated on him.'

'No she didn't.' I started to walk back towards the visitor centre, briskly. Phil set off after me.

'She was fucking around, Bird.'

'Did Michael, aka the Assassin of Ass, tell you that?' My eyes were fixed on the visitor centre.

'Yes. I bumped into him, as he was leaving work.'

I looked back over my shoulder, shaking my head. 'You went to find him again, didn't you? Phil, this thing you've got against Kim – it's weird.'

'She's no good. I know it.' I told myself not to engage, to stay focussed on getting back to my car. Phil trotted up alongside me and I lengthened my stride. 'You know it too, Bird, deep down. Otherwise you would have asked me what Mike said. You're scared to hear the truth.'

'I'm not.' I chuckled, wanting him to see my incredulity rather than my irritation.

Phil, muttering about the 'damned binoculars', fell back and then caught up with me again. 'I asked Mike if Kim was a cheating bitch and he said, "You'd better ask her about that."'

I stopped. 'Is that it? Is that all he said?'

'It's not what he said. It's the way he said it. She's guilty.'

'Phil, for the love of Darwin.'

'She's as guilty as sin.'

I shook my hands in frustration. 'You're lucky he didn't punch you.'

'He pushed me, but I don't mind that. I'm actually better at falling now.'

I stopped by the wooden bench across from Dulverton hide and asked Phil to take a seat. When he was seated, with his hands curled around the seat, I asked him not to speak.

'Kim wasn't the one who compromised their pair-bond, Phil. She can hardly bring herself to talk about, about… him. And the fact that he is dishonest about this – when confronted by a weirdo – proves nothing.

'And anyway, she is paired with me now and I trust her. Think about the way she responded when I told her about Charlotta. If she wanted freedom to procure extra-pair copulations surely she would have encouraged me to go to Sweden.'

'She wants the best of both worlds, Bird.'

'I haven't finished.' I pointed a rigid finger at him. 'This is not about Kim, Phil. It's about you. You didn't like Claire—'

'I can see I might have judged her a bit harshly in retrospect.'

'And surprise, surprise, you don't like Kim. I'm sorry that I don't have as much time to spend with you as I used to, but I'm not about to sever my pair-bond to suit you.'

'I'm not bothered about that,' he pouted. 'She's bad to the bone, Bird. I can feel it. She's a selfish, controlling man-eater. Look at the way she flirted with you when she was with Michael. And with me.'

I snorted. 'With you? Phil, *please*.' I stared up into the passing cirrus. 'Stop this. *Now*. You've just accused Kim of being a "cheating bitch" and a "man-eater". Can't you see how insulting that is? And it's all based on a gut feeling. What if it's just hunger Phil, huh? Next time you feel like insulting Kim please just make yourself a sandwich.' I paused, considering what else I needed to say. 'I never *ever* want to hear you insult her again. I mean it, Phil.'

I started back for the visitor centre, listening intently for his footsteps behind me.

'We could do an experiment,' he bellowed from the bench, 'to scientifically test her fidelity. Then you'd know.'

'One more word, Phil,' I said, staring straight ahead.

# Chapter 43

*Late summer*

'Wolfie, will you summarise our findings for Simon please?' said Mats.

I bent towards the speakerphone. 'Aren't we going to wait for Charlotta?'

'Ah, Charlotta won't be joining us,' said Mats. 'She went to Brisbane two weeks ago. There she will spend a year studying the predator-specific alarm calls of *Cracticus tibicen* to determine if these calls are instinctive or intelligent.'

'Sounds interesting... And Kev-in?'

'From what I hear he is mostly instinctive,' said Mats. I hadn't seen Mats for a year but I could still imagine the smile creeping on to his lips. 'They broke up some months ago.'

I was curious to hear more about Charlotta but Wolfie was clearly intent on sharing the outcomes of my pied flycatcher random territory experiment. He quickly got to the point: 'The females choose the males occupying the territories with the best food supply, regardless of the characteristics of the male.'

'Fascinating,' I said, because that was as close to gloating as I felt I could allow myself to get.

'You were right, Simon,' added Wolfie, which surprised me. 'But I might be right too.' That sounded more like the old Wolfie.

Mats cut in, 'Wolfie has added an ingenious element to your study design.'

'If we collect blood from all the fledglings again,' said Wolfie, 'we can assess if the females paired with "inferior" males indulge in more extra-pair copulations, thereby achieving the best of both worlds – resources and genes.'

'That's fiendishly clever, Wolfie,' I said. 'I love it.'

*\*\*\**

And I did love it; Wolfie's additional data would provide deep additional insight about female choice. The only problem was that I now had a large, unexpected round of DNA fingerprinting and paternity analysis to complete.

Kim was furious when I told her that I wouldn't be able to join her for Neil and Bel's gathering in Montenegro. I hated to disappoint her and I knew that I would miss her terribly, but secretly I was also relieved to have avoided ten days in the company of Narcissistic Neil *et al.*

*\*\*\**

Kim didn't give up. One evening, just a week or so before she was due to depart, she walked in to the bedroom in her latest swim wear acquisition.

Looking up from the June edition of *Courtship and Mating Behaviour* to see her framed in the doorway my thoughts turned instantly to copulation. Instinctively I released the periodical from my grip and gaped.

'Sorry, honey,' she said, a seductive smirk just discernible on her clever red lips, 'I was just trying on my new cross-front bikini. I didn't mean to wake you.'

'I was awake,' I said. 'Not as awake as this, but I was awake.'

'Good. I wouldn't want to disturb you.' She stepped towards me. 'Do you like it? I'm going to wear it in Montenegro.' She came to a halt by the side of the bed and I detected the aroma of vanilla and sandalwood that I had come to love by association.

'They say stripes are slimming, but I don't think they make my breasts look small, do you?'

'No,' I said. 'No, they definitely don't.'

'Good.' With the lightest of touches she brushed the tips of her fingers slowly across her abdomen from the underside of her right breast down to her left hip. 'Look, Simon, these little bikini briefs have these cute ties on them.' She flicked at the ties with her clever pink fingers. 'I bet you could open them with your teeth.'

I writhed across the bed towards her, teeth parted. But Kim backed away, so as to be just out of dental range. 'Sorry. I mean, I bet you *could* open them with your teeth – if you were coming to Kotor.'

'Kim.' I reached out for her wrist. She withdrew it, hiding both of her hands behind her striped bottom.

'We wouldn't copulate *all* the time, I shouldn't think,' she said dreamily. 'Just as much as you wanted. You could get up early to write the book and then we could copulate. You could write by the pool and then we could…'

'Copulate.' I rolled back towards the middle of the bed, exasperated. 'I can't, Kim, unless Neil has the best little poolside DNA fingerprint set-up in the former Yugoslavia. Mats is really grinding my genitals for the PF2 paternity data. And if there is one thing that Mats doesn't typically go in for, it's grinding.'

Kim slinked back over to the bedroom door. She turned to face me, one hand on the door handle. 'Well, Neil probably could get a little DNA thing. He's very resourceful. And, hmm,' she placed a finger on her lips, 'maybe Mats could get a little perspective?'

\*\*\*

It was the last time Kim tried to persuade me, but her apparent acceptance only heightened my guilt.

'You'll have a great time,' I said, as I drove her to the airport.

'I intend to,' she said, correcting her eye make-up in the vanity mirror. That eased my guilt, but it didn't eradicate it.

\*\*\*

For the ten days Kim was away I lived a dual life, though life as Birdman is less dynamic than Spiderman, say. By day, I worked on PF2. By night I worked on *The Feathered Ape*, determined to present Kim with a first draft when she returned.

\*\*\*

Kim and I spoke whenever we could. I always called before heading home from Empirical, but sometimes I couldn't reach her.

She always made a big effort to sound like she was having a good time, and I was grateful to her for that.

At the start of the week, above the sound of the surf mixed with swaying samba or bossa nova music, she told me about a group paddle-boarding excursion followed by the best little cocktails in the bay.

Later that week she started to tell me about a 'fabulous' helicopter tour, but then I heard excited vocalisations and a loud splash.

Holding the mouthpiece away from my face I yelled, 'Kim?' Fearing that she had been thrown overboard or hurt in some way I repeated my appeal, this time louder and more insistent only to hear her laugh. Apparently a few of Neil's band had leapt into the pool in unison, deliberately soaking her as she stood poolside. I didn't get a chance to hear more about the helicopter trip because Neil and a silverback buddy were trying to drag her in.

I pretty much stopped worrying about her after that.

\*\*\*

On the morning of the day that Kim was due to return I scheduled a teleconference with Mats and the team to share my PF2 findings.

Mats and Wolfie dialled in first and then Charlotta joined us from Brisbane. There was a brief exchange of greetings and news, but the team were not in the mood for reinforcing social bonds.

'Simon, I think we would all like to hear what you have discovered,' said Mats.

'Yes,' said Wolfie.

'Yes please,' said Charlotta.

'Very well. Gentlemen, Charlotta, the analyses have, as we hoped, given us a much deeper insight into female choice in the pied flycatcher. And I will share the analysis with you in a moment. But first I need you to make a choice: would you like me to slowly reveal the conclusion over the next hour or so or would you like to hear the headlines first.'

'Headlines,' said Wolfie. '*Headlines.*'

'Headlines,' said Charlotta.

'Simon, please stop toying with us,' said Mats.

'Sorry,' I smiled. 'Without further delay… it gives me great pleasure… to reveal… these findings… which are yet to be validated by a second biometrician.' Wolfie groaned. 'The females paired with inferior males, where inferiority is defined by small size, limited song repertoire and brown colour, are… more likely to produce young fathered by an extra-pair male.'

'Yes!' said Wolfie.

Maddie was right: it was possible to hear if someone was smiling and even if they were pumping their fist in the air.

'Yes, Wolfie, you were right,' I said.

'I'm sorry, Simon, there was a problem with the line. Could you repeat that,' he said.

'You were right, Wolfie.'

'I am the daddy,' said Wolfie.

'A fascinating response to the outcomes of an avian paternity analysis, but yes, Wolfie, the females are trying to have the best of both worlds.'

The call went on for another ebullient hour. Even Mats sounded like he was encroaching on the outer fringes of excitement.

I was excited about the data too, and there was now a second *Nature* paper to draft, but after the call ended I couldn't think about anything but the Kimminent return of my love.

# Chapter 44

*September*

I was very anxious when I arrived at the studio for the first of my weekly interviews with Cassie Ponting – national treasure and host of *The Human Race*. Unlike the rest of the planet, I was not an ardent follower of Cassie's. However, given that I had not spent an extended period of time in a coma or on a space mission, I knew who she was. Instinctively I felt suspicious of her brand of instant intimacy and emotional amplification. Maddie said she was sure to be a bitch's bitch.

\*\*\*

The stage for *The Human Race* was a raised orange platform in the shape of Africa. In its centre were two angled black armchairs and a table cut from a baobab trunk. Nat introduced me to Shaun the studio director and the two bearded cameramen and then she left me to relax in one of the armchairs while she went to 'see how Cassie was getting on'.

Bracing myself for a long prima donna style wait, I reached into my backpack for the script. However, a young make-up girl, her hair tied up in a colourful silk scarf, her breath smelling of sweet milky coffee, pounced.

When she returned to preen me again just five minutes after the first time, I laughed, saying I couldn't believe that my appearance had deteriorated so much already.

'I tell myself it's OK because they do exactly the same thing to Scarlett Johansson,' said a new yet familiar voice. The make-up girl immediately stepped back, and there was *the* Cassie.

'Hello, Dr Selwood,' she said in that lilting Scottish way of hers. Cassie's voice was like a shallow stream passing over pebbles. Just hearing her speak my name made my eyelids feel heavy.

The make-up girl left and Cassie stepped towards me. I stumbled to my feet. She was wearing a sparkly, peachy, thigh-length cocktail dress and she looked smaller than her televisual self, but the long red hair was just as shiny and the teeth were as white and as numerous. 'I'm Cassie,' she said, as if it was perfectly conceivable that I might not know. 'It's lovely to meet you.'

*Yes*, said the PC.

'I know... I know who you are,' I said.

'That's a shame,' she said, cringing cheerfully. 'Do you know, my dad thinks I've *finally* made it, now that I'm going to be working with a proper scientist? He always hoped that they would bring back *Tomorrow's World* so that I could host it,' she laughed. 'He's a science teacher, you see, and a bit of a back garden birdwatcher too, as it happens.' She beckoned me to sit again and she sat too, plaiting her legs. 'He's got this wee flock of red-faced, yellow-winged birds that come to his feeder. What are they called?'

'Those are goldfinches,' I said. 'In my opinion one of our most beautiful resident species. They were widely kept as a caged pet at one time.'

'Oooh, that sounds cruel,' she said. 'I don't like that. Dad says they are the only birds that come to that feeder. Why's that?'

I explained about thistles and teasels and imported niger seed, and that the goldfinch's close relative, the siskin (*Carduelis spinus*), could sometimes also be lured to such feeders, depending on location.

'I can't wait to see the expression on his face when I tell him that,' she grinned.

Cassie leaned forward a little. 'How did you get dragged into *this*?' she asked. And so I told her.

'What do we really know about life in those early clans on the African savannah?' she asked. Again I told her, this time drawing on the week's script as well as my own knowledge. I did the same when she asked me about ancient gender roles.

We'd been chatting away like that for about fifteen minutes or so and I was pleasantly surprised by how much interest she was showing and

214

then she got to her feet and for a moment I thought she had been bored all along.

Standing over me, with her palm outstretched, she said, 'There, not so difficult was it?'

'Not at all,' I said. 'I bet I clam up as soon as I see the autocue though.'

Cassie frowned and looked out on to the floor towards the studio director and then back at me. 'No, Simon, we just did it. We just recorded it. We've got everything we need for week one. You were great.' She looked out of the front of the platform again. 'Hey Shaun – we got all of that didn't we?' Shaun held out an upturned thumb. 'I thought so,' she said. 'See you next week, Simon.'

# Chapter 45

Returning to Kim's apartment after recording my Week 5 contribution to *The Human Race*, I happened to mention that Wednesday's programme had drawn over five million viewers. 'I mean, that's the size of the entire *Homo sapiens* population ten thousand years ago, at the dawn of the Neolithic.' Though we were in the lounge Kim immediately solicited a copulation. I had no idea she found early agriculture and semi-permanent settlements so arousing.

Later, clad in her pink dressing gown, I prepared pasta while whistling Kylie's latest slice of pop. Kim was on the phone when I took the bowls through to the lounge.

'Sara says hello,' she said.

'Hello Sara,' I said, plunging a fork into my fusilli.

Kim held out the phone, saying, 'She wants to speak to you', and picked up her own bowl.

'It's very exciting isn't it?' said Sara. 'Kim says you have to wait just like the rest of us to find out who is eliminated.'

'I'm afraid I do,' I said, watching Kim suck the tail of a piece of fusilli through her clever red lips. 'Every precaution is taken to avoid leaks in order to maintain the integrity of the project.' This amused Kim and a piece of part-masticated pasta almost slipped from her mouth. She knew that I only knew the names of three contestants and had only a vague comprehension of the rules of *The Human Race*.

'Kim says you won't even be able to watch it next Friday,' said Sara.

'No that's right, Sare, *I-won't-be-able-to-watch-it-next-Friday*,' I said, slowly repeating Sara's comment for Kim's benefit. 'It's a shame. Unfortunately, Cassie and I have to fly down to Ethiopia to film a piece on location.' Kim placed a hand to her lips as a precautionary measure.

'With Cassie,' said Sara, dreamily.

'I usually call her Cass. Or Cassowary. She likes that too.' My spontaneous fabrication sent Kim staggering out in search of kitchen towel.

Sara asked me what I thought was the secret of the success of *The Human Race*.

'People love transient pair-bonds,' I said. 'And *The Human Race* provides lots of those because that's what you get when you throw together fifty young, attractive, scantily clad attention seekers in an environment free of reality TV, social media and entertainment.'

***

Later, Kim and I snuggled up together on the pink sofa. She began to gently stroke the top of my head in a circular motion. 'Oh, did you tell Sara that you can't play golf with Tony this weekend, honey?' she whispered.

'I did,' I said.

'OK, good… What did you tell her?'

'I told her I was going to the Arsenal with Damien.'

'Oh, I thought you said you would rather "pluck a live duck".'

I opened my eyes and kissed Kim on her beautiful quizzical forehead. 'I told Tony that I was going to Arsenal with Damien. I told Damien that I was playing golf with Tony. I'm actually staying here with Kim the Copulatress.'

'Yum,' she said, slipping her hand inside my dressing gown.

# Chapter 46

*November*

A word of warning: always allow extra time at airport security if you are carrying a skull in your hand luggage, even if it is only a replica.

When I finally made it to the executive lounge, Cassie, wearing a green camouflage track suit, was already established in a secluded spot at the rear.

Leaving her in custody of my backpack and cranium, I went to the buffet. When I returned a pair of middle-aged well-wishers were conversing with her. I quietly took the seat opposite Cassie, but the female recognised me too.

After the pair departed, I eagerly went to work on my cubes of cheddar and oat cakes. Noticing Cassie looking at my plate, I held it out towards her.

'Good god no,' she said, scanning the lounge. 'I mean, thanks, but I can't let anyone see me eating *cheese*.'

Cassie explained that a significant number of British females believed that she lived on a diet of proprietary 'super juices' supplemented by star jumps.

'Don't you ever get tired of the constant requirements to display?' I asked, savouring more than ever the freedom to nibble cheddar.

Cassie's smile on this occasion, like one of her super juices, was a blend of ingredients that don't naturally coexist. 'It's fine, usually,' she said. 'Every once in a while, though, I do wish I had an invisibility cloak.' The blended smile reappeared.

Glancing furtively across the lounge, Cassie slowly extended finger and thumb, like a cautious mole-rat (*Heterocephalus glaber*), towards my plate. She held a single creamy cube up in front of her face. For a few seconds as she rotated and contemplated it, I felt the collective gaze of the executive lounge resting on her.

Grinning, she placed it on her tongue.

Despite the cheese sampling Cassie wore, for the first time in my experience, the kind of weary expression you might find on the face of a mortal. Not wishing to be a source of further weariness, I took a journal from my backpack. I began to read and chomp, but Cassie quickly said, 'You don't *have* an invisibility cloak in there by any chance?'

'Is this one of those days?'

Cassie nodded.

'I don't have an invisibility cloak,' I said, 'but...' thrusting my hand into the backpack, 'I do have a skull. That should keep most people away.'

\*\*\*

Leaving the plane next morning I was informed that Ms Ponting had already departed.

It took me a while to find Cassie at the baggage carousel because she had changed into a pale grey track suit. She was standing amidst the other passengers as they stared down at the passing cases like a siege of herons (*Pelecaniformes*).

When Cassie lifted the dark sunglasses from her eyes, I felt a sudden shock. Though her hair retained its vaunted lustre she looked tired. I knew I had failed to suppress my instinctive reaction when Cassie laughed and said, 'I know, I know. I need a super juice.'

\*\*\*

We made the short trip to the heliport in an old black Honda Civic driven by Rada, our pilot for the helicopter flight down to Omo. He was a slight man with skin the colour of muscovado and a Marvin Gaye beard. Cassie was busily thumbing her phone and so I looked out of the dusty windows and up at the kind of indecisive sky so familiar to Britain's naturalists.

The heliport consisted of a hangar with an unexpectedly low, gently sloping roof and an adjoining L-shaped, white-roofed office building. Rada took us through to a small unmanned waiting area and told us to help ourselves to the facilities, which comprised a three-legged vending machine with a marked lean, two identical rows of blue chairs, and a toilet.

I went over to the window to get a closer look at the helicopter. Beside it, Rada laughed with a larger man in a tattered blue boiler suit. The large man rubbed his hands on an oily rag.

Hearing Cassie emit an exasperated gasp, I turned in time to see her drop her phone into her handbag then zip the bag closed.

Noticing my stare she said, 'Why does it always have to be so difficult, Simon?'

'Don't ask me,' I said, 'I'm the novice.'

'No, I mean relationships. Why are they so hard? So painful?'

'Are you experiencing generalised relationship difficulties, or problems with a specific individual?' I asked, walking back towards her.

Cassie smiled. 'You don't read the papers, do you? I like that about you... I'm experiencing difficulties with a specific individual. Though to be fair to him, he is by no means the first such individual.'

I sat beside her, feeling the awkwardness that comes when I know that I am expected to say something yet have nothing useful to contribute. 'I used to have difficulties too,' I offered. 'I began to think I would never form an enduring pair-bond.'

'Cheers to that,' said Cassie, taking a sip from a bottle of water.

Encouraged by our shared experience, I continued, 'Before meeting Kim I had a previous pair-bond, but it failed and naturally I began to wonder...'

Cassie coughed. 'Just one?' she laughed, 'I really am screwed.'

Cassie was, I believe, inferring that she'd experienced a significant number of pair-bonds. However, having once been beaten over the head by a female for asking her for relationship statistics, I did not press her further.

'Aren't you going to ask me how many lovers I've had?' said Cassie, screwing the cap back onto the bottle.

'It hadn't occurred to me,' I lied. 'I'm more curious about the mean duration of your relationships.'

'That's a new one,' she smiled. She played with the bottle contemplatively. 'I would say about a year,' she said. 'About a year to six months.'

'That's interesting,' I said. 'People typically state the lower number first when providing ranges.'

'Perhaps those people don't *typically* exaggerate the upper number.'

'Hmmm. House wren,' I said, thinking out loud.

'Where?' Cassie stared over towards the window.

'No, I mean, you are like a house wren, kind of.' Cassie looked puzzled, but she said nothing. Inwardly I groaned; I had committed myself to what now seemed like a very unhelpful analogy. 'Approximately ninety per cent of birds are socially monogamous,' I said. Cassie picked at the corner of the label of her water bottle. 'But there are several different kinds of monogamy. Remember when you told me about your dad's goldfinches?' Cassie looked up from the bottle. 'Well, most birds are like goldfinches. They pair for a full breeding season. The following year they pair again, usually with a different mate. There are also a few birds, and it is just a few, that mate for life. They are usually large, long-lived species with small clutch sizes and their young take a long time to fledge. The albatrosses are perhaps the best known example.' Clearing my throat, I said, 'And at the other end of the monogamy spectrum there are some birds which only pair for a single brood. They might have multiple mates even within a single breeding season.'

'Like the house wren?' said Cassie.

'Very good, Cassie. Yes, the house wren is an excellent example.'

'*I'm* a house wren?'

Cassie was playing with the lid of her water bottle and I suddenly felt acutely aware of the incomparable dexterity of the human hand.

'Well, no, not literally, but I *was* thinking that there are some… parallels…'

'And you think I should be more like an albatross?' I estimated that Cassie's bottle was at least half full.

'No, not at all,' I said, happy that for once my instinctive drives for honesty and self-preservation were aligned. 'Do you?'

Cassie shrugged a shoulder. '*Why* am I a house wren, Simon?'

I had seen Cassie lachrymate before, as an expression of empathy for a *The Human Race* contestant. Now I feared that she was about to lachrymate for herself.

'I'm sorry, Cassie, I have no idea,' I said. 'I'm not a very useful person. I know a lot about birds, but a lot less about people, which means I'm of little practical, day-to-day use for anyone – not even myself.'

Cassie was looking away towards the vending machine now, but I knew that she wasn't longing for a Mars Bar or a packet of Quavers. She was lachrymating and I had, at best, failed to soothe her.

Ashamed, I looked down at my hand, the one resting on the thigh closest to Cassie's. I lifted it. For a moment I let the hand hover in our interpersonal space before touching it down, fleetingly, on Cassie's forearm.

'I do know this, Cassie,' I said. 'House wren or not, I like you, a lot.'

Cassie turned towards me, wiping the tears from her eyes with a tissue pulled from her track suit pocket. I was going to speak again, but Cassie, her masseters tightly clenched to keep tears at bay – shook her head. Touching my thigh she looked away again.

\*\*\*

I saw little of Cassie for the rest of the Omo trip. They filmed my piece at the site where the fossils were discovered and then I flew back. Meanwhile Cassie stayed on to interact with real live clan members.

When I saw her back in the studio in Week 7, I was delighted to see that the weariness of Omo had gone.

After the recording, I said my usual hasty goodbyes and headed to the exit. I had just stepped out of the door, when I heard her call my name.

'Thank god I caught you,' she said, breathing rapidly.

'Why?'

'I wanted to apologise, you know, for getting upset last week. That wasn't fair.'

I explained that I had felt no sense of injustice.

'Well, that's good. But I also wanted to say thank you, you know, for listening – and for not offering any advice. Everybody always wants to offer me advice.'

I explained that offering no advice was actually remarkably easy for me and told her that I would be happy to offer no advice whenever she didn't need it.

Cassie laughed. 'Well thank you anyway, Simon.'

'And you're feeling OK, now?' I asked.

'I am,' she said. 'I'm feeling a bit scared but I've decided that I want… I want to be an albatross. We're both going to try.'

Smiling, I wished her luck. And then Cassie Ponting, national treasure, put her arms around my neck, squeezed me just as firmly as if I were a raw ingredient in one of her super juices, and she kissed me beside my left ear.

# Chapter 47

Next morning I spent the first hour at my desk reviewing a second draft of Gustavo's zebra finch poster. Hearing a rap on the door, I took a moment to consider the most constructive way to convey my feedback to him. When I did look up though, it was Prof I saw striding towards me in his tweed jacket.

'What the blazes is this?' he said, slapping a newspaper against my desk top.

'I'm sorry, Richard. What's what?'

'This,' he said. 'This... this... excreta.' He shoved the folded paper across the desk.

Unfolding the paper I looked down at the front page. In the centre was a photo of a female locked in an embrace with a male, his face obscured. The image was a little dark and low resolution, but as I examined it closely I noticed that the female bore more than a casual resemblance to Cassie. But who was the male?

Confused, my eyes darted for the headline: *Cassie finds new love with The Human Race hunk*. Hurriedly, I started to read the article but Prof interjected.

'This thing has gone too far, Selwood. How much longer is the damn thing running?'

'Kim,' I said.

'What? Think of the reputation of the department, man – that's what you need to do. There's more *drivel* inside, and none of it's good.' He snatched the paper away from me, opened it and spread it out across the desk, rapping a rigid finger down on a montage of photos of bathing, pouting, jutting female clan members. In the centre of this halo of images was a picture of me crouching in the shorts provided by 'Wardrobe' for the Omo shoot.

'For god's sake man,' he continued, 'think of the damage. What do you expect me to say to the Chancellor? What is it they call you again?' Grabbing the paper from the desk once more, he began to read it like a manic commuter. 'Here it is: "Resident promiscuity pundit". Promiscuity pundit – I ask you…'

'All valid points, Richard,' I said. 'And I am feeling no joy about any of this either. But right now, I need to call Kim.'

***

As I anxiously waited for Kim to answer, I ingested more of the article's claims and insinuations. I learned that Cassie's partner Max was also a celebrity. He had achieved a measure of success in motor sport, but it was after meeting Cassie that 'Max Velocity', as the papers labelled him, had shot to prominence. Now the same journalists were suggesting that Cassie's days of riding pillion were behind her, and I was being tipped as the next Mr Cassie.

Kim finally answered as I read the snipey comments of a 'friend of the couple'.

'Sorry, honey,' she whispered. 'On a call. Can't speak now.'

'Kim, whatever you do don't—' The dial tone croaked like the courtship song of a male toad. 'Kim?'

I called again only to get voicemail. I didn't leave a message. Then I called a third time and left a long rambling message explaining my innocence. Kim did not call back. I sent her texts. She didn't reply to those either.

When Gustavo arrived I hurriedly explained, apologised and rescheduled.

'Congratulations,' he said, hand on door handle. 'I think you are the first behavioural ecologist Cassie Ponting has ever been linked with.' He closed the door behind him. It opened again. 'In fact, you must be the first behavioural ecologist anybody has been linked with.'

'Why am I not feeling like all my hard work and dedication has finally paid off?' I replied, still searching for Cassie's number.

I called Cassie, figuring that she was the only person who could corroborate that our embrace had not been a prelude to an extra-pair copulation. She didn't answer.

Then I became sure – surer than I ever am – that leaving voice and text messages for Kim had been a very, very bad idea. Throwing on my jacket, I set off for Cucumber Communications.

\*\*\*

'Do you have an appointment?' said the stern-looking man in the blue blazer and tie.

'No, I don't. I just need to speak to Ms McFale urgently.'

He asked me to take a seat over by the window. Twice he came over to suggest that I should come back another day. Twice I told him I was prepared to fossilise in his lobby if that's what it took.

Some thirty minutes later a heavily pregnant female arrived to escort me to the sixth floor. She deposited me in a seat in a narrow corridor beside a water cooler.

Having made it that far, I began to have grave doubts about how much Kim would appreciate me bringing our personal issues into her work place. When the water cooler belched, it unnerved me further and I was about to make a soft shoe retreat to the elevator when a door opened and Kim stood before me.

'Hi honey,' I said.

'You'd better come in,' she said, disappearing back into the room. I swallowed.

The room was dominated by a large grey oval table and eight empty chairs. There was a flip chart in the corner, a black speakerphone on the table and, more pressingly, a copy of *The Daily Digest* spread beside it.

'Why don't you sit just there,' she said, from the far side of the table. She made a show of looking at the double-page spread.

'It's not what it superficially resembles,' I said.

'So that's not you and Cassie Ponting after all?'

'Well, yes it is.'

'And according to your voicemail Cassie is expressing her gratitude because you have been talking through her relationship problems with her. That's very nice of you.'

'It's true, Kim,' I said. 'I swear it's true. I would never deceive you.'

Kim laughed, and I mean really laughed – like Pippa, almost. 'Of course I believe you,' she said. 'Silly boy. Cassie told me all about it. House wren? Honestly Simon, what are you like?'

'You've spoken... you've spoken to Cassie?'

'Yes, of course. When I asked her to help us.'

Though I still wasn't at all sure what was going on, I was getting the sense that I might not be in as much trouble as I had initially feared.

'Help us what?'

'Help us get a little bit more publicity – obvs. I couldn't tell you yesterday in case you bottled it. And it wasn't supposed to make the papers until tomorrow. I *was* going to tell you tonight.' Kim reached out across the table to me with both hands. 'I didn't know it was in print myself until about twenty minutes ago.' She squeezed my hands. 'House wren? Jesus, Simon.'

'I know.'

'You're *too* funny. Cassie's clearly very fond of you though. She genuinely wanted to help.'

'Won't Max whatsisname be mad?'

Kim laughed again. 'Well I know every man lives in constant fear of being ousted by a birdwatcher, but I imagine coming third in the Handsome Brit poll will help him to keep it in perspective.'

'Presumably,' I said.

'Oh, stop looking so worried, you,' she said. 'Come and give your clever girlfriend a big kiss and then buy her a coffee.'

'I think I should probably try to save my job first,' I said.

# Chapter 48

*November*

I was there when *The Human Race* finally ended.

This time when I hugged Cassie, Kim was there to witness it in person. 'I hope we can work together again,' said Cassie.

'Me too. I'm considering looking at the impact of flock size on pair-bond integrity in the goldfinch, if you're interested.'

Cassie laughed. 'Fair enough. But let's keep in touch, OK.'

As my taxi pulled away from the studio in the gentle rain, Kim's hand in mine, I was grinning.

I was as free as a bird.

\*\*\*

Or so I thought.

I had become used to noticing males noticing Kim, but now I noticed that people were staring at me. I pretended not to see the lingering glances and conspiratorial whisperings.

Then a stocky, stubbly man approached Pippa and I in the cacophonous café and directed his stocky, stubbly phalange at my chest and accused me of being 'that archaeologist fella'.

All of this attention was unexpected and unnerving, but at least it wasn't time-consuming and I didn't need to make any effort. However, in addition to becoming a curiosity I had become 'an asset' and others possessing a more acute olfactory sense than my own had detected the aroma of opportunity. *The Feathered Ape* was rushed into publication and before I knew it I was committed to a series of 'personal appearances'.

***

To mitigate my anxiety as the first 'gig' approached I kept telling myself that this was an opportunity to rouse, in a few at least, a latent love for birds, nature and/or science.

The first reading was at a small bookshop in Soho. I called the manager a few days before the event to talk it through.

'Will you wear your shorts?' she asked.

'Shorts?'

'Yes, shorts. You know – the ones you wore in Africa.'

'It's freezing.'

'I can turn up the radiators,' she said.

***

In advance of the event, I reread *The Feathered Ape*, to be sure that I could handle the Q&A with confidence. I shouldn't have bothered.

When I arrived the narrow bookshop was empty but for the manager, an assistant and a brace of browsers criss-crossing the floor like shorebirds.

Thirty minutes later, when the now visibly nervous manager introduced me, the shop had been transformed into a human roost. Every chair was occupied and some were multiply occupied. Latecomers crowded and craned in the spaces between the jutting bookshelves and behind the final row of chairs. And faces continued to appear in the spaces between other faces.

They applauded before I even said a word, but quickly fell into a respectful, almost meditative, silence. I began by explaining what I thought we could learn about ourselves by understanding the mating lives of birds. They continued to listen as I read from the opening chapter. Why, I thought, couldn't undergraduates be so attentive?

When I asked for questions, hands went up like alarmed partridge (*Perdix perdix*). I was torn between the upraised hand of a young female on the front row (rationale: she had arrived earliest) and that of the short, elderly female at the very back (rationale: she had endured the greatest discomfort), but a middle-aged male in one of those black tennis-type of polo shirts made a cupped-handed intervention:

'What is Cassie really like?' he yelled.

The young female nodded and her hand descended. I smiled at the smiles, nods and glances I saw spreading through the rows and columns. *Well, might as well get it out of the way*, I thought. I responded in good humour, expressing the warmth that I had grown to feel for Cassie and also took the opportunity to clarify that we had never been romantically involved. Then I asked the lady at the back for her question before anyone else could jump in.

'Thank you, Simon,' she said. Adjusting her glasses, she consulted the note in her hand. 'What did you learn from working alongside Cassie?'

And so on.

Not all of the questions were about Cassie – just the majority. There were also questions about *The Human Race* and individual clan members. There were no questions about the parallels between the mating lives of birds and humans, and just two which made any mention of birds at all. The pick of these, if I remember correctly, was: 'How come if pigeons are so mucky they get to breed so much?'

***

I thought this might be some kind of West End anomaly, but Cassie's ghost appeared at every reading.

Ealing was the final straw: 'If Cassie was a bird, what kind of bird would she be?'

'She's a house wren, but she's trying to be an albatross,' I said. 'Next question.'

By then, much as I liked Cassie, I had grown resentful. She had stolen my audience and I wanted them back.

# Chapter 49

*December, Papa's, South Kensington*

Salvatore, still in love with Kim, had finally left with our order and I was allofeeding her an olive when Phil barged into the restaurant, clutching a brown A4 envelope.

'Phil?'

'Ah, there you are.' Phil came towards us. He took a chair from the next table, placed it down, rear first, between us and lowered himself on to it, like Christine Keeler as portrayed by a HGV driver. He placed the brown envelope beneath his chair.

'Hi Kim,' said Phil.

'Hi Phil,' said Kim.

Phil's greeting for Kim was bright, but sarcastically so. Kim opted for pure distilled contempt.

'Erm, will you join us for a drink, Phil?' I said, willing him to say no. I looked from Phil to Kim and back again. 'Our food won't be here for a minute or two. What are you doing here anyway?'

'Lager please,' said Phil.

I waved Salvatore over. 'Don't feel you have to stay on my account, Phil,' said Kim as Salvatore arrived. 'Simon told me that you feel uncomfortable around light, healthy cuisine.'

'Half a lager for our guest please, Salvatore,' I said.

'Make that a pint, mate,' said Phil, smirking at Kim.

A hush fell when Salvatore left, but not a peaceful one.

'Well this is nice,' said Phil. 'Relaxing together. It's been a busy week for both of you hasn't it? Such busy, busy people. You were doing one of your readings last night, weren't you, Bird?' I said that I was. 'Did you go along, Kim, to see your man in action?' Kim said that she hadn't been able to go. 'Do you usually go, though? Do you ever go?'

It was true that Kim had never offered to come to any of my readings, but then I didn't really want her to. I explained that she'd been particularly busy with the EPCON account recently.

'What's this about, Phil?' said Kim. 'Are you missing your only friend? Have you thought about getting a new one, or aren't you ready to stop being a cock?'

Phil reached down to the floor and lifted the envelope on to the table. 'She's been busy all right, Bird.' He turned to Kim. 'Are you going to tell him what you got up to last night, or shall I?'

I looked at Kim. She smiled. 'No, you tell him, Phil. I'm curious to hear what I was doing.'

'Phil—' I tried to say, but Kim touched my hand.

'It's always struck me as very suspicious that she,' Phil tipped his head at Kim, 'keeps finding you all these little projects to keep you busy in the evenings. Don't you think it's a bit unfair that while you are writing this book to please her she goes out partying?'

'Actually, I'm quite happy to avoid group interaction,' I said.

'And then she pushes you into *The Human Race* and then after that it's a book tour. She even goes on holiday without you.'

'We were both disappointed about that,' I said, 'weren't we, honey?'

'Why's she keeping him so busy, I thought. What is she up to?' Phil paused to peel open the envelope. 'And so last night I decided to follow her.'

'What?' I said.

'You poor, sad, isolated little man,' said Kim.

'You can play it as cool as you like, Kim. Game's up.'

'Come on then Phil, let's see what you've got,' she said. 'Make Simon see. Expose me.'

'As so many have… Last night, Bird, while you were doing your thing, she was snogging other men in a nightclub.'

This, I don't mind admitting, unsettled me, but Kim looked calm. 'How many men would you say I "snogged", Phil? That might help Simon get a sense of just how much of a tramp I am.'

'One,' said Phil. 'To be fair it was just one. That I saw.'

'But you were watching me pretty closely, weren't you…? And what did this guy look like?'

Phil finally and triumphantly pulled the photo from the envelope. It was approximately A5 sized, but I only got to see it briefly because Kim promptly turned it over.

'See?' said Phil. 'See what she did?'

'We can all look at the photo in a minute,' said Kim. 'This way will be more fun. Tell Simon about this guy I kissed. What did he look like?'

'Early forties,' said Phil, a little of his early swagger had gone I thought. 'Tall. Well, tallish. Thinning at the front. Close-cropped reddish goatee.'

'Coloured trousers?' I asked.

'Maybe,' said Phil.

'Sounds like Neil,' I said, turning to Kim.

Kim nodded. 'Sounds a *lot* like Neil, doesn't it? And Neil was there last night. But then you would expect him to be at his birthday party, wouldn't you?' Kim ran a lovely pink finger back and forth across her lovely pink chin. 'Has anybody ever kissed you on your birthday, Phil?'

'Bird, they were tongue-jousting, I swear,' he said.

'That's right, Phil – I was tongue-jousting with my best friend's partner in front of my best friend. Does your photo show our tongues jousting?'

'No,' said Phil defiantly.

'I thought not… Simon, do you want to see Phil's photo?' Kim's gaze was unwavering.

'No,' I said. 'No, I don't.' I took the envelope and then the photo from beneath her hand and slipped it back inside as Salvatore arrived with bruschetta and calamari.

'I think it's time for you to leave, Phil, don't you?' said Kim as we made room for the plates on the crowded table.

'You've got to believe me, Bird,' said Phil. 'She's bad.'

Salvatore frowned down at Phil and glanced across at Kim. 'It's OK, Salvo,' she said. 'He's leaving.'

But Phil didn't budge. He pulled out the photo again and shoved it out across the table. Knowing that my response was being closely monitored, I looked away. A brief glimpse suggested only several heads in diffuse, dark pink light.

Salvatore tried to lift Phil to his feet by his elbow, but Phil resisted and so Salvatore called for Vincenzo. Phil was still holding the photo out as they led him to the door.

'I'm right about her, Bird,' he said. 'And what about Mike, Kim? Tell Simon the truth about that.'

When they'd bundled Phil outside, Vincenzo guarded the door. Kim hugged Salvatore and apologised.

I wasn't feeling hungry, but I picked at the calamari so that the evening would seem less spoiled. 'I don't know what got into him,' I said.

'He's still there,' she said, looking past me. Twisting in my chair, I saw Phil standing in the window, pressing the photo against it. Seeing he had my attention he began to yell and to point but I couldn't hear him.

'In five minutes I will call the police,' Vincenzo said calmly from the doorway.

'You need more positive influences in your life,' said Kim, picking a long piece of raw onion from the bruschetta.

# Chapter 50

*January*

I began to experiment with the readings.

I sprinkled some of the more arresting 'snippets' from the book into my opening comments and carefully monitored audience reaction. I stayed behind to speak to the audience, accruing their comments and opinions.

In this way, my talks evolved. Reading by reading, I began to make small gains on Cassie.

Noting that the audiences responded best to the quirkier content, I added more. I incorporated anecdotes about iconic scientists and unusual species. My audiences began to ask me more questions about birds, my book, me.

Next I added amusing stories about the sex lives of birds, mammals and *Homo sapiens*. I told them funny stories about my own experiences in the field. I even added a joke:

'Why did the chicken cross the road?'

'To get to the other side,' they would answer in unison.

'Yes, but what was the chicken's motivation?' At this point they were generally united in silent bafflement. 'Well, a behavioural ecologist would say that we don't have enough information to make a firm conclusion. However, we do know that feral jungle fowl spend sixty-one per cent of their time foraging, so there is a good chance that the chicken was simply looking for food.'

Here the audience was typically divided. Some frowned, some exchanged glances, a few smirked speculatively.

But I wasn't done yet. 'Would you like the dirty version?' I asked. (When I became more accomplished, I would take a small step towards the audience and I would lower my voice.)

'Yes,' they would say. 'Yes.'

'Promise you won't tell Cassie?'

'We promise,' they would say.

After taking another small step towards them, I would then say, 'It's possible that the chicken crossed the road...' here I tried to remember to pause for effect, 'to take a dust bath because this is the best way to remove parasites, skin irritants and excess preen oil.'

It never failed.

\*\*\*

Once, I accidentally embellished my opening remarks for so long that I ran out of time to read. I admonished myself as Maddie would surely have done. And yet, when the manager ushered me over to the signing table, the queue ran to the front of the store and along the till. After that, I dropped the excerpts entirely.

\*\*\*

The Foyles reading went particularly well, and afterwards a friendly young couple stayed to chat with me in the doorway while I waited for Kim. When she arrived I saw her glance down at the bulging plastic bag in the male's hand.

As we walked down Charing Cross Road in search of dinner, Kim's hand hooked inside my arm, she said, 'You're in a good mood.'

'I am,' I said.

'Tell me why then,' she said, lightly tugging at my arm.

'Guess how many questions they asked me about Cassie.'

'I don't know.'

'Guess,' I insisted.

'OK, I'll say two. They asked two questions: "Can Cassie fly unaided?" and "Does Cassie moult?"'

'Nice try,' I grinned. 'They didn't ask any questions about Cassie. Not one.'

'That's great, Simon. Really great.' Kim stopped outside a small white-fronted Thai restaurant and dragged me over to look at the menu taped to the inside of the front window.

'If Cassie had walked in there tonight, I don't think they would have noticed,' I said. Kim was still intent on the menu. 'OK, they would have noticed. But they enjoyed themselves, and I enjoyed myself too. I think I'm getting quite good at it.'

'Of course you are, honey. I'm sure you're great.' Kim tapped the menu. 'This looks OK. Shall we try it?'

As I followed Kim and our tiny silk-wrapped hostess across the restaurant I realised I was feeling dissatisfied, despite the wafting flute melodies. I wanted Kim to observe my transformation for herself.

I was still feeling that way when the prawn crackers arrived. 'Come and see me next Monday evening, Kim,' I said, dipping the rim of a cracker into the tiny dish of satay sauce.

# Chapter 51

*Monday, Piccadilly*

'Great turnout,' beamed Nigel, my host for the evening, but I wasn't happy. Numerically he was correct, every seat was occupied, but Kim's perfect rump was not lodged amongst them.

When Nigel asked if I was ready to start for the third time, I sullenly assented.

*Damn EPCON*, I thought.

The smile I wore as I got to my feet was not a natural one. As the gentle applause petered out I appealed to myself to make an effort for my audience because, after all, they had left *their* workplaces on time.

I began, as was my custom, by suggesting that our everyday language reflected recognition of the similarities between the courtship behaviours of birds and *Homo sapiens*. I waited a moment to allow my congregation to start to wish they had gone home instead.

'Think about it,' I said, holding out my right hand. 'Lovebirds.' I gripped my little finger. 'Broody.' A second finger. 'Nesting instinct. And what about "bird", as per the once popular expression, "Oi, mate, take your eyes off my bird"? Or "chick", its North American equiv—'

Detecting a discontented vocalisation, I hesitated. 'Does someone have a question?'

'It was me,' said a male in a grey rolled-collared cardigan. 'Sorry but "bird" is a *really* outmoded expression. I mean, it went out with *The Sweeney* and flares.' The female to his side, possibly his mate, turned to look at him. 'And it's patronising,' he added.

'Oh, I agree,' I said. 'And I'm not here tonight to lobby for the reinstatement of these expressions. I'm simply suggesting that our everyday vernacular suggests that we used to be more aware of the bird-like qualities of human courtship behaviour.' I swept my gaze from left to right across the audience and sensed that their judgement was still in the balance. 'And, look, males don't exactly get off scot-free.' The discontented male's arms, and even his face, remained folded. 'After all, "cock" is hardly an expression of admiration.'

Some of the audience chuckled, and some of those chuckled only begrudgingly. And because their first expression of appreciation was muted I was able to hear footsteps patting across the wooden floor. Turning towards them I felt a fresh flinch of disappointment when I discovered the footsteps were not Kim's.

The new arrival, a non-Kim female, made her way to the back of the seating area. An instantaneous assessment of posture, gait and hair led me to conclude that the non-Kim female was of approximately the same age as Kim. However, this female also appeared to be a very different creature. Kim didn't own a hoodie or a backpack for one thing, or possibly two. The female was a little shorter than Kim and her hair was white-blonde, scrunchier (you know what I mean) and less lustrous.

I found myself thinking that if her hair was shorter, the non-Kim female might resemble, from the posterior at least, Charlotta.

Thinking no more of it, I quickly told the audience about the great cock irony (i.e. male birds don't have penises). As they chuckled for a second time, I looked over to the late-arriving female again. She appeared to be engaged in a reciprocal altruistic exchange with an older male; he was offering her his chair and she was declining it. She stooped to speak to him, pushing her hair back behind her ear, and I noticed that she also resembled Charlotta from the lateral perspective.

The late-arriving female must have detected my attention because she turned towards me. Her anterior looked *remarkably* like Charlotta's.

'Charlotta?' I said.

The audience twisted in their seats.

'Hi, Simon,' said Charlotta. 'Erm, hello everyone.'

'What are you doing here?' I said. 'And how in Darwin's name are you?'

'I'm good thanks, but...' she looked around the audience.

'Yes. Yes,' I said. 'Of course. Let's catch up at the end.'

\*\*\*

Eventually all of the books and *The Human Race* memorabilia were signed and Charlotta and I stepped out on to Regent Street. The cold wind groaned, rebuffed by the surrounding buildings. Mindful that Charlotta had only a hoodie for warmth, we slipped into a nearby Italian complete with hanging hams. Inside there were long rows of marble-topped tables and several deer antler lampshades. *Kev-in would love it here*, I thought.

While waiting to be seated, I slyly slipped my phone from my pocket and read and huffily deleted Kim's explanation and apology. 'So, what brings you to London, Charlotta?' I said, slipping the phone back into my coat.

'The third Worldwide Congress of Animal Vocalisation and Communication. Global Vocal for short.' Charlotta unzipped her hoodie to show me a white T-shirt with a logo featuring a cheesy cartoon of a superb lyrebird (*Menura novaehollandiae*).

'Never heard of it,' I said. 'Is it annual?'

'Yes,' she laughed. 'Next year is Boston.'

A waiter at the far end of the bar acknowledged us. 'Oh, by the way, Charlotta,' I said, 'if the waiters or anybody make a fuss about me, don't take any notice.'

'OK,' she said, hesitantly.

'It's just I was in this popular TV show and then I was linked with a celebrity in the tabloids. Erroneously, of course.'

While the waiter led us to a table I wondered if *The Human Race* phenomenon had reached Australia and also if Charlotta had enjoyed my gig.

'I think I might just have the soup,' said Charlotta when the waiter left with my coat. 'You don't get a lot of soup in Brisbane.'

A discussion about Australian magpies (*Cracticus tibicen*) turned back to pied flycatchers. After the food arrived we talked about Mats and Wolfie and reminisced about nest boxes, ladders and the minibus. I asked after Nelly and Bertil. Charlotta asked about zebra finches and living in London.

However, when she laid her spoon down inside the empty bowl, there was still much that we had not discussed. We hadn't spoken about Kev-in or Kim or our near-miss copulation. And, most surprising of all, Charlotta still hadn't told me what she thought about my gig.

When Charlotta returned from the bathroom, I said, 'So, what did you think of the reading, Charlotta?' I picked up a Mint Imperial from the tiny chrome platter and began to squeeze it from its plastic wrapper.

'I'll get this,' she said lifting the bill. 'You can buy me a Guinness.'

***

Charlotta was keen to find a karaoke bar but I explained that this was probably inadvisable given my transient celebrity status.

We stumbled out of the rain into the nearest pub. Holding two pints before me I went in search of Charlotta, finding her staring into a flashing quiz machine.

'Hmm. Silver coronation, I think?' she said, pressing a blinking button. 'Yes! I am a historian.' I passed her the drink and we looked down at the next question.

'I think it's Michael Johnson, no?' she said.

'I will defer to female choice,' I said.

Charlotta insisted on my help with the next question, though my knowledge of equatorial countries was not superior to that of athletics world record holders.

'I don't know, Brazil, possibly?'

'Brazil?'

'I don't know. It could be Colombia or Venezuela. Aren't there any questions about passerines?'

Panicking, Charlotta pressed the button corresponding to Brazil. 'Oh, Venezuela. Shame.' She sipped her Guinness. 'Shall we play again? Or would that be inadvisable for a celebrity?' she smiled.

'Very humorous. You still haven't told me what you thought about the talk.'

'Let's play again,' she said.

***

We played and failed three more times and still Charlotta didn't mention the talk. By the time we sat at a nearby table I was feeling very quizzical. To reassure myself I thought back to the smiling faces, the applause, the line of people clutching *The Feathered Ape*. Had I imagined it?

'You didn't like it, then?' I said. 'The talk.'

Charlotta's cheeks inflated then deflated. 'No, no. It was... entertaining.'

'Am I not allowed to be entertaining?'

'Simon, look...' Charlotta had begun to slide her glass slowly back and forth across the table. 'Most people clearly enjoyed it...'

'But...?'

'But,' Charlotta sighed again, 'would you *really* rather be telling jokes about chickens than doing fieldwork?'

'So *that's* what this is really about,' I said, clamping my hands on to the damp table. 'Look, I'm really sorry I wasn't able to help with the fieldwork last summer. I did design the study though, don't forget that.'

Charlotta gently shook her head. 'No, Simon, that is not what this is about – not at all. The three of us managed very well. I just can't believe that you want to do this. I mean what was that thing about President Coolridge?'

'Coolidge, actually,'

'Coolidge.'

'It's a funny story, that's all. Legend has it that when President Coolidge and his wife visited a farm she was impressed by the sexual antics of a rooster. She asked the farmer if the rooster was like that every day and when he assured her that he was she asked him to tell the president. And so he did and the president asked him, "Does the rooster always chase the same hen?" When the farmer replied, "Oh no sir," the president said, "Tell that to Mrs Coolidge."'

Charlotta sighed. 'I know, Simon. I heard it the first time.'

'It's very popular,' I sulked.

'And a little bit cynical too?' Charlotta sipped. 'You went from one polygamy story to another...'

'Well, monogamy isn't commercially viable, you see,' I said. Hearing myself repeat Maddie's words, I cringed. Perhaps it was this shame that made me hurtle on with insufficient caution. 'And anyway, you haven't always been such a staunch advocate of monogamy yourself.'

Charlotta stared at me fixedly, but said nothing. The quiz machine made excitable electronic sounds.

'I'm very, very sorry,' I said. 'That was indefensible.'

'You should be,' she glowered and then looked down at her glass. 'I was lonely… With Kev-in I felt dead in that way.' She lifted the Guinness to her mouth. 'We spent a lot of time together. We both love behavioural ecology. It was a silly summer crash.'

'Crush actually,' I said.

'Crush,' she said.

# Chapter 52

'Even your friends will treat you differently,' Cassie had said, back in the early days of *The Human Race*. I returned to those words for comfort after my evening with Charlotta. It was a shame that she had reacted negatively, but I reminded myself that others, including Kim's family and friends and even Gustavo, were now treating me with greater respect.

And when Kim said she would take a half-day holiday in order to attend my performance at the Wibley Literary Festival, I forgot all about Charlotta's criticisms.

\*\*\*

When the day of the Wibley gig arrived, I got to Paddington early, bought two tickets and two take-out coffees and waited for Kim beneath the departures board. But when our platform was announced she still hadn't arrived. Noticing a missed call I called her back.

'How far away are you?'

'Didn't you get my message?' she whispered.

'No. I called you straight back.' An announcement echoed out over the tannoy.

'I can't speak, Simon, I'm in a telecom. Things are really unwinding at EPCON.'

I sighed and stepped backwards, almost colliding with a small girl excitedly running around. 'How late are you going to be?'

'Honey, I'm not going to make it. It's a big old mess. They're going to need body bags for this one. I have to go. Sorry...'

I dumped Kim's latte into a bin at high velocity and trudged to the platform at low velocity.

\*\*\*

Stepping into the auditorium at Wibley was like stepping through a portal into a lost world of music hall. The furnishings and décor were regal crimson and gold and the long crimson velvet stage curtains were festooned with sashes and tassels. The air was cool and musty and it smelled like a mouldy old canvas hide, or perhaps it was just my mood.

The audience was the largest I had encountered on *The Feathered Ape* tour. Tristan Griffs, poet and anthologist, had been appointed to interview me. He was tall with an outbreak of disobedient, oily, cormorant-like, dark grey hair and he wore a crumpled green shirt which hung down, unevenly, over the top of a pair of grey jogging bottoms. My own jacket, trousers and shirt for the occasion had been acquired by Kim, but I surmised that Tristan had not benefitted from female choice.

It sometimes seemed to take Tristan longer to ask a question – with his contorted formulation and reformulation – than it took me to answer it. As he spoke his hands writhed as if forming his questions from invisible clay.

'Do you mean what is the most fascinating species I have studied?' I asked after he had agonised his final question into existence.

'Yes,' he said, 'in a sense.'

I turned to the audience: 'How many of you have even heard of a bird called the pied flycatcher?' Three hands went up and one of these only partially. 'Well, it might seem strange to you then that we have spent thousands of hours obsessively monitoring the nest boxes of these tiny birds,' I said. 'The adults weigh only about as much as a compact disc or a breadstick, but their tiny lives are packed full of controversy. The male is a gentleman and a rogue. He works hard to provide for his family, but he's also a selfish opportunist and he will lure a second female if he can. The female is very careful to choose a male who can provide the support and resources to make the difficult task of raising a brood easier, but she's an opportunist too. If he lets her out of his sight and a superior male happens along she will copulate with him. So you see, when we study the courtship and mating behaviour of the pied flycatcher we are witness to the ancient tension between male and female, between monogamy and polygamy, played out in miniature.'

A bald male in a yellow golfing-style V-neck jumper nodded, slowly. A female with long grey hair, palest at the ends, smiled in a manner consistent with moderate intensity enjoyment.

\*\*\*

The first question posed by a member of the audience came from a male seated in the third row. I recall his hair was swept back like EO Wilson (the world's foremost ant specialist or myrmecologist). He requested clarification regarding the sea horse (*Hippocampinae*) gender controversy.

'Who else has a question for Dr Selwood?' said Tristan. We both scanned the audience eagerly. 'Come on, Wibley, discard your circumspection.' Still no hands. Tristan glanced at me and then addressed the audience again: 'Was it James Russell Lowell who said "Fate loves the fearless"?'

Because of Tristan's questions there had been fewer anecdotes and jokes than usual and, anxious about the lack of questions, I began to think of a way to work in the Coolidge effect story when a hand appeared at the rear of the auditorium.

'Wonderful,' said Tristan. 'Please, what is your question for Dr Selwood?'

I watched a young festival volunteer scuttle towards the raised hand with a microphone. The hand took the microphone and climbed to its feet.

The hand was female, and highly so. The hand had long, dark red wavy hair. Suddenly the rest of the audience seemed to be in monochrome.

*Screw seahorses*, said the PC.

*It's Lady Godiva*, I thought.

The hand gently tapped the microphone and looked at me over the sea of grey heads.

'Can you hear me OK?' she said.

Tristan and I said 'Yes' in synchrony, like obedient drones.

'Thank you so much for your talk, Dr Selwood.' The accent was unmistakably North American. 'I'm so excited to read your book.'

'Thank you,' I said. 'I hope you will enjoy it.'

246

'I'm sure I will. I have a cheeky little question for you first though, if you don't mind. I was wondering: how does a man like you celebrate Valentine's Day?' The audience laughed and the female beamed – providing a powerful testimonial to the proficiency of her homeland's orthodontists. She returned the microphone and sank down behind a male in a red checked shirt.

*Eject him,* yelled the PC.

'I'm sure we are all very intrigued to hear how Dr Selwood will respond,' said Tristan.

Dr Selwood was also intrigued. He didn't know at first. He only remembered Maddie telling him to always answer the question he wished he had been asked.

'I suspect that you're asking me about my own attitude towards love. Am I right?' I said. My reward was another glimpse: the beautiful redhead leaned over to nod between the shoulders of those seated in front. 'Well, I suppose I am more conscious of love as an evolutionary strategy than most people. But that knowledge has never conferred any immunity upon me, not in the slightest. For years I found it impossible to talk to an attractive female. I would get horribly nervous and tongue-tied and I would stammer. Love exhilarates and fixates me like a normal person, maybe even more so.' The lady with the long grey hair was smiling again. 'And why should I be immune? If I studied the way that pied flycatchers forage for insects do you think I would become less reliant on food?' The grey-haired lady didn't seem to think so.

I asked the red-headed female if I had addressed her question satisfactorily. She got to her feet again, delighting the PC, and took the microphone for a second time.

'Well, yes, thank you, it kind of does, but...'

'Do we detect lingering curiosity?' said Tristan.

'But, I still want to know if you buy your wife flowers.' The audience laughed again and this time they clapped too. I laughed and clapped my own hands a couple of times. She had earned the loudest laugh of the evening, but it was not resentment the PC was feeling.

'I'm not married, actually,' I said.

It wasn't a lie, merely a small deception.

\*\*\*

The Selwood Index of Mass Engagement (or SIMEn) is derived from the proportion of the audience that stay for the signing and by that measure alone my Wibley talk was another success.

As the end of the line approached, I got talking to an enthusiastic amateur naturalist with a beard of copper wire. When his wife finally pulled him and his two teenage sons away, the only person left in the queue was the beautiful red-headed female.

She smiled and stepped towards the table with a copy of my book pressed to her abdomen.

'Hi,' she said.

'Hi.'

She placed the book down, and slowly slid it across the surface towards me. As a member of the audience her beauty had given me pleasure, but now she was much too close and we were alone. The PC had occasionally appreciated the beauty of other females since the formation of my pair-bond with Kim, but there was something uniquely terrifying about this one. As she opened the book, revealing burgundy nails, I felt the old discombobulation grip me.

'I hope you didn't mind my question earlier. I was just teasing,' she said.

'Yes, teasing,' I said, looking down at her fingers as they pressed down on the inside cover. 'Good question.' I decided to keep looking at her fingers.

'Well, it was a great talk. I was *totally* transfixed.'

'Thank. You.' I looked up. She looked too happy, too relaxed and most of all, too beautiful. 'The inscription?'

'Hey, I don't know, I guess I hadn't thought about that.' She frowned for just a second and then the smile was back and wider. 'I've got it. Write this for me, please.' I drew the book closer and poised my rollerball. 'For Elise,' she said. I looked down at the blank page. 'And then, "Happy Valentine's".' I looked up into her eyes. 'Go on,' she said, 'it's just for fun.' I did as she asked, closed the book and handed it to her. She opened it and inspected the front page. 'Hey, whoever heard of a Valentine's gift without a kiss or two?' She passed the book back and, mumbling an apology, I complied.

'Thank you. You are very sweet. I will treasure it.' She slipped the book into the bag hanging from her shoulder. And then she said, 'I have a proposition for you, Dr Selwood.'

'Oh. Proposition.' I reached for my water bottle.

'I'm a journalist. I came here today to interview another author, but I got here early. Now I'm thinking it would be fun to interview you too.'

'I have to go London. Now,' I said. 'I, I live there. In London.'

'That's fine,' she said. 'I didn't mean now. I need to read my Valentine's gift first, don't I?' She patted the side of her bag. 'We could meet in London, next week maybe?'

I cleared my throat. 'Uh-huh.'

# Chapter 53

The Elise female suggested the following Tuesday evening for the interview. That worked well for me: Kim had plans after work that evening and so I figured I would be able to give the interview without disruption to our pair-bond. So it wasn't opportunism you see.

I didn't tell Kim that I had arranged to meet a journalist – well, she already had a lot on her plate with all that EPCON business – and so the fact that the journalist was beautiful was also irrelevant.

\*\*\*

By the time I arrived at the hotel a tingle of anticipation had transmogrified into a prickle of anxiety.

I scanned the wide, open lobby for Elise but couldn't sight her. I made my way across a massive pale grey rug towards a vacant low purple rectangle by the angular reception desk and sat facing the two large glass revolving doors.

Elise first spotted me as she stepped out into the lobby, though my heart had been pounding since I watched her emerge from the black cab. She waved and her lips parted in a perfectly terrifying grin.

*Over here*! yelled the PC.

Elise wore a flowing brown blouse made of a lightweight material which had clearly not been designed for fieldwork. Its sleeves were full and long, but the neck was cut away to reveal her shoulders. A thin brown cord strap from the neckline looped around the back of her neck.

*I love a revealing interview,* said the PC.

I rose to greet her, on jittery legs. *Remember, never trust a journalist,* I told myself as I prepared to shake her hand. However, Elise threw out her arms, causing the sleeves of her blouse to billow like the outstretched wings of an eagle. As we hugged millions of wonderful perfume molecules located the receptors in my nasal epithelium.

*Never, ever trust a beautiful, aromatic journalist,* I urged myself.

\*\*\*

Elise found seats for us between two white cylindrical pillars at the front of the lobby. Informing me that it was her birthday, she ordered two glasses of Prosecco, though I had set my mind on a strong black coffee. 'You don't mind having a little drink with me on my birthday do you, Simon?' she asked, though the waiter had already departed.

I shook my head compliantly and repeated my birthday wishes.

Elise crossed her legs and began to circle a brown stockinged kneecap with the tip of a long burgundy nail. I asked her where she was from; interesting questions were her domain, not mine, and in any case I was only asking in order to distract myself from the kneecap and finger. She told me about a youth in California spent surfing and playing beach volleyball.

*Ask her if she has pictures,* said the PC but there was really no need because we were already imagining a youthful Elise in blue micro-shorts and a cropped yellow T-shirt. We were imagining sand adhering to a perfect cinnamon thigh.

After the drinks arrived Elise asked me about my own childhood. I was forced to admit that there had been a lot of Top Trumps and almost no volleyball. Then I learned that modelling beachwear is not as glamorous a way to pay your way through college as it sounded, though it still sounded more glamorous than the Berkshire library service.

Lifting my glass to my lips I was surprised to discover it was already empty. Reminding myself that one should never get inebriated in the presence of a beautiful, aromatic journalist, I dangled the empty glass down by the side of my chair so she wouldn't order another.

When her own glass was empty, Elise took to rolling the slender stem up and down the length of her thumb as she chatted. I became transfixed by this and hardly noticed the waiter return.

'Sorry, sir,' he said. 'I was asking madam if you would like me to inform the restaurant that you will be joining us for dinner.'

I looked to Elise. 'Shouldn't we get on with the interview?'

Elise looked up to the waiter. 'Can you give us two minutes please? I need to discuss it with my husband.'

'Husband?' I said, as the waiter retreated.

'Oh, don't worry,' she said. 'We aren't actually married. Please let me buy you dinner though.' I wavered, pondered and vacillated. Elise changed strategy and position. Leaning towards me, she said, 'Simon, are you going to make me eat alone on my birthday? I mean I remember you telling us that true altruism is rarely observed in nature – but in Knightsbridge?'

\*\*\*

The restaurant was dark as a cave, and sparsely populated. Square pale blue glass plates mounted on dark wood walls emitted vaporous blue light. Small, dark wood tables were arranged in parallel, closely packed rows. In the centre was a tiny rain forest simulation.

A waitress, menus in hand, directed us to a table midway down the left-hand aisle beside a couple. The male, sitting with his back to the wall was rotund and approximately sixty years of age. A ring of grey hair circled his scalp like a grubby sweatband. The female was some two decades younger and her breasts, packed inside a tight brilliant white T-shirt, were probably much younger still. The pair continued to eat without acknowledging us or even each other. Elise whispered something to the waitress and we were on the move again. We travelled deeper into the restaurant where it was darker and even more sparsely populated.

'This is much cosier,' said Elise, when the waitress had gone, though I would have said 'isolated'. Elise rotated her menu so that we could read it together, though I had a perfectly legible copy of my own and no appetite. She ran her finger slowly down the menu's columns but I was aware only of her proximity, her perfume and the feather-light clashing of the silver bracelets on her slender wrist.

I ordered a light meal (scallops from Peru and black pudding from an unspecified location). Elise ordered sea bass and an expensive bottle of Chablis Premier Cru.

When the wine arrived Elise shot me a smile of satisfaction.

'I know,' I said. 'It's your birthday.'

'Did I mention that I lost my virginity on my birthday?' she asked, as I poured the wine into her glass. 'What about you, Simon?'

I gulped. 'Mostly airplane modelling kits and bird books as I recall.'

Elise's fingers only part concealed her smile. 'No, I mean when did *you* first get laid?'

'Laid is an interesting term, don't you think?' I said, folding and unfolding my brown napkin. 'It's another good example of the way that we have co-opted terms from the life cycle of birds.'

'He was a lifeguard,' she said, closing her eyes for a second. 'And it was in a red, white and blue lifeguard tower.'

*God bless America*, said the PC.

'I'd had my eye on him the whole summer. And then on my birthday I waited for his buddy to go off patrolling the beach and then I paid him a visit. There wasn't much room in the hut. There was just this one small desk; it was about the same size as this table actually.' Elise ran her finger slowly along the edge of the table. 'I had to push my hands back like this to stop my head from pounding against the wall.' Elise lifted her arms above her flawless shoulders, inverting her wrists. 'He said he didn't want anyone to hear us... I'm pretty sure they heard us anyway.' She laughed then dropped her hands back down. Breaking off a small piece of bread she placed it on the tip of her tongue. 'You don't mind me telling you about that, do you, Simon?'

'No. Not at all,' I lied. 'I can see why you became a journalist though. Very vivid.' I reached for a small white roll which I did not intend to eat. 'So what do your readers need to know, Elise?'

'Right, right,' she said, dipping her hand down into the brown leather handbag by her ankles. The hand emerged and a small black voice recorder dangled from it like an electronic rat. She slid it into the centre of the table, its red eye blinking.

'Not that I could ever forget anything *you* said,' she said. 'OK, to get us started, I want you to tell me everything you know about men. You are different – we get that – but how should we adapt?'

I had been looking forward to the moment when the sexual anecdotes stopped, but Elise's first question did not relax me.

'I don't follow you?' I said.

'Well, how do you think women should adapt so that they can get better, more fulfilling relationships with their men?' I was still puzzled and Elise saw it. 'Everybody wants better relationships, right?'

I pondered this for a moment. Did I? My love for Kim remained powerful, but it would be nice if she would acknowledge the importance of avian behavioural ecology. Also, it would be nice if she would attend the occasional reading. Oh, and I wouldn't have objected if she decided to find a completely new set of friends. And because of these thoughts, but mostly because it's oh so easy to agree with a beautiful journalist, I nodded pliantly.

'The women I write for want to know what men are really thinking and why they are thinking it. They would *love* to hear your advice,' she continued.

I gasped. 'I'm not a relationship counsellor, Elise.'

'No, but you understand why we love, isn't that what you said? And you are definitely a man – I don't need a PhD to see that.' Elise smiled as she had throughout the brief time I had known her.

'I'm not even capable of advising myself most of the time,' I said. Elise's smile was unwavering but despite her intoxicating presence I suddenly felt more jaded than ever before by public life and the petty preoccupations of contemporary *Homo sapiens*. As she resumed circling her kneecap I told her that I was only prepared to describe what we had learned from studying other species that form pair-bonds.

'That sounds awesome,' said Elise.

\*\*\*

I flitted, like a hummingbird (*Trochilidae*), from one evolutionary concept to another until our meals arrived.

Elise refilled our glasses and I looked down at the small black and white pile in the middle of the huge plate before me. She pressed a button on the voice recorder and the red eye ceased blinking.

'Time for a little break,' she said. We began to eat and almost immediately Elise quizzed me about my own sexual history. 'Come on,' she said, pointing at the recorder, 'it's off the record.'

'I'm not worried about that,' I lied. 'I just don't feel comfortable talking about that kind of thing.'

'Don't kiss and tell, huh?' said Elise. She placed the tip of her fork in her mouth, pulling the flakes of white flesh from it with her lips.

'I suppose not,' I said, attempting a knowing smile. In her company I actually felt ashamed of my two monogamous relationships. Eager to get back on safe ground I said, 'I must tell you about the great grey shrike.' Placing my fork down, I reached out for her voice recorder and fumbled around for the record button. I told Elise about the efforts that the male shrike has to make, sometimes over several weeks, in order to win the approval of the female. Most famously this includes collecting a cache of small rodents, birds and invertebrates to impress her. 'Eventually, he presents her with one last juicy piece of prey, completes a little "dance" and then, finally, they copulate,' I said.

'Fascinating,' said Elise. She ran a finger back and forth across her lips in a gesture that might have been interpreted as contemplative if it had been made by a member of the Life Sciences faculty. Sitting forward she turned off the voice recorder. 'Dinner then dancing: it's the classic combo... Do you dance, Simon?'

'No,' I said, hastily. 'Tight hamstrings.' Another small lie.

'Shame.'

I had barely touched my meal and so I began to pick at it. Elise had eaten little more than half of her sea bass (*Lateolabrax japonicus*) but she placed her fork down at the side of her plate and dabbed at the corners of her mouth with the thick brown cotton napkin. 'Who knew bird science could be so charming?' she said. She swept her hair over her shoulder and now the intensity and fixedness of her gaze seemed even more unsettling.

'I haven't even told you about barn swallows,' I said.

Unbidden, Elise reached across the table, placing her hand on top of mine. 'It's funny, I felt very comfortable with you right from the first time we spoke in Wibley,' she said. 'Why do you think that is?'

'I suspect that's because I was feeling uncomfortable enough for both of us,' I said.

'Simon, I'm going to be very honest with you.'

'Please don't,' I pleaded.

'I'm not all that interested in shrikes.' That was when I knew for sure that Maddie was right about journalists. 'I am *very* interested in *you* though.'

'Thank you,' I said.

Elise sighed. 'Do you think I am an attractive woman?'

*Yes!* said the PC.

'In what sense?' I asked.

Elise sighed again and more deeply. 'Let's start with visually, shall we?'

Unable to find a reply which was both candid and cautious, I gaped. Elise shook her head and then placed her hand on mine again. 'Would you like to make love to me, Simon?'

*In a beach hut?* said the PC.

I extended my gape.

'If you can't speak, Simon, just nod,' she said.

'Elise… Elise, you are a very, very attractive woman, but—'

Elise was now stroking my cheek which was bad because the last thing I needed was more dopamine. 'I'm no biologist,' she said, 'but as I understand it that attraction feeling is nature's way of telling you to make love to me.'

'Elise. Please stop.' I put my hand gently around her wrist and placed her hand back on the table.

*Coward!* said the PC.

'I don't understand,' she said. 'Didn't you just say you found me attractive?'

'You *are* very attractive… You are too attractive if anything. Look, in Wibley I said… I said I didn't have a wife.'

*Don't listen to him,* said the PC, who was now attempting to communicate with Elise directly.

'You have a wife?'

'Well no, but—' Panicking, I tried to scramble together a coherent defence, but Elise wasn't angry.

'That's OK,' she beamed. 'I've got a husband. He's in New York.'

'I have a girlfriend. And I love her.'

Elise was still beaming. 'I'm sure you do, Simon, and that's very sweet, I just don't see what that's got to do with it. I mean, when I heard you talking at Wibley I said to myself, that guy gets it. You *do* get it, don't you?'

'Of course,' I said. *Get what?*

'I knew it. It doesn't make sense does it? Why should we deny our instincts if nobody gets hurt? I'm still married *because* I allow myself a little freedom within my marriage… Especially around my birthday.'

Elise stroked the back of my hand. 'And when I saw you at Wibley I said to myself, "That's who I want for my birthday this year".'

Elise dipped down to reach into her handbag revealing more peri-shoulder flesh and the sheer black fabric of her breast-restraining garment. Then she pressed something into my hand and without looking I could tell that it wasn't a spare voice-recorder. It felt more like a credit card. Why had she given me a credit card?

'Room three thirty-eight,' she said. 'I got an extra key in case there were certain things that you would only reveal in private.' She lowered her voice, though there were no diners nearby. 'It's got a *huge* freestanding bath.'

Elise lifted herself from her chair with an artful, sinuous, almost choreographic grace. Clasping either side of the table she leaned towards me.

My desire for Elise had gained impetus as the evening progressed but it was only when she kissed me that I finally knew what I had to do. Her lips were warm and soft yet firm. They entreated mine. They promised and demanded. The kiss continued long beyond the moment when I might legitimately have pulled away or protested.

Sensing my yielding and without breaking the kiss, Elise came to sit beside me on the bench seat. She slid along until our hips were abutting and then I felt her hand slip inside my right thigh. I felt her nails pressing through the fabric into the soft flesh.

Breaking the kiss, I stared into her eyes. 'Did you say three thirty-eight?' I said.

*Yes!* said the PC. *Yes!*

'Good boy,' she said. 'Turn right outside the elevator.'

'OK. I will get the bill and allow my penis to subside a little. Why don't you go up and run us a bath?'

'Don't be long,' she said. 'And don't let your penis subside too much either.' She squeezed her nails into my thigh again, retrieved her handbag, kissed me and left. I watched her slink past the uncommunicative couple and then our waitress on her way to the exit.

'Wow,' I said as I watched her leave the restaurant.

*Wow* said the PC.

***

I paid the bill and slipped my wallet inside my jacket and the receipt and black plastic room key into my trouser pocket.

I thanked the waitress again and turned right towards the pale marble of the lobby. By the time I reached the purple rectangular sofa the PC had become suspicious. He started to bombard me with retained images of Elise. I saw her beautiful face, her green eyes, her wavy red hair and her wonderful shoulders. I saw her finger circling her kneecap. I saw her arms arched back over her head. I saw her fingernails bite into the blue plank walls of the beach hut of my imagination. I even felt her nails pressing into my thigh.

*Turn around*, the PC implored me.

*No*, I said.

*TURN AROUND, you idiot.*

*No*, I said.

*You deceived her! You deceived me!*

*I had to.*

As I stepped, head spinning, into the revolving door he screamed, *I demand a transplant.*

He was still livid when the taxi arrived. *I hate you*, he said.

*I know*, I said. *I'm sorry.*

# Chapter 54

The taxi was halfway to Acton when the compulsion to confess became too strong and I asked the driver to turn back to South Ken.

***

I let myself in. It was a little after ten pm and the lights were on in the hallway and the kitchen and so I suspected that Kim was back.

'Hi honey,' I hollered up the hallway, withdrawing my key from the lock. 'I felt like a conversation.' No answer. 'Kim?'

I walked down the hallway. The bedroom door was closed but the lounge door was open and the light was on so I stepped in there but it was empty. 'Kim?'

I heard her voice muffled by the bedroom door. 'What are you doing here, Simon?'

I stepped across the landing and placed my hand on the bedroom door handle and pushed, meeting against firm resistance. The door had opened only a tiny fraction before closing again.

'Simon. I'm doing my bikini line for god's sake.' Kim sounded anxious, but then I imagined I would be too.

I stepped back from the door. 'Oops, sorry. I'll wait in the lounge.'

I walked over to Kim's framed Lady Godiva print and spent a little time considering what I wanted to say to Kim and how I wanted to say it and then, still undecided, I returned to the hallway. 'How much longer will you be in there, honey?'

'A few more minutes yet.' Kim still sounded tense. 'Why don't you go and get a bottle of wine?' she said.

'I don't want wine. I just want to talk.'

Back in the lounge I spotted an old edition of *The Auk* journal perched on Kim's row of books. I sat on the sofa flicking through it but mostly thinking about how to make Kim understand.

Then I had a worrying thought: what if Kim and her newly valeted vulva wished to copulate? With memories of Elise still so vivid in my mind and genitals, I didn't feel comfortable about that. Deciding that I would need to demonstrate my commitment to Kim in other ways, I leapt to my feet.

'How about a cup of tea, Kim? Or some more wax? Do you want some tea?'

'Yes… Please…' Kim still sounded grumpy. I started for the kitchen. 'I mean no. No thank you.' I stopped. 'I might have one when I'm done. You could run me a bath.'

'A bath?'

'Yes, a bath. And keep a very close eye on the hot water. It's started going cold suddenly.'

'Has it?' Had it? 'That's funny.' I went into the bathroom and turned on the hot tap then I stepped out into the hallway again. 'Do you want anything in it, honey?'

'Actually, I would really appreciate five minutes to myself.'

'Fair enough,' I said. Kim was clearly experiencing pubic separation anxiety and so I went back into the bathroom to test the tap. I stirred the shallow water to no useful purpose.

Hearing the front door close I leaned out of the bathroom. Kim, in her pink dressing gown was striding up the hallway towards me. 'You left the front door open,' she said. She looked florid, poor thing.

'Did I? Sorry.' I'd never left Kim's front door open before and it made me realise just how much Elise had unsettled me. Kim went back into the bedroom and I went back into the bathroom to check the hot tap and then went into the bedroom to speak to Kim. 'The water seems fine… How was… it?'

'Same as always.' With her back to me she was putting washing away in her drawers.

'I thought you got a wax last week?'

Kim was balling socks but she looked at me in her mirror. 'She missed a bit.'

'Huh. Do they call that a Mexican?' I sat on the bed. 'Don't I get a kiss on surprise visits?'

'Let me clean my teeth first. My mouth tastes funny.'

Glad that I didn't have to endure cosmetic procedures so uncomfortable they made my mouth taste funny, I lay back on the bed and stared at the ceiling. Kim walked past on her way to the bathroom.

'I wanted to talk to you about something,' I said.

Kim appeared in the doorway, her electric toothbrush in her mouth. 'Huh huh.'

'Yes. I met with a journalist tonight.'

'Hid hoo?' Kim disappeared.

I got back to my feet and went through to stand in the bathroom doorway. Kim was standing at the basin. 'The journalist asked me a really annoying question about how women should adapt to male psychology. Well basically that was what he asked.' I felt that declining an EPC had earned me the right to deceive Kim about the journalist's gender.

Kim turned towards me, nodding. 'Oim lethin.'

'And I realised… I realised that I don't ever want to be asked a question like that again.' This time it was the bathroom mirror that Kim used to look at me. 'I've decided that I'm finished with the media. I'll do the existing bookings but after that no more readings, no more interviews, no more reality TV.'

Kim shrugged. 'Huh huh huh huh.'

'I've been outside of my natural environment for too long, honey. I want to go back to being a behavioural ecologist pure and simple. I want to get back into the field.'

I desperately wanted to know Kim's response but she pointed at her mouth and then pointed towards the bedroom and so I left. I laid back in my old spot on the bed.

When Kim came through she laid down beside me, her nose pressed against my neck. 'Do what feels right for you,' she said.

'Thank you, honey.' I wrapped an arm around her and kissed her on the forehead. 'I don't deserve you,' I said.

# Chapter 55

Fortunately Kim did not solicit a copulation that evening.

Waking the next morning with my nose in her hair, I felt truly ashamed of the seedy scenario that had played out in the crepuscular restaurant.

Kim left early for her office and I got to work on my punishment, forcing myself to consider alternative endings to my encounter with Elise.

What if Elise's husband had walked in as we were kissing? What if Sara and Tony had walked in? But neither scenario was tortuous enough because I knew the protagonists were in New York and Dorset respectively.

What about Neil and Bel then? This scenario initially showed more promise because Neil might well wish to check out the best little ostentatious and dimly lit hotel restaurant in Knightsbridge but then I remembered that Damien had hinted that they were experiencing pair-bond strain.

Finally, I found a way to truly terrify myself: what if someone – say our waitress, or the bored looking lady with the improbable breasts – had taken a surreptitious photo of the kiss? What if that someone had sold the picture on to the press? Faeces!

I dressed frantically and dashed the ancestor down to the newsagents, returning, gasping, to the flat with a heavy wad of tabloids.

Throwing them down on the Kim's kitchen floor, I spread them around me and crawled over them, maniacally turning their pages.

When my task was finally complete and I was satisfied I had evaded discovery, I wandered, zombie like, into the lounge and dropped myself down on to the pink sofa. My knees hurt from the maniacal crawling, but I could have wept with relief. I lay there, still clad in the coat I had worn for the speedy trip to the shops, loudly berating myself for what might have been.

***

When I arrived at Empirical, I sent a long email to Charlotta, belatedly thanking her for her great honesty, courage and friendship. I also told her that I was determined to get back into the field as soon as possible. For the sake of brevity I did not mention that a beautiful journalist had also contributed to my enlightenment.

***

Kim and I spent a pleasant weekend together. To reward her for being so understanding about my decision to shun the spotlight, I made her favourite – my famous chicken tagine with lemon and olives. She might have been a bit quieter than usual that weekend, but I put that down to EPCON exhaustion.

***

When Kim walked into her kitchen on Monday morning though, this did strike me as truly uncharacteristic behaviour. The kitchen was my territory on the mornings that I stayed at hers; I needed black coffee and toast with peanut butter but Kim was somehow able to absorb everything she needed from the 'nourishing extracts' in her body wash.

Rather than express surprise, I asked her if she would like a coffee.

'Yes, please,' she said and I heard the surprise in her own voice.

While preparing the second cafetière of the morning and trying to appear unruffled, I placed two mugs on the table and invited her to sit, as if she were a guest. I asked if she wanted toast – she didn't. I told her she looked nice – she did.

'Is that a new dress-skirt?' I asked.

She nodded. 'I bought it a while ago, but I haven't worn it before. I didn't know you knew what a dress-skirt was.'

263

'You've learned about behavioural ecology, "pine flysnatchers", and sperm competition. I've learned about PR, olives and female fashion.'

She smiled fleetingly. I poured the coffee and fetched the milk from the fridge.

We sat holding our mugs for several minutes, conducting the kind of conversation you might expect from two strangers in the aftermath of an unexpected copulation.

Kim took a sip of her coffee and then looked at her watch. 'I'd better be going,' she said, though it was still early. She lifted herself from the chair and leaned over the table to kiss me before heading towards the door. She stopped, hands clutching the door frame.

'It's a shame,' she said, her back still towards me.

'What is?'

She span around. 'It's a shame you're giving up now.'

I groaned. 'Kim...'

'I mean it's just a shame that you are giving up before you were able to do some good.' She walked back to the table. 'Curlew, nightingale, puffin, turtle dove. All endangered, Simon. There are sixty-seven species on the red list. But species like the red kite have been brought back from the brink – by education. Imagine what you could achieve if you harnessed your profile to actually educate people.'

She had never looked more beautiful.

# Chapter 56

*March*

While I knew a good deal more than most *Homo sapiens* about the plight of endangered avifauna, I knew a good deal less than almost anyone about how to go about making a TV documentary thing.

Fortunately, Kim sensed this (some might make reference to female intuition but science is yet to validate that phenomenon). 'I'll speak to Nat,' she said.

\*\*\*

We met Nat in the cacophonous café.

'Simon wants to make birdwatching accessible to everyone,' said Kim.

'With minimal equipment,' I added.

'And without making anyone look like a prick or feel socially isolated.' I turned sharply. 'Just joking, honey,' she said. 'And he wants to educate everybody about steps they can take to preserve our native species.'

'Honey, you said "our",' I said, unable to conceal the emotion in my voice. Was Kim finally beginning to care about birds?

'What do you think, Nat?' she said.

'Hmm. I mean, it's interesting… I like it… We need a hook though.' Nat held up a curled index finger, in case we didn't know what a hook was.

'I think you might be getting confused with fishing,' I said.

The obligatory hook proved elusive. We ordered refill coffees and a slice of seed cake for me. Kim and Nat continued to propose ridiculous, gimmicky suggestions.

With sarcasm my intention, I suggested that perhaps I could co-host it with Big Bird (*Aves major*) from *Sesame Street*.

Kim and Nat looked at each other.

'Cassie,' they said.

# Chapter 57

*April*

Cassie sounded genuinely excited.

'Can't wait to tell Dad,' she said. 'And won't it be fun to work together again? I've missed you, Simon.'

I reciprocated. While I had resented her omnipresence at my early gigs, I was looking forward to seeing her again. 'And this time I might actually know what I'm talking about,' I said.

\*\*\*

Nat said we needed to film 'a taster' and Cassie had just one free day, a Saturday, before heading off to make a celebrity yacht race thing.

'Working title, "Bloated B-listers on Boats",' said Nat, who might just have been wishing that she had come up with the concept herself.

\*\*\*

The WWT London Wetland Centre was very accommodating. Nat and I met with the general manager in the Kingfisher Café. Coffee and Danish were brought to our table and after expressing thanks I joked that I thought there would be more minnows and sticklebacks on the menu.

The general manager pulled her Danish apart with her fingers.

'Simon's a scientist,' said Nat.

Anyway, the general manager gladly agreed to give us access to the Wetland Centre one hour ahead of the public opening. Frankly, when she heard Cassie was involved I think she would have drained the reservoirs for her.

I was especially thrilled because Kim was able to attend the shoot. At last I would have a chance to display my talents for her.

\*\*\*

It was already a beautiful, bright, still spring morning when we left South Ken. We fell silent as we drove past the reception building because a few hundred people had flocked like geese outside its glass doors and they were also backed up across the footbridge.

'Huh. Must be a rare passage migrant in,' I said.

Kim laughed and slowed to allow an adult pair and two juveniles to cross. 'Or – just a thought – they might be here to see Cassie,' she said.

\*\*\*

Kim and I waited in the car until Nat and then the crew arrived. Then, forming a huddle by a notice board, we waited for Cassie. Kim stamped her feet and brrred at the cold that wasn't (it must have been ten degrees).

Cassie arrived right on time in a surprisingly ordinary looking green hatchback. And, another surprise, she was accompanied by a male.

The male was wearing a black biker-style leather jacket and black baseball cap with a deep, red peak that obscured his face. As they strode towards us, hand in hand, I turned to Kim. 'Is that…?'

'Max Velocity? It certainly is. I wonder if he's still jealous of you.' Kim grinned and I grimaced. 'He's quite little, isn't he?' I said.

'Hmmm.'

\*\*\*

Nat, Kim and the general manager decided that Cassie should first address those gathered to see her before we started.

'Sorry, Simon,' said Cassie. 'It might be best.'

The females quickly chose a venue for the public address – i.e. in the courtyard behind the visitor centre – but then it took a while for a male to locate a microphone and a bale of hay for Cassie to stand on.

When Cassie finally took hold of the microphone, Kim and I slipped back towards the visitor centre. Max was already there, leaning back against the building, his faded denim backside pressed back against the glass.

'Is it always like this?' I asked.

'It's a nightmare,' he said, adjusting his cap.

There was no time to develop the conversation further because Cassie had climbed on to the bale and the crowd was cheering loudly, though it was not an especially large bale.

'Well, that noise should see off most of the birds,' I said quietly to nobody in particular.

'Yeah,' said Max.

Unexpectedly, Cassie invited me to join her on the bale. Wobbling, I almost unbalanced her but she righted herself and so I wasn't torn apart by the angry mob. Cassie asked me to explain our project and then passed me the microphone and kick-started a little round of applause.

When I returned to Kim she patted my arm reassuringly.

'He's not Max Volume, is he?' I said, glancing over to our companion who was reluctantly signing a guide brochure.

'Don't be so snooty,' said Kim.

'I'm not,' I protested. 'I just thought he might be a bit friendlier.'

\*\*\*

At last, Cassie and I were on our way to the Peacock Tower. I felt like the pied piper, though of course it was Cassie the throng was following along the south route. Ahead in the tower the crew were waiting for us and volunteer wardens had set up scopes and were readying themselves to be interviewed.

'I'm looking forward to this,' said Cassie.

'That's nice,' I said, turning back to look for Kim amongst those trailing in her wake. A little way back Nat waved, two-handed, but I couldn't see Kim. To allow her time to catch up, I paused by a tall gorse in which I had spotted a small charm of goldfinch (*Carduelis carduelis*).

'Yes, that's what my dad gets,' said Cassie, excitedly.

'I thought so,' I said, looking back for Kim.

\*\*\*

269

I checked my phone before climbing the stairs of the Peacock Tower to where the crew were waiting; there was no message from Kim. I was about to call her, but Cassie saw me and said, 'Now, now, Dr Selwood. Let's focus, shall we?'

\*\*\*

We started out by looking out west over the main lake. Warden Gerald pointed out a few of the day's highlights. Luckily enough, a pair of great crested grebe (*Podiceps cristatus*) were engaged in a preliminary courtship dance over by the scrape. They didn't go so far as the weed dance, but it was still captivating. Cassie was genuinely charmed by their display of symmetry and mutual mimicry.

We got everything, including the bit where she said, 'Oh my god! They look Elizabethan,' and I said, 'I think you will find that they've been around for considerably longer than that.'

We had been filming for half an hour or so when Gerald tried to scope a common tern (*Sterna hirundo*) for Cassie. I took the opportunity to quickly pop downstairs to see if Kim was there. She wasn't and so I went straight back up to the second floor and, using my own binoculars, I looked out along the paths for her, first south and then east. *I bet she got drawn in by the sand martins*, I thought, but the entrance to their nest bank was obscured from view.

And then Cassie got excited by an avocet (*Recurvirostra avosetta*) that Gerald had scoped for her and my search for Kim was arrested.

\*\*\*

When we had most of what we needed from the Peacock Tower, I went over to the north-facing windows just to check we hadn't missed something interesting on the grazing marsh or in the reed beds. I couldn't see very much on the gridded marsh and so I turned the scope westward. And there, at the intersection between the marsh and the reed bed, right by the edge of the Headley lagoon, I spotted a grey heron (*Ardea cinerea*). As if aware that he was being watched, he made the great, slow, deep-squatting effort to get airborne, and set off west.

Flicking the scope up just a fraction I spotted a distinctive red Gortex jacket. I steadied the scope. Kim was over by the Wildside hide. 'Ah. She went down the west route. Silly girl,' I said under my breath.

'What was that, Simon,' said Cassie. 'Have you seen something?'

Adjusting the focus, I pressed my eye to the lens again. Light shot off the water, blinding me briefly but I found her again. She was sitting on a bench near the hide. At first I was so relieved to have found her I didn't notice somebody was with her. I increased the magnification. Her companion was male. The male wore a black biker-style jacket just like Max Velocity's but wasn't wearing a cap. Ah, but there was a cap in his hand.

Optics have improved immeasurably since I got my first second-hand pair of bins. They are lighter, easier to use, more affordable and much, much more powerful. Take Kim and Max for example, they must have been at least two hundred metres away, but I could see them with stunning clarity.

I could see that she was smiling, and that she was smiling at him.

I could see that he was smiling back at her.

I could see that they were holding hands.

Finally, and the clarity was still excellent, I saw Kim kiss Max Velocity. She kissed him for an unbearably long time. I observed their two bodies move towards and press against each other. Next, I saw Kim's hand reach up around Max's neck. It was a gesture I had often experienced myself. Often, but not always, I had experienced it as a prelude to copulation.

'Simon, let me see,' said Cassie, now standing by my shoulder.

'Just a second,' I said without taking my eye from the lens.

Finally the kiss broke. Kim quickly planted another kiss, this one brief but firm on Max's lips and then they stood. They were still holding hands. Max, his cap now back in place, was speaking to her.

I saw him attempt to lead Kim back to the visitor centre.

'*What is it?*' said Cassie.

I saw Kim resist.

I saw her entreat him.

I saw him yield.

I saw her tugging him towards the hide. I saw them disappear into the hide.

'It's over, Cassie,' I said. I lifted my eye from the scope and stood face to face with her. 'I mean, it flew off.' Cassie squinted. 'Has Gerald shown you an oystercatcher yet? Oystercatchers are wonderful. Let's see if we can spot one on the wader scrape.'

# Chapter 58

When the male blue tit (*Cyanistes caeruleus*) suspects his mate may have participated in extra-pair copulations he reduces feeding visits and nest defence. Similarly, the male reed bunting (*Emberiza schoeniclus*) reduces paternal care if his nest carries eggs fertilised by another male.

The male shrike (*Lanius minor*) takes things one step further. If he suspects his mate has copulated outside the pair he may resort to physical aggression. He might peck her, chase her from his territory or force-copulate with her, since in his world the last sperm often wins.

An evolutionary psychologist visiting from a distant culture might predict that male *Homo sapiens* would respond more robustly to a threat to his pair-bond than even the shrike. After all, the human male often makes a greater investment (i.e. decades) in fewer progeny.

Fortunately, the response of the human male is rarely so harsh. While he might feel distress, anger and pain – especially immediately after discovering the infidelity – it is perfectly feasible for the male to contain and control his behavioural response.

In extreme cases he might not even mention his awareness of the infidelity to his erring mate. He might sit silently beside her as she drives them home and while she chitters cheerfully he might wonder how many times previously she has deployed a positive demeanour in order to conceal an infidelity from him. He might turn to see if she looks different to him, now that he knows the ugliness she is capable of. And he might discover, perversely, that she looks more beautiful to him than ever.

The thought of physical aggression or forced copulation probably won't ever enter his mind.

He might still say nothing when they are back within the privacy of her flat. When she asks him if he wants to go out for lunch, he might shrug. When she asks him what he wants to eat he might say, 'I'm not really hungry.'

He might go into her bedroom and without even consciously planning it he might pack his bag. Then, picking up his faithful old backpack from the hallway he might walk out of the door.

# Chapter 59

The Life Sciences library seemed like the best place to go. I could have gone back to Acton, but my instincts told me that the presence of other nerdy *Homo sapiens* would somehow make me feel less alone.

Settling myself into a desk in a corner at the back with the latest draft of the PF2 paper as an excuse for my visit, I tried to focus on the most urgent decisions about my future. However, I hadn't yet processed the immediate past; time and again I returned to the scene that unfolded before me at the Wetland Centre. And not content with what I had observed, my imagination insisted on dragging me inside the hide with Kim and Max. I tried closing my eyes but this only intensified the horror.

Eventually I managed to focus my mind on the most pressing issue of all: where would I roost for the evening?

I didn't want to spend the night alone in the flat but I couldn't very well go to stay with Phil. Firstly, he and I hadn't spoken post the Kimfrontation at Papa's. Secondly, the flat he and Cammie shared was small and she was in the late stages of gestation. But most of all I couldn't go to stay with Phil because I wasn't feeling strong enough to face hours of 'Told you, Bird'.

Mum was also out because she had an over-developed capacity for worry and an acute desire for grand-progeny.

Surely there had to be someone I could impose my despondency upon. On the back of the pied flycatcher manuscript I started to list my other significant kinship and social bonds. Looking up from the page I saw an uncharacteristically sombre-looking Pippa walking up the aisle towards me. I flipped over the manuscript to conceal my scribblings.

Pippa moved a chair around and placed her hands flat on my desk.

'Kim's outside,' she whispered. 'When she couldn't find you at home she came here, but they won't let her in.' I nodded. Restricted membership was an unanticipated advantage of the library. 'She won't tell me what she's done but she says she's sorry.'

With my pen, I pointed up at the 'Silence Please' sign on the end of the bookshelf.

Pippa took the manuscript from beneath my hand and the pen from my fingers. When she finished writing on its back she turned the manuscript around to face me. It said:

*You have to talk it through.*

She handed me the pen.

*I'm not ready to talk.*

I slid the pad back across the table.

*She's really, really, really sorry.*

I nodded, though I suspected that Pippa had inflated Kim's remorsefulness. Pippa passed me the pen, but I shook my head.

*She loves you very, very much.*

I shrugged and declined the pen again.

*She wants to explain.*

I shook my head. Pippa held out the pen. I shook my head again. Pippa jabbed the pen forcefully towards me. Reluctantly, I took it and wrote:

*I can't*

I watched realisation travel down Pippa's face and she took the pen back.

*Has the silly girl done it again?*

*I'm afraid so*

Pippa grimaced.

*Do you need someone to talk to?*

I shook my head.

*Where will you stay?*

*With Phil,* I wrote.

\*\*\*

When Pippa left I called Phil and immediately apologised for ignoring him for the last few months. He didn't say anything. Then I gave a little cough and explained that Kim and I were experiencing strain on our pair-bond.

'Well I never,' he said. 'Did you try to come between her and her humanitarian work?'

'I need somewhere to stay for a couple of days.'

'Have you tried Airbnb?'

'No, I mean I really need a friend…'

'I know, Bird,' he said. 'What time shall we expect you?'

\*\*\*

Cammie hugged me and asked me how I was doing. Phil made a show of hugging me like a genial wrestler and asked me if I wanted a beer.

I sat beside him on the long grey-black futon that was to be my bed with a stubby green bottle resting on my thigh. Cammie sat on the grey bean-bag chair by the kitchen door, caressing the superior surface of her distended abdomen.

It had been more than a year since I had visited their flat and things had changed. The green patterned carpet they inherited had been replaced by one which retained much of the natural character of the fleece from which it was obtained. The walls had been painted a very pale yellow and they had erected a set of compartmented shelves above the sliding kitchen door. Small, brightly coloured bottles and vases were displayed in the individual compartments. I complimented Cammie on the tastefulness of the room. She thanked me, then, shifting her hands to the inferior aspect of her abdomen, she explained that they were looking for a bigger place.

'I told her you would only be here for a few days, but she thinks you are going to be single for a while,' said Phil.

On the wall facing the futon was a large framed colour photograph of Phil dating back to the initiation of his pair-bond with Cammie. It was almost life-size and showed him bearing down on the camera at the end of a run down a hillside covered in wild flowers. In the picture he wore only a pair of striped boxer shorts and a demonic grin. His skin looked pale against the out-of-focus lushness. It was one of those pictures that reveal something new every time you saw it; invariably it was something you wished you hadn't seen.

Phil noticed me looking at it. 'I would take it down, but Cammie loves it,' he said.

Cammie rolled her eyes.

'Does Kim know where you are, Simon?' she asked.

I nodded. 'Thank you. It's thoughtful of you to ask,' I said, glancing at Phil.

Her question prompted me to fish my phone from my pocket. I was still refusing to listen to any of the voicemails Kim had left, but I was now feeling strong enough to ingest text messages. There were three new ones from Kim and one each from Judy, Aman and Damien the Solicitor. They implored me to go home, to talk it through and to forgive. I put the phone on the table and took another swig from the warming beer.

Cammie spoke: 'Simon, you are very welcome to stay, you know that, but if you want to go and talk to Kim, don't mind us.'

'That's right, Bird,' said Phil. 'The futon's a pain in the arse to make up.'

\*\*\*

We hunched over a Chinese takeaway watching the pilot episode of some gruesome American crime thing. Halfway through, Cammie asked me if I would rather watch something else, but I said I thought it was good, though I had spent the last thirty minutes watching repeats from the Wetland Centre and miscellaneous highlights of my pair-bond with Kim.

Later, when my phone began to vibrate across the table, I felt Cammie's eyes on me. I changed the settings and slipped the phone into my back pocket.

When the crime thing finished, Cammie pulled herself out of her chair, supporting her abdomen with one hand, and said that she was going to bed, though it wasn't yet 10 pm.

'Why don't the two of you go out to The Swan for a bit?' she said.

'I've got a better idea,' said Phil.

\*\*\*

Phil's great idea comprised *Call of Duty* and two more beers.

'This is great,' he said. 'Cammie never plays. She hates the Xbox.'

'I hate the Xbox,' I said, but Phil was already on his knees at the base of the TV fiddling with consoles, cables and controllers. I reminded Phil that I found video games a) pointless and b) disorientating.

'Let's just play for a bit,' he said, his eyes glued to the screen and his backside perched on the edge of the futon – my bed – with his knees widely splayed.

Soon he was laughing loudly at my gaming inadequacies. After a few minutes I became so angry that I became determined to beat him. If anything though, I just became more incompetent. Game after game he beat me and game after game he laughed.

Eventually I felt nauseous from repeatedly turning my hapless infantryman left and right. I leaned against the back of the futon, refusing to defend myself.

'I'm getting tired,' I said, for the fourth time.

'Just a bit longer,' he said. 'I want to see if I can beat you with my bare hands.'

It was after eleven thirty when Cammie came through to complain about Phil's noisy victory dance.

I could have kissed her.

# Chapter 60

I left next morning before Phil and Cammie arose. I sat in a café with an untouched bacon roll until the library opened.

When my thoughts crowded me out of the library I spent an hour at the Wildlife Photography Exhibition at the Natural History Museum. Claire and I had always gone to the photography exhibition together, but I hadn't been since she departed. At first, as I had hoped it might, it tempered my monomaniacal grief. I enjoyed the images of a seal peering up from an ice hole, a bear framed by a cabin window and even a shamefully anthropomorphic image of a penguin spat. But then I saw the photo of a male northern gannet (*Morus bassanus*) presenting a gift of red campion to his mate and resurgent grief forced me back out on to the streets.

***

When I returned to the flat that evening, Cammie was sitting cross-legged (yoga style) on the futon with a childcare magazine, which she promptly laid to one side. Phil emerged a few minutes later. His hair was damp and he was wearing a very generous pair of stripy boxer shorts – not unlike the ones in the photo.

'Ah, Wing Commander Bird has returned safely,' he said, dropping himself gracelessly on to the futon and Cammie's magazine. 'Any progress at the front line of the battle of the sexes?' he asked, as he lurched over towards the remote on the coffee table.

'No,' I said, bristling. 'No significant developments.'

'Excellent news. Excellent. I was thinking we could either watch the TV or... or I wondered if you might want to take a look at my naughty Kim snaps, now that she's not here to scold you. Which do you fancy?'

Cammie scolded him and I told him that I thought TV would be preferable.

'Have it your way, Bird. Nip into the kitchen to get a couple of beers for us will you, oh, and get a folic acid for the little lady while you're at it.' Cammie slapped him hard on his bare thigh, only part playfully. Phil yelled and they began to wrestle. In their small kitchen I vowed to return to Acton next day.

Cammie briefly dozed off before the end of the episode and then woke, apologising. 'Are you two going to be up all night playing that stupid teenage boy game again?' she said as she bent to kiss Phil goodnight.

'I don't think so,' said Phil. 'I will end up in The Hague if I give him another battering like the one he got yesterday. Combat isn't really Bird's thing, is it, Bird?'

'No,' I said. 'Not really.'

When Cammie left, Phil began to hunt around the lounge. 'Have you seen the iPad?' he said, bending over to inspect their bookshelf. After completing a cursory lap of their lounge he demanded that I help him to look. He began to look in exactly the same places again, but more angrily. Finally he put his head inside the bedroom door and asked Cammie if she knew where the iPad was just as I had located it beneath the coffee table.

Taking the iPad from me, Phil sat back on the futon and asked me to get two more beers. I didn't want a beer, but I went to fetch him one. The electronic clock on the cooker said that it was 22:17 and when I went back through I said, 'Work tomorrow. I should really get a decent night's sleep.'

'Definitely,' he said, frowning at the iPad screen. I handed him his beer and sat back in the bean-bag chair, but he patted the seat beside him on the futon. When I joined him, he passed the iPad to me. 'There you go,' he said. 'This should be much more up your street.'

\*\*\*

But *Angry Birds* was not 'up my street'.

'Why don't you like it?' he asked. 'Is it because the birds have eyebrows?'

When his beer was finally finished, he placed the empty bottle on the table, laid the iPad down and said, 'Beaten at your own game. It's not your week is it?'

281

'No,' I said. 'It isn't.'

'Never mind. We can go to the pub tomorrow night if you like. Things might seem a bit less bleak from there.'

'Yes, they might,' I agreed, so as to get him off the futon.

With his hand on his bedroom door he said, 'I could see if Mike can join us. The two of you could swap stories about Kim Wrong Un.'

\*\*\*

Next evening Phil was standing at the bar when I walked in from the aerosol-fine drizzle.

'Ho, Bird,' he said, nodding over to our table where his green canvas jacket was hanging on the back of his chair and a brown A4 envelope was resting on the table. 'Incriminating evidence' was written on it.

*InKiminating*, I thought. I placed the envelope on Phil's chair and sat down. 'New Kid in Town' was playing. I hated 'New Kid in Town'. The table rocked over to the left just as it always had but this time it irritated me more than usual and so I placed a folded beer mat under the leg. Phil came over with the beers and settled himself in his chair.

'Well here we are again,' he grinned.

'Yes.' I told him to put the envelope away.

'Your call, Bird. I was wondering: do you think you should have stuck with the po-faced one? What was her name again?'

'I've been wondering too,' I said. 'I've been wondering... why do you always insist on being such a cock? What is it that makes you—' I pulled myself up short – Phil was grinning. He looked even happier than he did during his 'historic' *Call of Duty* 'massacre'. It was disarming.

'Go on,' he said. 'Get it out. Get it all out.'

'Why are you happiest when I am miserable? What kind of friend *are* you?' I had at that moment decided that this would be my last evening with Phil, ever. It would be *our* Swan Song.

'Good. You're angry at last. Angry's good.' He was still smiling. 'Tell me exactly what kind of cock I am. Get *really* specific.'

'I want to throw this beer in your face,' I said. 'I really do.'

'Well, if you think it would help…' he glanced over to the bar, 'but you know what Jim's like about spillages.'

'What? Look, I know you don't like Kim, Phil, but you know I valued our pair-bond. Why couldn't you show me just a little bit of empathy? Just once?'

'I didn't think empathy was what you needed.' He picked up his pint.

'You haven't even *tried* to talk to me about what happened.'

'You said you didn't want to talk about it.'

'I didn't... I don't... Not all the time, but you could have shown *some* interest. You could have expressed non-specific concern rather than spending two evenings indulging your own juvenile desire for superiority.'

'Would you have talked about it if I did?' He took an unflustered sip. Did he truly not care about anything but himself?

'Maybe not, but I'm ready to tell you now,' I said, threateningly. 'I'm willing to share every nuanced emotion with you, and, be warned, there aren't too many emotions I haven't felt since Saturday.'

'Good,' he said. 'Tell me everything.' He leaned back in his chair, rubbing his shoulders against the backrest the way a cow might rub itself against a fence.

I'd wanted to see horror in his eyes, but there was none. He was denying me even that. 'Are you... Are you asking me to take my Swan Song?' I asked.

'Jesus man, no! Don't bother with that. Just talk to me. Take as long as you like... I'll listen, I promise.'

What was going on? Was Phil so determined to remain in control that he was prepared to withstand unconstrained outpourings of emotion just so long as it was his idea?

Determined to make him suffer for his folly, I told him what had happened, what I thought about it and, knowing that he feared it the most, I told him how I felt. I told him what Kim meant to me. I spoke of love, jealousy, pain, anger, loss and of emptiness. He finished his pint and I kept going. My soundtrack included Paul Weller, Macy Gray, Van Morrison, Green Day and many more, as they used to say about compilations. Finally, as Bill Withers recalled his grandma's hands, I had said all there was to be said.

I braced myself.

'I'm sorry, Bird,' he said. 'That is totally messed up. What are you going to do?'

'I don't know yet,' I said, warily.

'Well, Cammie and I will… you know… well, we'll be there for you, you know, whatever you decide.'

'Thanks.'

'If there is anything we can do…'

'Thanks.'

'And you are right, you do deserve better. Much better.'

'Thanks…'

To buy myself some processing time, I gathered the glasses and went to the bar. While waiting to be served, I kept looking back over at the table. Phil saw me and nodded empathetically. He looked as though he too was trying to brave.

I was still expecting a Weapon of Mass Derision when I got back to the table, but Phil just thanked me for the beer. He even went over to the bar to retrieve the two packs of crisps and the change I left there without commenting.

'What do you think I should do?' I said.

He shrugged. 'Nobody can tell you that.'

I probed and prompted but Phil wouldn't be drawn. He wouldn't even joke. 'What's going on?' I said. 'First Kim betrays me and then you offer emotional support. Are none of my assumptions about the way the world works valid?'

'Cammie says I have to let you make up your own mind, whatever happens.'

'Wow, first a flat without a visible bong, then listening and now this. It's a lot to take in, Phil.'

'The thing is, Bird, my personal prejudices have no validity in the context of the challenges you are experiencing.' As he spoke I observed that the crisps lay unopened.

'Did Cammie say that as well?'

'Word for word.'

After this first small confession, it didn't take very long for Phil to engineer a way to share his full opinion with me. 'Here's what we'll do,' he said. 'You tell me about the options that you are considering. I will *listen* to each one of them. *I will not judge them in any way.* I will, however, hold up a mirror,' – he presented his highly non-reflective hand – 'to help you to see your comments from a fresh perspective, or some such bollocks. Does that sound OK?'

'Yes,' I said. 'But I still want to know why you've been such a cock until now.'

'I told you – I needed to help you to find your anger.'

'Was that Cammie's idea?'

'No, it was mine,' he said. 'She thought it was really stupid, but sometimes you just have to follow your instincts. Right, come on – tell me what you are thinking. Remember, *I won't judge*. You are in a safe place. Oh, we need another pint first though.'

\*\*\*

I explained that, as I saw it, I had two basic options. Phil was nodding at woodpecker-like frequency, to show his support. 'First, I'm considering not going back to Kim, which means starting again at the age of thirty-seven.'

'Sounds good,' he said.

'I thought you weren't going to be judging.'

'It's not judging when you agree is it? It's agreeing.'

'It's still judging.'

'Well I'm sorry about that – *if* you're right – but don't clam up now, Bird, keep going. You are doing great.' He smiled and patted me on the arm.

'My second option is the opposite.'

'How do you mean?'

'I mean I could go back to Kim. We could try to work through our differences. She sounds contrite in her messages.'

'I'm not judging,' he said, lifting his hands high in the air.

'In many ways it's the most rational option.'

'Boy, do you need to take a good, hard look in my mirror of wisdom.'

'Look, she made an error of judgement. It happens. But now she can see that she might lose me and she's scared, I can tell. If I can find a way to forgive her, I know she wouldn't take that risk again.'

'No. Maybe she'll hide your binoculars or next time she screws a guy she'll make sure she's at least five hundred yards away.' Sneering he opened the crisps.

'She didn't copulate with him,' I said, leaning over the table and lowering my voice.

285

'Of course she did.'

'She swears she didn't.'

'Ah, well, I stand corrected. She must have gone in there looking for a cormorant.' He lifted a crisp. 'Or maybe it was a shag. I still can't tell the difference.'

'That's not funny, Phil.'

'Maybe it isn't. I'm sorry, Bird.' And he genuinely did look sorry. 'It's her. The way she treats you. She's so selfish.'

'We're all selfish – to a certain extent.'

'The trouble with you, Bird, is you give your brain one vote and your balls a vote each.'

'That's not fair. My pair-bond with Kim was never just about copulation, though that aspect was certainly very satisfying.'

'It was, Bird. It was precisely about sex. It's powerful juju. Think about it this way: what advice would you give me if Cammie did the same thing?'

'I could never ever judge Cammie. Society owes her a great debt,' I said. Phil chuckled, finding an unintended compliment within my insult. 'I love her, Phil,' I said. 'I always will.' Phil closed his eyes, cocked his head back and slowly rubbed its top. 'And we really don't have much say in it. Male choice is an illusion.'

Phil lowered his head, slowly opened his eyes and spoke with unusual care and precision. 'Of all the not inconsiderable bollocks you have ever spoken, Bird, that is probably the worst. If you decide not to go back to Cruella – you don't go back. *Your choice.* I can see that it might be a *difficult* choice. I can tell that it isn't what you want to do – but you *can* choose it. Or you can, if you have no self-respect or dignity, *choose* to go back to her. And who knows? That might even make you happy for a while – until it makes you miserable. Either way though, at least have the courage to admit that it's *your* decision. You aren't a bird, Bird.' He pressed a hand against the table and began to stand. 'Now, I need a piss,' he said.

'When you come back, you can start judging if you like,' I said.

# Chapter 61

*June*

I went back to Kim.

Our re-pairing was demarcated into three distinct phases.

In Phase A, the A was for awkward. We were relieved to be reunited, but self-consciously so. It was as if we needed to draw up the rules and the rhythms of our relationship anew. And, of course, we were both very aware of the fragility of our pair-bond. Fortunately, Phase A was a short one.

The relief that accompanied the re-emergence of confidence and familiarity propelled us into 'Buoyant' Phase B. Holding hands beneath the table in Papa's we agreed that while un-pairing had been painful and neither of us wanted to go through anything like that again, it had made our pair-bond stronger and more resilient. Phil didn't buy this theory of course. However, he was too sleep-deprived by the arrival of his progeny for overt scepticism. We felt renewed confidence in 'Us', and an anxious determination to show the world that our pair-bond was impregnable and so I moved in with Kim.

At first I mistook the arrival of Phase C for a transient blip in Phase B, but transience does not, by definition, linger.

Phase C was not characterised by Conflict or Collapse. We were still Close. We Cuddled, Caressed, Copulated and Co-habited. But my feelings had Changed.

\*\*\*

And then I got distracted by Consuela ('Chelo'). Her work on sperm competition in rodents was highly respected, but the thought of collaborating with her had never occurred to me because, well, rodents aren't birds.

She sent an email, totally out of the blue, saying she wanted my opinion about something. Intrigued, I called her.

'I will make it fun for you,' she said. 'I will send you sixteen micrographs of passerine sperm at identical magnification. I will tell you which one of these is *Pyrrhula erythaca* (grey-headed bullfinch) and I will give you the names of the fifteen other species. I only want you to guess which sperm is from *Pyrrhula pyrrhula* (Eurasian bullfinch).' I was having fun already just listening to her; her Spanish tongue must have vibrated like the wing of a hummingbird as she spoke those names.

***

The sperm images she sent were from species as diverse as the tiny wren (*Troglodytes troglodytes*) and the raven (*Corvus corax*). Compared to Chelo I knew very little about sperm, but I still knew an acrosome from a flagellum, and I knew that comparative sperm morphology could be used to predict evolutionary relationships between species. I spent a few minutes staring at the micrograph of the *erythaca* sperm. It looked like a pretty typical passerine sperm to my eye. I pulled a ruler from my desk drawer and took some rough measurements. Then, since *Pyrrhula pyrrhula* is *erythaca's* closest living relative, naturally, I set about trying to identify which of the other fifteen images most closely resembled it.

I immediately eliminated Micrograph E because the acrosome was round (rather than helical) and the midsection was very short. I assumed that Chelo had included it as a joke because biologists can be like that. I also quickly eliminated a handful of the other micrographs on the basis of size. This still left me with half a dozen images to choose from. Chelo was right, it was fun.

Finding it almost impossible to decide between the remaining images I pulled my calculator out of the drawer and began to work up a few ratios (head length to total sperm length, that kind of thing). But for all that, when I emailed Chelo declaring that in my opinion the *Pyrrhula pyrrhula* sperm was probably Micrograph F, it was a guess, albeit one calculated to two decimal places.

Chelo called me back the next morning. 'And your second guess?' she asked.

'Ah... I don't know... B?'

'Wrong again.'

I guessed a third time. I was wrong a third time. At that point further guesses would have been, well, guesses.

'OK, I will tell you,' she said. 'The *Pyrrhula pyrrhula*...' – ah, the pleasure of that sound – 'sample is Micrograph E.'

'Very funny, Chelo,' I said. 'I spent over an hour messing around with the images. Tell me the real answer.'

'It's Micrograph E.'

'I don't mean to be rude, Chelo, but I think you've got your samples mixed up.'

Chelo didn't take offence. 'That's what I thought at first, but we sampled three more birds. There is no error, I assure you. What do you know about *Pyrrhula pyrrhula*, Simon?'

I couldn't tell her much. The Eurasian bullfinch, being shy of nature, hadn't caught the attention of the scientific community and so I knew only what any amateur ornithologist might know. I knew that the Eurasian bullfinch pair-bond was perceived to be very strong and that, once paired, the male and female rarely leave each other's sight. I knew that even a brief separation could be unsettling for them and that when reunited the male would regurgitate food into the female's beak to re-establish the bond. I knew that both genders contributed to feeding of the brood, and that the feeding continues even after fledging and that the feeding effort is so intense that both male and female develop temporary pouches in their mouths to enable them to take larger quantities of food back to the nest.

Chelo sounded disappointed. 'Why is the sperm morphology so unusual if there is little competition between males? It makes no sense.'

\*\*\*

I tried out Chelo's 'sperm competition' on Gustavo and Prof and it foxed both of them too.

I made myself a tuna sandwich when I got home that evening and sat on the pink sofa watching the news while I waited for Kim to get home.

When I finished masticating, I got out my laptop and went on to the publications database in search of deeper bullfinch insights.

As I suspected, there wasn't much. I had just found an article about comparative sexual anatomy in passerines when I heard Kim's key in the door.

She was slightly euphoric and her cheeks were bullfinch pink. She came over to kiss me and then kneeled by the side of the sofa to tell me a confusing story about a pizza. I smiled and moved the laptop off my lap so that she could occupy it, as per her request. With her head resting on my shoulder she began to stroke the opening of my shirt. When we heard the intro music for the local news she patted my chest and whispered, 'Time for bed.'

'Hmm. Getting that way.'

'I'm going to quickly jump in the shower.'

'I'll just shut the laptop down, and then I'll come through.'

And I fully intended to do just that, but when I opened up the laptop the comparative anatomy article was there and, figuring I had a few more minutes, I read on. I became very intrigued when I read that Eurasian bullfinch testicles are very small, even when corrected for bodyweight. *Hmmm*, I thought. The paper cited another paper about bullfinch ecology which also sounded interesting.

Kim arrived in the doorway, wrapped in a fluffy pink towel. 'What could possibly be keeping you in that chair when there is a clean, warm, and very naughty female waiting for you?' she said.

'Bullfinch,' I said.

'Precisely,' she said.

'I'll close it down.'

'Good decision,' she said, then, 'Oops! Clumsy me.' When I looked up Kim was gloriously naked and her towel was crumpled by her feet.

'Won't be a second,' I said. When Kim left I had every intention of shutting down the laptop, but I doubted that Kim would know precisely how long this would take and a couple of extra minutes became a few minutes became a while…

\*\*\*

The flat felt oddly silent when I finally closed the laptop. I placed it gently on the coffee table and tiptoed across the lounge. I stepped over the pink towel that resembled a melted scoop of strawberry ice-cream. The bedroom door was slightly ajar and I was able to slip quietly into the darkened room. Kim lay silent and motionless beneath the duvet. I undressed in the dark and carefully slid into bed. When my arrival didn't elicit a response, I assumed she was in a deep sleep. To avoid waking her I tried to cover myself as best as I could with the limited quantity of duvet available.

Lying on my back, gently gripping the edge of the duvet, I started to think about bullfinch sperm morphology once again. Kim shifted towards me, freeing a little more duvet. *Why should a species which appeared to be unusually monogamous have evolved such a unique sperm morphology?* Kim moved closer still.

Then it came to me: perhaps it was a *reduction* in selective pressure, rather than an increase, which had driven the change. Perhaps *Pyrrhula pyrrhula* sperm had gradually become, to use a very unscientific term, 'rubbish' because they *didn't* need to compete with sperm of other males.

This new hypothesis was so satisfying that a little 'Hmmmmm' escaped from my lips.

Kim shuffled across to rest pressed against my side and draped an arm across my abdomen. She kissed my chest then brought her lips close to my ear, whispering, 'Can't you sleep, honey?'

'Not really,' I replied, turning my head towards her as best as I could, 'I've managed to get myself too worked up about blessed bullfinches.'

Kim executed a slow half-roll away from me.

\*\*\*

I called Chelo early the next morning. Unable to contain my enthusiasm I blurted out my reduced selective pressure theory followed by a few of the many study ideas that had landed in the branches of my brain overnight. 'I really want to collaborate with you on this, Chelo,' I said. 'I can get us money. I know I can.'

She laughed throatily. 'Has anyone ever told you that you are an easy catch, Simon?'

\*\*\*

I hadn't felt so excited about the prospect of a study since meeting Mats. I told Kim about it at Papa's that evening. 'We want to dig much deeper to really understand why monogamy is so beneficial for that species. Time is short though, unfortunately and so I'm afraid I need to fly out to Barcelona on Friday evening so that we can formulate a plan on Saturday. You don't mind, honey, do you?'

'No, of course not,' she said. 'I could come with you if you like.'

I put a whole dough ball in my mouth and wondered why the idea of Kim accompanying me hadn't occurred to me.

'You hadn't thought about that, had you?' she said. I shook my head. 'And you've already booked your ticket haven't you?'

I nodded. 'We still might be able to get you a ticket.'

'It doesn't matter,' she said. 'It was a bad idea.'

\*\*\*

Chelo and I spent the morning cooped up in the red brick building of the Faculty of Biology of the University of Barcelona. At lunchtime she took me out into the spring sunshine. We crossed the road and walked over to the gardens of the Palau de Reial de Pedralbes, home to hundreds of squabbling parakeets.

We ate lunch at a rustic-style restaurant with red clay floor tiles, navy blue runners and napkins, and white marble table tops. When a bowl of fat green olives arrived I briefly broke off from my preoccupation with sample size and data collection concerns to tell Chelo about Kim's passion for olives.

'I know where to take you,' she said.

\*\*\*

We concluded our discussions that afternoon strolling through the city centre and taking in the modernist majesty of La Sagrada Familia.

With just a few minutes remaining before my departure, Chelo took me beneath the flying-carpet-like roof of Santa Caterina Market. There, she led me briskly past the displays of fish, cured meats and vibrant, tightly packed fruit to her favourite olive stall.

\*\*\*

Kim's hair was piled up and her feet were curled beneath her thighs on the pink sofa when I returned. A magazine was open in her lap and the TV was on low in the background. I kissed her and gave her the olives.

She thanked me and then put them down on the carpet. I sat down beside her.

'You don't love me like you used to,' she said.

'I thought you loved olives,' I said.

Kim gave a short laugh that was short on pleasure. 'I do love olives. This isn't about olives.'

# Chapter 62

*September*

When the estate agent's mini pulled up, I pulled up the hood of my waterproof, though the rain had almost stopped, and got out of my car.

I didn't lower the hood until we had climbed the stairs and entered the lounge. Detecting volatile paint molecules in the air, I looked around at the four white walls, the three bare shelves, the two curtain poles and the one black velour sofa.

The estate agent turned to face me. Able to see my face for the first time, she appeared perplexed.

'Did I show you 42 Cowper Road the other day?' she asked.

'Not me,' I said. Keen to avoid recognition I asked how far away the tube was, though I already knew.

When I had completed my brief tour of the flat the estate agent was on her phone in the lounge. I waved my hands to signal that I was happy for her to complete the conversation, but she ended it.

'Shall I show you the bedrooms?'

I shook my head. 'I looked already.'

She pursed her lips. 'We should have more two-beds coming on in the next week or so.'

'I like this one,' I said.

'Oh. I thought—'

'That I didn't look very enthusiastic?' Her head wobbled. 'I used to live just a couple of streets away. I just wasn't expecting to be coming back so soon – that's all.'

\*\*\*

While there were zero ways to determine whether Kim and I had done the right thing, there were a seemingly infinite number of ways to brood upon it.

Work was the only thing that seemed to help and so I plunged into it like a peregrine (*Falco peregrinus*) into a flock of starlings (*Sturnus vulgaris*). I flogged poor Gustavo into submission (of his PhD thesis). And I sent bullfinch grant proposals to every funding body known to *Homo sapiens*.

\*\*\*

When Chelo and I heard that one of the applications had been successful we were relieved but we weren't in the mood for pyrrhula pyrotechnics because we were only awarded money for a single year, rather than the two we had requested.

Given the short tenure of the grant I was worried we wouldn't attract high-quality Post Docs but applications quickly began to arrive. Prof drily suggested that applicants might be thinking they would get a chance to 'snog' Cassie.

Of the first four CVs only one made it into my green 'shortlist' folder. Scanning the fifth CV I was jolted when I read that the applicant had worked in the group of Dr Mats Carlsson in Uppsala. I quickly turned back to the front page and there at the top in bold type was the name of Charlotta Ronja Anderson. Charlotta!

My initial delight lasted for just a few moments. With just one year of funding, we needed to generate results quickly. While Charlotta was undoubtedly talented, with a string of high-impact publications in her own field, we needed someone who could establish a bellowing of bullfinches, not a vocalisation expert.

\*\*\*

I developed a simple plan: I identified four high-quality candidates. Of these, Nuri from Cornell, who had done first-class work with *Emberizidae*, was my alpha candidate. I also included Charlotta, making five.

Before the interviews I called Chelo to inform her about my friendship with Charlotta. I did not tell her about Charlotta's injury-time EPC proposition. As I spoke I could hear Chelo inhaling sharply on her cigarette. 'I know Charlotta doesn't have the right experience,' I said, 'but I feel that I owe her an interview. Do you understand?'

'No problem,' said Chelo, exhaling.

Finally – and this was my masterstroke – I asked Prof to join us for the interviews. I figured that this would allow me to tell Charlotta that I had been outnumbered when delivering the bad news.

***

When the Toronto candidate withdrew, we were down to four. We met Constance (*Lyrurus tetrix*) from Edinburgh first and later that same day we conducted the interview with Nuri of Cornell via video conference.

Nuri was ahead, for me, at the end of the first day. But over dinner Chelo expressed reservations about his emotional maturity. I nodded and made a mental note to read more about emotional maturity considerations in the context of candidate selection.

***

I woke early the next morning, dreading the interview with Charlotta.

I met the AV technician in the conference suite at Empirical just before eight am and he initiated the call. A black chair, empty, appeared on the wall-mounted plasma screen in front of me. I looked at my watch and towards the door, willing Prof and Chelo to arrive. But Charlotta, or, to be more specific, her torso, clad in a navy blue V-neck T-shirt, appeared first.

The T-shirt disappeared from view and then her face appeared. She sat close to the screen, too close, and because the top of her head was cut off she resembled a face with blonde curtains. Her eyes seemed paler than when I last saw her. Or was it just that her skin was darker now?

I could tell that the PC wished to express an opinion about Charlotta, but since splitting with Kim I had learned to suppress him more effectively.

'Sorry! Big scary face!' said Charlotta, rolling the chair back. 'How are you, Simon?'

'Hej, Charlotta,' I said, looking towards the door again. 'Great to see you.'

'Can I go now, Dr Selwood?' said the technician, sweeping his long brown hair back over his head.

'Just stay a few minutes longer, please,' I said, not wishing to be left alone with Charlotta.

'It'll be fine now,' he said.

'Give it a couple of minutes, just in case, please.'

Fortunately, Prof and Chelo arrived with coffee and pastries before the technician left.

***

The format for the interviews was tightly prescribed to reduce variables and thus minimise subjectivity.

After completing the introductions, I spoke about the insights that sparked the study, our research objectives and an outline of the proposed methodology. Charlotta listened intently and made occasional notes. I deviated from my script only once and at the end of the intro: 'And so you see, there won't be a vocalisation component.'

'Yes, I see,' said Charlotta.

I felt terrible for her, but I had no choice. 'Unless you've got any initial questions we would like to understand a bit more about how you would approach the study,' I said.

'I've got lots of questions,' said Charlotta brightly, 'but they can wait.' Was that a slight Aussie twang I was detecting?

'OK,' I said, taking a deep breath. I really wished I didn't have to ask the first, brutal question. 'Given that we will have to establish a captive bullfinch colony to address the research objectives, can you tell us about your own experience of establishing a captive colony.' As I awaited her answer, I thought back guiltily over the efforts Charlotta had made to make me feel welcome in Uppsala and of the courageous feedback she had offered after my Piccadilly reading.

'Well,' she said, 'over the last twelve months I have set up a superb fairy wren colony. Is that the kind of thing you mean? I know that the aviculture of *Pyrrhula pyrrhula* can be challenging, but *Malurus cyaneus* are tricky too and I'm pretty stoked about how it all worked out.'

'Stoked?' I said, as I flicked back to Charlotta's publications, running my finger down the list. I couldn't recall seeing any *Malurus cyaneus* publications. My finger was running down the list again when I heard Charlotta's once so familiar laugh.

'Sorry,' she said, 'I meant we are optimistically cautious about the study.'

'Cautiously optimistic perhaps?' said Prof.

'Is that better?' she asked and this time I heard the Australian accent for sure. Her better was definitely bitter.

I looked up to the screen again. 'I'm sorry, Charlotta, I can't see anything about *Malurus cyaneus* here.'

'Oh, no,' she said, 'Sorry, I'm working on the manuscript. JAB want another couple of graphs.'

'JAB?' I said. 'Good for you.'

'Is that good?' said Chelo.

'It's pretty good,' said Charlotta.

'It's a *really* good journal,' I said.

'You must be "stoked", Dr Anderson,' said Prof.

'Reckon,' said Charlotta, laughing for a second time.

I wasn't laughing though. We still hadn't addressed the core issue regarding Charlotta's candidacy. I plucked the white plastic lid from my coffee and as the steam rose up, warming my face, I considered the most humane way to state my follow-up question.

'And what did you learn about the song of *Malurus cyaneus*?' I said, glancing at Chelo so she understood the significance of the question.

'Oh, I wasn't studying song,' said Charlotta.

'OK,' I said, now just slightly annoyed by her evasiveness. 'What did you learn about *Malurus cyaneus* vocalisation?'

'I wasn't studying vocalisation either.'

I put my pen down on the table. 'OK, Charlotta, why *were* you studying *Malurus cyaneus*?'

'Well,' Charlotta smiled, 'a colleague discovered something very interesting. He found that there are two distinct types of male *Malurus cyaneus*. One type have short, fat-headed sperm. The other type have long, slim-headed sperm.' I heard Chelo's chair edge closer to the screen. 'And I started to wonder *why*. I mean *why* should these two types of male sperm coexist?'

\*\*\*

298

It took us a full hour to get past that question. Chelo just couldn't let the *Malurus cyaneus* sperm question go and Prof was clearly fascinated too. After almost two hours and with questions still swirling around Charlotta like a murmuration, I had to draw the interview to a close because we were late for the final candidate.

\*\*\*

After the final interview, Chelo needed a cigarette. Outside the lift, I suggested we should debrief over lunch before Chelo's flight, but Prof had another appointment.

'It's your call, Selwood,' he said.

'I agree,' said Chelo, the cigarette already in her fingers. 'You need to choose. It's you who will have to work with her or him every day.'

'Her or him?' I said.

Prof and Chelo looked at each other, each trying to read the other's thoughts. The lift door opened.

'Well it has to be Charlotta Anderson,' said Chelo. Prof nodded. 'She is easily the best candidate. *Easily*. And, this isn't the main thing, but she can also start immediately.' She looked at Prof.

'No, I agree,' he said. 'I mean, like I said, it's one hundred per cent your choice, Selwood, but you would be crazy to go for anyone other than Anderson. In my opinion.'

And so my choice was made for me.

# Chapter 63

*January*

I wondered how Charlotta would feel about flying away from the Australian summer, but she seemed to rejoice in the frosts that accompanied her first days in London.

Chelo had suggested that Charlotta might feel isolated for a while, and so I enlisted the support of Pippa, Judy and also Nat. I also researched local karaoke facilities, in case of emergencies.

However, in our first meeting in my office, Charlotta seemed as happy as a skylark (*Alauda arvensis*). As the meeting drew to a close she confessed that she still had a 'little bit' of *Malurus cyaneus* writing to finish. Instinctively I felt a 'little bit' concerned; after all, we didn't have long to get everything organised, but I said nothing.

Remembering that she was late for an appointment with a prospective landlady Charlotta hastily packed away her pen and notebook. I had been going to suggest a lunch with Pippa later in the week but she was in too much of a hurry. *It can wait for tomorrow*, I thought.

But I didn't see Charlotta again until the end of the week. Whenever I'd looked in on her desk she hadn't been there and so I thought I would try the library and it proved to be a lucky hunch.

'Is everything OK?' I whispered.

Nodding vigorously, she grinned and pointed at one of those 'Silence please' signs that I had previously used to suppress Pippa. She began to write a note on the back of a photocopied paper: *Need me to come out?*

*No*, I wrote beneath it, *Just wanted to say hi.*

\*\*\*

By the end of the next week I was getting more worried. I had hardly seen Charlotta at all and I was becoming concerned that the superb fairy wren was taking more of her time than we could afford.

And then she walked into my office with a full plan. She had secured space at the Croxton Park Campus for twenty aviaries. She had quotations for the aviaries themselves, including assembly. She had recommendations regarding vegetation and nesting, sensibly plumping for baskets rather than natural hawthorn and blackthorn. She had also given extensive thought to nutrition so as to reduce the risk of atoxoplasma. As she sat across the desk from me in a navy blue University of Queensland hoodie with her pale hair cascading, I was full of admiration.

\*\*\*

Chelo shouldn't have worried about Charlotta because she quickly formed a number of social bonds. In fact, if anyone was feeling socially isolated it was me post the birth of Phil and Cammie's progeny.

It was good to hear that Charlotta and Pippa had hit it off. Pippa told me that she had already introduced Charlotta to Sebastian and 'Dukie' and that Charlotta had introduced her to the delights of karaoke. The thought of Pippa with a microphone sent a shudder down my auditory canal.

\*\*\*

After the formalities of the naming ceremony were over Phil suggested a pint in The Swan. It was there, as he bounced Trinny on his knee that I presented Cammie with my gift: a silver-plated swan money box.

'Look, Phil,' she said. 'It is cute, no?'

'Thanks, Bird. She's down to her last four money boxes. Aren't you my angel?'

Cammie swiped at his arm.

'Don't worry, Cammie. He doesn't get to me anymore,' I said.

'I thought you said you were bringing someone, Simon,' she said.

'I said I might. It was just an idea.'

'Uncle Bird's been blown out, hasn't he?' said Phil, rubbing his nose against Trinny's. 'Yes he has. *Yes* he has.'

'Charlotta is an old friend, Cammie,' I said. 'I just thought she might enjoy meeting some people, given that she's new to the city.'

'Ah, so just a friend?' said Cammie.

'A friend he almost *intercoursed*,' said Phil, rubbing his nose against Trinny's.

'As usual, that's not *exactly* true, Cammie,' I said. 'And it was several years ago, pre-Kim obviously.' Knowing that Phil was impervious to explanations, I told Cammie that Charlotta unfortunately already had plans for the afternoon.

'Sounds like that particular bird has flown,' said Phil. 'Never mind, you're bound to meet someone narcissistic and self-centred eventually.'

\*\*\*

I was away at a conference when the first bullfinches were due to arrive. Charlotta texted me to let me know that most of the birds had been delayed and that only a solitary male had arrived. I was concerned, because bullfinches are sociable birds, but Charlotta said she could handle it.

She sounded confident, and I trusted her judgement and skill, but all the same I headed straight to Croxton Park when I landed.

'Simon, meet Dominic,' she said as we approached the aviary.

'Dominic?'

'Yes, the popular name for *Pyrrhula pyrrhula* in my country is dom,' she smiled. As we stood there looking into the cage with our fingers pressed against the mesh the male surprised me by flying over towards us. He landed on an apple branch just a few inches away from Charlotta's wind-pinked face, then slowly he edged along the branch towards us. When he was almost beside her, he regurgitated. Charlotta held out a finger, tentative with guilt, to accept his gift.

When he flew back across the aviary Charlotta's eyes avoided mine.

'Charlotta,' I said.

'Uh huh.'

'Charlotta, if he imprints on you he may not form a pair-bond. You know that.'

She nodded as he flew back across the cage towards her once again.

'I know. I'm sorry,' she said.

\*\*\*

302

However, Dominic did form a pair-bond. He and 'Dominique the Dominatrix' as she became known, quickly became inseparable. They paid little or no attention to the birds in the adjoining aviaries.

\*\*\*

A week later, as per the study protocol, we introduced a second female to Dominic's aviary. Charlotta observed that Dom, like the majority of the males, was all but oblivious to the presence of the second female.

When, again as per protocol, we removed Dominique, Dom still ignored the impostor female. He spent the whole of that afternoon flying back and forth across the cage making a low mournful call.

\*\*\*

Though she hadn't actually complained, I could tell that Charlotta was finding this phase of the study stressful and so I headed down to Croxton Park to provide moral support.

From the end of the long row of mesh cages I could see Charlotta crouched inside Dominic's aviary in her now familiar black woollen hat and green coat. At first I feared that she was infringing the study protocol, especially when I heard and saw the cage door crash back in the breeze. Walking along the row of aviaries towards her I carefully considered what to say, if, as I suspected, her actions were jeopardising the study.

As I got closer I could see that she was slumped back in the aviary doorway, her back resting against the cast-iron frame. She must have heard my steps on the path, but she didn't look around. I grabbed the door of the cage just in time to prevent the wind from crashing it into her back.

'Charlotta?' I said, quietly. She didn't move. 'Charlotta, what's wrong?' She said something, but I couldn't hear it in the wind. 'Charlotta, tell me.'

She looked up. Her face, raw from the days spent patrolling the aviary, was streaked. 'Dom's gone,' she sobbed.

She lifted her right hand. Cupped in it was Dom's small corpse. He was lying on his back with his black bead eyes closed; his rose-coloured breast feathers were ruffling in the breeze.

303

And that was the moment, as I gazed down at her cheeks, wet with lacrimal fluid, that I realised how powerfully I had become imprinted on Charlotta.

I reached down to touch her on the shoulder. 'I'm sorry.'

She nodded, her eyes still fixed on Dom.

Kneeling beside her, I felt the cold rain seep through my chinos and the powerful emotions rising within me, but I had absolutely no idea what to say.

# Chapter 64

*May, The Swan, Acton*

'I need some advice.'

'Inevitably,' said Phil, sliding his empty glass towards me.

When I returned with beer *and* crisps I confessed the depth of my feelings for Charlotta.

Phil laughed. He also looked up towards the ceiling, shook his head and pushed his tongue into his bulging cheek. Mostly though, he laughed.

'Thanks, Phil, that's been very helpful.'

Phil began to explain my predicament to an imaginary bystander. 'Finally he meets a woman who isn't po-faced or demonic. Which would be great, except he's her boss. He's got a genetic death wish, I swear he has.'

'What should I do?'

'Do? Well, as one who has spent years helping others to navigate the dark human resources marshland—'

My expression – pure stupefaction – actually stopped him, briefly.

'Do you want my advice or not?' he asked. 'I thought so. In my highly sought-after *professional* opinion, you've got three pretty shitty options. You could resign, but then what else could *you* do? Plus, she might not dig you.'

'Well, she did solicit a copulation.'

Phil picked up one of the packets of crisps. 'Years ago, Bird. It might just have been a momentary engorgement. Plus she knows you better now. *And* I haven't finished.' Phil paused to pop open the crisps in his underarm – like a corvid he is skilled at devising novel ways to access food. 'Given that you are highly institutionalised and couldn't survive if released into the real world, you should consider either *waiting* for her to leave your employ or, and this is my strong recommendation: *get-the-hell-over-it.*'

'Waiting?' I said. 'Charlotta's here for another eight months.'

'Where do you stand on self-immolation?' said Phil.

***

And so the waiting began. Waiting for the tube, for example, or for a pied flycatcher to return to a nest box, is a passive act. Such waiting is characterised by an absence of effort. The effort required to wait for Charlotta, however, was considerable. This was especially so because, as Phil had kindly pointed out, Charlotta gave no indication that she continued to 'dig' me. And, as the PC kindly pointed out on a daily basis, she was a very attractive female.

Ranked below in ascending order of anguish are some of the waiting challenges I endured over that seemingly endless spring and summer:

1. First, Pippa alerted me that she intended to introduce Charlotta to the same Daniel who had failed to charm Janet.
2. The Life Sciences summer barbecue: there I observed Charlotta flitting to and from the makeshift dance floor with Gustavo and thereafter with a seemingly endless stream of male members of staff, each a more accomplished dancer than his predecessor.
3. Learning that Charlotta had formed a transient pair-bond with an unknown male.

But worse, much worse, was yet to come.

***

Initially, when Charlotta suggested that she should spend September in Barcelona with Chelo in order to start pulling together the bullfinch analysis, I was actually slightly relieved. Observing her on a daily basis had been emotionally exhausting.

On the morning of her return Charlotta bounded and beamed into my office in red jeans and a grey jumper with black shoulders. Getting to my feet, I tried to appear merely very pleased to see her.

In the fourth-floor common room I made coffee. I felt tiny, high-frequency adrenaline tremblings in my fingers as I stirred them.

As we walked back to my office Charlotta informed me that the analysis had gone well. 'But I need more time,' she said.

'Sure,' I said, closing my office door behind me. 'I wasn't expecting it to be finished. Any surprises?'

'Urm, no… But, yes.' Charlotta looked into her coffee. 'I need to talk to you about something.'

'Right…' I said, distending the word. Charlotta's tone sounded ominous. Was it something or some-Juan?

'About the Royal Society Fellowship,' she said.

I relaxed again – so that was all it was. We had discussed the fellowships before she went away; while highly competitive, they were her best opportunity to find independent funding and also the gateway to building her own group.

'Yes, you can't miss the deadline,' I said.

'I didn't.' Charlotta's coffee was still fascinating her.

'Oh,' I said. 'Last time we spoke you were still undecided between *Passer domesticus* and *Parus major*. Which way did you go?'

Charlotta placed her mug down on my desk. Reflexively I pushed a coaster towards it.

'Thanks… I went… I went for *Mus musculus* in the end,' she said, bashfully.

I laughed, because there was no way that Charlotta was going to study mice because, well, mice are not birds. 'Great idea. I can see it now. "Short communication: Visually impaired common mice (*Mus musculus*) utilise speed to evade the spouses of agriculturalists." Or, no this one's even better: "Identification of a rare Dutch mutant that goes clip-clippety-clop on the stairs."'

'Simon, I'm serious,' she said.

'Oh,' I said. 'But—'

'This doesn't mean that I don't love birds anymore.'

'No. Of course not,' I said, though I couldn't see how that could possibly be true under the circumstances.

'I will probably study birds again, one day.'

'Well there are over nine thousand species you haven't studied yet,' I said. I might have sounded a tad defensive.

'I know. I know… It's just… I got talking with Chelo about her rodent work.'

'Chelo,' I said, glaring over towards my office door, as if daring my Spanish collaborator to walk in to face my wrath.

'It's not Chelo's fault, Simon.'

'Well whose fault is it then? I mean *Mus musculus*? What are you planning to do with… with… with… them?'

'I'm going to study their song,' Charlotta smiled and leaned forward, unable to suppress her enthusiasm. 'They utilise ultrasonic vocalisations during courtship. Did you know that? It's always been assumed that it's the male who does all the singing, but I've been looking in to it and I suspect that the females are singing too. I'm going to untangle the mysteries of mouse song.'

'*If* the panel approve the proposal,' I said. Charlotta's mouth opened and then closed again. She reached out for her mug. 'Charlotta? Is there something else you aren't telling me?'

'They did approve it. I heard last Thursday.'

'Congratulations, Charlotta,' I said, getting to my feet. Leaning over the corner of my desk, I hugged her briefly, loosely and asexually. 'You totally deserve it and I'm thrilled for you.' While all of this was true, and I didn't want to detract from Charlotta's joy, I would have been majorly more thrilled for her if she was going to spend the next five years studying *Parus major*, for example. 'A Royal Society Fellowship will set you up to achieve wonderful things with, with… that species.' I retook my seat.

'Thank you, Simon,' she said, sitting back down herself. 'I appreciate that. I know this isn't easy for you.'

I fluffed together another batch of the most supportive vocalisations I could muster.

Charlotta thanked me, again. 'And as difficult as this is, I would really want your opinion about something,' she said. There was that word again. 'The Royal Society stipulates that I can take the fellowship money to any UK university with a Life Sciences department. I can base myself literally anywhere.' I realised that I was about to lose Charlotta for the second time in the same calamitous conversation; first I had lost her to the Mammalia and now I was going to lose her to Darwin knows which university. 'Chelo says that Glasgow has a great reputation for murine behavioural work,' she said. 'What do you think?'

'I'm afraid I don't know the first thing about the requirements for working with *Mus musculus*, Charlotta,' I said, as evenly as I could.

She smiled, weakly. 'Please think about it, Simon. I don't have to decide until February.'

# Chapter 65

*January. The Swan, Acton*

The first Swan Thursday of the year found me in a despondent mood.

'All right, Bird,' said Phil, as he slapped the table top to the rhythm of 'The Boys are Back in Town'. 'If you agree to drop the Claire-face, we can start planning Project Ladybird now. Charlotta is finishing soon, isn't she?'

'Three weeks,' I said.

'Don't luck so glum, Bird, your wingman buddy is re-engaging just in the nick of time,' he grinned.

I sighed. 'It's too late for that.' I explained the whole *Mus musculus* situation. 'And she's right, Glasgow is the place – I checked,' I said.

The hand that Phil had been striking the table with was now covering his face and from behind it I detected a low, pained mumble.

'What did you say, Phil?'

He removed the hand but his eyes remained closed. 'I didn't say anything. Words are inadequate.' He opened an eye. 'You put your balls on ice for eight months for this woman and then when the great ball thaw is just around the corner you advise her to go to Glasgow?'

'She asked me where I thought would be the best place for her to do her work. What could I say?'

'Has she confirmed that she's going to Glasgow yet?'

'No not yet, but—'

'Good. And she's definitely not po-faced?'

'Not in the slightest.'

'Not too mousey either? And you're *sure* you wouldn't feel weird about fucking a fellow?'

'Ha. Ha.' I took a deep lug on my beer.

'All right, Bird, tell me about her.'

***

Timing is crucial.

Pied flycatcher numbers are declining alarmingly because of timing. Springs have become warmer and the caterpillars that the nestlings rely on are now at their most abundant *before* they hatch. Climate change has pushed the young pied flycatchers dangerously out of phase with their narrow window of opportunity (WOO).

Phil thought I still stood a chance of winning Charlotta. But even if he was right, my WOO was also extremely narrow. On Friday January 26 I ceased to be Charlotta's supervisor; on Saturday February 3, just one week later, Charlotta was going to Sweden on a three-week vacation. And before she left for Sweden she had to commit to where she would spend the fellowship years.

Clearly, the future of *Homo sapiens* didn't hinge on my ability to forge a pair-bond with Charlotta, but as my WOO approached, my limbic system and amygdala conspired to make me feel like my personal survival did indeed depend on it.

***

As January 26 approached, I became progressively more anxious about Phil's Project Ladybird plan.

'Couldn't I just tell her the way I feel?' I asked.

Phil scoffed. 'There's too much at stake,' he said. 'You need to *show* her how you feel. She needs a full-blown courtship display.'

***

Finally, at just before seven pm on Tuesday January 30 I stepped out of Ealing Broadway station. Phil was standing on the pavement, his hands pressed deep into his pockets against the cold.

'Take that cap off,' was the first thing he said. 'You look like Richard Dawkins doing Justin Bieber.' He swiped at it, but I moved away and clamped a hand over it 'I don't want to be recognised,' I said. 'I want to be able to focus on Charlotta.'

Phil shook his head and glanced at my backpack. 'Have you got everything?'

I nodded. 'Are you *sure* this is going to work?' I said as we started walking to the High Street.

'No,' he said. 'But it should be entertaining either way.'

\*\*\*

The restaurant was just a short walk from the station, but my heart was pounding heavily as I spotted its fronting. When we arrived on the threshold I asked Phil to go inside.

'Right,' he said, saluting a finger to his eyebrow, 'recon.'

He returned with news. 'OK,' he whispered, looking around furtively, 'here's the deal.'

'Phil, why are you acting like we are planning a hit?'

Phil continued, 'She's in there all right. She's looking cute, Bird.' He jabbed at my arm, approvingly. 'That Pippa from the blues festival is there too. They are right at the back of the restaurant. There are six of them in all.'

'Damn. We're going to need reinforcements,' I said. 'Let's get Spike and Ginger on the blower.'

Phil swiped at my cap again. 'I spoke with the owner. Told him what was going down. He's cool. But we need to go *now*, Bird, before their food arrives. You know I won't be able to concentrate if their food arrives.'

I sighed deeply and pressed my back against the wall to the side of the restaurant.

'Don't go chicken now, Bird,' he said.

I passed him my backpack and pulled my cap down over my eyes. 'I'm ready,' I said.

'Roger that,' said Phil.

\*\*\*

With my head lowered I followed Phil down the centre of the restaurant. He raised a thumb and at the far end of the restaurant another thumb rose in reply. The restaurant manager disappeared beneath the bar and the frenetic string and pipe music suddenly stopped.

At that moment I got my first glimpse of Charlotta, seated as Phil had said she would be in the very last chair at the very last table on the right and wearing a red and grey checked shirt.

*Yes*, said the PC.

As yet unaware of me, Charlotta was smiling at Pippa and Judy, seated opposite her.

The thing about highly anticipated moments, I have observed, is that I spend so long anticipating them that I am always somewhat taken by surprise when they actually arrive. The long walk down the restaurant made it feel as though I would never reach Charlotta's table and would therefore never actually have to make my courtship display. But then I was standing beside Phil and Phil was standing beside Charlotta's table and he was chiming Pippa's spoon against Judy's water glass and it all felt very real.

'Delivery for Charlotta Anderson,' said Phil. Snatching my cap he stepped aside allowing Charlotta to see me for the first time.

'Simon?' she said. The puzzled expression on her face – the kind that might be provoked by an anomalous data point – only heightened my sense of anxious discombobulation.

'Simon,' said Judy, twisting around in her chair.

'Simon?' said Pippa. 'What a lovely surprise, but what…?'

'Nice to see you, P, Judy. I'm here to see Charlotta.' Turning to Charlotta, I said, 'For some time now, Charlotta, I've had very powerful feelings…'

'He loves you, basically,' said Phil, placing a small black portable speaker from my backpack on the table between Pippa and Judy.

'Thank you, Phil,' I said, my eyes still fixed on Charlotta. 'But I think I can handle it from here. He's right. I do love you, Charlotta. I'm only sorry that it took me a while to realise that.'

*I apologised already*, said the PC.

'And then when I realised I loved you, there wasn't anything I could do about it, because of, well, the circumstances. I decided to wait until I could tell you, hoping that you might feel something for me in return. Except even that isn't easy because you got the fellowship – which is *great* – but it does make things even more complicated. But whatever happens in the future, I want you to know how much you mean to me. And when I was trying to think of the best way to show you that, I remembered all the times when I refused to sing with you in the minibus and at William's, which I am also sorry about, by the way. I suppose I didn't want to look stupid, but that seems pretty stupid now.'

'Silly, stupid, Bird,' said Phil, resting his hand on my shoulder.

'And so, tonight, belatedly, Charlotta, I want to sing for you, if you don't mind.'

'I don't mind, Simon, but…' said Charlotta.

'Such a silly, gorgeous man,' said Pippa.

'Music please, Phil,' I said. But then, as the first high, sweet piano notes rose from the small speaker, I remembered that there was something else that I needed to say and so I raised my hand.

'And I should have been more supportive when you said you were going to work with *Mus musculus*.' Phil, grumbling, stopped the music. 'I don't care what you study. You can study mice, macaques or mosquitos as far as I'm concerned, I would love you anyway. You could study Mahler or muons or mudslides and it wouldn't matter a mite. And I don't care whether you go to Glasgow or Greece or the Galapagos – although the Galapagos would be really cool actually. The point is I will follow you wherever you go—' Phil cleared his throat. 'If you want me to.'

I asked Phil to start the music again.

'Sing like a bird, Bird,' he said.

And I did. In the first verse I sang of the mysterious way that birds also desired to be close to Charlotta. As I paused, waiting for the second verse to begin, I hadn't yet determined unequivocally if Charlotta also longed to be close to me.

The original lyrics of the second verse refer to stars falling out of the sky, which is frankly a bit far-fetched, and so I sang my own modified version:

'Why do mice have to interfere?
Singing songs, we can't hear…'

By now I could hear Pippa giggling, but telling myself this could mean absolutely anything, I sang on.

An unfamiliar voice from a female member of a nearby social group yelled, 'Sing up son. We can't hear you.'

And so I sang the next verse – the one about an imaginary celestial collaboration – with increased vigour. I sang with all of the four chambers of my heart and with as much of my diaphragm as I could muster.

It wasn't a virtuoso performance; most sonographers would have said that I displayed a limited repertoire of strophes; but there was only one sonographer that I cared about, and she was now smiling at least.

When I began to sing the first verse for a second time, I became aware that people were gathering around me. In my peripheral vision I saw a small flash and then another one quickly afterwards and Phil said, 'No photos please. Unless you sing, too.'

And so as I sang the first verse a third and then a fourth time, it was not a gathering of angels but rather a small flock of warm-hearted *Homo sapiens* who helped me try to make my dream come true.

When the song ended, though I felt relieved, I also felt a sudden sense of powerlessness. I realised that I had done all that I could, and that my destiny was once again dependent on female choice. There was clapping and a request for an encore, but my eyes never left Charlotta. She was on her feet and clapping and beaming. I tried to make my way towards her, but there was a table between us and then Pippa hugged me and laughed in my ear and the manager of the restaurant wanted a photo but at least my hearing was returning by then and Phil had pulled the table away from the wall, creating a narrow channel for Charlotta to squeeze through.

'What do you reckon?' I whispered into his big fleshy ear as she edged towards me.

'Could go either way,' he said. 'You went a bit too Dionne Warwick for my taste.'

I kissed him hard on his big square jaw and went to Charlotta. We embraced and she still felt small like a bird and her hair still smelt of the woods. 'Thank you, Simon,' she said, kissing me beside my ear.

Still clinging to her I said, 'Are you going to tell me what you are thinking?'

'I'm thinking that perhaps it's best that I didn't hear you sing before,' she said, but I definitely heard her smile.

'Singing's not everything,' I said. 'I've still got all my original plumage, a cosy little nest box and a good heart.'

'All important criteria,' she said.

The music started up again and we turned towards it together. Phil, Pippa and Judy, staring intently down into Phil's phone, sang the opening to 'Sex on Fire'.

'How about a duet?' said Charlotta, slipping her fingers between mine.

I smiled down at her. 'Why not? I love singing. Now.'

'What do you think we should sing?'

'Oh, I don't know,' I said, glancing down at our intertwined hands. 'Why don't you choose?'

# Acknowledgements

Thanks must first go to Arne Lundberg and the late Rauno V Alatalo. I read their book *The Pied Flycatcher* and the original research articles over and over again. Like them, I became hooked on this fascinating little bird. Thanks also to Dr Malcolm Burgess of the RSPB for generously allowing me to accompany him as he studied pied flycatchers in the field (especially because he initially suspected I was 'a mate taking the piss').

For encouragement, enthusiasm and constructive advice I would like to thank my early readers: Judy Stewart, Miriam Kenrick, Alex Adams, Jan Keegan, Cathryn Smith, Simon Freedman, Tracey Brader and her book club, Antony Fulford-Smith and Richard Glover.

I am indebted to Maggie Hamand, Naomi Wood, Christie Watson and Howard Cunnell who all taught me so much about this writing malarkey.

Huge thanks to my agent, James Wills, for belief, insight and invaluable guidance. And to Abbie Headon, my editor, who made the process so much more enjoyable than I had expected.

To Phil Atherton, the real-life inspiration for Phil: thanks for being you, bud. I think.

Fond regards must go to the beautiful bullfinch that kindly appeared in my garden when I most needed a boost.

And finally, to Unette: thank you for a most miraculous pair-bond.

# About the Author

Lee's childhood was spent on a dairy farm in
Lincolnshire alongside a pet cow named Stupid.
When Stupid's grazing days were over, he headed to
Newcastle to study Genetics. He eventually gained a PhD in
molecular biology but then hung up his lab coat and headed
into industry. After more than fifteen years in strategic
marketing he kissed the corporate world goodbye
to spend more time writing.

Lee lives in Berkshire. He doesn't have any cows, but does
have two adult children and a large collection of bird feeders.

# Note from the Publisher

To receive updates on special offers and news of other humorous fiction titles to make you smile – sign up now to the Farrago mailing list at farragobooks.com/sign-up.